Don't Look Back in Ongar

For Humphrey

Don't Look Back in Ongar

ROSS O'CARROLL KELLY (AS TOLD TO PAUL HOWARD)

Illustrated by Alan Clarke

SANDYCOVE

an imprint of

PENGUIN BOOKS

SANDYCOVE

UK | USA | Canada | Ireland | Australia
India | New Zealand | South Africa

Sandycove is part of the Penguin Random House group of companies
whose addresses can be found at global.penguinrandomhouse.com.

First published 2024
001

Copyright © Paul Howard, 2024
Illustrator copyright © Alan Clarke, 2024

Penguin Books thanks O'Brien Press for its agreement to Sandycove using the
same design approach and typography, and the same artist, as O'Brien Press used
in the first four Ross O'Carroll-Kelly titles.

Set in 12/14.75pt Dante MT Std
Typeset by Jouve (UK), Milton Keynes
Printed and bound in Great Britain by Clays Ltd, Elcograf S.p.A.

The authorized representative in the EEA is Penguin Random House Ireland,
Morrison Chambers, 32 Nassau Street, Dublin D02 YH68

A CIP catalogue record for this book is available from the British Library

ISBN: 978-1-844-88629-6

www.greenpenguin.co.uk

Contents

Prologue

The old man is smoking a Cohiba long enough to inseminate a rhinoceros and he's acting like absolutely fock-all is wrong.

He's there, 'I've had Boris on the phone this morning! Seems he saw the piece in the *Gordian* saying that Irexit was failing! He said to me, "When they tell me that Brexit is failing, I remind them that they said the same thing about the Reformation! Then along came the King James Bible and changed the whole game!" Take your clothes off, Ross!'

I'm there, 'Excuse me?'

'Your clothes!' he goes. 'You'll bloody well sweat to death!'

Yeah, no, I should mention that we're sitting in the sauna that he had installed in the Áras and I'm being slow-baked like a jacket potato, except the jacket is by Helly Hansen.

I'm there, 'I'll leave my clothes on if it's all the same to you.'

He goes, 'Please yourself! Must be nice to have Ronan back in the country after his little sojourn across the – inverted commas – pond!'

I just, like, glower at him.

I'm there, 'I can't believe you're acting like nothing has happened.'

He goes, 'What are you talking about, Kicker?'

I'm like, 'Dude, you will get your focking comeuppance.'

'I'm afraid I'm not following you,' he tries to go.

I'm there, 'The dildo of consequence seldom arrives lubricated – as Jamie Heaslip texted me after Eddie O'Sullivan lost the Ireland job.'

He's there, 'I must confess, I'm struggling to understand what Eddie O'Sullivan has to do with –'

'A woman is dead!' I go.

'Yes, I know,' he goes, 'I watch the news, like you.'

I don't watch the news – just for the record.

I'm there, 'And you focking killed her!'

He stands up and – Jesus Christ! – his towel falls from his hips to the floor. I'm still sitting down on the bench, by the way, and I suddenly find myself face-to-face with his – I'm going to have to use the word – *mickey* and it's just, like, hanging there, all pale and limp, like an uncooked pig in a blanket.

He's like, 'What the hell do you mean by that?' and I haven't seen him this angry since he walked into Riverview and the new girl on reception asked him if he was there for the Seniors Water Aerobics.

I'm there, 'See-mon,' closing my eyes and turning my head away, 'or Sea-mon, or however the fock you say it –'

He's like, 'Yes?'

I'm there, 'She died in a cor crash. Dude, can you *please* cover yourself up? I'm going to focking vom here.'

Yeah, no, thankfully he picks up his towel and he wraps it around him and sits down again.

He goes, 'It said on the *Six One News* that the Gordaí were treating it as an accident!'

I'm there, 'It's all a bit convenient – for you, I mean.'

He's like, 'If you're implying –'

I'm there, 'She no more burned down the Dáil than I did.'

'She was a very disturbed young woman!' he goes. 'That much was evident from her diaries – or so I gather!'

'Well, we'll never know. Because there's obviously not going to be a trial now.'

'A tragedy on so many levels!'

'But she knew shit – as in, she had shit on you.'

He goes, 'Like what?' and I can hear the outrage growing in his voice again.

I'm there, 'She knew that *you* burned down the Dáil – as in, you and Hennessy.'

He's like, 'What kind of talk is this?' and he goes to stand up again.

I'm there, 'Dude, sit the fock down – please!'

'The Dáil was burned by sinister pro-European interests,' he tries to go, 'who wanted to stop us taking back control of our own country! They used a girl – a vulnerable girl – to burn down our national porliament as a warning!'

I'm there, 'Like I said, we'll never know if that's true now. It's funny, though, how she was refused bail and then she was suddenly let out. It's almost as if someone wanted her out of prison and out in the open where she could be –'

He goes, 'I'll not listen to a word more of this! This is your sister talking, isn't it?'

I'm there, 'Half-sister,' and I don't know why I feel the need to correct him – probably because I've been with her.

He goes, 'I know that Erika's angry that I wasn't there for her growing up, but to try to use this poor, mentally ill girl and her tragic death as a stick to beat me with, well, it's beneath contempt! I have a gravely ill wife and I'm trying to steer the nation through the birthing pains of –'

I'm there, 'Dude, the country is focked.'

Yeah, no, you basically can't buy anything that wasn't made or grown in Ireland.

I'm there, 'Dude, face it, you haven't had one good day since you put that focking wig on your head. And neither has the country.'

He goes, 'As Boris Johnson said, it'll come good! As long as we all just keep our nerve! He was asking after you, by the way! I think you've got a bit of a fan there!'

I'm looking at him sitting there, his skin all white and wrinkly, like my fingers when I've stayed too long in the bath, and I'm suddenly wondering *was* it him? As in, could he really be capable of, like, killing someone? Or burning down the – *his* word – *porliament*?

That's my problem, see. I'm too soft.

It's at that exact moment that the door of the sauna is suddenly torn open and Erika is standing there, looking about as pissed off as I've seen her since the time I let her walk around the library in Lillie's one night with a length of toilet paper attached to the sole of her Loub.

'Come in and shut the door!' the old man goes – the focking nerve of him. 'You're letting all the heat out!'

I'm there, 'Take your clothes off, Erika,' and then I realize that it

sounds possibly pervy, so I go, 'Although only if you want to obviously.'

She fixes the old man with a look and goes, 'It was you! You focking killed her!'

I'm there, 'Erika, look away! He's going to –!'

Except it's too late. The dude stands up, losing his towel again.

He goes, 'What the hell do you mean by that?' and I can't help but notice that they're the exact same words he used to me, so that it sounds like something he's rehearsed.

Erika goes, 'You focking know what I mean.'

I'm there, 'Erika, take your clothes off!'

I think there's definitely something wrong with me.

He goes, 'You would believe that of me? Your own father?'

She's like, 'What, that you'd take someone's life? I wouldn't doubt it for a second! Because that's how drunk on power you are – you *and* your focking sidekick!'

He's there, 'I'll not stand here and listen to you traduce the good name of Mr Hennessy Coghlan-O'Hara!'

I go, 'Erika, I honestly don't know how you can stand there looking at him. Pigs in blankets was the first thing that crossed my mind. That's one thing I *won't* be eating this Christmas?'

She doesn't respond either way. She keeps just staring at him. She has a stronger stomach than I do.

Then she goes, 'You killed Sea-mon!' and she roars it at him. 'You killed her in cold blood! And I am going to get justice for her – and see that you go to prison forever!'

Erika turns on her heel and pushes open the door. The old man goes to follow her, but she slams the door in his face and I'm left sitting there, staring at his pale, saggy orse, like two week-old chicken breasts.

And like he's forgotten that I'm still there, he goes, 'Oh, Erika – you silly, silly girl! You should know by now – you play with matches, you are sure to be burned.'

She's Got One in the Oven

Roz is looking tremendous tonight, in fairness to the woman. She's wearing this black top that's clinging to her like a drowning man. I'm trying not to stare at her wabs, but it's easier said than done.

I'm there, 'You look well tonight. Tremendous, in fairness to you.'

And she goes, 'Are you talking to me or my breasts?'

I go, 'Er –'

But she laughs and goes, 'I'm teasing you, Ross!'

I'm like, 'Oh, right. Yeah, no, good one, Roz.'

Jesus Christ, I've a boner on me that could churn butter.

'What are you going to have?' she goes, looking down at the menu.

Yeah, no, we're in a restaurant on Camden Street called Comté.

I'm there, 'Everything looks great. And I'm pretty horngry. I mean, hungry. Jesus, I'm sorry, it's just that top –'

She laughs – again, I think she's, like, *flattered*? Then, in a whisper, she goes, 'Oh my God, we only did it, like, two hours ago.'

I'm there, 'I honestly don't know what's wrong with me,' and I *literally* don't? I don't think I've ever been more turned on by a woman in my life.

'Well,' she goes, 'we've got the house to ourselves tonight.'

Yeah, no, Sincerity is having a sleepover with Honor in ours and Erika is, I suppose, babysitting them, so it's, like, happy days.

The waitress arrives to take our order. I don't even clock whether she's a looker or not. That's how genuinely loved-up I am.

'For my storter,' Roz goes, 'I'm going to have the roast Jerusalem ortichoke –'

The waitress is like, 'It's actually a Beara Peninsula ortichoke tonight. We can't get the Jerusalem ones – because of Irexit.'

'And does it still come with the crème fraîche and the Pink Lady?'

'It's actually a Golden Delicious.'

'That's fine. And for my main, I'll have the wild halibut–'

'We've had to substitute that for cod.'

'– with kohlrabi –'

'Turnip.'

'– and chorizo –'

'Annascaul pork sausages.'

'That's all fine. I'll have that.'

The waitress turns to me then.

I'm there, 'Yeah, no, I've heard good things about the ricotta –'

'It's cottage cheese now,' she goes. 'Because of –'

'Irexit. Fair enough. And for my main, I think I'll have the monk-fish with, like, prosciutto –?'

'Honey-roast ham.'

'– and gnocchi.'

'Baby potatoes.'

'Yeah, no, whatever. It all sounds good to me.'

We hand her our menus and off she jolly well focks.

Roz goes, 'This is nice, isn't it – having an actual *date* night?'

I'm there, 'Yeah, no, it's all good. And, like you said, we've the run of the house later – you know, to do whatever we want . . . to each other, like.'

She sips her water and goes, 'It's lovely that Sincerity and Honor are getting along so well, isn't it?'

I'm there, 'Yeah, no, definitely,' not wanting to sound too enthusiastic because Honor is like a faulty firework – it's all fun and laughter until she takes the focking face off you.

She goes, 'The change that's come over Sincerity in the last few months, it's so lovely to see. She used to be such a goody-goody.'

I'm there, 'Well, Honor's definitely the one to knock that out of her.'

'She never really had a lot of confidence before. Now, she's bursting with it. She's outgoing. She's got friends. She's got boys who are interested in her. And that's all thanks to Honor.'

'I hope it stays well for her – that's all I'm going to say on the subject.'

All of a sudden I hear a voice from across the room go, 'Look at these two lovebirds!'

I look over my shoulder and it ends up being Raymond, Roz's ex-husband, who pretends to be sound but who's actually a dick. He doesn't even want Roz, but he can't stand the thought of her being with someone else. Of course, *she* is blissfully unaware of this fact, despite being married to him for, like, ten years.

'The fock are you two doing here?' I go.

Yeah, no, he's standing there with his current wife – we're talking Gráinne.

Roz is like, 'Ross, don't be rude!' because – yeah, no – him and her are still, like, best friends.

I'm there, 'I'm just making the point that it's a bit of a coincidence, isn't it, that of all the restaurants in Dublin they could have gone to tonight, they chose this one?'

That's when Roz goes, 'Ross, they own this place.'

I'm there, 'Excuse me?'

'Comté,' she goes. 'It's Gráinne's restaurant.'

Of course I'm the one who ends up being made to feel like a knob.

I'm there, 'I didn't know it was their place,' even though I remember her mentioning that the second wife was a chef.

Roz goes, 'Ross, I told you when I was booking it. And I mentioned five minutes ago that Gráinne was hoping to get a Michelin Stor.'

'Probably too busy staring at your chest,' Raymond goes. 'I was watching him from across the room,' and then he laughs and places a patronizing hand on my back. 'I'm only winding you up, Ross! Look at his face there!'

Roz goes, 'I'm sorry, Raymond. I'm sorry, Gráinne.'

And Raymond's like, 'Hey, it's cool. Like I said to you before, Ross, there's no need for you to feel threatened by my friendship with Roz. No need at all.'

I'm there, 'I *don't* feel threatened?' which is absolute horseshit.

He goes, 'That's good, then. What did you goys order?'

Roz is like, 'I ordered the Jerusalem ortichoke followed by the halibut.'

9

He's there, 'You know it's a Beara Peninsula ortichoke now and the halibut is cod?'

'Yeah, no, I know,' Roz goes. 'The waitress explained all the substitutions to us.'

The dude puts his orm around Gráinne's waist then and goes, 'Gráinne here is working absolute miracles, day after day, to keep coming up with menu items made up of only home-grown food,' and then he's like, 'Of course, Ross, we've *your* old man to thank for the fact that we can't import anything from the EU or beyond.'

I'm there, 'He says it's just a temporary thing. It's just, like, *teething* problems?'

He goes, 'I hope he's right, Ross. I really do. I know that Gráinne and I didn't vote for Irexit. Nor did you, Roz, did you?'

She's like, 'I didn't, no.'

I can't listen to any more of his bullshit, so I excuse myself by announcing that I need a whizz.

'Second door on the right,' the dude goes, like I couldn't have figured that out myself.

Into the jacks I go. Thirty seconds later, I'm standing at the urinal, chasing one of the little disinfectant soaps down the trough with my piss – I'm never *not* competing in some way? – when Raymond walks in, stands beside me and whips out his piece.

'You're really struggling out there,' he goes, unleashing his own stream.

I'm there, 'In terms of?'

'Maintaining the nice guy act.'

'Look who's focking talking.'

I'm trying to sneak a look at his chopper, to see if it's big – like I said, never not competing.

He goes, 'This person you're pretending to be when you're with Roz – the loving, attentive boyfriend – it might fool her, but it doesn't fool me. I know what you are.'

I'm there, 'And what's that?'

He laughs.

He goes, 'You're just a basic rugby wanker.'

I'm there, 'Is that right?'

He goes, 'You don't think I'd allow you to become potentially a stepfather to my daughter – my only child – without doing my research on you, do you? It's a small world, Ross. I've heard a lot of stories about you.'

I'm like, 'What kind of stories?' because there's a lot of them out there and the ones that sound made-up are the ones that tend to be true.

'About the way you treat women,' he goes. 'Funnily enough, I work with a girl who knows you – or *knew* you, back in the day.'

I'm there, 'A lot of girls claim to know me.'

He goes, 'I'm sure they do,' and then he's like, 'Jesus Christ, are you trying to look at my penis?'

I'm there, 'No.'

'You were,' he goes, at the same time laughing. 'You were trying to see was it bigger than yours. Well, here you go – have a look.'

He turns to face me.

I'm there, 'No.'

He goes, 'Go on, look at it!'

I'm there, 'I've no interest in your penis!' but – yeah, no – I end up having a quick glance. To my great relief, it's not enormous – it's around the same size as mine.

I decide to go on the attack then. I'm there, 'Dude, you need to get over Roz,' as I shake the last few drips of venom from the snake's head, 'because she's definitely over you.'

'Leopards don't change their spots,' he goes. 'This, I don't know, rugger-bugger who's out for a meal with his girlfriend, it's not you, Ross. It's just a persona you're trying out. Deep down, you know that.'

I'm there, 'I love her – and she loves me.'

'Well, I'm sorry to disappoint you,' he goes, 'but this is not happening. Like I told you, I'm going to make it my business – no, my absolute priority – to break you two up.'

I'm like, 'What the fock *is* that thing?'

We're in this, like, humungous warehouse in Sandyford Industrial Estate, staring at what looks very much to me like a giant *oven*?

Erika doesn't get a chance to even answer.

'It's a Resomator,' Sorcha goes, taking her seat in the row behind me. 'One of my first decisions as Ireland's first Minister for Climate Action was to award individual grants of up to half a million euros to allow places like this to be built.'

I'm there, 'So is See-mon being, like, cremated?'

'No, *Sea-mon* was very much *anti* cremation?' Erika goes, not even looking over her shoulder to acknowledge Sorcha's presence. 'Cremation releases CO_2 into the atmosphere –'

'Four hundred kilograms per body,' Sorcha adds in her Mount Anville Head Girl voice. 'Then, don't forget, cremation fumes can also include vaporized mercury from tooth fillings and other toxic emissions from burnt prosthetics and melted bone cement used during common surgeries such as knee and hip replacements. How *are* you, Erika?'

Erika finally turns around and gives her a look. I haven't seen a filthy like it since the time I shushed Doireann Garrihy during *Mad Max: Fury Road* in Dundrum.

She goes, 'How *am* I? I'm sad, Sorcha – because my *friend* just died?'

Sorcha's there, 'Yeah, no, I meant it in more of a *general* sense?' and then, in a sulky voice, she goes, 'She was *my* friend before she was ever *your* friend, can I just remind you?'

I'm in cracking form because Ireland beat Scotland in the opening match of the World Cup in Japan this morning. I actually think they're going to win the thing, although that could have something to do with the six beers I had for breakfast. The time difference would kill you.

I'm there, 'So, if she's not going to be cremated, what's going to actually happen to her?'

'Her body will be put into that pressurized cannister over there,' Sorcha goes, 'and submerged in a mixture of 150 degrees Celsius water and potassium hydroxide solution for three to four hours until the flesh is dissolved –'

Erika huffs and shakes her head. She's right. It's a definite case of TMI, even though I *did* ask?

'– leaving behind only soft, greyish bones,' Sorcha goes. 'They'll be dried in that oven there, then ground down into a paper-white powder, which can be put into a hole in the ground to nourish the roots of a new tree. Is she going the tree route, Erika?'

Erika doesn't answer her. It's hord to believe they used to be bezzy mates and now Erika can't bring herself to even look at Sorcha. I know it's wrong, but I'm a little bit turned on by it.

'Then the water that remains, which is obviously full of nutrients, is used to fertilize the soil,' Sorcha goes. 'How are you, Ross? How are things going with Roz? A friend of mine – she's actually the Secretary General of my deportment – said she saw you in Comté on Camden Street and you looked all loved up.'

But I don't get a chance to answer her because Paul Byrom, the tenor – who I know through Gordon D'Arcy – launches into the opening number, which turns out to be 'Saltwater' by some randomer named Julian Lennon. It's a sign that the family have finally arrived.

Yeah, no, they make their way to the chairs at the front. Over my shoulder, I can sense Sorcha moving around, trying to get Simone's old pair and sister to notice her. Then I hear her, almost in a whisper, go, 'Hi, Benoîte – oh my God, I'm so, so sorry,' but I'm pretty sure the sister hasn't seen her.

The poor girl looks broken up.

I'm there, 'He has some set of lungs on him, Paul Byrom, doesn't he? I went on the lash with him and Dorce after the final of *Celebrity Jigs 'n' Reels* and lost three days of my life.'

Erika doesn't say shit. I suppose there's nothing *to* say?

'Such an amazing song,' I hear Sorcha go. 'Julian Lennon. I actually bought the single with my Confirmation money. Did you hear he's making a documentary for Netflix about regenerative agriculture?'

Again, it's a tumbleweed moment.

I turn around to Erika and I go, 'So is it going to be, like, Mass?' and I can hear the dread in my own voice. 'I didn't think See-mon believed in any of that shit.'

Erika's there, 'It's Sea-mon,' again correcting me.

I'm like, 'Yeah, no, I'm pretty sure I'm saying it the exact same way as *you*, Erika?'

'And, no,' she goes, 'it's not going to be a Mass. She was an atheist.'

Thank God for that, I think.

The dude finishes singing, then – yeah, no – Benoîte stands up with her back to the famous Resomator and goes, 'Thank you all for coming this morning.'

I look around. There's only, like, thirty or forty people here. Simone didn't have many mates. She was a bit of a weirdo, in fairness to her.

Benoîte's there, 'It's an unusual setting for a funeral, I know, but at least we can say with absolute certainty that it's what Sea-mon would have wanted, because she left very clear instructions. She was a big believer in alkaline hydrolysis –'

'I know,' Sorcha – under her breath – goes, 'she was the one who told me about it and persuaded me that it had a vital role to play in the culling of the national herd,' and I don't know who the fock she thinks she's talking to other than herself. 'Disposing of all cows and sheep using this method is hopefully going to be port of my legislative agenda for 2020.'

Benoîte isn't great in terms of looks and I'm only saying that to provide a bit of background colour. She's got, like, punky hair, which looks like it's been spray-painted blue, then a yellow mohair jumper that looks itchy as fock, black jeans and black Converse, which are wrecked.

I'm just saying, it's a funeral – she could have made an effort.

She goes, 'My sister believed that we should die as we live – causing as little harm to those around us as possible. Which is why it was so painful for her to have her name and her reputation slandered in the last few months of her life. This much I know about my beautiful baby sister – if she didn't believe in cremation, she most certainly did not believe in arson.'

Members of the family stort – yeah, no – applauding her, and me and Erika join in. I look over my shoulder and I notice that Sorcha *isn't* clapping?

'As a matter of fact,' Benoîte goes, whipping out her phone, 'on the night that Leinster House was burned to the ground, she sent me a text message that said, "Oh my God, I am sick here thinking about all the contaminants being released into the environment and the amount of water that it's going to take to put the fire out." Does that sound like the kind of person who would deliberately set fire to a building?'

'No,' most of us go, panto-style, although – again – I don't hear *Sorcha* respond?

I turn to Erika and I go, 'That's a very good point she made about the girl being basically anti fire?' but I notice that she's sobbing away quietly to herself.

Benoîte's like, 'Those of us who knew Sea-mon,' and she looks straight at Erika when she says it, 'who cared about her, we knew in our heart of hearts that she wasn't capable of doing what she was accused of doing. Just as we know that her death wasn't the accident that the Gardaí are claiming it to be.'

She pauses for, like, dramatic effect, then she goes, 'My sister was murdered to stop her from revealing things that she knew about the Government. And it sickens me to my stomach that the same Government that ordered her execution has sent someone to represent it here today.'

She just, like, glowers at Sorcha, and everyone, including me, turns around and looks her.

Sorcha's there, 'Oh my God, I'm not wearing my ministerial hat this morning. I'm here in my capacity as, like, a friend?'

Benoîte goes, 'A friend? *Really?*'

Simone's old man stands up and turns around then. He goes, 'She wouldn't want you here. Get out of here, you ghoul.'

Sorcha is, like, devastated. She stands up and storms out of the place and I can hear her bawling her eyes out as she goes.

Benoîte goes, 'Now I'm going to invite Paul Byrom to sing "Big Yellow Taxi", which was Sea-mon's favourite song, by Joni Mitchell.'

I stand up and I chase after Sorcha. Her State cor is porked outside and I notice Kennet sitting behind the wheel with the engine idling. So much for the focking environment.

I call her name and she turns around.

She goes, 'I was the one who got her into Joni Mitchell? She thought the Counting Crows version was the original.'

She's lashing out because she's hurt.

I'm there, 'I'm sorry – about what happened in there.'

'It's not that I think that I should be above criticism as a minister,' she goes, 'but I can mourn the passing of a friend while also believing that she was a dangerous extremist. The two things are not mutually *incompatible*?'

I'm there, 'Look, it's a funeral. Emotions are bound to be running high.'

There's, like, silence between us, then she goes, 'Do you think your dad was capable of ordering her murder, Ross?'

I'm there, 'He says he didn't, so I suppose we're going to have to take his word for it.'

All of a sudden, I hear Kennet, from the driver's seat, go, 'How's thing's, Rosser? G . . . G . . . G . . . G . . . Great to hab Ronan back, idn't it? Arthur putting all that Amedica b . . . b . . . b . . . b . . . b . . . boddicks behoyunt him. It woatunt be long now befower him and Shadden is throying for anutter b . . . b . . . b . . . b . . . b . . . '

I turn back to Sorcha, totally blanking him. I'm there, 'Are you going to be okay?'

She dabs at her eyes with the tips of her fingers and she's like, 'I'll be fine. I need to get back to work. The most fitting way for me to honour Sea-mon is by continuing with the drive towards corbon neutrality.'

Kennet is still going, 'b . . . b . . . b . . . b . . . b . . . b . . . b . . . '

I'm like, 'Do you want to hug it out?'

But she goes, 'No, I'll be okay. I meant what I said. I'm actually delighted for you – *and* Roz. And Comté is supposed to be amazing. It's on the list.'

I'm there, 'Mind yourself,' because I still care about her. I watch her get into the back of the cor, while Kennet goes, 'b . . . b . . . b . . . b . . . b . . . b . . . babby.'

The old dear says she wants a gin and tonic, but the nurse who's looking after her goes, 'You're not in The Westbury, Fionnuala. You're in a nursing home in Wicklow.'

The old dear is like, 'How dare you? I've been drinking in this establishment for more than fifty years. I pay your wages, you ugly little tart.'

Me and Honor are watching this scene play out from the doorway of her room.

'A gin and tonic,' the old dear goes, 'or I'll see the manager this instant.'

Honor steps into the room and fills a glass from the tap.

She's like, 'Here you go,' offering it to the old dear. 'One gin and tonic.'

The old dear stares at her – I shit you not – not a clue who she even *is*?

She's like, 'Oh! You're new!'

Honor's there, 'Yes, I am,' as the old dear grabs the drink from her, then sips a mouthful.

'Well, you've stinted on the gin,' the old dear goes. 'I can tell I'm going to have trouble with you.'

The old dear spots me standing in the *doorway* then?

She's like, 'Ross, you came!'

I'm like, 'Er, yeah, no, I did.'

She goes, 'This is Elspeth,' pointing out Honor to me. 'She's new here and she makes *the* most ghastly cocktails. But she's keen to learn, aren't you, Dorling?'

Honor smiles at her and goes, 'That's right, Fionnuala.'

The old dear's like, 'Elspeth,' like she's trying to figure out where she's heard the name before. 'Are you from somewhere foreign?'

'No,' Honor goes, 'I'm from Ireland, Fionnuala.'

The old dear is like, 'What's that accent, then? Is it Limerick?'

'No, it's South Dublin.'

'I can't abide Limerick people. They're light-fingered.'

On her way out the door, the nurse turns around to me and goes, 'We don't indulge patients in their fantasies here. It just increases their sense of confusion.'

The old dear's there, 'What's that bitch saying to you? What she fails to realize is that I could have her sacked . . . like that!' and then she snaps her fingers.

I move over to her and sit down on the side of her bed.

She goes, 'How are you, Ross? Your hair is nice like that.'

I'm there, 'It's always been like this. Blade one at the back and sides and a quiff at the front.'

She goes, 'I like it,' and she hands Honor her glass. 'Put some manners on that, would you, Elspeth? Less tonic, more gin. And I'll know if it's not Hendrick's.'

Honor takes the glass over to the sink.

'Limerick,' the old dear whispers to me out of the side of her mouth. 'Keep an eye on my handbag, would you, Ross?'

Honor arrives back from the sink and the old dear fake-smiles her. She takes the drink from her, has a sip and goes, 'Better, Elspeth! Much, much better!'

I'm there, 'So, like, how have you been and shit?'

'Busy,' the old dear goes. 'Honestly, Ross, between one thing and another, I haven't had a minute to myself. How's Audrey?'

'Who the fock is Audrey?'

'Your wife!'

'Yeah, no – it's *Sorcha*?'

'Are you sure?'

'Yes, I'm sure. And she's fine – even though we're, like, *separated*?'

She's there, 'You were always too good for that girl,' and I notice that even Honor has a little smile to herself. 'She was always a bit too desperate for my liking. She used to ring the house at all hours, crying her eyes out on the phone to me. She'd say, "You know him, Fionnuala. You know what makes him tick. How can I *make* him want me?" Used to getting whatever she wanted, you see. Spoiled rotten by that father of hers. Sometimes, I'd put the phone down, go off and fix myself a cocktail, come back and she'd still be pouring her hort out.'

I laugh.

'Honor!' the old dear suddenly goes, pointing at – yeah, no – Honor. 'You're my granddaughter!'

Honor's there, 'Er, *yeah*?'

'So why did you tell me your name was Elspeth?'

'I don't know.'

'As if I'm not confused enough already.'

'Sorry, Fionnuala.'

'And how long have you worked in The Westbury, Honor?'

My phone all of a sudden beeps. It's, like, a text message from Roz. It's like, 'I just bumped into Raymond. Your ears must have been burning! How's your mum?'

I text her straight back. I'm like, 'Confused but fine. What was Raymond saying?'

She texts me back, going, 'Lovely things. He's a big fan!'

Shit. I know I've got a fight on my hands with this dude.

The old dear goes, 'I was just saying to Honor that this place isn't what it once was, Ross.'

I'm there, 'Er, is it not?' because I'm wondering what the focker is planning.

'Where's the tree?' she goes.

Honor's like, 'What tree?'

'The Christmas tree.'

I'm there, 'It's September.'

'Is it? Doesn't the year fly?'

The nurse from earlier returns. She goes, 'Fionnuala, it's time for your bath,' and then the woman turns to me and goes, 'Mrs Melchiot wants to see you.'

I'm there, 'Who the fock is Mrs Melchiot?'

She goes, 'She's the Managing Director. Follow me.'

We say our goodbyes to the old dear, then we're directed down the corridor and to this, like, waiting room. We end up sitting there for two or three minutes before the door is opened and a woman in her – I'm *guessing*? – late fifties invites us into her office.

She goes, 'And you are –?' and it's obvious she's not a rugby fan.

I'm there, 'Ross O'Carroll-Kelly. I'm *Fionnuala's* son? And this is my daughter, Honor.'

'Oh, right, well, I'll come straight to the point,' the woman goes. 'We believe that the care we offer here in St Aednat's is no longer appropriate for your mother's needs.'

I'm there, 'What's that in English?'

Honor goes, 'They want to throw her out,' and I can hear the anger in her voice. She loves my old dear. They just, like, *get* each other, both of them being, I suppose, *sociopaths*?

'We're not throwing her out,' the woman goes. 'We're suggesting transferring her to a hospice where she can receive care that is commensurate with her condition.'

I'm there, 'Which is?'

'Ross – is that what you said your name was? Your mother is deteriorating very quickly.'

Me and Honor look at each other. This is, like, heavy shit.

I'm there, 'So, like, how long has she got left?'

The woman goes, 'That depends on a number of factors. But, based on my experience, I would say no more than a matter of months.'

Honor bursts into tears.

'You're full of shit,' she goes, 'you focking ugly bitch.'

Yeah, no, the woman has a face like a witchdoctor's rattle. I just didn't want to be the one to say it.

'I know it's upsetting,' she goes. 'That's why we want to transfer her somewhere she can get the specialist attention she requires during this stage of her illness.'

I'm there, 'So where *is* this supposed place?'

'Ongar,' she goes.

I'm like, 'No way. No focking way.'

'It's near Blanchardstown.'

'I know where focking Ongar is. I used to work as an estate agent.'

Yeah, no, we were trained to accentuate the positive, but Ongar stretched the limits of even *my* bullshitting abilities.

'A focking shithole of a place,' I go.

The woman's there, 'I can assure you that the hospice is absolutely wonderful.'

Something suddenly occurs to me.

I'm there, 'Hang on, why is it *my* decision to make? Should you not be talking to my old man?'

She goes, 'We haven't been able to contact him.'

'Excuse me?'

'We've e-mailed. We've written to him. We've phoned him and left message after message. He is simply refusing to engage with us.'

I'm there, 'Refusing to engage? Are you telling me he hasn't been in to visit her?'

'No, he hasn't,' she goes. 'Not even once.'

'What the fock?' is my opening line. 'What the focking fock?'

The old man looks up from his desk.

'Ross,' he tries to go, 'I'm rather busy right now!'

I'm there, 'So I believe. Too busy to go and visit the old dear.'

He's like, 'Did you, em, watch the Scotland match, Kicker?' trying to weasel his way out of it. 'I thought CJ Stander was wonderful!'

I'm there, 'Stop trying to change the subject.'

He's like, 'How do you think they'll fare against Japan this weekend? I'd imagine you're thinking about little else! I know how that mind of yours works!'

I can't help myself, of course.

'Japan are no great shakes,' I end up going. 'But you can't afford to be complacent against the tournament hosts. Joe Schmidt will have a plan for them.'

'I'm relieved to hear it!'

'They want to move her. I'm talking about the old dear. To Ongar. It's near Blanchardstown.'

'I know where Ongar is!' the old man goes, suddenly looking all dewy-eyed, like he did when Chorlie Haughey left him his dollar-sign cufflinks in his will. 'I used to own quite a bit of land out there! Made an absolute killing when I got it rezoned for housing! Great days – eh, Hennessy?'

Yeah, no, Hennessy has stepped into the office behind me.

Hennessy's there, 'How did *he* get in here? Do you want me to have him thrown out on his head?'

The old man actually chuckles.

He's like, 'There'll be no need for that, old scout! No, I was just about to explain to him the emergency we're facing as a nation!'

I'm there, 'Is this the one where we basically can't import or export anything because you thought it would be a good idea to leave the European Union?'

'A temporary state of affairs! No, the Supreme Court has, this very morning, ruled that the Government is in breach of the Constitution by failing to reconvene the famous Dáil in the wake of the fire that destroyed Leinster House!'

I just shrug and go, 'And this affects me *how* exactly?'

He's there, 'It means the Dáil is going to have to sit, for now at least, in the National Convention Centre! And I'm going to have to listen to Messrs Varadkar and Mortin complaining that their constituents are unable to buy, I don't know, brie and lapsang souchong! And they call it – quote-unquote – democracy!'

'You could always defy the Supreme Court,' Hennessy goes.

'I've a bloody good mind to!' the old man goes. 'But no, let them have their superficial appeasements! *Panem et circenses!* You'll know that, Ross, from your Juvenal! *Iam pridem, ex quo suffragia nulli, vendimus, effudit curas; nam qui dabat olim –*'

I'm like, 'What the fock are you banging on about? I came here to give out shit to you for abandoning your supposed wife.'

'I'm sure your mother will be in very capable hands in Ongar, Ross! I'm afraid that, for now, the country's needs must come first! *Ducit amor patriae* – eh, Hennessy?'

And Hennessy's there, '*Faciam quodlibet quod necesse est!*'

'Hennessy, you'll phone the nursing home, won't you? Make the necessary arrangements!'

Hennessy goes, 'Yes, Taoiseach. And I'll tell Kennet to be on stand-by to drive her to Ongar.'

I'm there, 'They're saying she might only have a few months left, by the way.'

The old man goes, 'Yes, I'm well aware of that, Kicker!'

I'm like, 'Okay, I've said my piece – and now I'm out of here,' and I make sure to give Hennessy a serious, *serious* filthy on the way out the door.

I walk along the corridor – this is in, like, the Áras, by the way? – and I suddenly hear a voice coming from the office three doors down. Yeah, no, it ends up being Ronan.

I stand at the door and I'm like, 'Ro, how the hell are you?'

Except he can't hear me because he's got, like, AirPods in?

He's chatting away to someone – presumably on his Bluetooth.

He's going, 'MiNYA zaVUT Ronan. Kak vaz zaVUT?'

I put my hand on his shoulder and he pretty much levitates off his seat.

'Moy fooken Jaysus, Rosser,' he goes, his hand clutched to his hort, 'I nearly shit me bleaten jockeys, so I did. The fook are you sneaking up on me fowur?'

'Sorry, you were on the phone.'

'The phowunt?'

'Yeah, who are talking to? Buckets of Blood or one of that crew?'

'Rosser, I was thalken Rushidden.'

'Russian?'

'That's reet – Rushidden. Ine learning it, so I am.'

'I just thought –'

'Is that what you hea-or, Rosser, when Ine thalken to the likes of Buckets and Nudger and Gull?'

'Pretty much, yeah. I usually catch every third or fourth word and try to get the gist from that.'

He just shakes his head and goes, 'You've libbed a sheltored life.'

And I'm there, 'Yeah, no, thank fock for that. So how are things?'

'Ah, you know yisser self, Rosser.'

'Must be shit being back, is it?'

'Is what it is – know what Ine saying?'

'Only too well, Dude. Only too well. And you're back with Shadden, I believe – as in, like, *properly* back?'

'Ine in the speer roowum. She hadn't fuddy fogibbon me yet.'

'The focking nerve of the girl. *She* wasn't exactly loyal to *you* – riding that Mixed Mortial Orts dude. While also living rent-free in my old pair's gaff in Foxrock –'

'We woatunt be theer for much longer, Rosser. Shadden's wanton out. She hates Foxrock.'

'Well, I know for a fact that the feeling is mutual. Between her focking karaoke nights and her thongs on the washing line, she's the talk of the village.'

'Ine godda ast Heddessy if he'll loaned us the muddy to buy eer own gaff.'

'Ro, don't ask Hennessy. You don't want to be in debt to him.'

'Ine already in debt to him.'

I feel instantly shit. The poor dude gave up his girlfriend, Avery, and a place in Horvard to stop me going to prison.

I'm there, 'I feel guilty, Ro.'

He's like, 'Doatunt feel giddlety.'

'I keep thinking if I hadn't taken my orse out in the Thomond Bor in Cork that time, you'd still be in the States. Instead, you're back here doing Hennessy Coghlan-O'Hara's dirty work.'

'Look, me thaughter's hee-or, Rosser. And hopefully I can persuade Shadden to take me back properdy.'

'Seriously, the focking nerve of her,' I go. 'You think she'd be grateful to get you back. Don't take any shit from her – or her family, Ro.'

He's there, 'Like I says to you, I joost hab to put me head dowun and gerron wirrit.'

Something suddenly occurs to me then.

I'm like, 'Why are you learning Russian anyway?'

He goes, 'Two or tree yee-ors, Rosser, and we're alt godda be learding it.'

'You know,' JP goes, 'I think I'm actually getting used to this stuff.'

He's talking about the Hanijan, the knock-off Chinese piss that we're all still drinking in the absence of Heineken.

I'm there, 'I'll never get used to it.'

Dave Kearney puts my bottle down on the bor – yeah, no, it's Saturday lunchtime and we're all in The Bridge – and he goes, 'Well, we've got your old man to blame for that,' even though I'm getting sick to death of people reminding me.

I turn around to Christian and I'm there, 'I think I might join you on that shit,' because he's drinking just, like, Ballygowan now that he's back on the wagon.

We're all in foul form. Ireland lost to Japan this morning, which means we're going to be playing the All Blacks in the quarter-final.

'The focking All Blacks,' I go.

JP's there, 'That's if we even get out of our group.'

I'm like, 'We'll get out of the group. Russia and Samoa are no great shakes.'

Christian goes, 'I remember you saying the same thing about Japan.'

I'm there, 'Why do they always do this to us? I thought Joe Schmidt had a plan.'

'I said it during the Six Nations,' JP goes. 'We peaked too soon. Seriously, we've been found out.'

I change the subject. I turn to Christian and go, 'Any word from Lychee?'

He's there, 'No – and neither will there be. I don't know what I was thinking there.'

I'm like, 'There was no talking to you, Dude. I said it. Twenty years is too big an age difference. Focking ridiculous.'

JP's there, 'At least you don't have to take any more photos of her for Instagram.'

And Christian goes, '*Take it again, but this time make my orms look thin,*' and it's a pretty good impression of her, it has to be said. '*Why are you trying to make me look cross-eyed? Oh my God, why are you giving me two chins?*'

I'm there, 'I don't know how you put up with it for so long.'

JP goes, 'Hey, we were all twenty-two once.'

I'm like, 'So is there anyone else? My advice would be to get back in the saddle straight away.'

'No time,' he goes. 'I'm flat-out with work. I've got an order for ten thousand Vampire beds for Malingrad and they want them by the end of December.'

Fionn's like, 'You mean there's going to be people living there by the New Year?'

'Yeah,' Christian goes, 'you'd want to see the place. It's a concrete focking jungle.'

I'm there, 'Something else to thank my old man for. Do you miss it, JP? I'm talking about the vertical bed business.'

He's like, 'Not really – and that's no offence to you, Christian. I really love what I'm doing now.'

Yeah, no, he's using some of the moolah he made from inventing the whole sleeping-standing-up thing to set up a charitable foundation to help those less fortunate – which in JP's case means everyone in Ireland except the twenty or thirty people ahead of him on the *Sunday Times* Rich List.

Christian's like, 'So what are all these good works you're doing? Who's benefiting from your philanthropy?' and I notice JP and Fionn exchange a look.

'Well,' JP goes, 'I'm setting up a Social Justice Bursary Scheme for Castlerock College.'

I'm like, '*Bursary?* Is that even a word?'

Fionn's there, 'Yes, Ross, it's a word,' because he can't help being a dick about it. 'When I took over as Principal of Castlerock, my first priority, as you know, was to make the school co-educational.'

I'm like, 'You and your big gobstoppers. You mean allow girls in – even though a mixed school has never won the Leinster Schools Senior Cup in the history of the competition.'

'My second priority,' he goes, deciding to just ignore my point, 'was to waive the fees and education costs for ten per cent of the student population.'

'Belvedere College does something similar,' Christian goes.

I'm there, 'Yeah, because a load of kids from Sheriff Street walking around speaking Ancient Greek is just what the world needs.'

'Well, thanks to JP's generous offer,' Fionn goes, 'from September of next year a quarter of all students attending Castlerock College will receive their education free of chorge.'

I'm there, 'What?' and I can hear the absolute disbelief in my voice. 'You're opening the doors to, like, poor people?'

Fionn goes, 'We *live* in a world of social diversity, Ross. As an educator, I have a duty to prepare our students for that eventuality.'

JP's there, 'When you think about it, Ross, we spent all of our school years mixing only with people from the same social class as us and the same two or three postcodes.'

'Didn't do us any horm,' I go.

Christian laughs. He's there, 'Are you shitting me?' and I realize

that it's suddenly three-against-one here. 'We were obnoxious fockers, Ross.'

I'm like, 'We could afford to be – that's what being privileged is
all about. Dude, I've a better idea. Why don't you pay the school
fees for a load of poor kids to go to Blackrock and Michael's and
Mary's and Gonzaga? Focking flood them with absolute howiyas.'

Fionn goes, 'Ross, the world is changing – and we have to change
with it.'

I'm there, 'I'm glad Father Fehily isn't alive to hear you say that
because that would kill him. Anyway, I thought your priority would
have been your son.'

Yeah, no, Hillary is living with him in a little gaff on the grounds
of the school. His sister, Eleanor, minds the kid during the day. I've
ridden Eleanor twice. Although I'm not sure *why* that's relevant?

'Just because I'm making changes to the ethos of the school,'
Fionn tries to go, 'doesn't mean I don't have time for my son.'

I'm there, 'It's just that Sorcha thought he'd be better off with
you because she's busy trying to save the planet. Sounds like you've
taken on a bit too much work as well.'

I'm out of order and I know it.

He's there, 'How we raise our son has nothing to do with you, Ross.'

I'm like, 'Fair enough,' and then I go, 'Jesus! Focking! Christ!'
because – yeah, no – Delma has walked into the pub. I keep thinking I'll get used to the sight of her humungous sink-plunger lips but
I still *haven't*? Every time I see her, I end up like this. 'Jesus Christ,' I
go, trying to get my breathing under control. 'Jesus. Jesus. Oh, fock.'

'Is there something wrong?' Delma goes.

I'm there, 'No, no. Jesus. Er, it's just – yeah, no – a surprise to see
you, that's all. A *nice* surprise?' and I suddenly stort taking a keen
interest in the label on my Hanijan. 'Bottled in Wuhan. Is it just me
or do a lot of placenames sound made-up?'

I notice that Christian and Fionn are struggling to look at her
as well.

'Four per cent alcohol content,' Fionn goes. 'That's actually *less*
than Heineken, isn't it?'

Delma looks at JP then. She's like, 'Are you ready?'

I'm there, 'Ready? Ready for what?' and I pick a point on her face – her left eyebrow – and I try to focus on that.

'I've still got half a bottle here,' JP goes. 'Can I get you a drink? Glass of Pino Grig, is it?'

I'm there, 'Goys, ready for what?'

Delma goes, 'We're going for lunch – a family lunch.'

It's at that exact point that I spot her son and daughter walking through the door – we're taking Belle and Bingley. The names are focking comical.

I'm there, 'Belle! Bingley! How the hell are you?' happy to have someone new to focus my eyes on.

But the two of them give me major filthies. Yeah, no, in fairness, I was the one who suggested that Delma get one or two bits of work done – the lips were specifically mentioned – to make herself look more like JP's wife and less like his old dear. I didn't know she'd end up looking like she's been smashed in the face with a snow shovel.

I'm there, 'So what's the occasion? And the only reason I'm asking is because we said we were going to watch the rugby together and then make a *day* of it?'

'We're going to The Ivy,' Delma goes. 'It's my birthday.'

I'm there, 'And is it a biggie? I suppose they're all biggies when you hit your age.'

Shit is just pouring out of my mouth now. I think it's, like, *nerves*?

Bingley goes, 'The restaurant is booked for two o'clock. It's *already* that.'

And JP's there, 'I'll tell you what, why don't you three go ahead, I'll knock this back and I'll follow you on in an Uber?'

The three of them just stare at him. Belle eventually goes, 'Come on, Mom – let's just go,' and off the three of them fock.

I do feel a little bit bad about Delma. She was a fine-looking woman before she let that butcher in Istanbul go at her face. Sure I rode her myself in my old dear's side passage. Even though – again – I'm not sure how that fits into the story.

'I take it all is not good on the home front,' I go.

JP's there, 'I can't even bring myself to look at her,' because he's a bit jorred.

'I don't know,' I go, 'I think it's definitely settling down. It's a bit like the Hanijan. I'm sure there'll come a day when I can't remember what it *used* to be like?'

He's like, 'We'll go for dinner, then a few drinks in The Shelbourne, then we'll go home and she'll want sex.'

I'm there, 'It's her birthday, Dude. She's fully entitled.'

He stares off into the distance. I honestly haven't seen him this upset since Sibéal Houseman spat Robbie Arlen's spunk into his mouth at the height of the snowballing craze in the late 1990s.

He goes, 'She likes to do it with the lights on. But I can't, because I –' and then he suddenly stops. For a second or two, I think he's about to burst into tears. 'I lose my erection as soon as I look at her face. So I have to either do her in the dork, or do her from behind.'

I'm like, 'Fock!' because it's the only thing to say in the circumstances.

Fionn goes, 'Is it reversible? Can they remove whatever they put into her lips?'

I'm there, 'Very good question, Fionn – in fairness to you.'

JP shakes his head. He's like, 'They said she could end up looking even worse.'

I'm there, 'It's hord to imagine how she could look any worse than she does – and that's not me being a dick to you.'

It's, like, hort-breaking. He fancied Delma from the time he was, like, fifteen and she was, like, forty. He used to hang around outside her interiors shop in Ranelagh after school every day, staring through the window at her, the little focking deviant.

He turns to Dave Kearney and goes, 'Same again, Dude.'

Fionn goes, 'Are you sure? Bingley said the restaurant was booked for two.'

I'm like, 'Bingley! Where the fock was she going with the names, can I just ask?'

'Hey, like I told them,' JP goes, 'I'll follow them in a taxi.'

Fionn's eyes meet mine and we both know in that moment that the dude is going nowhere.

★

So I'm sitting on the wooden bench underneath the Witch's Hat at the top of Killiney Hill and I'm listening to Honor chatting away to Sincerity while the two of them stare at their phones.

Honor's going, 'What about the white one?'

Sincerity's there, 'The *white* one?' and then she laughs. 'Oh my God – that's, like, *way* too short?'

'Are you saying your mom wouldn't let you go out in it? Just do what every other girl does – wear it underneath a longer skirt, then take the longer skirt off in the toilets of Eddie Rocket's and stash it in your bag.'

In some ways, I should be flattered that my daughter feels comfortable enough to say shit like that in front of me – the whole cool dad thing – but sometimes I wonder am I actually parenting the girl at all? Oh, well, it's too late now.

Sincerity's there, 'No, my mom is totally cool with, like, *whatever* I wear? It's just, I don't know, I hate my actual legs.'

Honor goes, 'Oh! My God! You have amazing legs!'

'Do I – *actually*, like?'

Honor laughs. She's there, 'Oh my God, totally!'

Sincerity's face lights up like a runway. There's no doubt that Honor is really helping her confidence.

'They're gorgeous,' Honor goes. 'You should definitely show them off more.'

I sort of, like, zone out then because I'm keeping an eye on Brian, Johnny and Leo. Yeah, no, it's one of my famous unsupervised access days and the boys wanted to go on a – *their* words – *nature trail?* I shit you not, they are literally picking leaves up off the ground and using some app on their phones to identify what tree they've fallen from – three focking weirdos.

'*Das ist von einer Eiche!*' Leo goes, pushing his glasses up on his nose.

Brian's there, '*Ich habe einen Tannenzapfen gefunden!*' holding up a pine cone and my hort *literally* breaks?

Yeah, no, they're definitely not the kids they used to be. A year ago, before Sorcha's old man took a hand in raising them, they'd have been causing absolute mayhem up here, with other children fleeing them in fear of their lives. It's not a nice thing to say about your own kids but they honestly focking bore me now.

I call out to them. I'm there, 'Goys? Goys?'

Johnny looks up from the berries in his hand that he's spent the last twenty seconds examining. He's like, 'Ja?'

I'm there, 'English, please – you're not in focking school. Yeah, no, I was just thinking, why don't we try to break *into* the Witch's Hat? One of you could stand on my shoulders and climb over the rail onto the ledge up there. Then you could try to jemmy the metal door open.'

They stare at me like I've just asked them to drink their own piss.

I'm like, 'What do you think? There could be treasure in there.'

Johnny goes, 'Granddad Lalor said the reason they blocked up the entrance is because it's dangerous.'

I'm like, 'Did he now?' and I'm thinking, who the fock does he think he is, filling their heads with shite-talk like that?

Leo's there, 'He also said that if we injured ourselves, we wouldn't be covered by insurance.'

I'm like, 'Focking insurance. Your granddad is a knob,' and then I turn to Honor and I'm like, 'The man is a knob, Honor.'

She just ignores me. Her and Sincerity are in their own little world.

Sincerity goes, 'Oh my God, where are you doing your Transition Year work experience?'

And Honor's like, 'Nowhere. I didn't bother my hole arranging anything. I'll just pretend to the school that I'm doing it in my mom's office, then I'll just hang around Dundrum Town Centre every day.'

I'm there, 'Honor, it's nice that you feel you can open up like this in front of me, but I wouldn't be doing my job as a parent if I didn't step in and say something here – like, what about you *actually* doing it in your old dear's office?'

She goes, 'With *her*?'

'She'd really love it, Honor. It might be a chance for you two to properly connect again.'

'Yeah,' she goes, 'focking spare me.'

31

Hey, no one can say I didn't try.

Sincerity's like, 'I'm doing mine in Comté – as in, like, Gráinne's restaurant? I'm going to be, like, *waitressing* for her? Oh my God, why don't I ask her if she could take you as well?'

I'm thinking, a choice between that and two weeks hanging out in Dundrum? Good luck with that, Sincerity.

But Honor goes, 'Oh my God, I would *so* love that!'

I'm there, 'Waitressing?' and I actually laugh. 'Honor, it'll mean having to take shit from people.'

She's like, 'So? I can take shit from people. I can try.'

All of a sudden then, I hear what would have to be described as a piercing scream. Yeah, no, a boy is trying to push Leo down the hill into the focking – I presume – *sea*? And poor Leo is holding onto a tree for dear life and – like I said – screaming at the top of his lungs.

I'm there, 'Isn't that the little focker from St Brigid's who kept jabbing Johnny in the ribs with his hockey stick a few weeks back?'

'Yeah, Morcus,' Honor goes.

The dude is karate-chopping Leo's orms to try to get him to let go of the tree and while this is going on – I can't emphasize the screaming enough – Brian and Johnny are just standing there, watching it happen.

I'm like, 'Why aren't they kicking the fock out of that kid?'

Leo is going, 'Please don't hurt me! Please don't hurt me!'

Sincerity stands up and she's like, 'I'll go and talk to him. He probably doesn't even realize that what he's doing is bullying.'

And off she goes to try to reason with the dude.

I have a little chuckle to myself. I'm there, 'Doesn't realize that it's bullying – yeah, good luck with that, Sincerity.'

Honor goes, 'She tries to see the good in everyone.'

'And that's suddenly a positive thing in your view, is it?'

'What does that mean?'

'I'm just making the point that you seem to be getting on very well together these days.'

She's like, 'So?' on the big-time defensive.

I'm there, 'It's just an observation. You used to hate her guts.'

'That was before I gave her a chance. Would you prefer it if I went back to being a bitch to her?'

'God, no. That'd make things very awkward between me and her old dear. Yeah, no, you keep doing what you're doing. It's earning me major Brownie points with Roz.'

The two of us are looking at Sincerity, who's trying to persuade Morcus to leave Leo alone. Suddenly, out of literally nowhere, the dude shoves her in the chest and then – I swear to fock – spits in her face.

'What the fock?' I hear myself suddenly go and I jump to my feet.

But not before Honor. She covers the distance between here and there in, like, ten giant strides and then – without even saying a word – kicks the little focker between the legs.

I actually laugh. A kick in the balls is never *not* funny? Except when you're the recipient, of course. I'm there, 'Jesus, I felt that one myself.'

The kid turns white, hits the deck and storts groaning.

Of course, that's when his old dear decides to make herself known.

She's going, 'Morcus! Morcus!' and you'd swear he just got a knife in the back rather than a kick in the doo-dahs. 'You horrible girl! You could have killed him!'

I had words with her at the hockey, of course. She's one of *those* women – high-pitched voice, straight to outrage, like everything's a five-alorm fire.

I'm there, 'So you saw him taking a kick in the jewels, but you didn't see him trying to throw my son off the hill?'

'Or spitting in my friend's face,' Honor goes.

The woman's there, 'That was just horseplay,' helping Morcus to his feet. 'Boys being boys.'

He's cupping his nuts with both hands. I reckon they'll be a long time dropping now.

Honor asks Sincerity if she's okay. All the girl can do is just nod. Honor pulls the sleeve of her top down over her hand and wipes the honk off Sincerity's face with her cuff. Then she puts her orm around her shoulder and goes, 'Come on, let's get you back to the cor.'

That'll learn her to try to reason with pricks like Morcus, whose old dear hasn't finished having her *say*, by the way?

Yeah, no, she's going, 'You haven't heard the last of this! You'll be hearing from our solicitor! He's with one of the top five!'

'Yeah, sit on your focking thumb,' Honor goes, without even looking back at the woman, 'you unfuckable, horse-faced tramp.'

I crack up laughing. Of all the things I love about my daughter, her one-liners are definitely, definitely *up* there?

But I'm absolutely furious as I follow Honor and Sincerity back to the cor. I turn around to Johnny and I'm like, 'How can you just stand there watching your brother get the shit kicked out of him like that? There's, like, three of you! Why can't you stick up for each other?'

The three of them have their heads down – looking ashamed of themselves, and so they focking should be.

I'm there, 'Why can't you be more like your sister? Gives the little focker a kick in the mebs and then comes up with a cracking smack-down for his ugly-as-fock mother. Come on, I'm dropping you home.'

'What about the nature trail?' Brian goes.

I'm there, 'The nature trail is over. I'm disgusted with the three of you.'

Oisinn and Magnus want to see me – except they won't say *why*? Yeah, no, it's actually Oisinn who asks me to pop down to Brittas Bay 'for a little chat' and straight away I'm wondering have they found out that I'm potentially the father of their surrogate baby?

I send him a text back, going, 'Can I ask you what it's concerning?' and of course I'm wondering then does that make me sound guilty?

He texts me straight back, going, 'Ffs just come down. We need to ask you something.'

I go to text Sorcha's sister. I'm going to find out her name, by the way, even if it focking kills me. I just go, 'Have you told Oisinn and

Magnus that the baby's possibly mine?' but in the end I don't send it. I decide not to give her that power over me.

So instead – yeah, no – I point the cor in the direction of Wicklow with not a focking clue what I'm about to walk in on.

I'm on the M11, passing the turn-off for Ashford, when my *phone* all of a sudden rings? It ends up being Roz, so I answer it.

I'm there, 'Hey – how the hell *are* you?' doing my famous sexy voice.

She's like, 'All good. I'm just out of hot yoga,' and I'm suddenly picturing the woman in tight-clinging Spandex, sweating like a trumpet player's orse crack.

'Ross?' she goes. 'Are you still there?'

I'm there, 'Yeah, no, sorry, the signal dropped there for a second.'

She goes, 'I really enjoyed last night.'

Yeah, no, we had unbelievable sex. It's mad to think that, after all these years, I'm finally getting good at it.

She goes, 'Even though I'm sore all over today. Where are you, by the way?'

I'm there, 'I'm, em, popping down to Brittas to visit Oisinn and Magnus.'

'Oh my God, they must be *so* excited about the baby, are they?'

'Yeah, no, hopefully – still.'

'Anyway,' she goes, 'the reason I'm ringing is that Sincerity's asked me if she can go to the cinema with Honor tomorrow night. I think there's going to be boys there.'

I'm there, 'Boys?' because it's the first I'm hearing about it. 'Which boys?'

'Someone Honor knows called Johnny Prendergast and a few of his friends.'

'Johnny Prendergast. I've never heard of the dude. Although he *sounds* Protestant. Which is obviously a good thing.'

'Is it?'

'Yeah, no, I just trust Protestants. I don't *know* why? It's just something in me.'

'Right.'

'Like, back in the day, if I was going through the phonebook, looking for an electrician or a plumber to do a job, I'd always pick someone who sounded Protestant. I think I got it from my old man.'

'Well, this boy goes to Wesley College.'

'I rest my case.'

'So you wouldn't have any qualms about letting them go?'

'Like I said, none whatsoever.'

'Let's make sure to tell them to look out for each other.'

'Good thinking. Anyway, listen, I better head here. I'm just about to take the turn-off for Brittas. I'll ring you later.'

'I love you,' she goes.

My hort skips a beat – I'm just not used to this – and I end up nearly swerving off the road.

I manage to get control of the cor and I go, 'I love you too, Roz.'

Five minutes after that, I'm driving up the driveway towards Drayton Manor with a literally knot in my stomach.

The in-patient treatment facility for former employees of American fintech companies, which Oisinn and Magnus opened in Gerald Kean's old gaff, is up and running and at full capacity and you'd have to say fair focks to them. There's people being let go by the likes of Facebook and Google and Accenture and they're struggling to readjust to a world without free Coca-Cola, four-hour-long town halls to discuss Bike to Work schemes and paintball outings aimed at encouraging team-building and maximizing employee productivity.

There's, like, fifteen or twenty people standing around out front, smoking and vaping and whatever else. Magnus is standing in the doorway.

'Rosh!' he goes. 'It ish great to shee you!' and I'm thinking, does he mean that literally, or am I being lured into a trap here?

I'm there, 'Yeah, no, it's good to see *you*, Dude.'

I give him a high-five, which turns into a chest-bump – he's got onboard with all the South Dublin customs – and then he invites me in.

I'm there, 'This place is hopping. I'm going to say fair focks.'

'Yesh,' he goes, 'you've probably heard that there ish talk of a lot of lay-offsh in the tech world. We are already at maxshimum capashity, but in the nexsht few yearsh, Ireland will need thirty to forty reshidential fashilitiesh jusht like thish one.'

'Yeah, no, cool,' I go, because I'm not picking up any hostile vibes from the dude.

He's like, 'Anyway, come through. Oisinn ish making lunch,' and he leads me down to the – yeah, no – *kitchen*?

Oisinn is delighted to see me. He's stirring a humungous pot of presumably soup when I walk in and he goes, 'Ross! How the hell are you?' and he steps away from the hob long enough to give me a high-five-turned-chest-bump.

I'm there, 'I was just saying to Magnus, this place seems to be flying,' because – yeah, no – I'm storting to relax.

He goes, 'Yeah, we've two or three very severe cases, but we've just hired a therapist who's an expert in Stockholm Syndrome. He's been involved in actual *hostage* negotiations?'

I'm there, 'Actual hostage negotiations? Someone is going to have to say fair focks again and it might as well be me.'

'So how are you? How are all the goys?'

'Yeah, no, they're all good. Fionn is talking about allowing poor people into Castlerock College – *with* JP's help – but they can't be focking told.'

'I'm sorry we couldn't make it – the day of the Japan match.'

'You missed nothing. I don't know what the fock is wrong with the team.'

Yeah, no, we've beaten Russia and Samoa since, but I wouldn't be putting money on us to beat the All Blacks tomorrow morning.

He goes, 'I really wanted to go that day but, you know, there's so much happening here, between the treatment centre and then obviously the baby. Speaking of which –'

Oh, fock. Sorcha's sister suddenly steps into the room, looking *very* heavily pregnant.

She goes, 'Hi, Ross!' looking me up and down and really drinking me in. 'I didn't know *you* were coming!'

Magnus is there, 'Yesh, we have shomething to ashk you both. I wash jusht about to call you becaush I wanted you together for it.'

'Oh?' the sister goes. 'I wonder what *this* is about. I'm a bit nervous, are you, Ross?'

I'm like, 'Er, no. I've hopefully no *need* to be?'

'But first,' Oisinn goes, 'I want you to taste this, Ross, and tell me what you think.'

He puts a bowl of – I *was* right – *soup* down in front of me?

He goes, 'It's my mom's minestrone recipe.'

I'm there, 'Fabulous,' because he knows I'm a fan of his old dear's cooking.

I taste a spoonful and out of the corner of my eye I can see Sorcha's sister biting her lip while checking out my guns and my pecs.

'Oh, by the way,' she suddenly goes, 'I was passing Antoine's room and he was singing the Google initiation song.'

'What?' Oisinn goes. 'Why didn't you tell us sooner?'

Magnus is there, 'If the other patientsh hear it, it will shet all of them off!' and the two of them suddenly peg it out of the room and up the stairs, leaving me alone with the girl.

She goes, 'How are you, Ross?'

I'm there, 'Yeah, no, all good. It's a bit random being back here. It's totally changed since the days when I used to crash Gerald Kean's porties. People slag off the Celtic Tiger but we had some nights in here. I actually made a move on Glenda Gilson in this very kitchen but we decided – well, *she* decided – that we were better off as mates. And then she ghosted me for about three years. But it's not one bit awkward whenever I meet her now.'

I'm babbling. I know it and she knows it.

'Am I making you nervous?' she goes, walking around to my side of the table.

I'm there, 'Not really. Maybe a little bit. How's it all going? The pregnancy, I mean?'

'It's fine,' she goes, touching my hair, 'except my hormones are all over the place at the moment. I am *so* focking horny.'

I'm there, 'And, em, I wouldn't imagine there's too much quality on the dating apps in this port of the world?'

'I'm not interested in dating apps, Ross.'

She leans down and moves her face close to mine. She smells of apple and spinach smoothie and *Twilly d'Hermès*.

I'm there, 'The thing is, I'm actually going out with someone.'

'Oh, *are* you?' she whispers in my ear. 'That's *very* interesting.'

She tries to kiss me, but I pull away. Well, no, that's not true, I actually get off with her for a little bit – all of this, what, half an hour after telling Roz that I love her? – but then I come to my senses and I pull away from her.

I'm there, 'Yeah, no, her name is Roz. She lives in Goatstown but she's from Donnybrook originally, although a lot of people would call it technically Milltown.'

She goes, 'She sounds amazing,' and she kisses me again while tugging at my chino buttons.

I'm there, 'What the fock are you doing?' but I'm not exactly pushing her away.

'I told you. I'm horny.'

'And I'm trying to tell you that my relationship status has changed since we last –'

She tears my trousers open like she's opening a packet of Hunky Dorys – we're talking salt and vinegar.

I'm like, 'Jesus Christ,' as she reaches inside my boxers and pulls out my plonker.

'Oh, someone *else* is turned on,' she goes, because – yeah, no – I've a focking horn on me like a pepper mill. 'I don't think this Donnybrook girl is doing enough for you.'

I'm there, 'Like I said, she lives in . . . Goatstown now.'

She's wearing a light, cotton maternity dress and she hitches it up around her waist and then she – and there's no getting away from the word – *straddles* me?

I'm there, 'What if Oisinn and Magnus come back?'

She goes, 'Be quick – not that I have to tell *you* that, of course,' and she laughs in what I would have to say is a *cruel* way? 'Come on, you'll be finished before your soup has even cooled.'

I'm like, 'No, wait. You need to tell me first – am I the father of that baby you're carrying?'

'I'll tell you what,' she goes, 'if you sort me out, I'll tell you the truth. That's a promise.'

Then she pulls the gusset of her pregnancy knickers to one side, moves the old chess pieces into place and suddenly my nose is jammed between her Himalayas and she's bouncing up and down on me with her eyes clamped shut and her lower jaw sticking out like an open cash register.

All I can feel, though, is her humungous Ned Kelly rubbing off mine – it's very, *very* off-putting – and after twenty or thirty seconds, she goes, 'This isn't working,' and she suddenly stands up.

I'm *kind* of relieved? I suppose you could say I've only *technically* cheated on Roz.

But then she goes, 'Let's try it this way,' and she turns her back to me, pushes my soup to one side and assumes the position that's popularly known as reverse cowgirl. Then, suddenly, we're back at it and it's funny because I have a sudden flashback to a Lalor family Christmas when we were playing Cords Against Humanity and I had to use the words 'reverse cowgirl' in front of Sorcha's old pair, then the sister mentioned casually that it was her favourite sexual position and her old dear was so shocked that Sorcha's old man had to call the doctor, who put her on a course of benzodiazepine.

Sorcha's sister is leaning forward, with her big, swollen belly resting on the table, and she's bouncing up and down like I'm giving her a crossbor on a mountain bike on a cobbled road.

And there I'm going to bring the story to a close, having provided all the detail necessary to put my point across. All I'm going to add is that she absolutely goes to town on me, grinding herself backwards and forwards and left and right on my joystick until the whole interaction comes to a juddering halt with her shouting, 'How do you like that, Sorcha? How do you like that, little Miss focking Perfect!' and me biting her bra strap and digging my fingers into her swollen orse.

She stands up and without saying a word she grabs the napkin off my bread plate and cleans up our spills. I put my flute away and I'm like, 'Well?'

She goes, 'Well, what?' as she drops the napkin into the Brabantia.

I'm there, 'Stop focking around. You said you'd tell me the truth about who the father of the baby is.'

She smiles at me.

'Okay,' she goes, 'the truth is . . . I still don't know.'

All of a sudden, Oisinn and Magnus step back into the room.

'I know what you've been doing,' Oisinn goes.

I'm there, 'Dude, she was the one who came on to –'

But he goes, 'You've been asking her which of us she thinks is the baby's father.'

I'm there, 'Er –'

And the sister gets straight in there and goes, 'Like I keep saying, I honestly don't know. Some days I think it's Oisinn's. Some days I think it's Magnus's. And then other days –'

Magnus is like, 'Other days, what?'

And she goes, 'Other days . . . I think it's Oisinn's again.'

We all laugh at that. I've no idea why. Although it's almost certainly relief in my case.

'Are you okay, Ross?' Oisinn goes. 'You're very red in the face there.'

I'm there, 'Am I?'

The sister goes, 'Maybe his soup is too hot?'

I try a spoonful. Yeah, no, she was right. It's still roasting.

I'm like, 'Yeah, no, I'm all good, goys. I'm *all* good.'

Oisinn looks at Magnus and goes, 'Okay, well, like we said, there was a reason we asked you to drive down here today. We wanted to ask you – ask you both, in fact – would you be our baby's godparents?'

'Wow!' the sister goes. 'Isn't that amazing, Ross?'

I'm thinking, yeah, no, at least there's a chance I might find out her actual name.

I'm like, 'Er, yeah, no, I'd, em, love to.'

And the sister laughs and goes, 'Oh my God, Ross, are your trousers open?'

'How are Oisinn and Magnus?' Erika goes.

I'm there, 'Fine? Why do you ask?'

She's like, 'Jesus, Ross, I was only making conversation,' because – yeah, no – it may have sounded a *bit* defensive?

I'm there, 'Yeah, no, they're good.'

'And what about Sorcha's sister?' she goes.

'Why are you asking me about *her* all of a sudden?'

'Er, because she's carrying their *baby*?'

I'm there, 'Oh, er, yeah, good point. No, she's good,' and I suddenly can't look her in the eye. 'Sorry, I'm in a bad mood. The rugby was a horror show this morning. And I actually storted to believe before kick-off that we could repeat the heroics of Soldier's Field.'

Seven focking tries the All Blacks scored and that's it, over for another four years.

She goes, ' Where's Honor tonight?'

I'm there, 'She's at the cinema with a Protestant and his friends. Oh, and Sincerity, of course.'

'They're inseparable these days, aren't they?'

'Yeah, no, it's definitely random. I've never known her to let anyone get this close before. I'm sure it'll all end in tears.'

I notice that Erika is sort of, like, *smiling* to herself?

I'm there, 'What?'

But she just goes, 'Nothing. I'm agreeing with you. I think it's nice.'

'I'm sure she'll be back to her old self before long. Bullying the girl and talking shit about her behind her back. Have you heard from Sorcha, by the way?'

'She's been ringing me two or three times a day. Trying to persuade me that *he* had nothing to do with Sea-mon's death. If she wants to be a sap for him, then let her.'

'So is that it? Is your friendship, like, totally over?'

'Hey, she chose her side. Oh, I have a bit of news, by the way.'

'It's not a new boyfriend, is it? Who is he? Go on, make me jealous.'

She just stares me out of it and goes, 'I sometimes think that chemical castration is the only way to go for you.'

'Sorry, it's hord to fancy the orse off someone for years and years –'

She's like, 'Jesus Christ.'

'– and then suddenly *stop* fancying them just because you find out that –'

'I'm your sister!'

'Exactly. *Half*-sister. Let's get our facts right. So what's this news if it's not you having unbelievable sex with some total and utter stud?'

'Sea-mon's parents have hired an independent crash investigator to find out if there was foul play involved in her death.'

'Whoa! That *is* big news!'

'They're a German company. They've investigated thousands of cor accidents and they've disproved the official version of events in dozens of cases.'

I'm like, 'That's fantastic,' and that's when we hear the front door slam and the entire house seems to shake.

I'm there, 'Is that Helen?'

She goes, 'No, she'd never slam the door like that.'

'Then it can only be –'

Ten seconds later, the kitchen door is thrown open and in Honor walks, looking seriously, *seriously* pissed off about something.

I'm there, 'Hey, Honor, what are you doing home?' but she totally blanks me.

She walks to the fridge, throws it open, looks inside, then slams it shut again.

I'm there, 'Honor –?'

And she's like, 'I focking *said* hello! Oh my God, are you *really* that *needy*?'

Erika's like, 'What movie did you see, Honor?'

And Honor smiles and goes, 'Oh, hi, Erika!' because girls of her age can be in two totally different moods at exactly the same time. 'We saw, like, *Joker*.'

I'm there, 'How was it? I've heard good things.'

She rolls her eyes and goes, 'It was fine. Except halfway through it, Sincerity storted scoring Johnny Prendergast right in front of me.'

I'm there, 'Honor, I'm sure this Johnny Prendergast isn't all *that* and a side of fries. There's plenty more dudes out there and one of them is bound to be for you.'

Honor looks at me like I'm a blackhead on debs night.

I'm there, 'What's wrong?'

And she goes, 'I'm going to my focking room. Night, Erika.'

Erika's like, 'Night, sweethort.'

Then up the stairs the girl tramps. Erika is just, like, smiling at me and at the same time shaking her head.

I'm there, 'You can't talk to them when they're like that, can you?'

She goes, 'You really don't know why she's upset?'

'Because a dude she liked got off with her mate instead of her. You know what girls are like at that age. It was Jonah from High School Rathgor a few weeks ago. Now it's Johnny from Wesley College. It'll be someone else next week.'

'Are you genuinely that slow on the uptake?'

I am, of course. I'm as thick as a bone-in ribeye.

She's there, 'You haven't been paying attention for the last few weeks, have you?'

I'm like, 'Paying attention in terms of what, Erika?'

And she goes, 'Honor has zero interest in Johnny Prendergast, Ross. Can't you see it? She's in love with Sincerity.'

2.

Maybe, I Don't Really Wanna Know

'Oh! My God!' Honor goes. 'What the fock is wrong with you?'

Yeah, no, this is while I'm driving her to school the following morning.

I'm there, 'Wrong with me? In terms of what, Honor?'

She goes, 'Er, you just drove through a red *light*? Then the man on the pedestrian crossing shouted at you – and you didn't even give him the finger.'

I'm there, 'Yeah, no, sorry, Honor. I'm not myself this morning. Probably still thinking about Ireland getting knocked out of the World Cup.'

Except that's horseshit, of course.

Honor's phone beeps. She looks down at it and laughs.

I'm there, 'Who's that? As in, who's texting you at this hour of the morning?' and I realize that I sound like a paranoid person.

'It's Sincerity,' she goes. 'Oh my God, she is being *so* funny this morning.'

I'm there, 'Is she? I'll be the judge of that.'

'So we do this thing where we just talk in, like, GIFs and memes?' she goes. 'She just sent me this one.'

She shows me her phone and – yeah, no – it's a GIF of some ran-domer, tapping his temple. I have no idea *why* it's funny? I say it to her as well and she gets in a bit of a snot with me then.

She goes, 'It's only really funny in the context of the conversation.'

I'm like, 'I'll have to take your word for it.'

I know what I'm doing and I hate myself for it.

I'm there, 'Do you know what *was* funny? Do you remember the time she baked brownies for Miss Durand – just basically trying to

45

suck up to the woman to get better morks – and you put the bag on the ground and stamped all over it?'

'Why are you bringing that up?' she goes.

'You made absolute shit of the things. I'm saying it was funny.'

'But that was, like, years ago. We were in primary school.'

'A good joke is timeless, Honor. And I backed you – do you remember when you were dragged into the Principal's office and you tried to blame it on another girl?'

'It was a mean thing to do. And, anyway, that was before I liked her.'

I'm there, 'Liked her, in terms of –?'

'Why are you being so weird?' she goes. 'She's my friend now.'

'Your friend?'

'Yes, my friend. Seriously, *what* is your problem?'

'I don't have one.'

I turn on the radio. Some random dude reading the news says that Taoiseach Chorles O'Carroll-Kelly is expected to come under heavy pressure from the opposition when the Dáil sits for the first time in almost two years in the Convention Centre in Dublin today.

He goes, 'Irexit is expected to dominate the agenda, with TDs keen to quiz the Taoiseach about Ireland's poor international credit rating, as well as the lack of basic foodstuffs on the country's supermarket shelves, following Ireland's decision to leave the European Union and renege on its international debt obligations.'

'Friend,' I go, because I'm thinking – yeah, no – Erika might have got it wrong. 'Two mates. Like me and Christian are mates – am I right, Honor?'

But she totally blanks me and storts giggling at Sincerity's latest text.

I'm there, 'Enough already!' and I actually *shout* it?

Honor just stares at me with a pitying look on her face, then goes, 'I think you're having a nervous breakdown,' and then she doesn't speak to me for the rest of the journey to the school.

I don't know why I'm being like this. Am I, like, homophobic? But then Oisinn is gay and so is his husband and I've no issue with that. So am I cool with the whole gay thing until it's one of my own kids?

My head is literally melted thinking about it. After I drop her off,

I decide to go and talk to Sorcha, to find out if it's as much a shock to her system as it was to mine. I turn the cor around and I point it in the direction of – what did the dude say? – the *Convention* Centre? I'm there in, like, twenty minutes.

There ends up being a humungous crowd outside – we're talking protesters – and they're not happy, which protesters seldom *are* in fairness to them? They're holding up placords saying shit like, 'EU-Turn!' and 'CO'CK Out!' and they're causing massive traffic delays on the north quays.

I ring Ronan.

I'm there, 'Ro, how the hell *are* you?'

He goes, 'Ine sowunt as a powunt. Ine learden me Rushidden hee-or.'

I'm like, 'Yeah, no, fair focks. Dude, I need to get into the Convention Centre.'

He's there, 'Are you looking for Cheerlie? He's not theer, Rosser.'

I'm like, 'No, I need to talk to Sorcha – we're talking face-to-face. Hang on, what do you mean he's not there? I thought the whole, I don't know, *thing* was back on today.'

'He's playing golf with Heddessy. He's arthur aston Sudeka to take questions from the Opposishidden.'

'Typical of the sly focker. Anyway, I need to get inside the building.'

'You and half the cunterdoddy, Rosser.'

'Please, Ro. This is important.'

'Alreet – there'll be a visitodderr's pass waiting for you at the securitoddy desk. Hee-or, Rosser, what are you doing tomoddow neet?'

I'm like, 'Fock-all, Ro. Most of the World Cup matches are on in the mornings.'

'It's joost we're habbon a few thrinks in the gaff for Shadden's burtdee if you're arowunt?'

Shit, I shouldn't have said I was free until I found out what it was about. Now I've focking committed myself.

I'm there, 'Yeah, no, I might show my face.'

I pork the cor, then I squeeze my way through the angry crowd of people outside. Some of them shout shit like, 'That's his son there! With the big nose in the yachting jacket!' But I blank out their voices like every experienced out-half is trained to do.

I grab my security pass and I'm directed to the public gallery, which turns out to be absolutely rammers, unlike the chamber itself, which is half empty – and we're talking my old *man's* half? Not only has he not shown up, most of his mates haven't either and – like Ronan said – he's left Sorcha to face the music.

She's doing an alright job from where I'm standing. She received an Honourable Citation for her performance in the 1997 All Ireland Debating Championships and they don't give those out to dummies.

She's going, 'I, along with the Deputy, share the public's frustration at seeing empty supermorket shelves. But we've said from the very stort that leaving the European Union – which was the expressed will of the Irish people, remember – would require a period of adjustment.'

There's, like, boos from the opposite side of the chamber.

She goes, 'I would further add that, in line with this Government's commitment to achieving corbon neutrality in the short term, we are going to have to give up many of these air-mile-intensive foods you mentioned, such as avocados, tamarind and goji berries.'

There's uproar in response to that. I'm guessing it's the line about avocados.

I suddenly spot her old man. He's sitting to my right, three or four seats in, hanging on her every word.

I'm there, 'She was never fond of avocados anyway,' and that's the first time he actually notices me standing there in the aisle. 'She always said they taste of nothing and they make you fat. Do you remember she put on a shitload of weight when she went to San Diego for that symposium about saving the Great Barrier Reef?'

He gives me a look shorp enough to shave off a three-day growth of beard.

'Although she blamed that on being back on the pill,' I go. 'She's doing alright, though, isn't she?'

Out of the corner of his mouth, he's like, 'She shouldn't even *be* there!'

And suddenly, *she's* going, 'If I might be allowed to finish –' because the other crowd are still shouting shit at her like, 'This has nothing to do with protecting the environment and you know it!' and then, 'Where is the Taoiseach? Why isn't he here today?'

Sorcha goes, 'As I explained, the Taoiseach is with his wife, who is ill at this time,' which is horseshit, of course. He'll be teeing off in Portmornock round about now.

She goes, '*If* I may be allowed to finish –' which was a favourite comeback of hers when she was being heckled by the girls from one of the Loretos. '*If* I may be allowed to finish –' but then she gives up and sits down.

She's always looked down on Loreto girls, even though she'd never admit it.

Simon Harris is on his feet then. I only know the dude because (a) I once skipped him in the coffee queue in The Happy Pear in Greystones and he made sure to tell me and everybody else in the place who he was – 'I am Simon Harris, *Teachta Dála* for the constituency of Wicklow, and I *will* have service!' – and (b) Sorcha had an erotic dream about him after a drunken cheese-tasting night in the French Paradox in Ballsbridge and whatever crazy shit went down she wouldn't do anything but missionary with me for about three months afterwards.

The dude goes, 'The Taoiseach is showing contempt for this house and contempt for our democracy!'

It all kicks off again – absolute murder.

The dude in chorge calls for order, but he's pissing into the wind. The shouting gets louder and louder until he eventually bangs his little wooden hammer off the table and announces that he's suspending the Dáil for the morning.

Sorcha's old man stands up and I make the mistake of catching his eye.

I'm there, 'It's hord to believe she once had a thing for that dude, isn't it?'

It's the most pissed-off I've seen him since the time I accidentally posted a video of me, totally naked, doing the Buffalo Bill Mangina dance, to the Lalor family WhatsApp group when it was meant for the Castlerock College Team of '99 WhatsApp group.

I follow the dude out of the public gallery, down the corridor, left, through a door and into another corridor, where Sorcha is waiting for him.

He goes, 'Dorling, I thought you acquitted yourself wonderfully well given the circumstances,' and it's while she's hugging him that she cops me standing there behind him.

She's like, 'Ross? What are you doing here?' making me feel about as welcome as a Mormite sandwich in a bridal shop.

I'm there, 'I need to talk to you. It's about Honor.'

Sorcha goes, 'Honor?' and then she turns to her old man. 'Dad, would you mind –?'

He's like, 'This will be some sort of cry for attention, no doubt.'

She's there, 'Would you wait in my office? It's the second door from the end on the left,' and off the dude focks.

Sorcha goes, 'Ross, I don't have capacity for any more drama right now. Your dad has hung me out to dry this morning.'

I'm there, 'Er, you know that Honor is really good friends with Sincerity now?'

She's like, 'Yeah? So what?' and she seems to genuinely mean it.

I'm there, 'Like, really, *really* good friends.'

She goes, 'Well, I wouldn't know what's going on in her life, because I friend-requested her on Instagram and she never accepted it.'

I'm there, 'Do you not think that's unusual – that she used to hate her guts and now she's suddenly her bezzy mate?'

She goes, 'Knowing Honor, there'll be some kind of angle.'

'In terms of?'

'It's probably another one of her schemes. Like the time she pretended to be interested in saving the planet. And the time she pretended to be transgender. She's up to something.'

'Do you think?'

'If there's one thing we've learned about Honor, Ross, it's that there's always an ulterior motive.'

Jesus, they've wrecked the gaff. And I mean *really* gone to *town* on it? There isn't a focking stick of furniture belonging to the old dear in here. Literally everything has come from Ikea, which is Shadden's idea of quality.

If God had ordered the Tuites to build an Ark, it would have been made of MDF.

I'm there, 'I love what you've done with the place,' meaning the exact *opposite* of course?

I'm glad my old dear will never see the inside of this gaff again because the dimmable LED ceiling light that replaced her mock Louis XIV chandelier would be enough to finish her off altogether.

'If you're wontherden wheer your ma and da's auld foornichor is,' Shadden goes, 'it's up in the bleaden athic.'

'I caddent belieb you eeben kept it,' her old dear – the famous focking Dordeen – goes. 'Full of bleaten woodlice, I'd imagidden.'

My old dear has chairs that are worth more than *her* focking house.

Kennet goes, 'You should hab f . . . f . . . f . . . f . . . f . . . fooken bleaten thrun irrout.'

I'm just looking at Ronan – who's staying quiet – and I'm thinking, he gave up an incredible life in America for this and it absolutely kills me.

He goes, 'Will you hab a thrink, Rosser?' and I need one – I *definitely* need one?

I'm there, 'Yeah, no, I'll have a stick of Heinemite, Ro.'

He goes out to the kitchen and returns a few seconds later with a stick of – yeah, no – Hanijan and he doesn't even feel the need to explain it, which says much about where we are as a country.

'How are the n . . . n . . . n . . . n . . . n . . . n . . . n . . . neighbours?' Kennet goes. 'Are thee addy bethor?' suggesting that *they* – and not Shadden – are the problem here.

Shadden goes, 'They're stook-up bastoords, so thee are. Altwees looking dowun their noses at ye.'

And I'm there, 'They're entitled to be,' unable to help myself. 'The people around here are the crème de la crème of our society. They're allowed to be dicks if they want to be. They've earned it. Or they've paid people to earn it for them.'

Dadden – Shadden's brother – goes, 'You'd wannt to move ourra hee-or befower you and Rihatta-Barrogan pick up one of them fooken yuppy accedents – like that fooken dope theer,' and – yeah, no – he means me.

Kadden – the sister – goes, 'I doatunt know how you purrup wirrit, Shadden. It's a hoddible peert of the wurdled. It's not nee-or athin,' and I'm about to say something when Ronan suddenly silences me with a look and a little shake of his head.

'Ine tedding you now, whor I'd do,' Dadden goes, 'if I was libbon in this kip, I'd burden it to the growunt for the insurdance.'

I'm there, 'Yeah, no, it's not their focking house,' because I can see that Shadden is actually thinking about it. 'So they'd get fock-all – just so you all know that.'

'Ronan,' Kennet suddenly goes, 'you're being v . . . v . . . v . . . v . . . v . . . v . . . v . . . v . . . v . . . v . . . v . . . veddy quiet. You moostn't be glad to be back, are ye not?'

Ronan's there, 'No, I am, Kennet – I swayor!' and it kills me to hear him having to talk in, like, a grateful tone.

'Are you sh . . . sh . . . sh . . . sh . . . shewer?' Kennet goes. 'Are you not missing your boord – the b . . . b . . . b . . . b . . . b . . . b . . . b . . . b . . . b . . . b . . . black wooden?'

I feel like nearly punching the focker in the face. God knows, he's had it coming for years.

He goes, 'Wh . . . wh . . . wh . . . wh . . . what's this her nayum was?'

'Avoddy,' Kadden goes.

They all laugh. I've no idea why. Avery is worth more than all of them combined, except Ronan doesn't point *out* this basic fact?

He just looks – yeah, no – totally cowed by them, like he's pre-pared to take any shit they throw at him.

'Getting above he's stayshidden,' Dordeen goes. 'Weredent you, Ro?'

Ro's there, 'That's reet, Dordeen.'

'Your auld fedda theer,' Kennet goes, 'fidding yisser head wit sh . . . sh . . . sh . . . sh . . . shite about Amedica and going to c . . . c . . . c . . . c . . . c . . . coddige. I nebber went to coddidge.'

I wait, like, ten seconds to find out the moral of this story, then I go, 'Sorry, Kennet – and?'

Ronan's like, 'Rosser, leab it.'

I'm there, 'No, I'm just waiting for Kennet to tell me what this is proof of – him not going to college, I mean.'

Ronan's like, 'Rosser, it dudn't mathor.'

Kennet goes, 'Listen to yisser s . . . s . . . s . . . sudden, Rosser. He's s . . . s . . . s . . . speaken the troot. He was happy until you steerted unsettling him – f . . . f . . . f . . . f . . . f . . . f . . . fidding he's head with d . . . d . . . d . . . d . . . d . . . dree-ums.'

Dadden goes, 'Fooken Avoddy. Black as the ace of spayuds, she was,' and I feel like nearly smashing his head through that flatpack armoire.

All of a sudden, the living-room door swings open and in walks Rihanna-Brogan, holding – yeah, no – a birthday cake for her old dear. She goes, 'Happy birthday, Mom!'

And Dordeen's there, 'What was that?'

'M . . . M . . . M . . . M . . . Mom!' Kennet goes, mocking her. 'Where are you going with that bleaten accedent?'

Rihanna-Brogan's like, 'Soddy, I meant to say happy birthday, Ma,' because – yeah, no – they've *embarrassed* her now?

'Happy boortday,' Dadden goes.

Rihanna-Brogan's like, 'Happy birthday.'

'Boortday.'

'Birthday.'

'Boortday.'

'Birthday.'

'Boortday.'

'Boortday.'

'Happy boortday.'

'Happy boortday.'

'That's it,' Kennet goes. 'Doatunt ebber forget where you're f . . . f . . . f . . . f . . . f . . . f . . . from – do you get me? Not like yisser bleaten auld fedda theer – what, Ro?'

He doesn't get a chance to answer because all the Tuites are suddenly off. They're like:

Happy boortday to you,
Happy boortday to you,
Happy boortday, dear Shadden,
Happy boortday to you.

Shadden blows out the candles and then Dordeen's like, 'What did you wish fower?'

Kadden goes, 'Anutter babby, I hope! Keep this fedda nailed dowun this toyum!'

I stand up and I'm there, 'Okay, I'm out of here,' because I can't listen to any more of this.

Dordeen goes, 'Are you not staying for cake? It's Ballack Fodest Gatho.'

I'm there, 'I'd rather eat two metres of my own shit, Dordeen.'

'What,' Kennet goes, 't . . . t . . . t . . . t . . . t . . . t . . . t . . . t . . . too good for us, is it?'

I'm there, 'Miles too good for you, Kennet. And so is my son,' and I give Ronan the eyes as if to tell him to see me out.

Ten seconds later, we're standing at the front door and I'm going, 'Why do you take that shit from them, Ro?'

He's there, 'I've no utter choice, Rosser.'

'Of course you have a choice.'

'Not if Ine wanton to get back in the big, round bed.'

They have a big, round bed. Nothing says 'sex people' like a big, round bed.

I'm there, 'But do you? Want to get back with Shadden, I mean?'

He just shrugs and goes, 'Joost for the sake me thaughter, Rosser. The geerdle needs her mutter *and* fadder.'

And it breaks my literally hort.

'Oh my God,' Honor goes, 'you are going to come back with *such* an amazing tan!'

Yeah, no, Roz and Sincerity are going to Quints for the October mid-term break – them and the rest of South Dublin – and we've driven out to Goatstown to say our goodbyes.

Honor's there, 'I wish I was going with you.'

Roz smiles at me – like she finds this adorable. I'm wondering – yeah, no – *is* this another one of Honor's scams?

'We can still text,' Sincerity goes.

And Honor's like, '*And* we can, like, Facetime?' sounding like a bit of a – and I'm only being honest here – but *desperate* bitch? So maybe her mother was wrong about her.

This is the four of us in the kitchen, by the way. Roz is fixing me a flat white from the Nespresso when Sincerity gets a text message.

'Oh my God,' she suddenly goes, 'it's from Johnny Prendergast.'

I watch Honor's eye narrow.

She's there, 'Bit pathetic. You're not going to text him back, are you?'

Throwing shade at the opposition. Maybe she's learned more from me than I realized.

Sincerity's like, 'Oh my God, he's going to be in Quints! He's going with his mom and dad!'

Roz goes, 'His dad is a partner in Arthur Cox. It turns out that Raymond plays Padel with his brother.'

I'm there, 'Small world,' and at the same time I'm checking out Honor's face for her reaction.

As is *Sincerity*, by the way?

'What,' she goes, 'you don't think I should text him back?'

Honor's there, 'I'm just saying that you don't want to spend your week in Portugal hanging out with someone from, like, *Rathmines*?'

Oh, she's good. She's very, very good.

'It's actually *Ranelagh*?' Sincerity goes, which I'm presuming Honor knows well.

Honor's like, 'Whatever. I'm just saying, it's not a holiday if you're just going to spend it with people you know from home.'

I'm thinking, there's no way Honor would embarrass herself like this, whatever her endgame might be. No, it's suddenly obvious to me that she's got it bad for the girl.

'Oh my God,' Sincerity goes, 'Mom, can I show Honor the three bikinis I bought?'

Honor is out of that chair like a focking Death Row inmate who's had a last-minute reprieve from the Governor.

Roz is like, 'Of course you can!'

But I suddenly hear myself go, 'No!' and they all look at me like I'm a crazy person.

I'm there, 'What I mean is, we should think about maybe hitting the road. I'm sure you have packing to do, Roz.'

Roz is like, 'No, we're all packed.'

'But presumably you've to be up early?'

'No, we're not flying out until the afternoon. Anyway, you haven't even had your coffee yet.'

Roz puts my flat white down in front of me. Honor glowers at me and goes, 'Oh my God, you are *such* a focking weirdo,' and then they disappear out of the room and up the stairs, Sincerity leading the way and Honor trotting after her like the focking dog from *As Good as It Gets*.

Roz goes, 'It's so lovely to see them together, isn't it?'

I'm there, 'Is it? Do you definitely think?'

And she laughs and goes, 'Of course. I'm so happy that they're friends.'

'Friends, yeah. Sincerity seems to be, em –'

'What?'

'Big into boys. And that's not me slut-shaming her.'

'She reminds me of myself at that age.'

'Boys, was it? *All* boys?'

'Absolutely. I like what Honor said to her, by the way.'

'In terms of?'

'About not texting that boy back. I'm talking about Pete Prendergast's son. I don't want her to have a boyfriend.'

Neither does Honor, I'm thinking.

She's like, 'I want her to get to know lots of boys.'

I'm there, 'Again, no judgement from me – even though you don't want her getting a reputation.'

I sip my coffee and she smiles at me.

She's there, 'I'm going to really miss you.'

I'm like, 'Yeah, no, I'm going to really miss you too,' and I'm thinking, okay, Sorcha's sister was a one-off – she always knew how to push my buttons and I only really rode her for information – and from now on I'm staying faithful to Roz.

My girlfriend.

I move in and I throw the lips on her. Suddenly, I've a focking horn on me like a T-Rex's shin-bone. Nothing I can do about it, of course – not with our children upstairs.

It gets definitely hot and heavy, though, before she pulls away, going, 'Ross, there's kids in the house.'

'Yeah, no, I was thinking the exact same thing. We'd have to be very quiet if we did anything –'

I'm looking at her face.

'– or,' I go, 'we should possibly wait until we have the house to ourselves again.'

This seems to be pretty much what she's thinking too.

'Oh,' she suddenly goes, 'Raymond called in today – just to see Sincerity before she goes away. I actually think he has a bit of a man-crush on you!'

I'm like, 'Does he?'

'Oh my God, you're all he can talk about. Asking me question after question about you.'

'Yeah, no, he certainly *sounds* obsessed?'

'I love it that you two get on so well.'

'And that's definitely important to you, is it? As in, like, a deal-breaker?'

'I suppose it is. It's just that all of the relationships I've had in the last ten years broke up because the men I was with couldn't handle me being best friends with my ex-husband.'

'Funny that, isn't it?'

'What do you mean?'

'Just that every single one of them turned out to be jealous of you two.'

'Well, as you know, we're very, very close. What about you and Sorcha?'

'What about us?'

'Do you think you two will ever be friends?'

'I doubt it. I'm on the record as saying that men and women *can't* be friends?'

'That's a ridiculous thing to say.'

'All I know is that it's true for me. I couldn't be friends with a woman and not want to sleep with her.'

'What about you and Erika?'

'A case in point.'

'Excuse me?' she goes.

I'm like, 'Sorry, what I meant to say was that we're pretty much sister and brother.'

Then, totally out of left field, she goes, 'What about Sorcha's sister?'

Holy focking shit-fock. I can feel my face go all hot.

I'm there, 'Er, wh . . . wh . . . wh . . .' turning into Kennet all of a sudden, '. . .why are you bringing *her* up?'

She goes, 'I'm sorry, I wasn't being nosy, I just noticed when I was making your coffee that you had a text message from her.'

Fock. I left my phone next to the sink. I'm getting sloppy in my old age. I stand up – I'm still as hord as Belfast, by the way – and I grab the thing.

It turns out that I've got, like, *two* texts from her? The first one is a message going, 'When are you coming to see me again?' and the second one is a photograph of her upright wink.

'Does she have a name?' Roz goes.

I'm there, 'Yeah, no, I'm sure she does.'

'I'm just saying it's weird that you have her in your phone as *Sorcha's sister.*'

'It's, em, something-something. Or maybe something-something-something. It begins with –'

'A vowel?' Roz goes, a big smile on her face.

I'm there, 'Yes.'

'*Or* a consonant?'

I'm there, 'Possibly,' and she laughs out loud.

I think she gets a genuine, genuine kick out of me.

She suddenly remembers something then. She goes, 'Oh, can you look after Tobey while we're away?'

I'm there, 'Who's Tobey?'

She goes, 'He's my spider,' and then she disappears into the utility room.

I'm like, 'A spider? Is he named after, like, Tobey Maguire?' and then she steps out of the utility room with – I shit you not! – a focking tarantula clinging to her forearm.

'Holy fock!' I go, jumping up from the table.

Again, she laughs.

She's there, 'It's fine. He's not dangerous.'

I'm like, 'Jesus Christ.'

'You've watched too many scary movies.'

I've watched one. I went to see *Arachnophobia* with Nuala Carey off the weather back in the day and I spent the whole two hours screaming like I was on a focking rollercoaster.

'What kind of a focking man are you?' she asked me – not unreasonably – as she drove me home.

There was no kiss and no second date.

I'm there, 'I don't think Erika would let me have that thing in the house, Roz.'

She goes, 'I'm not asking you to bring him home with you. Just pop in two or three times to feed him.'

'What does he even eat?'

She's there, 'Live locusts. They're in a box on the shelf above the washing machine,' and she must see the dubious look on my face because she goes, 'It's fine. I'll ask Raymond.'

That's why I end up going, 'Yeah, no, *I'll* do it. I'll definitely do it. Leave it to me. No better man.'

She goes back into the utility room and returns Tobey to his – I want to say – *tank*? A second or two later, Honor and Sincerity arrive back into the kitchen.

'Oh my God,' Sincerity goes, 'Honor says I look amazing in *all* my bikinis!'

Again, I have another sly look at Honor's face and it's, like, all her focking Christmases.

I'm there, 'Come on, Honor, we better hit the road.'

We say our goodbyes and we head off. Ten minutes later, we're sitting in the cor and neither of us is saying a word. The girl is smitten. There's no doubt about that. The gay thing – and I'm being totally honest here – doesn't bother me in the slightest, I've realized. I don't care *who* my daughter loves? I just don't want to see her hurt and I think she's heading for a definite fall.

I go, 'Will we swing into Donnybrook for an Ed's on the way home?'

But she doesn't seem to even hear me. She just stares into space with the tiniest little smile playing on her lips.

We've all been there.

Sorcha's old man is not happy to see me. But then, when is he ever? This is a man, bear in mind, who turned around to me after walking Sorcha up the aisle and went, 'I prayed last night that you'd die in your sleep.'

And – yeah, no – that's pretty much the same energy he's giving off right *now*?

He goes, 'What the hell are you doing here?'

Here, by the way, is St Kilian's in Clonskeagh, where Brian, Johnny and Leo are in school.

He's there, 'This isn't one of your unsupervised access days.'

I'm like, 'So? I'm allowed to turn up to watch my children play hockey, aren't I?'

Hockey. I feel sick to my stomach even thinking about it. But here we are.

'You're not,' he tries to go. 'Sorcha has explained to you that you can't just show up willy-nilly.'

I'm like, 'Willy-focking-nilly! Do you *ever* take a day off from being a focking knob?'

We're having this borney next to the ortificial pitch, by the way, in front of, like, thirty or forty other parents.

He goes, 'You're disrupting the schedule that Sorcha's mother and I have worked out for them and you're threatening to undo all of the progress we've made with them.'

I'm there, 'Talking out of your hole – as per focking usual,' and I walk straight past him, making sure to give him a good, solid

60

shoulder nudge as I do – the same move I pulled on Craig Doyle a few years ago outside the Natural Bakery in Donnybrook, when he was off to watch his beloved Blackrock College play with a blue-and-white jersey tied around his shoulders. Except there's no grudging respect in this. This isn't school rivalry shit – this is, like, pure hatred. Just like Craig, he ends up spinning around, I don't know, *however* many degrees and nearly losing his footing.

I walk over to the sideline and I wait for the two teams to come out. Yeah, no, they're playing St Andrew's today, although I have to admit there's a definite lack of atmosphere about the place. It's as if, ultimately, it doesn't really a matter a fock who wins – funny that, huh?

The two teams walk out onto the pitch and I try to get the crowd going by shouting, 'Come on, Kilian's – let's show these focking dickheads who's boss!'

Two or three – or maybe more – of the parents stort trying to pull me up on my language by reminding me that these are children. I make no apologies, though, for trying to turn the place into a bit of a cauldron for the visitors. If I've learned one thing about St Andrew's College over the years it's that if you give them an inch, they'll take the piss.

I'm looking at the Kilian's team and – randomly? – I can't see Brian, Johnny *or* Leo.

I'm looking around me, going, 'What the fock? What the actual fock?' but no answers are forthcoming.

The players are out on the pitch doing their stretches and – yeah, no – it turns out my eyes are *not* deceiving me. My kids aren't there. And, slowly, the horrible realization dawns that they haven't been picked. I look over at the bench and there the three of them sit, side by side, not looking remotely pissed off to be left out of the storting line-up.

I end up seeing red. The referee is just about to blow her whistle, but that doesn't stop me morching straight across the pitch to confront Mrs Kremens, the hockey coach.

I'm like, 'What's going on? Why aren't *my* kids playing?' and I realize in that moment that I possibly sound like one of *those* parents – as in, the *pushy* kind? Which I'm obviously not. I just want someone to explain to me, like I said, what the fock?

Mrs Kremens isn't happy to see me either. Yeah, no, let's just say we've interacted like this before.

'Mr O'Carroll-Kelly,' she goes, 'as I've already explained to you, it is my job to pick the team –'

I'm there, 'I want a straight answer. Why aren't they in it?'

Then she ends up *giving* me a straight answer?

'Because,' she goes, 'they are not very good.'

I'm there, 'What do you mean, not very good?' because she's from, originally, Germany and I'm wondering is something being lost in translation here.

'They are not very good at hockey,' she goes. 'As a matter of fact, they are very bad at hockey.'

I look at the three of them sitting there. If I'm expecting a reaction from them, I end up being disappointed.

Brian goes, 'Daddy, I don't actually *want* to play?'

And Johnny's there, 'I don't even like sport. I much prefer drama.'

I can't believe I asked Leo Cullen to be their godfather. I'm only grateful that he never got back to me. Yeah, no, according to mutual friends, he dropped his phone down the toilet with all of his contacts in it and didn't know it was me who was texting him.

Mrs Kremens says something then that's like a dagger to my hort.

She goes, 'You see? Your boys have no desire and no hunger.'

I'm there, 'Would you mind if I gave them a little pep-talk? If I had a word with them, would you think about maybe changing the team, even at this late stage? It's the sign of a good coach – being able to change your mind.'

She's there, 'You are not listening to me. They are not sporting children.'

I suddenly spin around on my heel and I point at Sorcha's old man across the pitch.

I'm there, 'This is what *you* call progress, is it?'

He's like, 'Go home. The boys don't want you here. Nobody wants you here,' and there ends up being a humungous cheer from – yeah, no – all of the other parents.

The referee – even though it's none of her focking business – goes, 'I have to admit, I quite agree. You're holding up the match.'

I'm there, 'The *match*? It's focking hockey. Get a hold of yourself.'

Sorcha's old man storts jabbing his finger in my direction then. He'd want to be very careful.

He goes, 'I won't be bullied by the likes of you – you're nothing but a thug,' which is pretty much the same thing that Craig Doyle said to me as he bent down to pick up his vegan sausage roll.

Yeah, no, I forgot to mention that he dropped his vegan sausage roll.

I'm there, 'I certainly took the wind out of your sails with that shoulder nudge. And that was me using maybe a quarter of my power.'

He's like, 'You have no idea who you're messing with.'

Again, word for word – Craig Doyle.

What I don't realize, of course, is that he's got something in his back pocket. And it's not a Blackrock College Union Blue and White Support Group membership cord, like the one Craig flashed at me. Yeah, no, this is, like, *information*?

He goes, 'You know, it's great to see my daughter not only thriving politically but getting on with her life and putting her bad marriage behind her.'

I'm there, 'In terms of?' and I feel like definitely decking him.

'Oh, haven't you heard?' he goes. 'She's met someone new.'

I'm like, 'Who? What school did he go to?'

He just shit-smiles me.

He's there, 'I'm sure you'll meet him in time. He and Sorcha are very serious about each other. And the boys absolutely love him.'

I'm like, 'What, they've met him already?'

'Oh, yes,' he goes.

I'm there, 'I'm going to repeat my question. What school did he go to?'

But he doesn't answer me. Wouldn't give me the pleasure. Although it's probably St Michael's. She always had a thing about Michael's boys.

He just goes, 'Look what you've done. Look how upset the children are.'

I look back at them and Leo is crying his eyes out – a focking disgrace to the name I chose for him.

And Brian shouts at me, 'Daddy, go home! We don't want you here!'

And in that moment, it would not be an exaggeration to say that my warrior's hort – which couldn't be broken by Clongowes, Belvedere, Blackrock, or any of them – cracks right down the middle.

Sorcha is on the phone to me – yeah, no – within, like, *hours*?

She's like, 'What the hell are you playing at?'

And I'm there, 'What am *I* playing at? Our three sons were dropped from the hockey team – the focking *hockey* team, Sorcha – and they didn't even give a shit.'

She's like, 'What *should* they have done, Ross?'

I'm there, 'They should have been in the coach's ear, telling her that she was making the biggest mistake of her life.'

I get this sudden flashback to me driving to Bishopstown to confront Declan Kidney after he didn't put me on the Ireland team for the U-19s World Cup, even though I was the best outhalf in my age group at the time, certainly in Ireland, and maybe even the world. Yeah, no, I was stood on his road, pressing the horn of my cor, screaming, 'Come out here and face me, you focking coward! You wouldn't know a rugby ball if you sat on one in a focking sauna!'

Now, it turned out that I had the wrong house and all I really succeeded in doing was putting the fear of God into Cork's oldest woman – she looked incredible for ninety-eight – and her granddaughter, who was also her carer. My point is that at least it provoked a *reaction* from me?

'And you'd have done what?' Sorcha goes. 'Found out where the hockey coach lived and spent an hour screaming in her letterbox?'

Yeah, no, I definitely pushed it too far that time. Hennessy ended up having to send the woman a threatening letter. In my defence, I was doing a hell of a lot of creatine around that time.

I'm there, 'Your old man has ruined those boys.'

She's like, '*He* ruined them?'

'That's what I said, Sorcha.'

'No, *you* ruined them. By letting them do whatever the hell they wanted.'

'And who got hurt?'

She's there, 'Lots of people got hurt,' which I'm not going to bother denying. 'They were banned from Tayto Pork. They were banned from the Disney Store. They were banned from the Natural History Museum.'

I'm like, 'Those places are just paranoid about insurance claims.'

As we're having this conversation, by the way, I'm letting myself into Roz's gaff in Goatstown.

I'm there, 'They had an energy about them, Sorcha. And, fine, sometimes it resulted in a man in a Buzz Lightyear costume getting a happy-slapping. Or the skeleton of a giant elk being knocked off its – I want to say – *plinth*? But he's taken all of that energy away from them.'

She's like, 'Yes, he's taught them boundaries. He's taught them how to control their impulses. He's taught them to respect other people and their property.'

I'm there, 'Some focking rugby players *they're* going to make.'

I make my way through the kitchen to the utility room.

'Anyway,' Sorcha goes, 'I'm ringing you just to warn you, Ross, that if there's any repeat of your performance today, I'm going to take away your visitation rights.'

I'm there, '*You're* going to take them away or *he's* going to take them away?' because I know who's driving this.

I'm looking at Tobey the focking tarantula through the glass of his, again, *tank*? He really is an ugly little focker.

Sorcha goes, 'Ross, you terrified the boys with your behaviour today.'

I'm there, 'Everything terrifies them. Including other kids. *He's* turned them into little – and I'm sorry if this sounds sexist, Sorcha – but *pussies*?'

I'm thinking, maybe I'll send them chicken feathers in the post anonymously, like I used to do to Oisinn back in the day whenever

I thought he wasn't putting his weight in at scrum time. It always made him up his performance by a good ten to fifteen per cent, although I never did tell him that it was me.

I spot the box containing the – yeah, no – locusts on the shelf above the washing machine. I take it down and I open it slowly and look inside.

'Jesus Christ,' I go, because the box is, like, crawling with them and they're disgusting things.

Sorcha's like, 'What?'

I'm there, 'Nothing.'

She goes, 'Anyway, I've said my piece, Ross. I never want to see the boys upset like that again.'

I suddenly spot an opening – an opportunity to turn the ball over if we're talking in rugby terms.

I'm there, 'Maybe they're upset for another reason?'

She's like, 'What do you mean by that?'

'I heard you've a new man on the scene.'

She doesn't say shit. Busted and disgusted. I take the lid off the top of the tank and I pour a shitload of locusts into it.

I'm like, 'So what school did he go to?'

She goes, 'Why is that important?'

'Sounds like Michael's to me.'

'It doesn't matter what school he went to, Ross.'

'Someone's changed their tune.'

'All that matters,' she goes, 'is that he's good to me and that he gets on well with my dad.'

I'm there, 'I'm delighted for you. And does he have a name?'

'Why do you need his name?'

'You've already introduced the dude to my children. I think I'm entitled to know what he's called.'

'His name *happens* to be Mike,' she goes. 'And no, Ross, he didn't play rugby.'

That *was* going to be my next question, in fairness.

'And what does he do,' I go, 'this supposed Mike?'

She goes, 'He's a pilot,' in the same smug voice she uses for telling people she grew up on Vico Road.

I'm there, 'Let me guess – Ryanair?' because I feel this sudden need to piss on her parade.

'No, not Ryanair,' she goes. 'He's a pilot on the Government jet.'

'Is he now? You said that the exact same way you tell people that you grew up on Vico Road. There's an unspoken *fock you* in there.'

'All you really need to know, Ross, is that he's romantic and faithful and that both of my parents say they wish I'd met him years ago.'

'And you know all that about him after, what, a few weeks?'

She's like, 'Ross, I don't have time for your pettiness. I've made my point. If you ever upset the boys like that again, I'm cutting off your access,' and then she just, like, hangs up.

I'm so angry in that moment that I feel like nearly hopping my phone off the wall. But then I spot something that nearly stops my hort. I've accidentally left the lid off the tarantula tank – and Tobey is missing.

Oh, holy fock-sticks.

I check all the surfaces in the utility room, then I get down on my hands and knees and stort scouring the floor, but there's no sign of the little focker and – fock, fock, fock! – I'm suddenly remembering what a bad track record I have with other people's pets.

I pull the washing machine out from the wall and I check behind it. No sign of him. Then I do the same with the back-up fridge-freezer. Same shit.

I'm storting to get really worried when I suddenly spot him out of the corner of my eye. My peripheral vision was one of the things that made me the rugby player I very nearly could have been and Denis Hickie – for one – has been known to tear up when he remembers some of my no-look passes. It's a relief to know that I haven't lost it. I see Tobey – like I said, out of the corner of my eye – moving across the floor of the kitchen like Keith focking Earls.

I hare after him and I think he knows straight away that the game is up, because he stops and stays still. I grab a bowl off the draining board and I cover him with it. Then I go looking for a piece of paper. I find a flyer for a company that installs solar panels on your roof – promising substantial savings on your home heating bills, if you're into that kind of thing – and I slide it underneath the bowl. Then I tip the whole thing over, trapping Tobey inside.

I'm there, 'Held up just on the line,' because everything comes back to rugby.

I drop the tarantula into his tank and replace the lid and I'm thinking, all's well that ends well, when I suddenly notice that I've managed to knock over the box containing the locusts and the things are hopping all over the place.

There's, like, twenty or thirty of them on the floor and I end up having to stamp on them. Yeah, no, all of a sudden it's like focking Whac-A-Mole in there. Wherever I see movement, I bring my foot down hord, crushing the little fockers under the soles of my famous size nine Doobie, Doobie, Dubes.

I'm pretty sure I've killed them all, as well as a few more that were hopping around on the surfaces. I put the lid back on the box and I return the box to the shelf.

And I think to myself, I must send Keith Earls a text and tell him that I was thinking about him today. Earlsy will get a great kick out of this story.

Helen has done her famous Nigella Lawson aromatic lamb shank stew for Sunday lunch and I'm milling into it like a man who hasn't eaten in days.

I'm there, 'This is incredible, Helen – in all fairness to you.'

She's like, 'There's plenty more, Ross,' and she smiles at me because she's always been a big, big supporter of mine, especially when I clean my plate.

'Although if your wife has her way,' Erika goes, 'we won't be eating it for much longer. It said in the *Sunday Independent* that they've storted culling sheep and cows again.'

She looks gorgeous at the moment, even though I feel like a bit of a pervert saying it. She's definitely doing something to plump up her lips – whatever that something is, I fully approve.

Helen goes, 'I honestly think I'd rather emigrate than turn vegetarian.'

Erika's there, 'I think by the time Sorcha's finished, those will be your only two choices.'

Honor's quiet, I can't help but notice. She's, like, sitting there, scrolling on her phone and not even *touching* her food?

I'm there, 'Honor, Helen spent a long time cooking that dinner – presumably you did, Helen, did you?'

Honor's there, 'I'm sorry, Helen, I'm sure it's lovely. It's just I'm not hungry.'

Helen's like, 'That's okay, sweetheart,' and then she ends up putting her foot in it by going, 'How's Sincerity?' because – yeah, no – Honor has only heard from the girl two or three times since she went to Quints.

Honor just shrugs and goes, 'I don't know,' and I notice Erika stealing a subtle look at me over a forkful of lamb.

I think I already mentioned her lips.

Helen's there, 'She's probably having too good a time to be thinking of home – meeting boys and all the rest of it,' because she clearly has no idea that Honor has a thing for the girl.

Honor stands up and goes, 'I'm going to go to my room. I'm sorry, Helen,' and off she focks.

Helen's there, 'Was it something I said?'

Erika looks at me for permission to say it, but I end up saying it instead.

I'm there, 'We think Honor has a bit of a *thing* for Sincerity.'

'Oh,' Helen goes, definitely surprised. 'I see.'

Erika's like, 'Has she spoken to you about it yet?'

I'm there, 'No, I was going to ask would *you* maybe have a chat with her?'

'It's *her* private business, Ross. I don't think any of us should say anything to her until she's ready to talk.'

'Do you think?'

'Yes, I think.'

'My daughter. A lesbian. Not that there's anything wrong with that.'

'It could be just a phase.'

'Could it?'

Erika shrugs. She's like, 'Lots of teenage girls go through it. God, I remember me and Meredith McTominay on the Sixth Year skiing holiday to Klosters.'

I swear to fock, I end up totally zoning out thinking about that, until I can suddenly feel a stream of dribble on my chin and I can hear Helen go, 'Is he okay?' and Erika's there, 'Maybe I should turn the fire extinguisher on him.'

I suddenly snap out of it again.

I'm there, 'Sorry, I was just thinking about . . . oh, Jesus Christ.'

Helen's like, 'Drink some water, Ross,' which is what I then do.

'What about Sincerity's mom?' Erika goes. 'Have you mentioned it to her?'

I'm there, 'Again, I don't know how to bring it up. It might weird her out. Not to mention Sincerity, who's into boys, by the way, not girls – she's made that *very* much clear?'

God, I remember Meredith McTominay. She played basketball for Ireland at schools level. She was about six-foot-three. I'd say she threw Erika around the room like a focking frisbee.

I finish clearing my plate and I go, 'Helen, that was a fabulous dinner.'

Then Erika puts her knife and fork down on her plate, sort of, like, clears her throat and goes, 'So I, em, have a bit of news, by the way.'

I'm there, 'News? In terms of?'

She goes, 'You remember the crash investigators that I told you about?'

She means the ones hired by Simone's family.

'Well,' she goes, 'according to Benoîte, they believe there may have been a second cor involved in the accident.'

I'm like, 'Whoa!' even though I'm not really sure where she's going with this.

She sees through my clever bluff, of course, because she explains it to me anyway.

'It means it wasn't a single-cor accident after all,' she goes. 'It means that someone may have deliberately run her off the road.'

I'm there, 'That someone being?'

She goes, 'Who the fock do you think, Ross?'

I presume she means someone working for my old man.

I can tell from the way Helen is looking at her that she's concerned about her. Erika can develop obsessions about things.

Erika goes, 'It was a black BMW X5.'

Jesus, they'll have some job finding that given that half of South Dublin has a second home in Roundstone.

I'm there, 'Good luck with that.'

Erika goes, 'What does that mean?'

'Means there's thousands of X5's driving around that port of the world on any given day. It's, like, needle-in-a-haystack shit.'

She goes, 'Well, the good news is that they've narrowed it down to five. They're going to find out who killed her, Ross. I'm absolutely sure of it.'

Then there's, like, silence at the table as she allows that to sink in.

I'm there, 'Whatever happened to Meredith McTominay?'

And she goes, 'Ross, will you focking forget about Meredith McTominay?'

And I'm going to try. I'm going to definitely, definitely try.

'Holy shit!' I go. 'She's swimming!'

Yeah, no, the new specialist care facility in Ongar is like a hotel. It's got, like, everything in it, including a music room, a cinema, a gym and a pool, where – like I said – the old dear is swimming, and we're talking lengths.

I'm there, 'I've never seen her swim before,' and I mean that literally.

Even when we went away on holidays, I'd be splashing around in the water while she was stretched out on a lounger with a Banana Daiquiri, or a Piña Colada, or a white wine spritzer. I'd be waving at her from the shallow end, going, 'Mommy! Mommy! I nearly swam!' and she'd sort of, like, toast me with her Mango Bellini, or her Cuba Libre, or her Elderflower Collins.

Or I'd go, 'Mommy, I was playing Morco Polo with a boy, but I found out he's from Shankill, so I'm not going to talk to him anymore!' and she'd go, 'Good for you, Dorling!' and sip her Gooseberry Gimlet, or her Long Island Iced Tea, or her Akaibara Cooler.

But I'm pretty sure I've never seen her *in* the water before.

I'm there, 'I didn't know she could even swim.'

And Dalisay, one of her full-time nurses, goes, 'Oh, she is very good. Every morning, she is swimming for one hour,' because the woman is from – not being racist – but the Philippines?

I'm there, 'It's like watching a focking elephant seal in one of those nature documentaries, isn't it? On land, they're, like, dragging their big, blubbery bodies around the place, then they get in the water and they cut through it like a knife through butter.'

Dalisay looks at me with her mouth open.

I'm there, 'That's just how we talk about each other. Don't worry, you'll get used to it.'

All of a sudden, I hear the old dear going, 'Ross! Ross!'

Yeah, no, she's stopped swimming and she's treading water in the deep end while waving and shouting at me.

She's like, 'Hello, Dorling!'

So I shout back. I'm there, 'Yeah, no, hey – how are things?'

She goes, 'I see you've met Dalisay.'

I'm like, 'Yeah, she's just given me the tour. It's some spot, isn't it?'

She goes, 'You'll have to watch *him*, Dalisay. He'll try to have sex with you.'

Jesus Christ.

I turn to Dalisay and I'm like, 'I'm sorry about that. I won't try to have sex with you. Not that there's anything wrong with you.'

She's a little focking cracker, by the way.

The old dear's there, 'He's a bit of a ladies' man, you see. He always was, weren't you, Dorling? But don't believe any promises he makes to you. Oh, the number of broken-horted girls I ended up having to counsel after he'd finished with them.'

I smile awkwardly at Dalisay.

I'm there, 'Her memory is obviously an issue.'

Dalisay smiles politely back.

The old dear goes, 'Are you getting in, Ross?'

I laugh. I'm there, 'I don't think so.'

She's like, 'Oh, come on – swim with your mother!'

I'm there, 'Er, I *can't* swim?'

But she goes, 'Oh, well, just get into the shallow end with me.'

Dalisay turns around to me and goes, 'I can get you some swim shorts.'

I'm there, 'No, you're alright, Dalisay – maybe some other time,' and then I shout to the old dear, 'Maybe some other time. Are you getting out or what?'

So – yeah, no – she swims over to the edge of the pool, then Dalisay bends down and helps drag her up the ladder. It's like watching Cheslin Kolbe pull Lood de Jager over a prison wall.

The old dear gives me a hug while she's still sopping wet.

She's like, 'How *are* you, Dorling?'

And I'm there, 'Yeah, no, all good.'

'Oh, look, I've soaked you. I'm so sorry.'

'Hey, it's cool. I was just saying to Dalisay here, I've never *seen* you swim before?'

'Haven't you?'

'No. I didn't even know you *could* swim.'

'Oh, I loved to swim when I was younger. Dalisay, could I get a Pomegranate Pimm's? Ross, you'll have one too?'

I look at Dalisay and she sort of, like, smiles. Yes, we're pretending.

I'm there, 'You know what? Make mine a double.'

And the old dear goes, 'What a wonderful idea! I'll have a double too.'

We both watch her turn and go.

The old dear's like, 'You're *not* going to have sex with her, are you, Ross?'

Jesus focking Christ.

I'm there, 'Er, I wasn't *planning* on it?'

'It's just that it would make my life more complicated – if you *did* have sex with her. We've become rather good friends, you see.'

'Fine – I won't do it so.'

'Thank you. I mean, I know how difficult it is for you –'

'It's *not* difficult. I don't try to have sex with *every* woman I meet?'

'I know you have a very high libido. All those rolled-up tissues I used to find under your bed.'

'I see you're having one of your clearer days, then.'

'I remember when you were a teenager – fourteen to sixteen were the worst years! – I'd be in the drawing room, reading a book – usually one of Maeve's – and upstairs I'd hear the bedsprings going and I'd say to your father, "Does that boy *ever* stop wanking?"'

I'm there, 'Can we possibly *change* the subject?' and we sit down on two sun-loungers, which are side by side next to the pool. 'I swung out to the Áras yesterday and I saw the kids.'

She's like, 'Oh! How wonderful!' and I can tell from the vacant look in her eyes that she has no idea what I'm even talking about.

I'm there, 'I'm talking about Hugo. I'm talking about Diana. I'm talking about Louisa May.'

She goes, 'Oh, lovely, lovely Louisa May,' and I see a flicker of, I don't know, *memory* in her face.

I'm there, 'I'm talking about Cassiopeia.'

'Cassiopeia is a biter,' she goes.

I'm like, 'That's right. I'm talking about Emily. I'm talking about –'

'Mellicent,' she goes.

I'm there, 'Mellicent – exactly.'

She smiles, delighted with herself.

Then she goes, 'How does your wife cope with it all?'

I'm like, 'What are you talking about?'

'I'm not being unkind, but what was she thinking bringing all of those children into the world – at *her* age?'

'They're not Sorcha's children – they're yours!'

'Are they?'

'You honestly don't remember?'

'Did I adopt them?' she goes. 'I always wanted to adopt a child from somewhere awful.'

'No, you froze your eggs.'

'If you say so.'

'Then they used the old man's sperm – actually let's change the subject again.'

She's like, 'You must swim with me.'

I'm there, 'I might. Not today.'

'Oh, Ross, do you remember the time, we were somewhere. It

must have been Praia da Rocha. And you were in the water and you said to me that you'd made a friend – from Shankill.'

'We were playing Morco Polo. I was only just thinking about that.'

'And I said to you, "You are not becoming friends with someone from Shankill."'

'Yeah, no, I remember it a *little* bit differently?'

'I said, "We'll go home and he'll want to stay in touch and the next thing we know his family will be asking us for money." So I went to his mother and I said, "You won't be getting a focking penny from us! So tell your boy to stay away from my son!"'

Shit, that *is* ringing a bell or two. I'm thinking, maybe her memory is better than I thought.

All of a sudden, Dalisay returns, not with our drinks – I didn't *really* think I was getting one? – but with the old man. I smile. I can't help myself. He came.

He smiles and goes, 'Hello, Dorling!'

Yeah, no, he's talking to the old dear, not me.

She's like, 'Hello.'

He's there, 'It's lovely to see you!'

And she goes, 'It's lovely to see you too.'

He's like, 'I just wanted to see how you were settling in! Hello, Ross!'

And I'm there, 'Yeah, no, whatever.'

He goes, 'You've been swimming, Fionnuala!'

'Yes, I swim every day now.'

'How wonderful! Well, I thought you might like to know that the job of rerouting the Liffey to place the Áras on the *south* side of the city is almost complete!'

'Is it?'

'It's meant knocking down considerably more houses than originally anticipated – about five hundred or so, although they're mostly in Cabra and Ashtown!'

And yeah, no, it's lovely to see them chatting like this.

'We've found temporary accommodation for all of those made homeless!' he goes. 'Well, many of them!'

The old dear's like, 'How lovely!'

And that's when she turns around to me – I shit you not – and goes, 'Ross, who is this person?'

I watch the old man's face just drop.

The old dear says it again. She's there, 'Who is he, Ross? Why is he talking to me about Cabra?'

The old man – I swear to fock – doesn't say a word. He just turns on his heel and he morches straight out of there.

I don't believe it. I don't *focking* believe it.

Yeah, no, Roz and Sincerity are arriving home from Quints tonight and me and Honor have turned up at the airport to *surprise* them? Except Raymond has had the exact same idea and he's waiting there ahead of us in the arrivals lounge, obviously trying to steal my thunder.

'The fock are you doing here?' I go.

He's there, 'Well, my daughter has been away for a week and I'm excited about seeing her. Is that okay with you, Ross?'

He makes me feel like an orsehole for bringing it up.

I'm there, 'Yeah, no, whatever.'

He goes, 'I got a text from Roz to say that they've landed,' and he is being a dick now – just letting me know again how close they supposedly are.

I'm like, 'Yeah, no, I got the exact same message,' even though I *didn't?*

We're carrying on like love-struck teenagers.

Speaking of which, Honor looks up from her phone, then goes, 'Sincerity says they're just waiting for their bags.'

I'm there, 'Did you hear that, Raymond? They're at the carousel. You didn't get that update, did you?' and I know how possibly *petty* it sounds?

The three of us stand there, staring at the arrival doors like Faf de Klerk waiting for the ball to pop out of a scrum.

All of a sudden, they slide open and Roz walks through, pushing a trolley, looking tanned and fit, with Sincerity behind her pulling a wheelie case.

Raymond moves first, but he just doesn't have my acceleration from a standing stort, having played what little rugby he did as a number eight, and even then it was for Bective's thirds – from what I hear – for only a season and a half.

Of course, Roz and Sincerity are shocked to the see the three of us chorging at them like the South African front row. I get there first and I throw my orms around Roz, while Honor – yeah, no – does something similar to Sincerity.

Roz laughs and goes, 'Oh my God! We must go away for a week more often!'

And it's only then that she cops Raymond standing there too.

She's like, 'This is quite the welcome,' and then she breaks away from me to hug him, which doesn't bother me in the slightest. No one cares who finishes second. Ask CBC Monkstown.

She goes, 'What a lovely surprise!'

I hear Honor tell Sincerity that she missed her – oh my God – so much and I feel like nearly telling her to rein it in, before Sincerity mentions that she ended up bumping into Johnny Prendergast after all and she has – oh my God – so much goss for her. Out of the corner of my eye, I can see that Honor is not a happy bunny.

Raymond goes over and hugs Sincerity then. He pretty much sweeps her up in his orms. Yeah, no, you'd swear we'd all been separated for years – like a bunch of screamy girls meeting outside McDonald's on Grafton Street on a Saturday morning, exactly sixteen hours after they last saw each other in school.

'So what are you all doing here?' Roz goes. 'I told you we'd get a taxi.'

I'm there, 'I came to surprise you. Raymond came just to be a –' and I'm about say 'focking bell-end' when the dude suddenly goes, 'Well, you haven't seen Ross in a week. I thought you two might appreciate a bit of time together – a romantic night in. I was going to offer to take Sincerity for the night.'

He's a smort cookie. I'll give him that.

Sincerity goes, 'Can Honor sleep over?'

The dude is like, 'Of course!'

'Raymond,' Roz goes, 'that is so thoughtful of you – isn't it, Ross?'

I'm there, 'Yeah, no, I'm admitting it.'

So basically what happens then is that Raymond focks off with the two girls and I drive Roz back to Goatstown in *my* cor?

She's happy to see me and she's making that much very obvious.

We've just taken the turn off the M1 onto the M50 heading south when she puts her hand on my thigh and storts – yeah, no – *massaging* it? I'm looking at her long, brown legs in her little cotton mini-dress and espadrilles and I'm thinking I might not be able to wait until Junction 13 for Dundrum, Sandyford and – yeah, no – eventually Goatstown.

'I might need to pull into the hord shoulder,' I go.

And she's like, 'No, keep driving. It'll be worth it.'

But it ends up getting hot and heavy very quickly, especially between Junction 4, for Ballymun and the Naul, and Junction 6, for Castleknock, Blanchardstown and the N3, when she storts tracing the outline of my battered sausage through the left leg of my chinos; then again between Junction 10, for Cookstown and Bally-mount Industrial Estate, and Junction 12 for Knocklyon, Firhouse and the R113, when she grabs my non-steering hand and storts, one by one – I shit you not – sucking my fingers.

I'm thinking, whose bright idea was it to put Goatstown this far away from the focking airport? But we eventually get there. I pull into the driveway and we both get out of the cor.

I'm there, 'Do you want me to grab your cases from the boot?'

But she's like, 'Leave them. Until afterwards,' and with her trembling hands she somehow manages to direct the front door key into the lock.

Into the hallway we go. I slam the front door behind me, then I push her up against the wall, our crotches touching, my mouth on hers, my hands all over her groodies, trying to push her bra up or down to get a better purchase on the things. She opens my belt and my buttons and pulls my chinos and my boxers down. Then she puts her orms around my shoulders and she jumps up, wrapping her legs around my waist.

I'm like, 'What, here? Up against the wall?'

And she's there, 'Yeah,' but then a second later she changes her mind and goes, 'No, in the kitchen. I want you to do me on the table.'

So, with my trousers around my ankles, I sort of, like, penguin-walk my way down the hallway towards the kitchen, with Roz clinging to me like she's shimmied up a tree to escape a bear, her breathing all ragged, her eyes turned in on each other and her mouth forming a perfect O.

I push the door to the kitchen and I end up getting the fright of my – *literally?* – life.

I'm like, 'Oh . . . holy . . . fock!'

Roz is there, 'What?' because she can see the shock on my face.

She turns around – still *clinging* to me, bear in mind? – and she can suddenly see what *I* can see?

Which is basically . . . a plague of focking locusts.

When I say a plague, I don't mean a couple of hundred, or even a couple of thousand. I'm talking about, I don't know, tens of thousands of the focking things. The air is, like, thick with them. They're on the walls, they're on the floor, they're on every focking surface.

It's like something from, I'm guessing, the Bible.

I'm still standing there with my trousers down, and Roz now clutching herself tighter and tighter to me, like she's trying to avoid a rising flood tide, and these things are suddenly flying into us and crawling all over us. They're in our faces, and they're in our hair, and they're in our mouths.

Roz screams. In terms of its intensity, the only thing I can compare it to is the noise that I made when Warren Gatland left Drico out of the third Lions test against Australia in 2013. It ends up nearly deafening me.

She's like, '*Aaaaaarrrrrrggggggghhhhhh!!!!!!*'

3.

Give Me Gin and Tonic

All I can say is sorry. Well, I don't *literally* say sorry, but I certainly make one or two apologetic noises.

I'm there, 'It's possible some of them may have jumped out alright – when I left the *box* open?'

And she goes, 'I told you not to leave the box open,' because she's a bit of a last-word freak is Roz.

I'm like, '*If* you did –'

She's there, 'I did, Ross.'

I go, '– then I genuinely don't remember you saying it. Either way, I had no idea that locusts could, like, *breed* that quickly?'

She's like, 'You've never seen, like, a nature documentary about locusts?' and I must really love her because if this was any other woman, I'd be getting out of this cor right now, even with the thing still moving.

I'm there, 'No, I've never seen a nature documentary about locusts,' although I can use my imagination.

We're on the road to Brittas Bay, by the way. Oisinn and Magnus are hosting a gender reveal porty in Drayton Manor. Sorcha's sister is obviously going to be there, so I'm already – yeah, no – nervous enough.

She goes, 'Well, it's a good job Raymond knew what to do.'

Which is a definite, *definite* dig at me. Yeah, no, it turned out that he played rugby – again, *thirds* rugby – with some dude who owns a pest control company and he sent someone round straight away.

I'm there, 'I did say I'd deal with it, Roz.'

She goes, 'You wanted to shut the kitchen door –'

'I was going to Google extermination companies the next morning.'

'–so we could go back to having sex?'

'They weren't going anywhere.'

'And you could *have* sex, could you – with a swarm of locusts downstairs?'

I could have sex with a herd of elephants downstairs.

I'm there, 'I was very turned on – and that was from pretty much Junction 4 onwards.'

She's like, 'Well, as Raymond said, it could have been a hell of a lot worse. *He's* just glad that Sincerity wasn't in the house at the time,' and then she goes, 'Oh my God!'

I'm there, 'What?'

'Were you about to open the door while the cor was moving?'

'No.'

'Ross, I watched you. You reached for the handle of the door.'

'Yeah, no, it might have been an *unconscious* thing? I was married for nearly twenty years, bear in mind.'

'Well, it's no wonder it didn't work out if you'd rather jump out of a moving cor than apologize.'

It's a low blow and she knows it.

I'm there, 'I did apologize.'

She goes, 'No, you didn't,' and she's actually shouting now. 'You'd prefer to just gaslight me.'

I suppose you could say that this is our first major row.

She's there, 'I trusted you to do something and you messed up.'

'And I'm admitting,' I go, 'that – yeah, no – I probably did leave the box open.'

'But you haven't said sorry.'

'Fine, then – I'm sorry!'

'That's not how you apologize to someone.'

'How do you want me to say it?'

'Like you actually mean it, Ross.'

And then we don't say anything for the rest of the drive to Brittas.

The gaff ends up being rammers, all the former Dell and Twitter and LinkedIn employees mixing freely with Oisinn and Magnus's family and friends.

I hear some randomer go, 'Do we know when the baby's due?'

And another dude is like, 'I think it's a goal for Q4/19 – definitely before Financial Year End.'

There's some really severe cases out there. The public doesn't know the half of it.

We spot Christian, JP and Fionn standing in the middle of the crowd and we tip over to them.

I'm like, 'Hey, goys – how the hell are you? Still planning to let skobies into Castlerock College?'

Neither Fionn nor JP takes the bait.

They're just like, 'Hey, Roz,' and it ends up being hugs and air-kisses and the whole bit.

I'm there, 'In case you were wondering, Roz, that was a reference to Fionn waiving school fees for – I don't know, what percentage was it again, Fionn?'

'Twenty-Five per cent,' Fionn goes – not even embarrassed about it.

JP's there, 'It's a bursary scheme that I'm funding, Roz. We want to give hundreds of kids from socially disadvantaged areas access to private education.'

Roz clearly hasn't forgiven me because she goes, 'What a lovely idea!'

A girl who went to Alexandra College. Eight focking grand a term. I can't see *them* opening the doors to people from, I don't know, Templeogue and Harold's Cross and if they did, I'm sure Roz would be the first one to call it a shitshow.

I decide to drop the subject, though.

I'm there, 'Delma not with you, JP?' but then she suddenly turns around – she had her back to us – when she hears her name mentioned and Roz quite literally screams with fright.

Delma goes, 'Are you okay?'

And Roz is there, 'Yeah, no, sorry, I just remembered that I, em, forgot to pay my property tax.'

The woman turns to JP and she goes, 'When is this announcement happening?' and she doesn't exactly sound happy to be here. 'We're missing all this time in the spa.'

JP's there, 'We're driving down to Monort afterwards,' and he doesn't seem pleased about that either.

It's a five-stor hotel, so she'll probably want the ride.

Christian turns around to me then – being a proper mate – and goes, 'Just to let you know, Ross, Sorcha's here.'

And all of a sudden I hear her voice and I see her coming towards us. She's going, 'Hi, everyone!' but her main focus is Roz.

She sticks out her hand to introduce herself, even though she's known the woman for years from the school run.

She goes, 'Lovely to see you, Roz! You're friends with Sally Sorley, who went to Mount Anville, aren't you? We did the exact same Special Study Topic for History in the Leaving! And you know Amy Madden from Zumba with Justyna! *My* mom used to play tennis with *her* mom in Glenageary!'

Sorcha does this when she's nervous about meeting someone – totally overdoes the whole connections thing. That's some focking background check she's done on her all the same.

She goes, 'Another mutual friend we have is Suzanne Dalby! She was in your Maths and Physics classes at school and I did Spanish grinds with her in the Institute! I'm still friends with her – although mainly just through Instagram!'

I'm there, 'Yeah, we get it, Sorcha – everyone in South Dublin knows everybody else,' because I'm wondering what the fock she's even *doing* here? She and her sister aren't exactly close and she's supposedly not happy about her even *having* this baby?

And that's when I get my answer.

'Everyone,' she goes, 'I'd like you to meet Mike!' and she suddenly hooks this random dude by the orm and she sort of, like, pulls him into the circle.

She's obviously decided this is the moment when they go public. It saves her posting it on all her socials, I suppose.

Everyone goes, 'Hi, Mike!' just to be polite, although *I* say fock-all, deciding to keep my powder dry.

Sorcha does the introductions while I just stare him down. Yeah, no, he's a good-looking dude, I'm saying that on the record, but he's wearing – I shit you not – an actual focking pilot's uniform.

I'm there, 'Fly to Brittas today, did you?'

'No,' the dude goes, 'I've actually just flown back from Italy,' and I go suddenly quiet because there's something in his voice – this is going to sound weird – that, I don't know, *does* something for me?

I manage to get my shit together to go, 'You couldn't have changed your clothes, no?' because he's even wearing aviators on his head, and I suddenly remember that the only time I ever caught Sorcha masturbating was while she was watching the Tom Cruise and Kelly McGillis kissing scene from *Top Gun* when she was supposably upstairs watching her *Emma Bunton Pelvic Floor Exercise* DVD, and then there was another time she accidentally called me Maverick when we were having sex on a city break to Dubrovnik.

'Italy!' Roz goes – because she's trying to punish me now. 'Wow!'

I'm there, 'Lot of air-miles involved in that trip, I'm guessing. Which you're very *anti*, Sorcha – am I right?'

He goes, 'Well, it *was* important Government business, Ross!'

He could be a DJ with that voice. I know this is going to sound random but it's, like, velvety or something.

Sorcha is like, 'Ross, don't be rude. I'm so sorry, Mike,' but I know her well enough to know that she's secretly delighted that it's pissed me off.

I'm there, 'Excuse me,' because I have to get away from here, 'I'm just going to go and look for Oisinn and Magnus,' and off I fock, leaving Roz with them.

I don't find Oisinn and Magnus, but I do end up running into Sorcha's – yeah, no – sister.

She goes, 'Hey, Ross,' sizing me up with her eyes. 'I'm so happy you're here.'

I'm there, 'Are you?' just making conversation with her.

She goes, 'Do you want me to suck you off?'

I'm there, 'Er, no, I think I'm okay, thanks.'

She's like, 'I could do it in the toilet. Like I did in Conway's that night during the Blackrock Folk and Bluegrass Festival, Including Appalachian Square Dance Fiddling.'

The Celtic Tiger was hilarious when you look back on it.

I go, 'I'm actually *here* with someone?'

She's like, 'Oh, is this your new *girlfriend*?' and she says girlfriend the way I say Gaelic football, like she doesn't believe it's a real thing at all.

I'm there, 'Her name is Roz.'

'*Roz!*' she goes – again, like she thinks I'm being ridiculous. 'Ross and Roz! That's hilarious! Does she do that thing that I do with your balls?'

I'm there, 'I'm not really sure I want to discuss my private life with you.'

'Really? Did you happen to mention to her that the last time you were in this house you pounded me to the point where I thought I was having uterine contractions the following day?'

Jesus Christ.

I'm there, 'I seem to remember it was more a case of *you* pounding *me*?'

She goes, 'You know, when Oisinn and Magnus do the big reveal, I was thinking of maybe doing one of my own.'

'What kind of reveal?'

'I'm going to announce that you're the father.'

'Please – I'm begging you.'

'Then answer my question – does she do that thing with your balls that I do?'

'No, she doesn't do that thing with my balls.'

'So what *does* she do?'

'Seriously?'

'I will shout it at the top of my voice that you are the father of this baby unless you tell me.'

'We do other things. We do, like, *tantric* sex?'

'Tantric? Is that the one where you go at it for hours?'

'Yeah, no, it *can* be hours, yeah. Not always, but it's happened.'

She's like, 'You've never had tantric sex with *me* before,' and she says it in a sort of, like, sulky way that I would say is typical of the youngest member in the family. 'Oh, speak of the devil.'

I look over my shoulder and – yeah, no – Roz has arrived over.

She's like, 'Hello, I'm Roz!' and she sticks out her hand to introduce herself.

And I'm thinking, here we go, I'm finally going to find out the
sister's name. But instead of introducing herself, she goes, 'Yeah,
I'm well aware of who you are!' and then she just, like, bitch-smiles
her and focks off.

Roz is there, 'Oh my God, what was *that* about?'

I'm like, 'The girl's eight and a bit months pregnant. She's not in
her right mind.'

'I meant the way she was looking at you.'

'What way was she looking at me?'

'Like she wanted to have sex with you.'

'That's very random,' I go. 'I've genuinely never noticed that before.'

She just, like, stares at me, like she knows I'm lying to her, but
then Oisinn ends up saving my skin by suddenly appearing with a
giant – yeah, no – cannon, which he wheels across the floor of
Gerald Kean's old bor and announces that it's finally time for us to
find out the gender of their supposed baby.

We're all looking at this thing, wondering, what the fock?

Magnus goes, 'Sho, I would like to ashk the baby'sh godfather
and godmother to shtep up here for a moment!'

So – yeah, no – me and the sister tip over to them.

I hear Roz go, 'Oh my God, you're sharing godparenting duties
with *that* girl?' because she's obviously got a vibe from her.

Magnus is like, 'Okay, sho what we have here ish a confetti
cannon. On the count of three, I am going to ashk Rosh to push the
button and out of the cannon will come perhapsh blue confetti or
perhapsh pink confetti. If the confetti ish blue –'

Oisinn goes, 'Yeah, I think they get the general idea, Magnus. Are
you ready, Ross?'

I move to the back of the cannon.

Magnus is like, 'On five . . . four . . . three . . . two . . . one!'

I press the button, but nothing happens – as in, no *confetti* comes
out of it?

I'm there, 'Sorry, I'm having a bit of an equipment malfunction
here.'

And Sorcha's sister – this is no bullshit – shouts, 'That's what you said last night, Ross!' and everyone laughs, except Roz and – presumably – Sorcha, who knows I've thrown my rod in those waters on at least one occasion in the past.

Magnus goes, 'On five . . . four . . . three . . . two . . . one!'

I press the button again and still nothing happens.

I'm there, 'I don't think it's going to go off.'

The sister goes, 'I've heard you say that as well, Ross!'

Again, there's, like, more laughter.

Oisinn goes, 'Okay, that thing's going back to the shop tomorrow.'

Magnus is there, 'Sho we can jusht tell them the newsh, yesh?'

And Oisinn goes, 'Right, let's do the countdown one last time.'

I've moved around to the front of the cannon and I'm staring into it, wondering is there some kind of, I don't know, *blockage*?

Magnus goes, 'On five . . . four . . . three . . . two . . .'

And in that exact moment the cannon decides to finally go off. There's, like, a loud boom and I'm suddenly showered in tens of thousands of pieces of shiny *blue* tinsel.

'It's a boy!' Oisinn and Magnus go, while everyone cheers.

I'm standing there, spitting out tinsel and pulling it out of my hair and I'm going, 'I wasn't expecting it to go off in my face like that.'

And Sorcha's sister goes, 'You're always so eager to finish, Ross! Maybe you and I should try tantric sex some time!'

Erika's there, 'How did yesterday go?' meaning the gender reveal porty.

I'm like, 'Yeah, no, pretty smoothly actually.'

And she's there, 'I heard the confetti cannon went off in your face.'

'Aport from that, I mean. I didn't see you there, by the way. I thought you and Oisinn were close?'

'I told him I didn't want to be there if Sorcha was going to be there. I heard she brought her new man along.'

'Oh, big time. Launching him on the social focking scene. He was wearing his pilot's uniform, by the way, and it wasn't until about three hours after I got home that I thought how funny it would have been if I'd called him *Hot Shots*.'

89

'What does that even mean?'

'Yeah, no, it's a movie storring Chorlie Sheen. It's a piss-take of – presumably – *Top Gun*? I watched it at a porty in Keith Gleeson's gaff back in the day. It was the dude's favourite movie. I'll hopefully get a chance to use it again in the future. If the opportunity arises, I will. Full stop.'

She's there, 'Anyway,' the way she does when she's about to change the subject, 'I had a call from Benoîte this morning.'

I'm like, 'Oh?' and I genuinely mean it.

She's there, 'I told you about this crowd who are investigating the circumstances of the –'

And I'm like, 'The crash – yeah, no, what?' because I'm genuinely *curious*.

She's there, 'The other cor that was involved in the accident –'

'The black X5.'

'It was a rental cor.'

I go, 'Interesting,' in a sort of, like, Yoda voice, even though I've no idea *why* I'm saying it that way?

She goes, 'The cor was rented by a couple from Kazakhstan.'

'Hmm.'

'What do you mean by *hmm*?'

'You're saying it doesn't exist?'

'No, it's a country, Ross.'

'Azkaban.'

'Kazakhstan! It's a former Soviet republic, but it remains very close to Russia.'

'I'm not arguing with you.'

'Meaning that it further points to Kremlin involvement in Seamons's death.'

'So what's going to happen?'

'The investigators are going to send someone over there to check out this couple. Ask them did they see something, while figuring out if they were somehow involved.'

All of a sudden, we hear the front door slam.

I'm like, 'Another angry slam. Definitely Honor.'

Erika's there, 'Honor, is that you?'

And Honor goes, 'Yeah, I'm just going to bed, okay?'

I'm like, 'She must be wrecked,' because – yeah, no – today was the first day of her work experience. 'I never thought I'd live to see the day. Honor working.'

'Even so,' Erika goes, 'it's only seven o'clock. Maybe you should see if she's okay.'

So – yeah, no – up the stairs I go. I knock on Honor's door and she's like, 'Hang on, I'm just changing into my pyjamas,' and I stand there for a good, I don't know, ten minutes before she goes, 'You can come in now.'

So I push the door and in I go. She's already in bed and the lights are off.

I'm there, 'How did it go? Your first day in Comté?'

She goes, 'I pissed in some stupid focking bitch's gazpacho,' and she sounds a bit – I'm going to be honest – manic.

So I just laugh along with her.

I'm there, 'Hilarious! Fair focks to you, Honor,' because I've always been a huge believer in positive parental feedback.

'Stupid focking bitch,' she goes.

And I'm like, 'Yeah, no, so you said. So, like, what actually happened?'

'I was working in the kitchen and Sincerity was out on the restaurant floor – just, like, taking *orders*? And this woman sent her gazpacho back because it was, like, *cold*?'

'Gazpacho? It's *supposed* to be cold!'

'Er, *exactly*?'

'I wouldn't blame you for being angry. The focking nerve of these people. So how did we get from that to you pissing in the thing?'

'She was, like, *so* rude to Sincerity.'

'Right.'

'She was like, "How old are you – ten?" and Sincerity was, like, full-on *crying*?'

'I'm one hundred per cent with you, Honor. Sincerity shouldn't have to put up with that shit – work experience or not.'

'So when the bowl came back to the kitchen, I took it into the toilet –'

'Second thoughts, maybe I don't need any more info.'

'– and I focking pissed in it,' she goes.

'Got it, Honor.'

'Then I focking stuck it in the focking microwave and focking heated it up for the stupid focker.'

'Please don't tell me she actually *ate* it?'

'She cleaned her bowl – the focking fock.'

Jesus Christ, I feel like nearly spewing here.

I'm there, 'Well, hopefully she won't catch anything from it – I don't know, *could* she catch something from it?'

'Er, *typhoid*?' she goes, at the same time laughing, 'or, like, urinary *schistosomiasis*?'

Of course, I just laugh along with her.

I'm there, 'Okay, *someone's* been Googling,' and I say it in a definitely non-judgemental way. 'And are either of those, like, fatal – just to put my mind at ease?'

'I don't care.'

'Well, hopefully it won't come to that. Much as the woman possibly deserved it, you hopefully don't want to kill someone on your work experience – certainly not on day one.'

She's like, 'Fock *her* shit. Sincerity was, like, *so* nice to her and she made her cry. I hope she focking dies.'

And I'm there, 'Yeah, no, good talk, Honor – *definitely* good talk.'

She turns over in her bed and goes, 'Yeah, *now* fock off.'

And what I can't help but notice, as I back out of her bedroom, is the faint whiff of alcohol in the room.

Roz says there's something she wants to talk to me about. She certainly knows how to pick her moments.

She's like, 'What do you think Sorcha's sister meant – when she said that thing about, you know, you and her having tantric sex?'

I'm there, 'Who even knows what goes in women's heads half the time? Present company accepted. Like I said to you at the porty, her hormones must be all over the shop.'

She's not letting it go, though.

'But it *was* pretty on-the-money,' she goes, 'wasn't it? Like, you didn't tell her that we – well, you know – *do* this, did you?'

92

That's what I meant when I said she knows how to pick her moments. We're actually *on* the job while this conversation is taking place, the big row about the locust infestation firmly behind us.

I'm there, 'Jesus, Roz, what do you take me for?'

This is possibly a case of Too Much Information, but I'm lying on my side, propped up on my left elbow – so is Roz, by the way – and I'm riding her from behind, while her right leg is sticking up in the air, crooked at the knee, and I'm reaching around with my right hand to cop a feel of her heavers.

Again, it's just a bit of background.

She goes, 'Sorry, I'm being paranoid . . . oh, that's nice, Ross. Keep doing that . . . what was I saying? Yeah, no, there's something about that girl that I just don't trust.'

I'm there, 'Sorcha's sister?' acting the total innocent. 'Yeah, no, I've known her almost as long as I've known Sorcha.'

She's like, 'She has a thing for you, Ross.'

'Are you serious? Jesus!'

'See, you can't see it. Girls pick up on these things.'

'Like I said, this is genuine, genuine news to me.'

I hate myself for lying to her. I didn't want Roz to be just like all the other girls. I realize that I'm on a slippery slope here.

She goes, 'I think it's nice that you're so trusting of people. But just be careful of her, Ross.'

I'm there, 'I'm going to take that advice on board, Roz – one hundred percent,' and then she asks if we can switch positions because her elbow has gone numb.

We've been going hord at it for, like, twenty minutes at this stage.

She wipes her sweaty forehead with the back of her hand and goes, 'This is *such* good sex,' like she's talking about, I don't know, a flat white from 3fe, or a plate of mushroom risotto.

She has literally no embarrassment about discussing it. It's very different from having sex with most South Dublin girls, who go about the job as if the eyes of every nun who ever led them in a chorus of 'Ag Críost an Síol' are fixed upon them.

I'm there, 'Yeah, no complaints this end either,' then she tells me to lie on my back and she casually throws her leg over me like she's climbing on board her yoga bolster.

She puts our various nuts and washers back into position and then we stort going at it again, her sliding up and down on me, with one eye open and one eye closed and her lips pursed like she's blowing out a candle, while I'm lying underneath her with my two orms stretched out in front of me, my fingers working her nubbies like I'm scratching a spaniel behind the ears.

She goes, 'Oh my God, Ross, you're *so* deep inside me now. Oh, I've been meaning to ask you, by the way, what are you doing on Saturday week?'

I'm there, 'Daytime or night-time? Oh my God, your nipples are so hord.'

She's like, 'You're the one who has them that way. Night-time.'

'Yeah, nothing in the diary,' I go. 'Jesus, they're like two light switches here.'

She's like, 'It's just that it's Gráinne's birthday and Raymond wants us to go out for dinner with them. How's *that* speed?' because – yeah, no – she's suddenly quickened the pace.

I'm there, 'Oh, that's the stuff! Oh, that's the definite stuff! What restaurant were they thinking in terms of?'

'Gráinne loves Glovers Alley,' she goes. 'Oh my God, you're not about to finish, are you?'

I'm like, 'No, no – all this admin is helping me keep the old swimmers between the safety flags. Who *doesn't* love Glovers Alley, by the way?'

She's there, 'Gráinne's really good friends with Andy McFadden. Do you mind if I turn around?'

I'm like, 'Turn around? In terms of –?' and I go to sit up.

She goes, 'No, you stay where you are. I just want to face this way. Yeah, no, they both worked for Neven Maguire back in the day.'

She hunkers down onto me – the famous reverse cowgirl again! – and I'm suddenly looking at her bony spine bouncing up and down in front of my eyes.

I'm there, 'I got a reservation for us for Neven Maguire's place. It's for, like, 2028 or something. Oh, that's lovely what you're doing.'

94

She goes, 'Yeah, I like this angle. Andy was very supportive of Gráinne when she set up Comté. Oh my God, I love this – don't stop what you're doing. Yeah, no, he's given her loads of ideas about how to get around – you know – the various food shortages since Irexit.'

I'm there, 'Fair focks to him. How are you in terms of, like, *closeness*?' because the old porridge is very close to bubbling over here.

'I'm *very* close – just keep doing what you're doing,' she goes. 'Anyway, I was thinking that maybe *we* could pay for dinner?'

I'm thinking, fock that. Raymond's loaded.

I'm there, 'Yeah, no, that sounds like a good idea. Okay, I'm very close here, Roz. I've crossed the twenty-two if you're looking for a rugby analogy.'

She goes, 'Like I said, I'm nearly there. Anyway, I was thinking it'd be a nice way for us to say thank you to Gráinne for agreeing to take Sincerity and Honor on work experience.'

'Yeah, no, I've *said* I'll go halves with you.'

For fock's sake.

She goes, 'Oh, that's the other thing I wanted to talk to you about. Keep doing that, Ross – oh my God, I am *so* nearly there.'

I'm like, 'What? What did you want to talk to me about?'

'Raymond rang me the other day. He was really embarrassed about bringing it up with me –'

'Bringing what up?'

'Well, he said that a bottle of gin went missing from the restaurant one morning when it was just Sincerity and Honor there. Oh my God, I'm about sixty seconds away from coming here.'

'Did he say what kind of gin?'

'I don't know,' she goes. 'Gordon's, I think. Why does it matter?'

I'm there, 'Doesn't. I'm just making conversation here.'

'You don't think one of the girls –'

I'm like, 'Not a chance,' and it's a good job she can't see my face.

'I mean, I asked Sincerity,' she goes, 'and she said it definitely wasn't her.'

I'm there, 'And it definitely wouldn't have been Honor. So – like the whole Sorcha's sister thing – it looks like it's going to remain a mystery.'

'Oh my God,' she goes, 'I'm coming, I'm coming, I'm coming!'

Dalisay sort of, like, intercepts me in the corridor when I'm on the way to my old dear's room.

She goes, 'Hello, Ross.'

I'm there, 'Er, is everything okay?'

She's a ringer for Angel Locsin and I hope that isn't me being racist.

She goes, 'Your mother is having not such a good day today.'

I'm like, 'If this involves her spitting out her dental plate again, can you put it in this time? I just don't think I'd have the stomach to do it again.'

'She is very confused, Ross.'

'Right.'

'More today than other days. She is asking for Conor.'

'Conor? I don't know any Conor?'

'I don't know if he is real or if she thinks you are Conor.'

All of a sudden I hear her voice coming out of the room, going, 'I can hear you talking about me, you know?'

I smile at her and I go, 'Yeah, no, thanks for the heads-up, Dalisay,' and she smiles back at me.

Like I said, very, *very* like Angel Locsin.

She leads me into the ward, going, 'It's Ross – your son, Fionnuala.'

The old dear is sitting in an ormchair in the corner.

She goes, 'I know who he is! What were you talking about out there?'

I'm like, 'Nothing.'

'Was he trying to seduce you, Dalisay?'

Jesus, *always* with the sex.

I'm there, 'I wasn't trying to seduce you, Dalisay,' and I don't know why I feel the need to explain it.

The old dear's like, 'She's very pretty, Ross.'

And I go, 'Yes, I know she's very pretty.'

'Don't believe any of the promises he makes to you, Dalisay. He'll use you and then discord you and I don't want your parents complaining to me. Accosting me in The Gables, or when I'm coming out of Richard Alan, and saying, "Tell your son to stay away from my little Princess!" '

I actually laugh. Her memory isn't as bad as Dalisay said.

She goes, 'I *always* made a point of telling them to fock off – didn't I, Ross?'

I'm there, 'You did, in fairness to you.'

'Fock off, I told them. And when you get there, you can go and fock off some more. These people didn't understand, you see, that Ross was a highly sexual person. He's *still* a highly sexual person. That's why I'm telling you to watch out, Dalisay.'

I go, 'Anyway, can we change the subject? I brought you a present,' and I reach into the bag between my feet and pull out a book – we're talking a *hordback* book? I hand it to her and she stares at the cover for a few seconds before reading the title out loud.

She's like, '*Criminal Assets*,' and then she looks up at me and goes, 'Is it good, Ross? Is there lots of sex in it?'

Seriously, she's obsessed.

I'm there, 'Yeah, no, it's full of sex – embarrassingly for me when it came out. It's about a woman who rediscovers the lustful side of her nature after her husband is sent to prison for bribing Dublin County Councillors to rezone land.'

I'm quoting from the dust jacket now, but I'm hoping it rings a bell with her. She looks down at the cover again.

'Oh, look,' she suddenly goes, 'the author has the same name as me!'

I'm there, 'Er, that's because you *are* the author?'

'Me?' she goes.

I'm there, 'You're saying you don't remember it?'

She goes, 'I'm saying I never wrote it.'

I always predicted this day would come – although I thought she'd be saying it out of mortification more than anything else.

Dalisay goes, 'Your mother wrote this book?' and she sounds impressed.

I'm there, 'She actually wrote a few.'

I reach into the bag again and hand the old dear the next one.

She goes, '*Mom, I've Never Heard of Sundried Tomatoes?*'

I'm like, 'That's a misery lit novel, set in the wake of the 2008 financial crisis, involving a little girl struggling to come to terms with the new economic reality and a mother who – yeah, no – rediscovers the lustful side of her nature.'

'The same woman,' she goes. 'Fionnuala O'Carroll-Kelly.'

I'm there, 'You genuinely don't remember writing it?'

She shakes her head from side to side.

'Okay,' I go, reaching into the bag again, 'what about this one?' and I produce my copy of *Fifty Greys in Shades*.

I've honestly no idea why I kept these. In my defence, I focked them in the bin a few times over the years – usually when I was pissed off with her about something – but Sorcha always found them when she was sorting through the recycling and returned them to the bookshelf.

'And what's this one about?' she goes, taking it from me.

I'm there, 'It was an attempt to cash in on the whole BDSM romance novel – except aimed at an *older* audience?'

She goes, 'What's BDSM?'

And I'm like, 'It stands for Bondage, Dominance and Sado –' and I get suddenly embarrassed saying it in front of Dalisay. 'Actually, it doesn't matter. It's about a bunch of elderly people who jet off to the sun and – again – rediscover the lustful side of their nature. You might be storting to spot a pattern here.'

'Oh, and these elderly people,' the old dear goes, 'are they the greys in shades? It's very clever, isn't it?'

'You definitely thought so at the time.'

'And it's written by the same woman as these others, is it?'

'Fionnuala O'Carroll-Kelly, yes.'

She opens the book on the page where it's been signed and she reads the inscription out loud.

She's like, 'To Ross, my number one fan, love Mum.'

She stares at it for a long time and for a second or two I think she's storting to remember something.

She goes, 'Well, she's certainly got a high opinion of herself, this woman, doesn't she?'

I laugh.

I'm there, 'Like you wouldn't focking believe.'

Dalisay goes, 'If you like, I can read them to you, Fionnuala.'

The old dear's there, 'That would be lovely, Dalisay.'

I'm like, 'There's a lot of graphic scenes you could maybe skip. You'll know them because I've written shit in the morgins, like "She's a focking pervert" and "This is sick shit."'

The old dear goes, 'Put them on my bedside table, would you, Dorling?' which is what I do.

And that's when she goes, 'Conor is on his way, Ross.'

I'm there, 'Conor? Who's Conor, Mom?'

She's there, 'My husband, Ross! Your father!'

I suddenly realize that she's talking about Conor Hession, the dude she nearly married *before* she met my old man?

I'm there, 'Right – and he's coming in, is he? As in, he's coming in here today?'

She goes, 'Ross, why are you acting so strangely? My husband is coming to visit me in hospital. Why is this difficult to understand?'

I give Dalisay the eyes to say, can I talk to you outside? Ten seconds later, she follows me out of the old dear's room into the corridor, where I'm like, 'Just to let you know, Conor is dead.'

She's there, 'I am very sorry to hear this.'

She seems like a genuinely lovely person – nothing like the nurses you'd meet in Copper Face Jacks.

I'm like, 'Hey, I never even *knew* the dude? Yeah, no, he was just some randomer that the old dear was engaged to before my old man was on the scene. Anyway, he definitely died – we're talking three or four *years* ago? – because I remember she went to his funeral in Donnybrook Church and ended up having a major borney with his widow, because she insisted on sitting in the front row, even though she hadn't seen the dude since, I don't know, the 1970s, and the widow told her that the front row was for family only and the old dear ended up calling her a dowdy frump of a woman – this was in front of, like, three hundred mourners.'

I don't know how much of this Dalisay is actually getting, but she nods and goes, 'So he is *not* coming?'

I'm there, 'He's not coming, no – what with him being dead since 2014, maybe 2015 – we're definitely talking *that* kind of ballpork?'

And from inside the ward we hear the old dear go, 'He'll tell you absolutely anything you want to hear, Dalisay, just to get inside your knickers.'

Johnny says he's bored. That's, like, *literally* the word he uses?

I'm there, 'Bored? How the fock could you be bored?'

Yeah, no, admittedly it hasn't been vintage Leinster tonight, but they're only leading Benetton Treviso by a converted try as the game enters its final phase and there's not a single person in the RDS who'd say that they were bored by what they're watching – except obviously my sons.

And Honor, by the way, who's permanently on her phone.

Leo goes, 'How long is left?'

I'm like, 'Seriously? *That's* what you're wondering?' because *I'm* thinking about the match still hanging in the balance and I'm thinking about Caelan Doris, who was forced to go off for a HIA – *and* on his European Champions Cup debut – after carrying the ball into contact.

Leo's there, 'I have homework to do,' and I'm looking at him sitting there with his stupid focking glasses.

I'm like, 'Homework? It's, like, Saturday night,' and I turn around to Honor and go, 'Tell your brother he's a focking disgrace,' but she doesn't even hear me. She's, like, glued to Instagram.

Leo doesn't even have the decency to look ashamed of himself.

Instead – yeah, no – he turns around to Brian and goes, '*Unser Vater ist ein Idiot*,' because they always talk to each other in German when it's something they don't want me to hear. '*Ich hasse Rugby.*'

Johnny's there, '*Ich hasse Rugby auch!*' and I'm like, 'English please, goys,' and that's when I hear a sudden roar and I look up to discover that I've managed to miss a Leinster try.

Like everyone else in the old D4tress, I'm punching the air because the game is suddenly in the bag, but I still end up having to turn around to the dude behind me to go, 'Who scored it?' and he says it was Garry Ringrose.

I'm there, 'Did you hear that, goys? Garry Ringrose has bagged himself a hat-trick!' but they look at me like I'm Fionn reciting the Periodic Table of Elements backwards, which was his genuine porty piece when we were in Sixth Year and port of the reason he was a virgin until well into his twenties. 'I'm admitting it hasn't been a vintage Leinster performance, but a lot of these goys are still coming down from the disappointment of the World Cup,' and that's when Brian asks Honor if he can borrow her phone.

I'm there, 'What the fock for?' because Ross Byrne is about to kick the conversion and it's massively disrespectful to the dude.

Brian goes, 'I want to text Granddad Lalor to ask him if he knows what time this match is over.'

I'm there, 'Honor, do not give him that phone,' because Sorcha's old man genuinely hates rugby. 'You'd only be giving the focker ammunition. Just watch, will you?'

So – yeah, no – Ross Byrne ends up nailing the kick and I go, 'He's the dude I told you was going to be the next Johnny Sexton. Remember we saw him once coming out of Molton Brown in Dundrum?' but they've no idea what I'm even talking about.

The match finally comes to an end and – yeah, no – it's a relief to get the European campaign off to a winning stort.

Leo's there, 'Can we go home now?' pushing his glasses up on his nose.

I'm like, 'No, we can't go home – because I have a little surprise in store for us all. Come on, Honor, let's go.'

Yeah, no, what I haven't told them yet is that I've splashed out on Meet and Greet tickets, meaning that we're going to get to talk to two of tonight's match-winners in the VIP area once they've had their showers and all the rest of it.

I deliver the good news and it ends up not being the mic drop moment I *thought* it'd be? Honest to fock, it's like I've just said we're going to pull each other's teeth out with rusty focking pliers.

Johnny goes, 'Is this something we have to do?'

And I'm there, 'I'm not going to dignify that with an answer.'

So – yeah, no – we head for the hospitality tent. On the way there, I turn around and I look at Honor.

I'm there, 'Can I ask you a question?'

She goes, 'Yeah, what?'

I'm like, 'Did you –?' and I'm just about to ask her did she steal the gin from the restaurant – and is that what the whiff of alcohol in her room was that night? – but I end up wussing out.

She goes, 'What?'

I'm there, 'I was just going to ask, what are you looking at on your phone?'

She's there, 'Sincerity's Instagram,' and I'm thinking, fock, she *really* has it bad.

I'm like, 'Where is she tonight?'

'The cinema.'

'With the Protestant?'

She just nods and I can see that her hort is breaking.

We reach the hospitality tent. I turn around to the dude on the door and I go, 'Do you know which two players have been selected for the Meet and Greet?' and he says he doesn't.

Behind me, Honor's like, 'I'm going to wait outside.'

I'm there, 'What? Are you sure?'

And she nods her head and goes, 'I just want to be by myself. Enjoy yourself, boys.'

In we go. And it's hilarious because I'm so nervous that I can't even eat the miniature beef and goat's cheese crostini or the tomato and feta skewers that are doing the rounds, although I do ask the waitress if she knows which two players have been selected for the Meet and Greet and she says she doesn't.

Literally, thirty seconds later, I hear this huge round of applause and I look up to see Josh van der Flier walking in.

I'm like, 'Happy focking days – come on, goys,' and I make a bee-line for him.

I'm there, 'I thought you played great today, Josh. I'm going to have to say fair focks.'

The dude's like, 'Thanks,' and he takes a step backwards.

I probably *am* standing a bit too close to him.

I'm there, 'These are my sons – this is Brian, this is Johnny and this is Leo.'

He smiles at them and goes, 'So do you play rugby, goys?' and you can tell straight away that he's a people person.

Johnny goes, 'No, hockey.'

I'm there, 'Don't worry, Josh, they're shit at it.'

I think he's a bit taken aback by my bluntness. It's just me calling it. Peter O'Mahony could tell him one or two stories next time he's on Ireland duty.

He's like, 'Well, it's, em, important to try as many different sports as possible when you're young,' and I'm thinking, if that's what they're teaching them in Wesley College, it's no wonder they haven't won a Leinster Schools Senior Cup since the 1800s.

It's possible he's just being nice, though.

I'm there, 'They can't even get their game. They're on the focking bench.'

He looks over my shoulder and goes, 'I'd, em, better go mingle,' because there's, like, forty or fifty other people here to meet him as well.

I'm there, 'Can you sign my ball first?' because – yeah, no – I brought the old Gilbert with me, along with a Shorpie.

While he's putting his name on it, I ask him if he knows which other player has been selected for the Meet and Greet, but he says he doesn't know, then he moves on to the next punter.

I give Johnny an absolute filthy.

'Focking hockey,' I go. 'Why would you bring that up?'

Then all of a sudden there's a humungous cheer, followed by a round of applause, because the second player selected for the Meet and Greet turns out to be the man of the moment – we're talking Garry Ringrose himself.

I'm straight over to him, nudging some random dude and his two daughters out of the way to get to him first. I shake his hand, then I hand him the ball.

I'm there, 'First things first, let's get this thing signed,' and while he puts his autograph underneath Josh van der Flier's, I go, 'A hat-trick – fair focks,' and then I ask him if he remembers a night a few years ago when he was having his birthday dinner with his girlfriend in Etto and I sent a bottle of champagne over to their table. He says he doesn't and I'm thinking it probably happens to him so often, but then I remember that I didn't do it in the end because his birthday was, like, two weeks before the stort of the Six Nations Championship and there was no way he was going to drink it.

I don't get to tell him any of that, though, because he hands me back my ball and then the dude with the two daughters comes in from the side and suddenly gets in his ear – although not before telling me that I'm very rude and that I knocked his daughter over.

I suddenly remember my own children and I realize that they're not *with* me? I turn around and I spot them over the other side of the hospitality tent, chatting among themselves, no even interest in meeting Garry – we're talking literally – Ringrose.

I don't know why I do this, but I shout, 'Leo!' and when he looks at me I throw the ball across the tent to him, although it's more of a pass than a throw, a beautiful pass – not to sound big-headed – that travels in a perfect orc over the heads of maybe ten or twenty people who are standing around. Leo stands there, watching the ball arrive, but he doesn't move a muscle and it ends up hitting him square in the face, knocking him off his feet and sending his glasses flying across the floor.

I turn around and of course Garry has seen it. His peripheral vision is as good as mine – think of all the offloads. He's standing there looking at Leo with his mouth wide open. I've never been so embarrassed by my own flesh and blood. And that really is saying something.

So I'm in the cor on my way to The K Club in Straffan – not to play golf, by the way, but to check out the new gaff that Ronan is supposedly interested in buying. Yeah, no, I follow the instructions on the satnav and I arrive outside this gaff in, I don't know, whatever port of the country Straffan happens to be.

The place is focking humungous – we're talking twice the size of the old pair's gaff. As I'm porking the cor, I'm trying to figure out what the mortgage would be on a place like this and I'm thinking there's no way Ronan would be able to afford it on whatever pennies Hennessy is paying him.

I get out of the cor and I notice one or two people looking out their windows. Oh, they're going to love Shadden around here. Wait until it's Eurovision Night. Or one of her famous Morgarita Monday porties.

I spot Kennet's State cor porked in the driveway next to Hennessy's chocolate-brown Rolls. Into the gaff I go, and they're all standing around in a hallway that's like something from, I don't know, *Dynasty* back in the day – we're talking Ronan and Shadden, we're talking Hennessy, we're talking Kennet and Dordeen.

I can tell straight away that Hennessy isn't happy to see me there. I'm there, 'Hi.'

Kennet goes, '*Hi!*' doing an impression of me and Dordeen laughs like it's the funniest thing she's ever heard.

I look at Ronan and I go, 'So, what, this is where you're moving to?'

Ronan's like, 'What do you think of it, Rosser?'

I'm there, 'Ro, there's no way you could afford the mortgage on a place like this. It'll be, like, five Ks a month.'

'*It'll be, like, five Ks a month,*' Kennet goes – again, doing the voice.

Seriously, there are people out there who think you're hilarious just because you don't talk like you're selling cigarette-lighters on Henry Street.

'Forget about the mortgage,' Hennessy goes, a fat turd of a Montecristo burning between his fingers, 'what do you think of the house?'

Ronan's there, 'It's lubbly, so it is, Heddessy.'

'It's situated in one of Ireland's most exclusive private developments,' Hennessy goes, 'offering easy access to more than five hundred acres of spectacular grounds, with two world-class golf courses, the five-stor K Club hotel, spa and leisure centre, tennis courts and a host of restaurants and bars.'

I sold too many gaffs in my estate agent days to be taken in by his bullshit.

I'm there, 'It's a bit, I don't know, *soulless* or something, isn't it?'

He looks at me like a taxi driver who's just been asked does he accept cord payments. We're talking pure and utter contempt.

He decides to just ignore my comment and goes, 'It's finished to an exquisite standard, having undergone a complete refurb, and now features a contemporary kitchen with state-of-the-art appliances, luxury bathroom suites, a new heating system and stylish décor throughout,' and that's when I suddenly cop that Hennessy actually owns the gaff.

I'm there, 'Here, didn't you buy two or three gaffs out here at one stage?'

Again, he doesn't say shit to me.

He just goes, 'And, best of all, the back bedroom overlooks the eighteenth fairway of the Arnold Palmer-designed golf course.'

Ronan's there, 'I doatunt play goddelf, Heddessy,' and Hennessy laughs like he finds it hilarious that anyone could be so naive.

He's like, 'Oh, you will, Ronan. You will.'

Then he slips his orm around Ronan's shoulder and goes, 'I'm going to tell you something that I told your grandfather – oh, must be forty-five years ago now,' and he storts leading him around the downstairs of the house with the rest of us following. 'Success starts when people start to think of you as successful – do you get me?'

Ronan's like, 'I think so, Heddessy.'

Hennessy goes, 'Some of the so-called richest people in Ireland haven't got a penny to their names,' his big voice bouncing off the walls of the empty living room. 'If you called in their debts tomorrow, they'd be poorer than anyone living on the streets. But they project an *image* of being rich and successful.'

He turns to Shadden then and goes, 'Can you imagine a big TV on that wall?' knowing what buttons to press with her. 'Imagine having one of your karaoke nights in here.'

Ronan goes, 'The muddy, but.'

Hennessy's there, 'You can have it for a thousand euros per month.'

A grand a month, I think. You wouldn't get a focking hot-press in Cherrywood for that.

I can see that Shadden's not convinced, though. It's probably too far from Finglas.

Hennessy – still with his orm around Ronan's shoulder – goes, 'There's a saying that I have, Ronan – build your own dreams, or someone else will hire you to build theirs,' and I suddenly remember the famous Mortyn Turner cortoon in the *Irish Times* of the day Hennessy took the old man out to West Dublin, showed him thousands of acres of just, like, fields and persuaded him that he could have it all corruptly rezoned and set himself up for life.

The Temptation in the Wilderness was the caption on it.

Hennessy goes, 'Do you want to be the kind of person who makes money or the kind who makes money for other people?'

Shadden answers for him. She goes, 'The foorst koyunt,' because – yeah, no – Shadden loves money like I love rugby.

Hennessy's there, 'So be brave. As I said to Charlie all those years ago, when he was living in – believe it or not – Sallynoggin, fearlessness is not the absence of fear. It's the mastery of it.'

It's Dordeen who throws a spanner in the works.

'What peert of the cunterdoddy are we eeben in?' she goes.

I was kind of wondering the same thing myself.

Ronan's there, 'It's County Kildeer, Dordeen.'

Kennet's there, 'Your ch . . . ch . . . ch . . . ch . . . childorden will eddend up playing for the bleaten L . . . L . . . L . . . L . . . Liddywhites – ast me boddicks.'

I'm like, 'What children? There's only Rihanna-Brogan.'

'That's for now,' Kennet goes. 'How many b . . . b . . . b . . . b . . . b . . . b . . . b . . . bethroowums has this place, Heddessy?'

Hennessy's like, 'It has six bedrooms.'

'Theer you are, Ro. Are you m . . . m . . . m . . . m . . . m . . . madden enough to fiddle them, but? Look at Ro's face theer, Dordeen!'

I'm guessing it's the same as mine.

'Me ma's right, but,' Shadden goes. 'I'd be a veddy long way from howum out hee-or.'

Honest to fock, if you offered Shadden the Taj Mahal, she'd say it was too far from Finglas.

Hennessy goes, 'You wouldn't be far from home. This would *be* your home,' but he's wasting his focking breath on them.

Kennet goes, 'You hab to wontherstand, Heddessy, we're v . . . v . . . v . . . v . . . v . . . v . . . v . . . veddy much Dubbalin people – ardent we, Dordeen?'

'Oh, veddy much,' she goes. 'Veddy, veddy much.'

'There's a thing thee wouldn't know athin about out hee-or,' Kennet goes, 'and that's c . . . c . . . c . . . c . . . commudity spidit. We've the best neighbours in the w . . . w . . . w . . . w . . . w . . . wurdled, habn't we, Dordeen? We wouldn't leab them for all the muddy in the –'

'What if I offered you the house next door,' Hennessy goes, 'free of charge?'

Dordeen's there, 'Will you pay for eer moving costs?'

I look at Ronan and we exchange a smile, except it's not a happy one. It's a smile of, I suppose, resignation?

Shadden and her old pair are hugging each other.

Kennet goes, 'It's like we're arthur widding the L . . . L . . . L . . . L . . . L . . . L . . .'

And the word he's trying to say is Lotterdoddy.

Helen says the bin is full.

Yeah, no, I'm trying to squeeze an empty milk corton into the Brabantia, using basically just brute force.

Erika goes, 'Ross, did you hear what my mom said? You need to change the bin bag.'

She's in an absolute fouler this morning.

Yeah, no, the crash-site investigators went to Kazakhstan to talk to the couple who rented the black SUV they thought might have been involved in the accident. It turns out that they passed Simone three minutes *before* the crash and they showed them the receipt from the rental company showing that there was no damage to their cor. And, anyway, they were a retired couple in their seventies – their granddaughter is studying in the University of Galway – and not exactly Brad and Angelina in *Mr and Mrs Smith*.

Erika goes, 'Ross, you need to change the focking bin bag!'

And I give her the line that I always gave Sorcha whenever she said that. I'm like, 'If God had wanted me to change the bag, he wouldn't have given me a set of guns like this,' and it goes down about as well as it used to with my soon-to-be ex-wife.

Helen goes, 'Ross, if you keep pushing it down, it'll tear when you pull it out.'

So I roll my eyes and go, 'Fine – whatever,' and I lift the lid off the Brabantia and go to whip out the bag.

Helen was right. The thing *has* torn – and as I pull it out of the actual bucket, the end falls out of it, sending rubbish skidding across the kitchen floor.

I hear the sound of glass bouncing off the tiles and three sets of eyes end up landing on exactly the same thing as it comes to rest in front of the cooker – it's, like, an empty gin bottle.

I automatically turn to Helen. I don't *know* why?

She's there, 'Well, don't look at me.'

Erika's like, 'Who the fock is drinking Gordon's gin?' because she's a snob when it comes to alcohol – and all other things too.

Quick as a flash, I go, 'Yeah, no, that's mine.'

Erika's like, 'I've never seen you drink gin.'

'Yeah, no, I like a gin and tonic before I go to bed in the evening.'

'Where's the tonic bottle?'

'Yeah, no, I usually have it *without* the tonic? *Or* the ice and lemon.'

'So you're just drinking gin in your bedroom straight out of the bottle? What are you, sixteen again?'

I laugh in a real 'what am I like?' kind of way, although I'm not sure if Helen knows what to make of it.

She goes, 'I have my Spanish class this morning,' and she leaves, while Erika shoots me an absolute filthy and goes, 'I'm having a shower. Clean that focking rubbish up.'

I wait to hear the water running upstairs, then I whip out my phone and ring Sorcha. I suppose, on some level, I feel like she deserves to know – and then I also think Honor's drinking is as much her problem as it is mine. I tell her that I need to see her and that it's, like, *urgent?* She says she's working from home this morning, so – yeah, no – I head out and I point the cor in the direction of Killiney.

Twenty minutes later, she's opening the front door to me and I can see straight away that she looks wrecked – like she hasn't *slept?*

I'm there, 'What's up?'

She goes, 'It's just politics,' like I wouldn't understand.

I definitely wouldn't. I remember Mortin McGuinness called to the door during one of the presidential elections and I thought he was there to fix the dishwasher. The thing was making a hell of racket and it was keeping me awake in the afternoons. I invited the dude in and – in fairness to him – he took a look at it and he reckoned we were probably overloading it, which he said was the source of most dishwasher problems. That was when Sorcha walked in and went, 'Who was that at the door?' and then she sees – yeah, no – Mortin McGuinness down on his hands and knees, checking the bearing ring and the spray orm seals.

Good times.

She goes, 'How are you? Roz seems nice,' except she says it as, like, one sentence.

I'm there, 'Yeah, no, things are going well there.'

'I know that her ex, Raymond, did a barista course with the husband of a girl who was the year ahead of me in Mount Anville,' she goes. 'I don't know if you remember Treasa Napier-Hall. She's *so* nice.'

I'm there, 'I'll take your word for it.'

'And he gets his hair cut in the same borber as Tom, who works in my deportment in Petroleum Affairs – do you know the Grooming Rooms on South William Street?'

'Sorcha –'

'And then he also bought a piece of ort from my friend, Étaín – do you remember she quit being an in-house lawyer and did that ceramics course? They sell her stuff in the Kilkenny Design shop.'

'Sorcha, he's a dickhead.'

'Excuse me?'

'Raymond. Her ex-husband. He's a prick of the highest order.'

'Are you sure that's not just jealousy? I'm not being a bitch, but I heard that him and Roz are still, like, best, best *friends*?'

'So?'

'Not nice, is it – when the shoe's on the other foot? I'm sorry, that was uncalled for. Do you want a cup of coffee?'

So – yeah, no – I follow her down to the kitchen.

She goes, 'What did you want to talk to me about that was so urgent?'

I'm there, 'Yeah, no, it's about Honor.'

But when she pushes the door to the kitchen, I see that her old pair are sitting at the island, having their breakfast. Boiled eggs and toast.

Her old man goes, 'What's *he* doing here?'

The two of them are still in their dressing-gowns and – yeah, no – *she's* flashing a bit of leg. Sorcha and her old man catch me staring at the pink, fluffy slipper dangling off the end of her toes, but it's only for a few seconds, and it does literally nothing for me – or very little anyway. I'm on the record as saying she has legs like the Brides Glen viaduct.

Sorcha goes, 'He wants to talk to me about – did you say, Honor, Ross?'

He's there, 'What's she done now, the little –?'

I'm like, 'Why do you always have to think the worst of her? Er, can I talk to you alone, Sorcha?'

But Sorcha's old dear goes, 'We are not a family that's in the habit of keeping secrets from one another,' which is (a) a definite dig at me and (b) complete and utter horseshit. 'Anything you say to Sorcha, she will tell us anyway,' and I'm watching her little fluffy foot bounce up and down again.

Sorcha's old man goes, 'Cover your legs, Dorling,' and she suddenly uncrosses them and pulls the two sides of her dressing-gown together while shooting me an absolute filthy, like it's five o'clock on Christmas Eve and I've just stolen the last porking space outside Thomas's in Foxrock.

Sorcha goes, 'Ross, what's going on with Honor? Has she done something?' and I suddenly realize that I can't do it to the girl. I can't let her down in front of these people who already hate her.

I'm going to have to deal with her drinking myself.

So instead, I go, 'Yeah, no, she's doing her work experience in Comté, which is owned by Gráinne – as in, Raymond's second wife – and she's apparently doing really well.'

Sorcha's old dear goes, 'You drove all the way out here to tell us that?' because her confidence is obviously through the roof now that she thinks I was checking out her getaway sticks.

I'm there, 'Anyway, that's all I came to tell you. That's one in the eye for Honor's critics, of which there are many.'

Sorcha goes, 'She chose to do her work experience in a restaurant?'

I'm like, 'I know – random, huh?'

'But I texted her,' she goes, 'and told her she could do it with me in the Deportment of Climate Action,' and I can tell that she's hurt. 'I thought it would be an opportunity for us to properly bond.'

I'm there, 'Yeah, no, she wanted to do it with Sincerity – her work experience, I mean.'

'They've gotten very close, haven't they? Do you want to see the boys while you're here, Ross?'

I'm there, 'Errr,' and I have to genuinely think about it. 'Where are they?'

She's like, 'They're upstairs, reading.'

And I'm there, 'Yeah, no, you're alright. I'll see them at the weekend.'

'What happened to Leo's glasses?' Sorcha's old man suddenly goes in an – it's not a word – but *accusatory* way.

He's really boiling my piss now.

I'm there, 'I threw a rugby ball at him to test his reflexes and it hit him full in the focking face. And if that's not your fault, then I don't know whose fault it is.'

Sorcha follows me to the front door and goes, 'Ross, can I say something to you?'

I'm there, 'It wasn't a sexual thing, Sorcha. It was just the way she was playing with her slipper. It caught my eye, that's all – whether that was her intention or not.'

There's definitely something wrong with me.

She decides to just ignore this and goes, 'I *want* to be proud of

Honor? But I've come to terms with the fact that she and I are never going to have the amazing, amazing relationship that I have with *my* mom?'

Honestly, I've seen better legs trying to rake my face in a ruck.

I'm there, 'You look wrecked, Sorcha – and that's not me being a wanker.'

She goes, 'I'm having doubts, Ross.'

I'm there, 'About?' hoping that she mentions Mike. 'If it's your new boyfriend, by the way, I just want to say what a focking dick move that was, turning up at Oisinn's porty in his pilot's outfit. It was a gender reveal porty, not a focking mickey-swinging competition, even though I find his voice weirdly soothing. He obviously knows you've got a thing for late-eighties Tom Cruise.'

She goes, 'I'm talking about the career I've chosen. Ross, the country is in trouble. We've isolated ourselves internationally. We're running out of good will. And there's all those people whose homes we knocked down just to reroute the Liffey. Was it worth it? I'm not thinking in terms of running for the leadership myself – there's no vacancy, as I said to Hugh Linehan on his podcast yesterday, so the question doesn't arise at this moment in time – but I have storted to wonder whether Chorles O'Carroll-Kelly is a fitting man to be Taoiseach.'

Raymond says that him and Gráinne have just bought a place in Crookhaven.

He goes, 'Do you sail, Ross?' because people who sail love to ask that question – then when you say no, they react like you've just said you don't like 'Fairytale of New York'.

I'm there, 'No, I don't sail.'

He goes, '*What?*' at the top of his voice. This is in the middle of Glovers Alley, bear in mind. People look up from their West Cork cod and their Wicklow Sika deer. 'You don't sail? Have you *ever* sailed?'

I'm there, 'No, Raymond, I've never sailed.'

'Jesus,' he goes, then he's like, 'Sorry, Ross, I've embarrassed you.'

I'm there, 'I'm not embarrassed in the slightest.'

Which I'm not. But Roz puts a patronizing hand on my orm and goes, 'It was just a joke, Ross,' making me feel petty for not laughing.

And Gráinne's there, 'It's just Raymond's sense of humour. It's an acquired taste.'

The dude goes, 'I'm sorry, Ross,' holding his hands up in surrender. 'I didn't realize you were so sensitive.'

Gráinne goes, 'You'll have to come to Crookhaven. We can lend you the house.'

Roz is there, 'That would be amazing, wouldn't it, Ross?'

And I'm like, 'Yeah, no, whatever,' and I go back to my tiramisu.

Roz goes, 'Gráinne, we wanted to say thank you again for taking Sincerity and Honor on work experience. They're really getting a lot out of it, aren't they, Ross?'

I'm like, 'Yeah, no, definitely.'

'By the way,' Raymond goes, because he loves the sound of his own voice, 'did we ever solve the mystery of the missing bottle of gin?'

Gráinne's there, 'Raymond, do we have to talk about this now?'

I look up and the dude is staring at me. I can feel my face suddenly redden. I decide that attack is the best form of defence.

I'm there, 'You're not implying that it was –?'

Gráinne goes, 'We're not implying anything, Ross.'

I'm like, '– either *Sincerity* –' and I put a lot of emphasis on her name.

'Definitely not,' she goes.

I'm there, '– or even Honor?'

'Well, it *definitely* wasn't Sincerity,' Raymond goes. 'That's not how she was raised.'

And I'm like, 'And it wasn't Honor either,' although I don't go making any great claims for how she was raised. There's no point in leaving myself open.

'Is it possible,' Roz goes, 'that one of the staff took it?'

Gráinne's there, 'Absolutely not.'

'Or maybe,' Roz goes, 'someone accidentally knocked the bottle over and they were too embarrassed to say anything?'

I'm there, 'That's sounds possible. I'd definitely go along with that.'

Gráinne's there, 'Can we *please* just drop the subject!'

We all go quiet then. It's, like, *awks* much? We finish our desserts, there's more talk about sailing – 'I can't *believe* you've never sailed!' Raymond goes. 'What have you been doing with your life?' – and then me and Roz end up settling the bill.

Raymond suggests we go for a late drink.

He's like, 'Kehoes?'

I'm there, 'Or we could hit Bruxelles? The music is great in there.'

But for some reason he has his hort set on Kehoes. So – yeah, no – we tip down Grafton Street and take the turn for South William Street. Roz and Raymond are walking a few feet ahead of me and Gráinne.

I go, 'That was an incredible meal,' just making conversation with the woman. 'I believe you're actually mates with Andy McFadden?'

And she goes, 'It was Honor who stole the bottle of gin.'

I'm there, 'Do you have proof of that?' thinking that a solicitor's letter couriered to her first thing in the morning might soften her cough. 'Because that's a very serious allegation –'

'Yes, I have proof,' she goes. 'I caught her on CCTV.'

'Right – and is the footage in any way grainy?'

'There's nothing wrong with the footage.'

'Fair enough.'

'She stole the gin and then she stole a bottle of Smirnoff today.'

Smirnoff? For fock's sake, Honor. I know it's beside the point, but it's one of the cheapest vodkas on the morket.

I'm there, 'Why didn't you say it at the table?'

She goes, 'Because I didn't want to embarrass you in front of Roz.'

'But why didn't you tell Raymond?'

'Because I can see that he's giving you a hard time – and he'll only use it against you.'

'That's very decent of you.'

'But I want the money.'

'What money?'

'The money for the vodka and gin.'

Jesus Christ. I nearly feel like reminding her that I just paid for half her focking dinner.

I whip out my wad.

I'm like, 'So what are we talking here? Thirty, forty yoyos per bottle?'

She goes, 'That's the cash-and-carry price, yeah. But if I'd sold them as measures –'

'You're asking me to pay the mork-up price?'

'Yes, I am.'

I roll my eyes, then I peel off five fifties, which she takes from me without even saying thanks.

She just goes, 'You know, you should have a long, hard talk with your daughter. She's very young to be drinking – especially spirits.'

I'm there, 'I'm dealing with it, okay?'

Into Kehoes we go. Roz gets the round in – even though Gráinne has two hundred and fifty snots in her pocket – while Raymond says he's just spotted some of his work crowd and he focks off to talk to them.

Literally two minutes later, the dude arrives back. I'm taking a sip of my Hanijan when he suddenly goes, 'Ross, I've got a surprise for you.'

I turn around – casually, like – and I notice that he's standing next to a woman who's roughly my age. She's short with, like, black hair and for a split-second I think it's Colette Fitzpatrick off the Virgin Media News.

I even go, 'Colette, how the hell are you?' wondering does she remember me telling her I loved her when I drunkenly crashed the porty to celebrate the changeover of the station name from TV3.

But she goes, 'It's Anna!' in a sort of, like, sing-song Cork accent. 'I went out with your brother!'

And in that moment, I suddenly remember her – and my life flashes before my eyes.

'Your brother?' Roz goes, her eyebrows halfway up her forehead. 'I didn't know you had a brother.'

Anna's there, 'Yeah, his name is Jamie. They're twins, like.'

And Raymond goes, '*Identical* twins!' and I suddenly remember him saying that he worked with a girl I once knew. He's had this in his locker for weeks now

'My friend Vanessa went out with Ross,' Anna goes, 'and I went out with Jamie. And neither of us could tell them apart!'

Yeah, no, this all happened back in the day – the summer of, I want to say, '01? – when I was seeing her and her mate under two different identities. I was young and much in demand. I met Vanessa in Club 92 and – yeah, no – I threw the lips on her. Then I told her I needed a whizz and for some reason she was under the impression that I was coming back to her. But on the way to the jacks I met another girl – Anna – and ended up getting off with her as well. Then I'm suddenly looking at Vanessa over Anna's shoulder and she's giving me serious daggers and going, 'That's my cousin, boy!'

Anyway, I took a punt and told her that I had a twin brother, we're talking Jamie, and that this kind of thing happened all the time. We had a good laugh about it, then I said I needed a whizz and focked off, about twenty seconds before I returned as Jamie, acting the innocent, going, 'What's going on? What are you laughing at?'

I ended up seeing the two of them for, like, four weeks before they realized that they'd never seen me and Jamie in the same room together and then they both storted to put the pressure on to arrange a double-date. Eventually, the stress of it became too much for me, so I bailed on Vanessa, although I carried on seeing Anna under the name Jamie for about another four weeks, until Sorcha very nearly saw us walking out of Davy Byrne's one Friday lunch-time, so I ended up just ghosting the girl.

'How is Jamie?' Anna goes – because I think she was a little bit in love with him.

I'm there, 'Yeah, no, he's great – he's in fantastic form,' because I kind of liked the dude myself. I put a lot of thought into the charac-ter, inventing little personality quirks for him, like he was deaf in one ear, spoke with a skanger accent and had a phobia about any-thing rubber, including condoms.

I'm there, 'Anyway, Anna, it was great to catch up,' trying to give her the big kiss-off.

But Raymond goes, 'Anna, you'll join us, won't you? What will you have to drink?'

Roz is just, like, glowering at me, shaking her head. She goes, 'Why didn't you tell me that you were a twin?'

And suddenly I remember promising that I wasn't going to lie to Roz any more and telling myself that I was going to treat her better than I treated Sorcha and the hundreds of other girls who've had the pleasure of my company. But it's like when you buy a brand-new MacBook Air and you take it out of its super-smooth, super-white packaging and you tell yourself, 'I am definitely, *definitely* not going to sully this beautiful new laptop by looking at pornography on it.'

And, well, we all know how that ends up going.

She's like, 'Ross, tell me the truth – do you *really* have a twin brother named Jamie?'

And even though I know I'm digging a seriously, *seriously* deep hole for myself here, I end up going, 'Yes, Roz, I have a twin brother named Jamie.'

4.

You Ain't Never Gonna Burn My Heart Out

The old dear tells me that I smell ghastly. She's sitting in a chair next to the window with the sun on her face and she looks actually *well*?

'I mean it,' she goes. 'The smell. It's vile. You haven't been using public transport, have you?'

I'm there, 'No, I haven't been using public transport.'

'Because you *know* how I feel about public transport.'

'You think that it should be banned.'

'I think it should be banned.'

Yeah, no, I remember her once sacking a cleaner because she claimed she 'smelled of bus'. Dominika was her name and she was from, I don't know, *somewhere* originally. Anyway, when she got the job, the deal was that she'd come to the gaff in a taxi, paid for by the old dear. But this one particular day the old dear insisted that she could smell subsidized travel off her – 'you absolutely reek of it' – and she ordered the woman to turn out her pockets. And there, in the back pocket of her jeans, was a bus ticket. Poor Dominika broke down and admitted taking the 46A, then pocketing the taxi fare, because she was saving for – could have been anything – her son's Christmas present, or her sister's lung replacement operation. The old dear sacked her on the spot. I remember her shouting, 'Everything smells of bus now! I can smell it in every room.'

It's nice to reminisce like this.

On the old dear's bed, I notice, lying open and face-down, is the copy of *Criminal Assets* that I brought in for her.

I'm like, 'Oh, you're reading it, are you?'

'No, Dalisay is reading it to me. The woman who wrote it has exactly the same name as me.'

'What are the chances, huh?'

'Fionnuala O'Carroll-Kelly. It's on the cover, look.'

'So is it any good?'

'Oh, it's filthy.'

'Filthy?'

'I think the woman who wrote it must have been sexually frustrated.'

I laugh.

She's there, 'Will you read to me, Ross?'

I'm like, 'You must be focking joking me.'

'Oh, please,' she goes, 'I shan't sleep unless I know what happens next. It's all about this woman, who's called Valerie Amburn-James. Her husband has been sent to prison and she's going through a sexual reawakening.'

So, being too nice for my own basic good, I pick up the book and sit down on the side of her bed.

I'm like, 'Is this where Dalisay left off?'

'Valerie has just met a dark, handsome stranger,' she goes. 'A solicitor, no less!'

I find the bit she's talking about and I stort reading.

I'm there, '*Valerie felt her face collapse. Not another solicitor, she thought, remembering that it was the legal profession that had sent Richard to prison.*'

'No, no, no,' the old dear goes, 'we've had all that. Get to the bit where they're preparing a meal together in the kitchen.'

So I skim through the next few paragraphs, then I go, '*I'll, em, get on with the fruit salad,' he said tentatively, picking up a mango and cupping it in the palm of his big but sensitive left hand. With his other hand he used a Stellar James Martin paring knife to cut away the green and yellow outer peel, deftly following the curve of the fruit, leaving virtually no flesh left attached to the skin.*'

'I said it to Dalisay,' the old dear goes, 'there's a *want* in this Fionnuala person.'

I'm there, '*She watched in amazement as he laid it down on its side and, with a cool sleight of hand, sliced it lengthways, then cut the normally stubborn fruit away from the stone with the minimum of persuasion. She watched his sturdy, educated fingers carve away the few small pieces of* recalcitrant flesh that had attached themselves to the stone and suddenly she found herself having to fend off thoughts, impure thoughts that fixated on those thick, fleshy hands.'

'Didn't I tell you it was filthy? I think the woman had a problem – sexual frustration most likely.'

I'm there, 'Suddenly, unable to help herself, she was imagining him peeling a sensuous black silk dress over her head, then tenderly exposing her body, brushing her skin, then hooking two fingers inside her panties –'

I look up and – shit – I notice that Dalisay is standing in the doorway, smiling at me.

She's like, 'Hello, Ross.'

I'm there, 'Hey, Dalisay – how the hell *are* you?'

I think I mentioned that she's a ringer for Angel Locsin.

'I am well,' she goes. 'It's nice to see you.'

I'm there, 'Yeah, no, you too. I was just, em, reading to her. Even though it's filth.'

'You read so well.'

'Er, do I?'

'When you read, I feel like I am in the story.'

What the –?

She's there, 'Fionnuala, it is time for your medication. I will go and get it.'

Off she goes and I'm thinking, what the fock did that mean?

'It's coming from that bag,' the old dear suddenly goes.

I'm like, 'What is?'

She's there, 'The stench. Of subsidized travel. It's coming from that bag,' and she points at the tote that's balled up and stuffed into the pocket of my Henri Lloyd.

I pull it out and look at it – yeah, no, I just grabbed it randomly from the cupboard under the stairs – and it's from the *Titanic* Experience in Belfast. I can't help but smile. Helen went there with her book club after they read some historical novel or other that involved two of the survivors. And – yeah, no – they took the focking Enterprise.

'Yes, it's definitely the bag,' the old dear goes. 'Get it out of here, Ross.'

Seriously, the woman has a nose like a springer spaniel.

I'm there, 'I was going to head off anyway,' and I stand up.

I'm giving her a hug goodbye when she suddenly goes, 'Ross, who *is* that frightful man?' and I notice that her, I don't know, *gaze* is being drawn to the muted TV on the wall. 'He seems to be everywhere.'

I burst out laughing. Because it's the old man. I grab the remote and I stick the sound on. It's, like, the RTÉ lunchtime news. Some dude is saying that the Taoiseach is coming under increasing pressure in the midst of shortages of many popular foodstuffs, which have come as a direct consequence of Irexit, as well as the controversial scheme to reroute the Liffey, which has resulted in more than a thousand people being made homeless.

'At New Republic's Ard-Fheis in the RDS this weekend,' the dude goes, 'the Taoiseach is expected to repeat his message that the food shortages are temporary and that the decision to leave the European Union will prove to have been the correct one in the long run.'

'He's awful,' the old dear goes. 'How do I know him, Ross?'

I'm there, 'Er, he's the leader of the *country*? So-called anyway. He's always on TV, bullshitting about something or other.'

'No, no, no,' she goes. 'I've met him, Ross. I know him. I just can't think how.'

'Ireland is on the verge of a boom,' the old man goes, 'that will be boomier than anything we've ever seen in the past!'

That goes down about as well as me crashing Brian Ormond and Pippa O'Connor's wedding reception after a drunken round of golf in Enniskerry with Christian and one of the Easterby brothers. People are actually laughing. Which they definitely weren't in the Ritz Corlton, I seem to remember, especially when I storted heckling Pippa's speech and Brian Dowling – her chief bridesman – had to drag me out of there in a headlock.

The old man seems totally oblivious to the haters, though. I'm watching him from the wings as he goes, 'Our country is about to enter a golden age!' banging the podium with his fist for added emphasis. 'All of the conditions are in place! We have shaken loose the shackles of the enterprise-crushing European Union! We have let it be known that we, the Irish people, will no longer be paying debts that were racked up by greedy bankers and property speculators! And the international community respects us for it! For the first time it can be said that, under New Republic, Ireland has truly taken its place among the nations of the world!'

A chant storts up. It's like, 'O'Carroll-Kelly, you're a wanker, you're a wanker –' and I get a sudden flashback to Brian Dowling – who's a hell of a lot tougher than he let on when he won *Big Brother* – turning me upside down and body-slamming me on the wooden floor of the Sally Gap Bor and Brasserie, before the Easterby brother – I'd nearly swear it was Simon – put his hand on his shoulder and told him that I'd had enough.

'Don't believe those extremists on the Far Left,' the old man goes, 'who would have you believe that a few temporary food shortages are evidence of an economy that is failing! For the first time in our history, Ireland is winning! And we are winning like we deserve to win!'

The dude steps away from the podium, then waves and blows kisses to the crowd, even though half of them clearly don't believe his bullshit any more. He eventually steps off the stage and the first person he sees is me.

He goes, 'Kicker! What did you think?'

I'm there, 'Doesn't matter what I think. Listen to that.'

The crowd are in, like, full voice now, giving it, 'O'Carroll-Kelly, you're a wanker, you're wanker.'

The old man's there, 'A chant you're more than familiar with from your rugby-playing days! And I don't remember it ever throwing you off your game!'

It's a lovely thing for me to hear. Yeah, no, I used to take my shirt off in front of them, then stort fingering my abs like they were accordion keys, although I'm relieved that the old man chose not to go down that route.

I'm there, 'I'm here to talk to you about the old dear,' and there's not even a flicker of interest in his face.

He's like, 'Who?'

I'm there, 'Er, your *wife*?'

But I don't get to say any more than that because he's suddenly surrounded by flunkies, including Gordon Greenhalgh, the Minister for Housing, who claps his hands and goes, 'If there were any doubters out there before, Taoiseach, you've turned them all into believers tonight.'

The old man smiles and runs his hand through his hair slash wig. He loves hearing nice things about himself. I suppose I must have got it from somewhere.

Hennessy steps forward, hands him a hip-flask and goes, 'Well done, Taoiseach. You did good.'

The old man's like, 'Yes, I thought I lost them for a little bit somewhere around the middle, but by the end they were eating out of my hand!' and I'm thinking, were they listening to the same speech as me?

'Dude,' I go, shoving Gordon Greenhalgh – Lychee's old man, bear in mind – out of the way, 'I was in the middle of *saying* something?'

The old man's like, 'Oh, yes – about your mother! How is she, Ross?'

'Why don't you go and see her and find out for yourself?'

'She doesn't know who I am, Ross.'

'She does know who you are. She saw you on the news and she thought she recognized you. As in, she knew that she'd *met* you somewhere before?'

He looks away.

He goes, 'Painful as it is, Ross, Fionnuala has gone – or at least the Fionnuala that I knew and loved!'

I'm there, 'That's horseshit. She smelled public transport off me.'

'She what?'

'She smelled public transport. Off a tote bag I had with me. She's still the same Fionnuala. I'm sure if you went to see her more often –'

But he just goes, 'Ross, I have a country to run. Your mother would have understood –'

'Stop talking about her in the past tense. She's still here.'

'Your mother would have understood that there are people out there who need me!'

'Out where?'

'Out *there*!'

'The Simmonscourt Pavilion?'

'And beyond!'

'Are you focking deluded?'

'I *beg* your pordon?'

'Can you not hear that crowd?'

Yeah, no, they're still in the arena and they're still giving it, 'O'Carroll-Kelly, you're a wanker, you're a wanker!'

That's when – I shit you not – he goes, 'Pay no heed to them, Kicker! It's just rugby banter – inverted commas! Nothing more!'

I actually laugh out loud.

I'm there, 'They're not calling *me* a wanker. They're calling *you* a wanker.'

He's like, 'What? Why would they call *me* such a thing?'

I'm there, 'Er, because you've destroyed the *country*?'

'Destroyed the country?' he goes. 'I should think it's you that's delusional! Hennessy, who is it they're calling a wanker out there?'

Hennessy – without hesitation – goes, 'Your son, Taoiseach.'

I'm there, 'Why the fock would people turn up to hear you make a speech and then call me a wanker?'

'It was a popular song during your Senior Cup days,' Hennessy goes. 'And the people – the party grassroots, who absolutely love you, Taoiseach – are singing it in an ironic way.'

'Ironic!' the old man goes. 'Did you hear that, Kicker? *Quod erat demonstrandum!*'

I'm there, 'Are you going to Ongar to see the old dear?'

But he just goes, 'I'm sorry, Ross! I have a country to run! I have a nation to inspire!' and off the dude decides to fock.

I walk out of the place in the middle of this, like, tide of people, all of them talking about what a prick my old man is and how he's destroyed the country.

I whip out my phone and I notice that I have five missed calls from a number that I don't recognize. That's never good, I think. I ring back, but when the phone is answered – this is an old trick of mine – I let the person on the other end speak first.

'Ross?' a voice, very faintly, goes. 'Oh my God, thank God!'

I recognize her straight away.

I'm like, 'Sincerity? What's wrong?' because there's a definite note of, I don't know, *something* in her voice?

She goes, 'It's Honor.'

I'm there, 'Has there been an accident?'

'She's unconscious.'

I'm there, 'Unconscious?' suddenly shoving my way through the crowd. 'In terms of?'

'She drank an entire bottle of Smirnoff,' Sincerity goes.

I'm there, 'Smirnoff?' even though – again – the brand should be irrelevant. I suppose if you're stealing it from a restaurant, it's easier to conceal than a bottle of, say, Grey Goose. 'Have you called an ambulance?'

She's there, 'Johnny asked me not to.'

I'm like, 'Johnny?' still pushing people out of the way. 'As in, like, Protestant Johnny?'

'Johnny Prendergast,' she goes. 'As in, like, my *boyfriend*? His parents are *so* strict. They'll go absolutely mental if they find out he had a porty in the house.'

I'm like, 'Where's the house?' as I finally manage to get outside. 'I definitely heard Ranelagh mentioned,' because South Dublin people never forget these things.

She goes, 'It's in Mountpleasant Square. It looks really small from the outside but his parents also bought the house next door and they've knocked through the wall and also extended out the back.'

I'm not even thinking fair focks to them. That's how suddenly pissed off I am with Johnny Prendergast, who I had a lot of time for, remember, even though I've never actually met him and wouldn't know him from a crow in a field.

I'm like, 'Text me the Eircode,' as I sprint all the way back to the cor.

Fifteen minutes later, I'm pulling up outside the gaff. Sincerity was right. These houses do *look* small – I saw the inside of one or two of them during my famous TramCo days – but they're huge on the inside.

The front door is open. There's, like, thirty or forty young people standing around with, like, worried looks on their faces.

I'm there, 'Where is she? Where's my daughter?' and the crowd sort of, like, ports down the middle, directing me to a lorge kitchen – very similar to Delma's, I can't help but notice – where Honor is passed out on the floor, with Sincerity crouched over her, along with a dude, who I presume to be Johnny Prendergast.

I can usually tell Protestants from their bone structure.

I hunker down and I'm like, 'Honor? Honor, can you hear me?'

The dude goes, 'I rolled her over onto her side,' which was good thinking from him.

I'm there, 'Am I supposed to be grateful?'

He doesn't say shit back to me.

I'm like, 'You're Johnny, I presume? I'm surprised at you. That's all I'm going to say,' and he looks at me, utterly focking bewildered.

I notice that Sincerity is crying her eyes out.

I'm there, 'Who gave her spirits?' looking around for someone to blame other than my own daughter.

'She stole it,' Sincerity goes, 'from the restaurant.'

I'm like, 'Some mate you are,' just lashing out now. 'You'd give her up in a focking hortbeat.'

I stort trying to wake Honor up. I'm like, 'Honor? Honor, can you hear me?' and I lay my hand on her forehead.

She goes, 'Dad?' except she sort of, like, mumbles the word.

Yeah, no, she's storting to come around.

She's there, 'Where am I?'

I'm like, 'You're at a porty. Mountpleasant Square, in fairness.'

I look at Sincerity. I'm there, 'Was she drinking it with a mixer?'

Sincerity shakes her head. She's like, 'No, straight from the bottle.'

Like her focking grandmother, I'm tempted to say.

I'm there, 'And you said she drank the entire thing?'

'No, that's not true,' Johnny goes. He has a very commanding voice. He could be a barrister one day if he wanted and I dare say he will be. 'She only drank half of it. She spilled the rest when she collapsed.'

Like her focking grandmother as well.

I'm there, 'So that's not piss on the floor?'

He shakes his head.

I'm like, 'Okay, Honor, you're probably going to be fine. Can you stand?'

She goes, 'No,' again mumbling the word.

I'm like, 'Right, let's get you home,' and I pick her up and – in one fluid movement – throw her over my shoulder, like I used to when she was a child and I'd do the whole 'Where will I put this bag of rubbish?' routine, except there's no squeals of laughter out of her now, just the sound of her dry-heaving.

Sincerity catches my eye and she goes, 'Ross, please don't tell my mom about this.'

I'm there, 'I can't promise you that, Sincerity. Me and your old dear have *no* secrets from each other,' which, as well as being complete and utter horseshit, comes out a little bit sleazier than I intended.

I carry Honor to the front door. Behind me, I hear a voice go, 'What a focking wanker. Easy to see why his daughter drinks so much.'

I turn around to ask who said that and, in the process, I accidentally bang Honor's head off the frame of the door. She'll have some bump on it in the morning. Hopefully, she won't remember.

I carry her out to the cor and I open the front passenger door. I put her softly down on the seat and I go, 'Everything's going to be okay, Honor – let's get you home.'

And just as I say it, she opens her mouth and spews the contents of her stomach right down the front of my shirt.

'He's going to get away with it!' Erika goes, pacing the floor of the kitchen. 'He's going to focking get away with it!'

She's talking about the old man. The crash investigation crowd have decided that Simone's death was a genuine accident, caused by a combination of the speed at which she was driving and the fact that she was texting at the time.

Helen goes, 'Her family have accepted it, Erika. And you're going to have to accept it too.'

Erika's there, 'She was murdered. She deserves justice.'

Erika is wearing her jodhpurs and riding boots and – even though it's wrong – it's doing all sorts of things for me.

'And what *is* justice?' Helen goes. 'What does it look like?'

Erika's like, 'Justice is *him* spending the rest of his life in prison.'

Helen's there, 'And would that make you happy, Erika?'

Erika doesn't answer her. She decides to take it out on *me* then?

'Why are you looking at me like that?' she goes.

I'm there, 'Like what?'

And she goes, 'Like a focking dog staring in a butcher's window.'

Amelie wanders into the kitchen. She goes, 'Mommy, are we going horse-riding?'

Erika's there, 'Yeah, did you wake Honor?'

'I knocked on her door,' Amelie goes, 'and she told me to go away.'

She'll be hungover to fock, I'd imagine.

I'm there, 'I'll try.'

Erika goes, 'Tell her we're supposed to be picking up Rihanna-Brogan at eleven.'

So up the stairs I trot. I stand outside her door for a good, like, sixty seconds, trying to summon up the courage to knock, when all of a sudden I hear her go, 'Dad, just come in, will you – you focking weirdo.'

Which is what I end *up* doing?

She's been crying. She's lying in bed with mascara streaking her cheeks. She's as down as a fat kid on a see-saw.

I sit on the edge of her bed and neither of us says anything for a good, I don't know, minute or two. Then she suddenly leans her head into my shoulder and I put my orm around her to pull her closer and she storts sobbing – we're talking *uncontrollably* here?

I kiss the top of her head, then I rub my cheek against her hair and I tell her that I'm not angry with her and it's going to be okay.

After a minute or two, she stops crying and we're both silent.

Then suddenly, out of nowhere, I go, 'Why don't you just tell her that you like her, Honor?'

I brace myself for her reaction, expecting her to explode at me and tell me to mind my own focking business. Except she doesn't.

She goes, 'Because she likes boys.'

I'm like, 'Right. Jesus. So you're, you know –'

'You can say the word, Dad.'

'I'd nearly prefer if you said it first.'

'A lesbian.'

'A lesbian, yeah? Are you – *one*, like?'

'I suppose I must be.'

I kiss the top of her head again.

I'm there, 'How long have you felt this way – about Sincerity, I mean?'

'I don't know,' she goes. 'I just realized it – one day during the summer.'

'But she has no idea – that you like her?'

'Dad, I *love* her.'

'That you love her, then?'

She shakes her head. 'I can't tell her,' she goes. 'She'll think I'm a focking weirdo.'

I'm there, 'She might not.'

'She totally would – and then I'd lose her as a friend.'

'This isn't –?'

'What?'

'Don't go mad – but this isn't another one of your scams, is it?'

'No, it's focking not.'

'You can't blame me for wondering, Honor, after some of the stunts you've pulled over the years. You told us you were trans at one stage.'

'Well, I'm not trans – but I *am* in love with a girl.'

'And there's nothing wrong with that. Nothing, nothing, nothing. Nothing at all. But, listen, the drinking, Honor –'

'Dad, please don't lecture me.'

'I'm not going to lecture you. It's just, you know, I'm getting too old to carry you up those stairs. There's a list of the injuries that I've had on the inside cover of my Rugby Tactics Book.'

She laughs and wipes away her tears with the palm of her hand.

She goes, 'You and your focking tactics book.'

Me and Honor, we just *get* each other?

Her phone all of a sudden beeps. She looks at the screen, then goes, 'It's her. She's asking me how I'm feeling this morning.'

I'm there, 'That's nice, isn't it? Shows she cares about you.'

'Yeah, but just as a friend.'

'There's nothing wrong with being just friends.'

I hate lying to her, but here we are.

She's like, 'But how can I make her like me – as in, like, *like* me like me?'

I'm there, 'Unfortunately, that's not how attraction works, Honor.'

She goes, 'It's alright for you. You can have, like, any woman you want.'

It's a lovely compliment to get, even though now is maybe not the time to ask her to go into specifics.

I'm like, 'That's a subject for another day. This is nice, isn't it?'

She goes, 'What is?'

I'm there, 'Just talking honestly to each other. Oh, speaking of which, if Roz asks you if I have a twin brother, tell her yes, will you? His name is Jamie and we haven't spoken in years.'

'But you don't have a twin brother named Jamie.'

'Yeah, no, it's a long story, Honor. It's grown-up shit.'

'Well, as long as you don't tell Roz that we were at a porty where there was alcohol.'

'I don't know if I can keep that from her, Honor.'

'I don't want to get Sincerity into trouble – please!'

'Yeah, no, fair enough. Are you going horse-riding this morning or do you want to give it a miss?'

'No, I'll get up now.'

I take my orm from around her shoulder and I stand up.

She goes, 'I've got a bump here,' and she rubs the side of her forehead.

I'm there, 'Do you remember how you got it?'

She's like, 'No.'

And I think, thank fock for that.

She goes, 'Does Erika know – about me being gay?'

I'm there, 'Honor, it's not a major deal. And Erika is in no position to judge you. Ask her about a girl called Meredith McTominay.'

Her face lights up and she's like, 'Oh my God!'

I'm there, 'Happened on the Sixth Year skiing trip to Klosters.

Although I have no more details than that. Actually, do me a favour – don't tell her I told you that, will you?'

She's like, 'I won't. I promise.'

As I'm walking out the door, she goes, 'I know I give you a hord time and I make it really hord for you to love me sometimes –'

I'm there, 'You don't, Honor. I'm a focking mug for you. Was from day one.'

She goes, '– but you're an amazing dad.'

And I feel my eyes suddenly fill up because I know she means it and I know it's true. Aport from rugby, being a father is probably the only thing I've ever been good at.

'Okay,' I go, 'let's have a look at this famous menu of theirs.'

Yeah, no, I'm having dinner with Roz in Mister S on Camden Street.

I'm there, 'I've heard good things. I see that they only use sustainable fish stocks and they support local, ethical forming. Which is a relief, I think it's fair to say.'

She hasn't known me long but she knows me well enough to know that I'm trying to avoid talking about something.

I'm there, 'I especially love that line there. *We have built amazing relationships with some of the country's best ortisans and our job is to help their produce speak for itself.* Sums it up really. Sums it up.'

She goes, 'Ross, why won't you talk about it?'

I'm there, 'Because there's nothing to talk about. Would you be interested in splitting the Côte de Bœuf, by the way?'

She's like, 'You have a brother. A twin brother. And you never mentioned him to me.'

I'm there, 'I told you, we haven't spoken in years.'

'But that's all you've told me.'

'No, I told you that he's deaf in one ear. That he has a skanger accent. That he has a phobia of anything rubber, including condoms.'

'But that's it,' she goes. 'Nothing about your childhood. Nothing about your reasons for falling out. Nothing about, I don't know, where is he now?'

My mind is suddenly swerving all over the place – like my old man driving home from Leopardstown on Stephen Zuzz Day. A waitress comes and saves me.

She's like, 'Are you ready to order?'

I'm there, 'I was thinking in terms of the Burnt End Rendang Spring Rolls to stort –'

But it's only a temporary reprieve.

Roz goes, 'Can you actually give us a minute or two?'

The waitress is like, 'Yeah, no, fine,' and she focks off to take someone else's order.

'Ross,' Roz goes, 'I can't believe you would keep something this big from me.'

I'm there, 'It's, I don't know, painful to talk about, that's all.'

'Look, I don't want to pry, and I don't want to make you feel uncomfortable, but I hated being blindsided in Kehoes that night. When that girl mentioned your twin brother, I had literally no idea what she was talking about. Raymond could see it in my face.'

'What does it have to do with him anyway?'

'Because I told him that you and I are serious about each other. And, like I said, he really, really likes you, which is important, not just because he's my best friend but also because – as my boyfriend – you are effectively becoming a step-parent to my daughter.'

I think that's pushing it a bit, but I say nothing.

She goes, 'Obviously, if I'm bringing a new man into our home, I have a responsibility to make sure I know everything I possibly can about him. You must understand that. You've got five children.'

And quite possibly a sixth on the way, I think.

She's like, 'I was embarrassed, Ross. I had Raymond and Gráinne looking at me, thinking, "She doesn't know the first thing about this goy." As a matter of fact, Raymond rang me the next morning and said he was surprised that I hadn't done due diligence on you.'

I'm like, 'Yeah, no, I bet he did.'

She's there. 'He's concerned, Ross, and he's fully entitled to be.' And then after a moment's pause, she goes, 'When we were together, Raymond and I told each other absolutely everything,' and then she leaves it hanging there for me to make of it whatever I want.

The waitress is back.

'What's harissa jus?' I go. 'I think I know the answer to this one, but I've just forgotten.'

Roz rolls her eyes and she's like, 'Can you give us a few more minutes, please? As a matter of fact, *we'll* call *you* when we're ready to order.'

The waitress focks off again, rolling her eyes this time, and I realize that I'm going to have to come up with something good here because she's not letting go of this.

I'm there, 'What's there to say? We were – yeah, no – close. We were twins. How could we not be? It was all the usual stuff you see on TV. We dressed the same. We used to finish each other's sentences. But unfortunately –'

Shit, I've forgotten the focker's name.

She's like, 'Jamie?'

I'm there, 'Jamie, exactly. Unfortunately, the dude was jealous of me.'

'Why?'

'Who knows? Maybe it was because I was better-looking than him.'

I can't help myself.

'That girl in Kehoes said you were identical,' she goes. 'No one could tell you aport.'

Jesus, this is focking work.

I'm there, 'Well, maybe not better-looking, then. But I was definitely a bigger hit with the ladies.'

She goes, 'Did he play rugby too?'

I have to be careful here. That shit is checkable.

I'm there, 'No, he absolutely detested the game. He'd have been more into soccer.'

She goes, 'Soccer?' and I'm trying to figure out is she genuinely shocked or is she just trying to coax more information out of me.

I'm there, 'Yeah, no, he was always watching it. Like I said, he hated rugby. He'd think nothing of switching off a Six Nations match – or Five Nations as it was in the years before Italy joined. But what Jamie hated even more than rugby was the fact that I was amazing at it.'

'Did he ever go to see you play?'

134

'No – he refused point-blank.'

'That would explain it, then.'

'Explain what?'

'Well, I knew two or three girls who knew you back in the day – they were, like, major rugger-huggers – and none of them remembered you having a twin brother.'

Shit, she's doing her due focking due diligence now, in fairness to the girl.

'See what I mean? He totally disowned me. He refused to even be there the day that I lifted the Leinster Schools Senior Cup after absolutely destroying Newbridge College pretty much single-handedly in the final.'

I can never resist an opportunity to talk about it.

'So, what, you fell out over that?' she goes.

I'm there, 'Yeah, no, that would have been the stort of it.'

'But it wasn't the final straw?' she goes, staring at me across the table. She wants more so I end up having to *give* it to her?

I'm there, 'The final straw would have been over a girl – named, em, Harissa.'

Oh, fock. For a pathological liar of my experience, it's unforgivably sloppy. By some miracle, though, Roz either didn't hear me ask the waitress about it or she doesn't make the connection.

'Harissa,' she goes. 'That's a lovely name. Was she Indian?'

I'm there, 'Yeah, no, she was,' and I realize that I'm losing control of what Ryle Nugent always referred to as the narrative. 'Her old man was Indian. Her old dear was from Letterfrack.'

I don't know where the fock that even is. I might have made it up.

'And was Harissa *your* girlfriend?' she goes.

I'm there, 'Yeah, no, two years we were together.'

She's like, 'Oh my God,' her eyes wide with expectation, 'what school did she go to?'

I'm there, 'Er,' suddenly hating that this town is so small. 'I'm going to say King's Hos?'

'Oh,' she goes, sounding disappointed, 'I don't know anyone who went to King's Hos,' and I breathe a definite sigh of relief.

I'm there, 'Anyway, to cut a long story short, after I left school, I did the SportsMan Dip. course in UCD. That's how I ended up mates with Brian O'Driscoll – before he even *was* Brian O'Driscoll. I picked up an injury in my first year, which put me out for a few months and had a big knock-on effect in terms of my career. I sank into – I'm going to shock you now – a bit of a depression. I was a nightmare to be around. And – yeah, no, cords on the table – I storted pushing Harissa away.'

I feel like I'm describing a movie I've seen but half forgotten.

Roz has a look of confusion on her face. She's there, 'I know our memories can play tricks on us, but I thought you and Sorcha were together that whole time.'

I'm like, 'She was definitely on the scene around that time. But she sort of, like, dipped in and *out* of my life?'

'So what happened – to Harissa, I mean?'

'Well, after I storted pushing her away, she storted hanging out in The Pod with her friends. She loved dancing.'

'I used to go to The Pod. I wonder would I know her to see?'

'Anyway, it was there one night that she ended up meeting Jamie and, well, one thing led to another and he, em, rode her.'

I suddenly put my hand over my mouth as if to stifle a sob.

'Oh my God, I'm so sorry,' Roz goes. 'I'm such a paranoid, selfish bitch for making you relive this when it's obviously one of the most painful memories of your life. Let's leave it there,' and she signals to the waitress that we're finally ready to order. 'I'm so sorry, Ross.'

I'm there, 'Yeah, no, that's why I never talk about it. Even if you asked Christian, JP, Oisinn, any of those about my brother Jamie, they'd just stare at you blankly and probably say, "What brother?"'

I'm lining up my defence here like a tactical master.

'Oh my God,' she suddenly goes, with a big smile on her face, 'I don't know if this is, like, the universe talking,' because she's, like, *into* all that horseshit, 'but there's harissa on the menu!'

'We don't have any harissa,' the waitress shouts over, 'it's been subbed out for tomato ketchup, because of –'

And all three of us, at the exact same time, go, 'Irexit.'

*

Toneet Ine godda daddence
For all dat we'b been treeew,
But I doatunt waddant to daddence
If Ine not daddecing wit yeeew.

Shadden is absolutely slaughtering that Taylor Swift song, then kicking its corpse into an open grave and filling it in with topsoil.

Yeah, no, I'm at her and Ronan's housewarming in The K Club and they've gone early with the karaoke. I catch Tina's eye across the floor of the living room and I shake my head, which she takes as an invitation to come over to me.

She's there, 'Are you joost godda staddend by and do nuttin?'

'Yeah, no, I thought about maybe flicking the trip-switch,' I go, 'like I used to do whenever Sorcha and Fionn were having one of their Oscar-winning foreign film nights.'

She's like, 'Ine not thalken about Shadden's sigging. Ine thalken about Ronan – *our* sudden – throwing he's life away, hagging arowunt with these peepil.'

Yeah, no, she's no fan of the Tuites.

She goes, 'And joost so as you know, Ine blaming you for this.'

I'm there, 'Me? What did I do?'

'He had a life mapped out for heeself,' she goes, 'in Amedica. And he came howum – to save *your* bleaten neck.'

I'm there, 'I don't feel good about it, Tina, if that's what you're implying. I'm as pissed off as you are that he's ended up throwing his hand in with this family of scummy focking scumfucks.'

Shit, I notice that Rihanna-Brogan is standing about two feet away, although I'm not a hundred per cent sure she heard me over the sound of the applause for Kennet, who has the mic in his hand. He's wearing his driver's cap, I notice.

'If you were addy kind of fadder,' Tina goes, 'you'd do sometin abour it.'

Kennet storts singing. The song is 'You Can Leave Your Hat On'. Of course, it is. *The Fully Monty* is Dordeen's favourite movie of all time.

I'm there, 'I don't *know* what to do? Hennessy has him over a focking barrel.'

All of a sudden, some absolute giant of a dude appears at Tina's side – we're talking tall enough to play second-row for Leinster, except he doesn't look the rugby type.

'Howiya,' he goes – I'm such a shrewd judge of character, 'Ine Toddem.'

I'm like, 'Toddem.'

'No,' he goes, 'Toddem.'

'I'm not sure I'm getting it.'

'Toddem.'

'At the risk of being rude now, can I –?'

'Toddem.'

I'm there, 'Oh, Tom! You're saying Tom!' and I don't know why but my eyes immediately find Tina's hand and there on her ring-finger are three – small, in fairness – diamonds. 'Whoa! Congratulations! I didn't even know you were seeing anyone. Not that I take an interest in what you get up to, I don't know, sexually or whatever.'

There's no 'Thank you', '*We're* very happy that *you're* happy' or 'Save the date'.

Tina just goes, 'Toddem's a foyerman. Based ourra Phibsbuddha. Hee-or, teddle Rosser what Shadden's mutter and fadder did this morden.'

'Thee burdened out their owult gaff,' Tom slash Toddem goes.

I'm there, 'What? Why?'

Tina's like, 'Why do you think? They're libbon out hee-or now and thee wanted the insurdance muddy.'

'What insurance money?' I go. 'I thought the council owned it?'

Tom's there, 'Thee do. But they're claiming for all the contents that were supposedly desthroyed. And probably for emotionoddle disthress as weddle.'

Of course they are. As Hennessy always says, personal injuries claims are the libel awards of the working classes.

'Rosser,' Tina goes, 'fooken do sometin.'

I'm staring at Kennet, who already has his shirt off and who's unzipping his bootcut Levi's in a way that Dordeen seems to find sexy, judging by the way she's fanning herself with her hand.

It's true what they say – there really is someone for everyone.

I spot Ronan, standing in the doorway, holding a can of cider that *looks* like Bulmers, although it's actually spelt Bù'ěr Mò Sī.

I'm there, 'Hey, Ro, how the hell are you?'

He goes, 'Ine moostard, Rosser. Fooken moostard,' even though I know he's still putting a brave face on a shit situation.

I'm like, 'Congratulations. On the new gaff, I mean.'

He's there, 'Thanks, Rosser.'

I'm like, 'It's quite the porty, isn't it?' and I'm looking around at all the old faces – we're talking Nudger, we're talking Gull, we're talking Buckets of Blood.

Ronan's there, 'What's that apposed to mee-un?'

'Doesn't mean anything,' I go. 'It was a compliment, if anything.'

He's like, 'You said it with a towun.'

'A what?'

'A towun.'

'A *tone*? I honestly didn't, Ro. Yeah, no, you're hearing things.'

All of a sudden, there's a humungous cheer as Kennet's bootcut Levi's go flying across the room and end up landing on Nudger's head. Kennet is standing in front of a – *literally?* – panting Dordeen, wearing just his driver's cap, a pair of white Nike socks and – I shit you not – a leopard-print thong.

'Jesus focking Christ,' I go. 'He's got a focking horn on him!'

Although everyone seems to find this hilarious.

I'm there, 'There's focking children in the room.'

And Ronan turns on me then. He's like, 'That's you all oaber, idn't it, Rosser? Looken dowun on utter peepil.'

I'm there, 'I don't look down on other people.'

I do look down on other people. Most people, in fact. But definitely these people.

He goes, 'Ine arthur been looken at you all neet, Rosser, standing arowunt with a big smeerk on yisser face, judging evoddy wooden. Looken dowun yisser nowuz at Shadden when she was sigging "Hody Garrowunt". Sneerding when I invited evoddy wooden outside to look at Rihanna-Brogan's horse in the back geerden.'

Yeah, no, there's a focking horse in the gorden. I'm trying to imagine the conversation between the neighbours out here.

I'm there, 'Ro, I don't know what to say,' because I've never heard him defend Shadden's family like this. It's like he *has* thrown his lot in with this pack of lowlifes and now he's determined to double down on it, even though he realizes deep down that he's made the biggest mistake of his life. 'All I can do is swear to you that I don't look down on them at all.'

All of a sudden – oh, shit – Dordeen is morching across the floor towards me with Rihanna-Brogan by her side – *crying*, I can't help but notice?

'I wanth a woord wit you,' the woman goes.

She's red in the face, although I'm not sure if she's angry about something or just flushed from the excitement of having her husband's mickey waved in her face like a conductor's baton.

Very quickly, I get my answer.

'Did you call us scummy fooken scumfooks?' she goes.

I'm there, 'No,' acting the total innocent. 'It doesn't sound like the kind of thing I'd say.'

Which is true, strictly speaking. I definitely didn't pronounce it anything like that.

'Well, Rihatta-Barrogan heerd you,' the woman goes, 'wirrer owun ee-ors.'

I'm there, 'I didn't say that. Honestly, Ro.'

'You fooken did,' Rihanna-Brogan goes – my only granddaughter, bear in mind. 'I was stanton right beside you, you fooken lying bastoord.'

I look at Ronan, as if to say, 'Are you going to let her speak to me like that?'

But it turns out that he's totally cool with it.

He goes, 'Rosser, I want you to leab,' and I notice that every conversation in the house seems to have stopped.

I'm there, 'Leab?'

He's like, 'Gerrout, Rosser. You're not weddlecom hee-or.'

Tina says nothing in my defence, by the way. She keeps her beak out of it.

Kennet decides to get involved then. Yeah, no, he's suddenly standing in front of me, going, 'S . . . S . . . S . . . S . . . S . . . Scumfooks – is that what we are to you, Rosser?'

Yeah, no, he's standing there in just his socks, his hat and his little focking lolly bag.

I'm there, 'I would never use a word like that.'

'Scummy fooken scumfooks,' Rihanna-Brogan corrects him.

Kennet's like, 'There's g . . . g . . . g . . . g . . . g . . . gratitude, wha? Turdening he's nowuz up at a famidy that's oately ebber been n . . . n . . . n . . . n . . . n . . . n . . . nice to him.'

Ronan goes, 'Rosser, you'd want to speddend a bit less toyum slagging off utter people's famidies and a bit mower toyum concenthrating on yisser owun.'

I'm confused.

I'm like, 'What's that supposed to mean?'

'I rang me sister this morden,' he goes, 'to see was she cubbing today.'

I'm there, 'Yeah, no, she's playing badminton in school. There's, like, a Transition Year Blitz on.'

He goes, 'She was fooken pissed, Rosser.'

I'm thinking, oh, no – not again.

'She was bleaten fluthered,' he goes. 'A geerl of, what, fourteen? Thrunk out of her head at eleben o'clock on a Saturday morden.'

There's more than a few gasps in the room. I realize that it's time for me to get the fock out of here. I don't need Brian Dowling throwing me around the place like Scott focking Steiner to let me know when a porty's over for me. Except obviously that one time.

Oh, Honor. She promised me that was the end of it. A badminton blitz. I'm a gullible fool.

I stort making my way to the door. Dadden opens it for me and that's when I see a group of neighbours standing together in the gorden. It didn't take them long to form a posse.

One of them goes, 'We've been ringing the bell for the past

twenty minutes. I expect you can't hear us with all that bloody racket going on.'

I smile because they're my kind of people. Good people – obviously with money.

'Is that your quadbike porked out on the road?' one of the others goes.

There's, like, seven of the dudes – all dressed in golfing gear.

I'm there, 'Er, does it *look* like my quadbike?'

All of a sudden, Kennet is standing in the doorway behind me.

He's like, 'What's the s . . . s . . . s . . . s . . . s . . . stordee hee-or?'

The men's faces all drop. Yeah, no, he's still in his *Fully Monty* clobber.

'Is this your house?' the first dude goes.

Kennet's there, 'No, it's me thaughter's. Ine libbon n . . . n . . . n . . . next doe-er.'

'So it's *your* quadbike,' the other dude goes. 'Could you please put it in your driveway – or preferably your garage – as per the rules of the management company?'

Kennet's there, 'M . . . M . . . M . . . Madagement compoddy? I doatunt *take* orders from addy m . . . m . . . m . . . m . . . m . . . madagement compoddy.'

'Well,' the dude with the hang-up about the quadbike goes, 'you would have been given a copy of the rules when you moved in. If you'd taken the trouble to read it, you would have seen that it also contains three paragraphs relating to noise pollution.'

It's all very Ulverton Road, Dalkey – and I'm saying that as a compliment to them.

Dordeen appears at the door then. She's like, 'What's going on?'

Kennet's there, 'He's slagging off your sigging, Dordeen,' and he steps out of the house in a definitely threatening manner. 'He said it was noise pollution.'

'It's more about the volume,' the poor dude goes – put on the back foot, 'rather than the singing *per se*.'

There's no point in using French around these people. They're still struggling with English. Kennet grabs him by the scruff of his Moncler polo shirt and goes, 'Is this f . . . f . . . f . . . f . . . f . . . f . . .

fedda a mate of yoo-ers, Rosser?' and I don't know why he automatically thinks I'd know him.

One of the other dudes goes, 'Unhand Simon this instant!' and he storts trying to break Kennet's grip on the poor focker.

That's when it all kicks off. Dadden and Kadden come tearing out of the gaff, followed by Shadden, then six or seven others, and they set about the neighbours like the great Castlerock College team of 1999 putting manners on the Gonzaga pack.

More neighbours – again, they're golfers – arrive to support the advance porty and it turns into a full-on brawl on the front lawn, although a very much one-sided one. Violence is being met with threats of solicitors' letters and further references to paragraphs, not to mention subsections, in the famous management agreement.

And right in the middle of this bloodied battlefield, I spot Ronan. For some reason, he's removed his top as well and he's standing there with one of the neighbours in a headlock while he waves his fist at another, who's holding a golf putter like it's a Samurai sword, and Ro's telling him, 'Do you waddant some? Do you want yisser bleaten go?'

I turn my head and I notice that Nudger, Gull and Buckets are standing next to me, staring at me.

'Rosser,' Nudger goes, 'you need to get him the fook ourra hee-or. And Ine not joost thalken ourra *hee-or*. Ine thalken ourra the cunterdoddy.'

Sorcha rings me on my mobile and without even a word of greeting she asks me what the hell is going on with Honor?

I'm trying to figure out if I can hear anger in her voice.

'In terms of what?' I go – just trying to draw her out a bit more.

She's there, 'I can't believe what I'm actually hearing here.'

'Fine,' I go. 'But can I just point out that you were no angel yourself, Sorcha. I remember you getting gee-eyed at the Mount Anville Past Pupils Association International Women's Day luncheon one year and throwing your soup up on Josepha Madigan's shoes – although, granted, you weren't fourteen at the time.'

She's there, 'People are praising her, Ross, telling me that she's an absolute credit to me.'

I'm there, 'Wait a minute – where are you?'

'I'm here!' she goes. 'And so is she!'

I'm like, 'Where's *here*?' because the girl has been giving me a wide berth ever since Ronan told me about her being shit-faced on Saturday morning. Yeah, no, I tried to talk to her about it, but she told me to stay out of her private business and then when I asked her to promise me that it'd be the last time she ever drank, she went, 'I will, yeah,' and I couldn't figure out from her tone whether she meant it or whether she meant the opposite.

She goes, 'I don't know if you read the *Irish Times* this morning, but if we continue cutting greenhouse gas emissions at the current rate, then one year from this very day we will become only the third country in the world, after Bhutan and Suriname, to achieve corbon neutrality.'

I'm there, 'I'm sorry to urinate on your parade here, Sorcha, but what does any of this have to do with Honor?'

'Well,' she goes, 'she saw my post on Instagram this morning, about the letter I received from Al Gore, offering Ireland his congratulations and urging us to keep going, and she wanted to tell me in person how – oh my God – *proud* of me she was?'

This is all sounding very suspicious.

I'm there, 'And, what, she just turned up at your work? It's very random, that's all.'

'It's not random,' she goes. 'I mentioned in my Insta post that we were going to have a little porty in the Deportment, portly to celebrate and portly to launch my new Countdown to Zero initiative, which is going to increase incentives for sheep and cattle formers to cull their herds.'

I'm there, 'A porty?'

'Yes,' she goes, 'a porty. And Honor, by the way, is getting on like a house on fire with everyone.'

Oh, fock.

I'm there, 'Define getting on with everyone for me please, Sorcha.'

She goes, 'She's chatting. She's laughing. Oh my God, it's like she's had a personality transplant.'

Yeah, she's pissed alright.

She's there, 'People keep coming up to me and going, "Oh my God – is that your daughter over there?" Do you see what this means, Ross? It means me and Honor have turned a corner – like I knew we would.'

I'm like, 'Sorcha, don't take this the wrong way, but would there happen to be drink at this porty of yours?'

She's there, 'Of course there's drink at it. The people here have worked hord for this, Ross.'

'Okay, I'm on my way.'

'What, just because there's alcohol, you're coming in?'

'No, I'm proud of you as well, Sorcha. Bhutan and Shutan – like you say, that's a massive, massive achievement.'

I hop into the cor and I hit the road, trying Honor's mobile number every three or four minutes, but she just lets it ring out – obviously doesn't want an earful while she's having a skinful.

I'm in an absolute panic. I'm crossing O'Connell Bridge when Oisinn all of a sudden rings. I answer the phone.

I'm there, 'Dude, can't talk. I'll ring you back.'

'Don't bother,' he goes. 'I'm just going to send you something.'

I take the left turn off Pornell Square onto North Frederick Street and I throw the cor in a wheelchair space outside the Deportment of Climate Action.

I take the stairs like I'd take the Kardashian sisters – two at a time while shouting, 'I'm coming! I'm coming!' at the top of my voice.

I hear noise coming from behind a door. I push it and I step into a room full of people in suits, sipping – yeah, no – champagne from flutes.

Sorcha spots me and tips over. She's like, 'Hey, Ross! Do I have your consent to put one of these on you?' and she pins a badge saying, 'Countdown to Zero!' onto my Leinster training top.

I'm there, 'Where's Honor?'

'She's around here somewhere. Do you want a glass of champagne? I'm sorry for giving you a hord time about only coming here because there was drink.'

'Yeah, no, it's cool. I'm driving anyway.'

I'm looking around the room and all of a sudden I spot Sorcha's old man, along with the famous Mike, standing a few feet away. The two of them are straight over – terrified of leaving me alone with Sorcha in case I worm my way back in there.

I end up having to laugh. Mike is in his pilot's uniform again.

I'm there, 'Oh, did someone order a strip-o-gram?' because – yeah, no – I can't help myself.

He goes, 'Oh, it's, em –' and he clicks his fingers twice, pretending to have forgotten my name.

Sorcha's old man smiles. He obviously gets a kick out of him.

Sorcha goes, 'I had another letter of congratulations – this time from the UN Intergovernmental Panel on Climate Change. I don't know if you've seen my Insta in the last hour?'

I'm there, 'Er, no, I haven't.'

Her old man's like, 'Sister Austrebertha predicted this – after you delivered the valedictory speech at the Mount Anville graduation. She said you'd go on to change the world.'

'I think she just said I'd go on to achieve great things,' Sorcha goes.

But her old man's there, 'No, I remember very clearly that she said you'd change the world. Because I remember turning to your mother and saying, "Look at her up there! She absolutely will, you know!"'

I'm thinking, yeah, great focking story.

Sorcha goes, 'I'm, like, so proud of what we've achieved – I'm talking as a deportment – but I couldn't have done it without the help and support of the Taoiseach,' and I'm thinking, yeah, no, whatever doubts she had about my old man being suitable to be the leader of the country, they are well and truly at an end.

I'm there, 'Why isn't Honor at school, by the way?'

Sorcha goes, 'She had a badminton blitz.'

She's as big a mug as I am.

I'm there, 'I'm going to go and find her,' and I do the rounds of the various rooms on this level, except there ends up being no sign of her.

I check the jacks, which are multi-gender – of course they are. I push the door open and on the edge of the sink unit I notice a bottle of champagne – an empty bottle of champagne, I discover, when I pick it up.

The door of Trap One is closed. I take a punt and I tap on the door. I'm like, 'Honor? Is that you in there?'

Then I hear this, like, *vomiting* sound? Yeah, no, it's my daughter alright.

I go, 'Are you okay?'

She doesn't answer me.

I'm there, 'Look, I'm not going to give you the big talk. I'm just going to wait out here to make sure you're alright.'

There's more vomiting. We've all been that soldier.

I sit down on the floor with my back to the wall. I whip out my phone – just to pass the time – and I notice that I have a WhatsApp message from Oisinn. It's a photograph, as a matter of fact. I open it up and I go, 'Oh, holy shit.'

Yeah, no, it's a photograph of a tiny, newborn baby. The message alongside it says: 'Paavo Ross, born at 2:15 p.m. today. Mother and baby doing well. Love, Oisinn, Magnus and Paavo.'

I pinch the image to make it bigger.

'Well, fock-a-doody-hay!' I go, because the baby – I can't help but notice – is an absolute ringer for me.

I tell Roz that this is – oh my God – delicious and she says it's Jess Redden's cheddar, onion and asparagus frittata.

I'm like, 'Jess Redden? As in, like, Rob Kearney's girlfriend?'

'I follow her on Instagram,' she goes. 'Oh my God, I have a total girl-crush on her.'

'She looks great, in fairness to her.'

'Yeah, no, her thing is creating delicious and nutritious meals to optimize hort-, gut- and bone-health and to balance hormones and blood sugars. She's a qualified phormacist.'

'Fair focks to her – and I mean it.'

'It's just so hord to find recipes with, you know, only Irish-produced ingredients.'

We're sitting at the table in her kitchen, by the way. She'd just finished a yoga session when I arrived and I'm trying my best not to stare at her nipples, which are showing like hornet stings through the merino wool-blend of her lululemon base layer half-zip.

I'm there, 'Sorcha thinks I have a man-crush on Rob Kearney.'

She laughs. 'And do you?' she goes.

I'm like, 'Yeah, no, it's sort of complicated. See, he takes all the shit I say about Clongowes to hort. So one minute we're being literally pulled aport in the Nespresso store on South Anne Street after I've shouted something at him about going to a school for wankers and there's the usual finger-pointing and shouts of, "Take a look in the focking mirror, mate!" and then the next minute he's ringing me to say thanks for all the complimentary texts during the autumn international series and telling me that him and Seán Cronin and Scott Fordy have got themselves steak sandwiches from Boca in Spencer Dock and are heading to Glendalough to watch the deer rut if I fancied tagging along. And when I get into his Audi A10, lo and behold, there's a sandwich there waiting for me.'

'I don't think I'll ever understand rugby.'

'The hilarious thing is that, whenever we run into each other, we can never remember whether we're fighting or not. So, just to be on the safe side, I'll say something derogatory about his old school – Hogworts for pricks, or something along those lines – and the next thing we're throwing punches at each other in the middle of Alias Tom's.'

She laughs. I think she finds me genuinely funny. We finish our frittatas – or maybe *frittati*? – and, as she puts our plates in the dishwasher, she goes, 'I'm sorry, again, about bringing up the whole thing about your brother.'

I'm there, 'Hey, it's cool. It's just, you know, painful, that's all.'

She goes, 'I felt awful afterwards for making you talk about it.'

I'm there, 'Hey, I don't mind talking to you about it,' because Sincerity is staying at her old man's gaff tonight and I very much fancy my chances of batter-dipping the old corndog here. 'I honestly feel like I could talk to you about anything.'

She closes the dishwasher and she gives me the eyes across the table.

'Okay,' she goes, 'can I ask you one last question?'

I'm there, 'Fire away.'

'Did Jamie end up with her?'

'With who?'

'With Harissa. Your ex? As in, did they get married?'

Jesus, women love a good soap story. You can't blame me for giving them what they want.

I'm there, 'Yeah, no, they got married in the end. On Christmas Eve.'

I don't know where I'm getting this shit from. Probably episodes of *EastEnders* I've seen. 'A morquee in the square. In, em, Stoneybatter.'

She goes, 'And do they have children?'

'That's two questions, Roz.'

'Okay, that's definitely the last one.'

'They've got a son and a daughter. The son is Gus and the daughter is, I don't know, Celeste?'

Jesus, Ross, keep it focking simple.

'But you've never met them?' she goes. 'Okay, definitely, definitely the last question.'

I'm there, 'No, I've never met them – which hurts obviously. They're my cousins.'

'They're your nephew and niece – surely?'

'Yeah, no, sorry, I was trying to figure out the connection there. That's how weird the whole estrangement thing has been for me.'

She's suddenly looking at me with her sexy face – we're talking full eye-contact while licking her lips, although she could be wiping a bit of oregano off with her tongue.

But no, my instincts are absolutely spot-on. She walks over to me and she throws her leg over me so that she's sitting on my lap facing me. She kisses me, we're talking softly, for ten, maybe twenty seconds, then she sits back and storts playing with my hair.

'I love you,' she goes.

And I'm there, 'Yeah, no, I love you too.'

She smiles. She likes hearing me say it. Then her expression changes.

'Oh my God!' she goes, suddenly half standing. 'Have you got an erection already?' and she makes a grab for the old sludge pump, then laughs. 'Were you sitting there with that for the whole of dinner?'

I'm there, 'It's that base-layer half-zip.'

She's like, 'Oh, it does it for you, does it?'

She knows that it does it for me. It's not an accident that she wore it.

'It's a pity you like it so much,' she goes, 'because I was thinking of taking it off.'

I'm there, 'Don't let me stop you,' really getting into the flirty talk now. 'If that's what you want to, like, do?'

She kisses me again – more passionately this time – then she takes the top off over her head, leaving me face-to-face with her nay-nays. I stort going at them like a hungry newborn, while Roz reaches behind her and pushes my glass and side-plate back, a sure sign that she wants the action to move to the table.

So I lift her up and I sit her down on it, her mouth locked on mine, as I take the old Long Point skiff out of the boatyord.

And that's when she suddenly goes, 'Oh, fock! Fock! Fock! Fock!'

I'm there, 'What's wrong?'

'Raymond,' she goes, slipping her orse off the table and bending down to pick her base layer up off the floor.

I'm there, 'Er, what about him?' and I'm standing there – quite literally – with my dick in my hand.

She goes, 'I just heard his key in the front door,' and she puts her top back on and uses the camera on her phone to check that she hasn't got sex hair.

I'm there, 'What, he just lets himself in, does he?' because now I can hear him in the hallway.

'Ross,' she goes, then with a nod of her head she indicates for me to put the thing back in my chinos, which is what I do, and no sooner is it away than he bursts into the kitchen.

Roz goes, 'Raymond!' like it's a pleasant surprise to see him.

He's there, 'Not interrupting anything, I hope?'

Gráinne walks in behind him. I'm just going to throw it out there that she looks a little bit like Sydney Sweeney, albeit older and from South Lotts Road, the Sandymount end, originally.

'You're not interrupting at all,' Roz goes. 'We've just finished dinner,' and I watch his eyes rivet to the space that Roz has cleared on the table. He's obviously familiar with the routine. She didn't just think that up tonight.

He's there, 'I'll come straight to the point. Ross has been keeping something from us.'

Roz is like, 'What are you talking about?' and I've suddenly got three sets of eyes boring into me.

'A little secret,' the dude goes. 'Isn't that right, Ross? Do you want to share it with the room?'

I'm wondering which secret he's referring to. Is it about me being potentially the father of my sister-in-law's baby or is it about me inventing a twin brother years ago so I could continue riding two girls at the same time?

I sometimes think I should take Father Fehily's advice regarding lineout codes and apply it to my own life – simplify, simplify, simplify.

I'm there, 'No, Raymond, you share it with the room – seeing as I've no idea what you're about to even say.'

He goes, 'It seems that Honor has been drinking. Ross had to collect her from a house porty in Ranelagh and carry her, unconscious, to his cor.'

I'm like, 'Oh, that!' I go, laughing with – being honest – *relief*?

'Do you find it funny?' he goes. 'A girl of, what, fourteen, drinking herself into oblivion?'

Roz is like, 'Who told you about this, Raymond?'

'Pete Prendergast,' he goes. 'Sincerity was also at the porty. I asked her about it tonight and she told me everything.'

Roz is there, 'Was Sincerity drinking?' and she turns her head and looks at me, like *I'd* tell her the truth.

'Thankfully not,' Raymond goes. 'She said she didn't touch a drop.'

Yeah, the girl was off her focking face, but I'm not sure it would help my case any to mention it.

Roz goes, 'Ross, why didn't you tell me?'

I'm there, 'Tell you what?'

And she's like, 'Why didn't you tell me that my daughter was at a porty where alcohol was being consumed?'

I'm there, 'Because Sincerity asked me not to,' feeling not even one bit bad for ratting her out.

'Oh my God,' Roz suddenly goes, her eyes turning to Gráinne, 'so it was Honor who stole the alcohol from the restaurant?'

Gráinne's there, 'I, em, don't know' – again, covering up for her.

'It was clearly her,' Raymond goes. 'I've told Sincerity that I don't want her having anything to do with your daughter again. Do you understand?'

'You can't do that,' I go because I'm imagining Honor's response when I tell her. 'They're, like, best friends.'

I turn to Roz, expecting her to back me up, except she's looking at me with pure disgust on her face.

She's like, 'I cannot believe you'd keep this a secret from me as well.'

I'm not always the best reader of a room, but I'm pretty sure we're not going to Foxtrot Oscar Chorlie Kilo tonight. That's off the table – literally.

I'm there, 'Yeah, no, I possibly should have told you.'

And when I turn my head to look at Raymond, I can't help but notice that he has the slyest little smile playing on his lips.

Honor is devastated. And I *mean* devastated?

She's like, 'He can't stop me from seeing her.'

I'm there, 'Technically he *can*, Honor? He's her father.'

'Sincerity was drinking as well. Not as much as me. But she was drinking.'

'I thought about pointing that out, but then I thought it might make the situation even worse.'

'He's a focking prick.'

'You'll get no arguments from me on that score.'

She whips out her phone.

'I'm going to ring him up,' she goes, 'and tell him he's a focking prick.'

I'm there, 'Honor, you need to maybe think strategically here.'

She stops mid-dial and goes, 'What do you mean?'

I'm there, 'I'm just making the point that you're in the same school as her, right?'

'Er, obviously?'

'So you're going to see each other every day either way.'

'But you said we're not allowed to hang around together outside of school.'

'Yeah, but you just have to be a bit sneaky about it. Do it behind people's backs.'

'Sincerity won't. Not if he tells her not to.'

'What's she saying about all of this?'

'She's not saying anything. She e-mailed me to tell me that he made her delete my number from her phone.'

'That's a real dick move.'

'I focking hate him. I hope he focking dies in a cor crash.'

I'm there, 'You're fully entitled,' and then I pause for a second, wondering how to word what I'm about to say next. She cops it, of course, being super-defensive.

She's like, 'What?'

And I'm there, 'Well, maybe Sincerity's old man has a point.'

'Excuse me?'

'Honor, please don't take this the wrong way –'

'Here we go. Here comes the lecture.'

'It's not going to be a lecture.'

'You were drinking at my age.'

'I might have been a year or two older. And, anyway, it's different for boys.'

'I only drank once – twice, if you're counting that stupid focking climate action porty.'

'I had to carry you down the emergency stairs. I think we're counting it.'

'So twice, then.'

'And then don't forget that Ronan rang the house last weekend and you could hordly talk you were so off your face.'

'Fine – three times. I still can't believe Ronan told you that. It was just a phase I went through.'

There's, like, a lull in the conversation, then she goes, 'So will you tell Roz that?'

'Tell her what?' I go.

'That it was a phase I went through.'

'I can't, Honor.'

'Why not?'

'Because she's not talking to me at the moment. She's pissed off with me for not telling her about the porty.'

'So ring her up and apologize. Tell her you accept that you're a bad father and that's the reason I ended up turning to drink. If you take the blame, it'll at least take some of the heat off me.'

'I'm not going to do that.'

'If you don't do it, I'm going to go upstairs and smash up my room.'

'Honor, I just think I'd be better off giving Roz a bit of time and space to hopefully calm down.'

She ends up totally losing it then.

She goes, 'I focking hate you. I focking hate everyone.'

I'm like, 'Honor, please,' because I haven't seen a tantrum like this from her since Sorcha bought a water buffalo for a family in Malawi and tried to pass it off as one of her Santa presents.

She goes, 'I have to talk to her! I focking have to talk to her! Otherwise I'll go focking mad!'

Off up the stairs she stomps and I get a flashback to that famous Christmas and her going, 'Fock you! And fock the Chembezis!' which is one of my all-time favourite quotes of hers.

I decide to just let her cool off. Having her pissed off at me, though, reminds me that I should probably try to fix things with Ronan – it's been over a week now – either by apologizing to him or, depending on which way the conversation goes, preferably him apologizing to me.

I whip out my phone and dial his number. He answers on the third ring and goes, 'I've nuttin to say to you, Rosser.'

I'm there, 'Dude, it got out of hand that day – I'm accepting that.'

'How can you thalk about yisser own granthaughter in that way?'

'Dude, I wasn't calling *her* a scummy focking scumfock – it was more her grandparents.'

'And Shadden?'

I can't lie to him.

I'm there, 'I honestly wasn't referring to Shadden.'

Okay, it seems I *can* lie to him.

He goes, 'She's been veddy good to me in taking me back.'

I'm there, 'Oh, come on, what else was she going to do? Wait for Matt Damon? Come on, Ro, we used to have a right laugh about the Tuites.'

He goes, 'Well, like it or not, Rosser, they're me famidy now. And if you caddent threet them with the respect thee deseerve, I doatunt waddant nuttin to do wit you.'

And then the line goes dead.

Upstairs, I hear the unmistakable sound of Honor smashing up her room. I'm actually sitting there thinking, one day, just give me one focking day without drama, when the doorbell suddenly rings. There's no one here to answer it – Erika is at some bloodstock event at Goffs and Helen is returning a bolero to Monica John – so I end up having to answer it myself.

I open the door and who's standing there only Oisinn. I can tell straight away that he's – oh, fockity fock-it – upset about something.

I decide to just style it out.

I'm there, 'Oisinn! The Big O! You got my text, did you? Congrats on the baby! He's a little beauty! A world-class front-row in the making – like his old man, I bet!'

'Ross,' he goes, 'I need to talk to you.'

I'm there, 'Yeah, step in there,' opening the door wider and ushering him into the house.

'I feel so stupid,' he goes.

'Why, Dude? Let me be the judge of that.'

'Because Sorcha warned us and we didn't listen.'

'Didn't listen? Didn't listen to what?'

'She said that when it came to it, her sister would refuse to hand over the baby.'

'Are you saying that's what she's doing?'

'Magnus and I turned up at the hospital to collect Paavo and she said no, she wouldn't let us take him.'

'But she can't do that.'

'Yes, she can.'

'But you've got, like, rights.'

'Only if it can be proven that one of us is the father.'

Seriously, never mind one day without drama. I'd take one hour.

'One of you is the father of the baby,' I try to go. 'That's a fact.'

He's like, 'It's not a fact. Not according to Sorcha's sister. She says she had sex with someone – some married dude who she's apparently in love with – around the time of the sperm transfer. She's saying she's ninety per cent sure that *he's* Paavo's father,' and that's when the tears suddenly come.

I stand there just staring at him, hating myself as the dude sobs his hort out.

'So what are you going to do?' I go.

He wipes his tears away with the back of his hand. Then he's like, 'If she refuses to give us access, we're going to have to go to court to get it.'

I'm there, 'But what if she's telling the truth – as in, what if Paavo really isn't yours?'

He goes, 'Please don't say that, Dude,' and the tears stort streaking their way down his face again. 'I honestly don't think I'd have the strength to cope.'

5.

Me and You, What's Going On?

The duty nurse behind the desk smiles at me. Nurses have always had a thing for me. I don't *know* why? It's one of those things that can't be explained – like why do people from different countries speak different languages? It's a mystery. We accept it. It just *is*?

I'm there, 'I'm looking for my sister-in-law – she's just had a baby.'

'Oh, that's lovely,' the woman goes – which she doesn't *have* to? It's focking Holles Street. Everyone in here has just had a baby.

I'm like, 'Can you point me in the direction of her ward?'

'Of course,' she goes. 'What's her name?'

I'm there, 'Excuse me?'

'Er, you'll need to tell me her name – we have a lot of beds in the hospital.'

Oh, shit.

I'm there, 'Yeah, no, I know it's – it's, em, something Lalor.'

She looks at me dubiously.

She goes, 'Something Lalor?' obviously thinking, what kind of a fockwit doesn't know their own sister-in-law's name?

I'm like, 'Unfortunately, that's as much information as I have at this moment in time,' unable to stop myself from flirting.

She looks at a book in front of her, then goes, 'Oh, there she is – Lalor. She's in Saint Mary's Ward. Take the lift to the third floor.'

I give her the guns and I go to walk away, but then I double-back and I go, 'Can I just ask you – and I realize that this is going to sound random – but what *is* her actual first name?'

She goes, 'Did you not say she was your sister-in-law?'

'It's just – yeah, no – I've had a total brain freeze. Do you think you could just –' and I sort of, like, indicate the book with a nod.

She looks down at it and goes, 'It's, em . . . oh, dear.'

159

'What?'

'It was Nuala who admitted her and I have trouble reading some of her words.'

She turns the book around to me.

She goes, 'Can you make that out?'

Oh, for fock's sake, it's just a focking squiggle.

'I think that could be an M,' she goes. 'But then it could also be an R.'

I'm like, 'Yeah, no, thanks for your help.'

But before I get a chance to walk off, I hear my name suddenly called and I turn around and there she is, standing there.

She's like, 'You didn't bring me balloons, no?'

I'm there, 'No, I didn't bring you balloons. You know why I'm here.'

She's holding a baby – *the* baby – in one orm and an empty bassinet in the other. She turns the little dude around so that I can look at his face and I instinctively turn my head away.

She goes, 'Say hello to your daddy, Paavo.'

I'm there, 'I'm not his daddy. Not definitely.'

'Ross, look at him,' she goes. 'Look at his nose. Are you honestly telling me that you don't see the resemblance?'

The duty nurse is listening to all of this with her jaw on the floor – culchie lockjaw, I call it – and I'd imagine she hears all sorts in here.

I'm there, 'I want a DNA test done. Before I admit anything. And even then – when you think about it, what does a DNA test actually prove?'

Again, she goes, 'Ross, look at him,' and then louder this time, 'Ross, *look* at him!'

So I do look at him. And I can't deny it. There are certain similarities, including – yeah, no – the humungous Shiva Rose on him, the poor kid.

She goes, 'Hold him, will you?'

But I can't. I'm suddenly frozen.

I'm there, 'I, em –'

She goes, 'I want to put him in his bassinet. Just hold him, will you?'

So I take him from her – there's some weight in him, in fairness – and I'm there, 'I want you to know that just because I'm doing this . . .' my inner Hennessy really warming to the task now '. . . it doesn't mean that I'm legally accepting –'

'Oh, shut the fock up,' she goes, putting the bassinet down on the floor.

The baby stares into my eyes and – I shit you not – sort of, like, smiles at me and it's like I'm suddenly listening to birdsong.

Sorcha's sister takes him off me then – I nearly don't let go – and lays him down into the bassinet.

Then she goes, 'You can carry him to the cor.'

I'm there, 'Whose cor?'

'Er, *your* cor? You're giving me a lift home.'

I smile at the duty nurse, who's clearly still in shock at the conversation she's just heard.

I'm porked on Merrion Square, opposite the National Gallery. I carry the baby to the cor, with Sorcha's sister walking beside me, linking my orm. Passers-by smile at us – one or two go, 'Congratulations!' and one goes, 'You're so lucky!' – and I'm thinking, you haven't a focking clue, mate.

Sorcha's sister sits in the back of the cor with the baby while I reverse out of the space. I'm like, 'When you say home –?'

She goes, 'Honalee.'

'And are Sorcha and your old man cool with that?'

'I don't give a focking shit whether they're cool with it or not.'

I'm there, 'Fair enough,' and I drive on in silence.

We're passing through Ballsbridge before I talk again.

I'm there, 'You've broken Oisinn's hort, just so you know – same with presumably Magnus.'

She goes, 'Would you want them to think that Paavo was their baby when he's not?'

I'm like, 'No.'

Even though that's exactly what I'd want.

She goes, 'I think Magnus twigged it straight away. He kept staring at him. He was trying to see himself or Oisinn in his face and he couldn't.'

I'm there, 'Sorcha predicted this. She said that when push came to shove, you wouldn't hand the baby over. You love the drama too much.'

'Hey, you didn't *have* to have sex with me.'

'It was a one-off.'

'What about a few weeks ago in Brittas Bay?'

'That was a one-off as well.'

She laughs – I *think* it's a word? – *scorningly*?

I'm there, 'What's all this shit you told Oisinn about you and the baby's father making a go of it together?'

She goes, 'I just said that because I knew it would fock with your head.'

'Because I'm not an option for you. I want you to know that. I'm with someone – as in, like, *with* with?'

'Oh, spare me, Ross! I could have you any time I wanted you. I've proved it time and time again. If I told you to pull into the cor pork of Booterstown Dort Station because I wanted to suck you off –'

'Jesus Christ.'

'– you would do it.'

'How can you talk like that in front of a baby?'

'I'm right, though.'

'You're not right.'

She is right.

She goes, 'The funny thing is, I've never been that much *into* you in terms of looks. It's just that being with that stupid bitch's husband gets me off like no one has ever got me off, man or woman.'

There's no real answer to that. Twenty minutes later, we're on the Vico Road. I pull up on the path outside the gaff.

She goes, 'What are you doing?'

I'm there, 'Er, I'm dropping you off *here*?'

'You want me to carry your son up that long driveway?'

'Stop saying that he's my son. I just don't want Sorcha and your old man putting two and two together and coming up with, whatever, four.'

'You'll carry him to the door or I'll tell that skinny focking bitch you call your girlfriend that you've become a father again.'

I sigh and I get out of the cor. I take the bassinet out of the back and – holding it in my right hand – I walk with Sorcha's sister up the long, cobbled driveway.

'Just so you know,' I go, 'Oisinn is talking in terms of taking you to court to prove that either him or Magnus is the father.'

She's like, 'I'm quaking in my boots.'

We're still a good twenty feet from the front door when it's suddenly thrown open. Sorcha's old man is standing there with a look of shock on his face.

He goes, 'What the hell are *you* doing here?' meaning *her* – his own focking daughter.

'Thought you might want to meet your new grandson,' the sister goes.

Sorcha's old dear appears at his side.

She goes, 'What's *he* doing here?' because I wondered how long it'd be before my presence was acknowledged.

The sister's like, 'I texted him and asked him for a lift. Seeing as none of you came to see me in the hospital.'

Sorcha's old dear goes, 'You know how we feel about it. Having a baby for money. As a Minister for the Eucharist –'

The sister takes the bassinet from me and she's like, 'Just get out of the focking way, will you?' and she shoves her way past them like Drico squeezing between two tacklers back in the day.

Her old man's like, 'What are you doing?'

She goes, 'Sorry, did I not tell you? I'm moving back in. I've decided to keep the baby, by the way.'

'You can't do that,' her old dear goes. 'You made a promise – to those two gay men.'

'The thing is,' she goes, 'I don't know if it's even *theirs*?' and I can see that she's loving the look of pure shock on their faces. 'I had sex with a man – a *married* man – around the time of the intrauterine insemination. I'm pretty sure *he's* the father?'

I almost feel sorry for her old man. It's the most shocked I've seen him since the time he found an empty box of flavoured condoms in the waste-paper basket in Sorcha's room.

'Anyway,' the sister goes, 'thanks for the lift, Ross,' and then she disappears down the hallway and into the kitchen.

Sorcha's old man is just standing there with his bottom lip quivering and I can't help remembering that image of him from back in the day, staring at the packet in his hand, going, 'Fizzy? Cola?' like he couldn't figure out why a rubber Johnny would even need a flavour. But his wife – who knows I'm a dirty dog – is staring at me with a look of, I want to say, speculation on her face?

I just go, 'Families, huh? I'll leave you to it.'

Sixty seconds later, I'm sitting in the cor, just storting the engine, when I hear a sudden tap on the window. I look up and it ends up being Sorcha's old dear.

I open the window – just a little bit.

I'm like, 'Can I help you?'

She bitch-smiles me, then she goes, 'Is that child yours, Ross?'

I'm there, 'Excuse me?'

'That . . . *child* that our daughter has brought into our home. Are you the father?'

'Er, why would you think *I* was the father?'

'Because the baby is the image of you. I can see it and so can Sorcha's father.'

'Can't say I've seen the likeness myself.'

She stares hord at me.

'Look at you,' she goes, 'grinning away there.'

There was always something about my smile that made the woman angry.

I go, 'Oisinn is hopefully the father of the baby. Either Oisinn or Magnus.'

'You told Honor,' Erika goes, 'about me and Meredith McTominay,' and I'm trying to gauge her level of pissed-offedness.

I'm there, 'I was trying to make her see that it's not a big deal, her being, whatever, gay. So – yeah, no – I told her about you and Meredith on the school trip to Klosters.'

I keep having these visions of them unzipping each other's skiing clothes with their frozen fingers and then snuggling up together for warmth.

Erika smiles at me and goes, 'It's fine,' and I breathe a definite sigh of relief. 'I told her that there's nothing wrong with it. It's totally normal.'

I'm there, 'So she really opened up to you?'

This is us in the kitchen, by the way.

Erika's like, 'Please don't overreact when I tell you this, Ross –'

I'm there, 'Okay, let me be the judge –'

'I caught her drinking my mum's Grey Goose,' she goes, 'necking it straight from the bottle.'

I'm like, 'What?' trying to sound like a proper dad. 'This is the first I'm hearing about it and I'm bloody furious.'

'Don't be.'

'Well, I am.'

'She said it was a one-off.'

'Okay, that's put my mind at rest.'

'She was very upset. She said that Sincerity's dad has stopped them from seeing each other.'

'Er, did she say why?'

'No, she just said he thinks she's a bad influence on his daughter.'

'Right.'

'Ross, she's broken-horted. She tried to talk to her in school but Sincerity burst into tears and told her that her dad would stop her going away at Christmas if he found out they were still talking.'

'A dick move.'

'Well, what are you doing about it?'

'In terms of?'

'Can't you talk to Sincerity's mother? You're having sex with the woman, aren't you?'

'I'm, em, not really sure where I *am* with that at the moment?'

'Ross, Honor is head-over-heels in love with this girl.'

'Right.'

'Like, *totally* besotted. I'm actually worried about what she might do if she's not allowed to see her.'

'Fine, I'll talk to Roz. Or I'll try.'

She's there, 'So what's going on with Sorcha's sister?' suddenly switching the play.

I'm like, 'Excuse me?'

'I had lunch with Oisinn today. He said she's refusing to hand over the baby. She's saying it might not be theirs.'

'Yeah, no, I heard something about that.'

'So is it yours?'

'Excuse me?'

'She'd do anything to piss off Sorcha and her parents.'

'I'm insulted that you think I'd –'

'You've been with her before, right?'

'That was, like, years ago.'

She stares at me like she thinks she might find the truth in my eyes.

Then she goes, 'So are you going to talk to Sincerity's mother or what?'

I look at my phone. It's eleven in the morning.

I'm there, 'She'll be in the gym at this stage.'

And Erika's like, 'So go to the focking gym. This is your daughter's happiness we're talking about.'

So – yeah, no – half an hour later, I'm in Riverview and I'm watching Roz use the cross-trainer.

'Are you alright there?' some dude, well into his fifties, goes and I realize that I probably look like a pervert.

I'm there, 'Yeah, no, I happen to *know* the girl?' because I'm just trying to figure out what I'm going to say to her.

His mate – another old dude – goes, 'You've been staring at her for ten minutes.'

I'm like, 'Why don't you mind you own focking business?' and then I tip over to her – just before they complain to the manager.

I'm there, 'Hey there!' deciding to keep it light and breezy.

She doesn't respond – doesn't even look at me. Then I realize it's because she's wearing her Beats.

I stick my head into her line of vision and she suddenly screams with fright. I notice the two dudes looking over. Roz stops moving and takes off her headphones.

'Oh my God,' she goes, 'you gave me such a fright.'

I'm there, 'Yeah, no, sorry, I just wanted to talk to you. I was giving you your space – you know, after all that shit.'

She goes, 'All that shit?' and this is at the top of her voice. 'Is that what you call it?'

I notice the two dudes walking over to us. One of them goes, 'Do you know this man?' and for a second I actually think Roz considers saying no.

'Yes, I know him,' she goes.

He's like, 'Is he bothering you at all?'

I'm there, 'Dude, I could focking bench-press you and your mate there. Why don't you fock off back to your five-kilo weights.'

Roz goes, 'It's fine – thank you,' and the two dudes do as they're told.

She looks at me and shakes her head, but I can tell there's a hell of a lot of affection still there, as well as a physical attraction.

'Right,' she goes, grabbing two Swiss balls from the rack, 'let's talk,' and she indicates for me to sit down on one of them, which I do, while she sits down on the other.

I'm there, 'Look, I should have told you about the porty. It's just that Honor was embarrassed and obviously she didn't want her old dear to find out.'

She goes, 'You mean Sorcha doesn't know?' and I'm trying to figure out from her tone if she's shocked by that or flattered that I'd talk to her about it first. It turns out to be just shock. 'Ross, how can you *not* tell her mother that you had to carry her unconscious from a porty?'

I'm there, 'Because I thought she deserved a second chance.'

'Ross, why is she drinking?'

'Look, I get it – I wish she'd waited another year or two.'

'A year or two?'

'Or three. Or four. I'm not borgaining with you, Roz. I'm agreeing with you. She shouldn't be drinking at fourteen – not spirits anyway.'

'Is something bothering her?'

'In terms of?'

167

'Well, is she upset about something?'

'Not that I know of – thanks be to God.'

I can lie to Roz now just as easily as I once lied to Sorcha, and that makes me sad.

She goes, 'Well, there has to be a reason – why was she the only one at that porty who was drinking?'

It sounds like I'm not the only one who's spinning her yorns.

I'm there, 'She said she was just experimenting with drink and – yeah, no – she's finished her experiments now and hopefully that's going to be that.'

She goes, 'I did wonder whether she was jealous.'

I end up nearly falling off the ball.

I'm there, 'Jealous? As in?'

She goes, 'Well, Sincerity is sort of going out with Johnny now. And I wondered was Honor maybe keen on him too?'

I think about telling her the truth. But then – as they say in the States – it's not my truth to tell.

I'm there, 'No, I genuinely think it's an innocent case of her wanting to get absolutely out of her bin just to see what it felt like.'

She sort of, like, smiles at me. I'm definitely winning her around.

'Look,' I go, 'if you feel that you don't want to see me any more – even though I was only acting in my daughter's best interests – then I totally understand that. But please don't punish Honor by stopping her and Sincerity from being friends.'

She takes a deep breath, then exhales.

She goes, 'I'll talk to Raymond, okay? I'll see what he thinks.'

I'm like, 'Thanks. So, em, what about us? Are we still –?'

Before I can finish my sentence, she leans in closer and she kisses me on the lips. Again, it's only my famous core strength that stops me from toppling over. I can see the two dudes from earlier looking at me, obviously thinking, 'He's a fast worker.'

Roz goes, 'Do you fancy coming back to the house?' and she puts her hand on my thigh. 'I can make you lunch and maybe you can persuade me to forgive you.'

I'm there, 'I'll give it a go,' because I'm on fire all of a sudden.

We both stand up. Jesus Christ, I've got a boner on me like a baby's bottle.

She goes, 'I'm just going to go and have a shower. I'll see you in the coffee shop.'

I'm like, 'Yeah, no, I'll get two flat whites to go.'

'No more lies, Ross. I mean it.'

'There definitely won't be.'

And I mean it too – in that moment anyway.

Off she goes to get herself cleaned up. I walk past the two dudes. They can both see through my chinos that I've a humungous horn on me.

I give them a big wink and I go, 'That's how it's done, dudes.'

Yeah, no, it's *that* time of the year again. Four weeks out from Christmas – the day that we sit down with the kids to write their Santa Lists. We're talking pages and pages and pages of demands, spelled out over many tearful hours – *our* tears – which will all be changed anyway once they've watched the *Late Late Toy Show*.

But like I said, it's tradition.

Sorcha sends me a text to remind me and I think it's nice that she still wants me involved. But it says a lot about where I am in my life right now that I spend twenty minutes staring at the house, wondering is her sister home with the baby? And is she going to choose tonight to spill the beans?

Sorcha opens the door.

She's like, 'Hi,' and she gives me a hug, even though it ends up being a bit, I don't know, awkward. When she pulls away, she goes, 'Why aren't you wearing a Christmas jumper?' because – yeah, no – *she's* wearing a red one with a penguin on the front.

I'm there, 'I don't know. I just felt more comfortable in this,' meaning my Leinster training hoodie.

She looks over my shoulder and goes, 'Where's Honor?'

And I'm like, 'She's, em, not coming.'

I watch the disappointment register on her face.

She goes, 'I thought when she came to the porty on North Frederick Street that night that we'd turned a corner. But she hasn't replied to a single call or text since that night. I'm actually storting to wonder why she turned up at all.'

I'm like, 'Look, it's not you – it's Sincerity.'

'Oh my God, have they had a falling-out?'

'Er, sort of.'

'I knew it. She's always hated that girl. I think she was only making the effort with her because you were dating her mom.'

'Could be that alright.'

All of a sudden, I hear a baby crying upstairs, and I feel my hort quicken and my face flush.

'That's Paavo,' she goes. 'By the way, thanks for driving my sister home from the hospital.'

I'm like, 'Yeah, no, she rang me – totally out of the blue.'

She lowers her voice to a whisper. 'It's been awful,' she goes. 'Mom and Dad won't even look at him.'

I'm there, 'And what about you?'

She smiles. 'You know me and babies,' she goes. 'I can't help myself. Oh my God, he's gorgeous, Ross – and he's got that new baby smell.'

I'm there, 'Yeah, no, I'm *saying* fair focks?'

'It makes me miss Hillary. And it makes me feel guilty, of course, that he's not here in this house.'

'Fionn is doing a good job raising him – although I'm just guessing.'

'Oisinn is the one that I'm feeling sorry for right now. And Magnus – although they can't say I didn't warn them.'

'Has she dropped any hints as to who the real father might potentially be?'

'All we know is that he's an older man and he's married.'

'Jesus.'

'Well, who am I to judge her, Ross? I mean, I had a baby with a man who wasn't my husband, didn't I?'

Yeah, no, I'll point that out to her if the truth ever gets out.

'Again?' a voice suddenly goes from the other end of the hallway. 'He spends more time here now than he did when he lived here!'

No prizes for guessing who.

Sorcha goes, 'Dad, he's come to help the boys write their Santa Lists – then he's going.'

He pulls a face – I'd love to focking deck him – then goes back into the kitchen. We follow him down there. Sorcha's old dear is stirring a pot of mulled wine, which is another one of *our* traditions?

'Oh,' she goes when she sees me – just that, followed by, 'it's *you*.'

The boys are sitting at the kitchen table, freshly showered, in their pyjamas, their hair side-ported, and not a focking peep out of them. Usually, at this point of the night, they'd be rolling around the floor, beating the focking lord out of each other.

I'm there, 'Hey, goys.'

And they're like, 'Hi, Dad,' in barely a whisper.

Seriously, pulling them aport was like separating the Christmas tree lights after I just focked them in a box the previous January.

I'm there, 'Are you looking forward to telling Santa what you want? I hope you've got a lot of paper!'

But Johnny goes, 'Granddad said we mustn't be greedy.'

I'm there, 'It's Christmas,' talking to *them* but aiming it at *him*? 'It's a time for greed.'

The focker picks up his *Irish Times* and refuses to take the bait. And that's when the doorbell rings.

'That'll be Fionn,' Sorcha goes.

I'm there, 'Fionn's coming?'

'Of course,' she goes. 'Hillary is port of this family too, Ross.'

Twenty seconds later, Fionn walks into the kitchen with the little lad, who runs past his mother and straight to me, going, 'Uncle Ross! Uncle Ross!' because – yeah, no – he's a fan.

I pick him up. He's a great little kid, by the way.

I'm there, 'Hey, Hill! So what are *you* going to ask Santa for?'

He takes a breath, then he goes, 'A bike! And a train! And a robot! And a Buzz Lightyear! And a truck! And a rugby ball! And a surprise!'

I look at Brian, Johnny and Leo and I go, 'You see? That's how it's done!'

Sorcha takes the little dude from me and we sit down at the table. Sorcha's old dear keeps stirring the mulled mine – usually *my* job, by the way, although I'm not petty enough to point that out – while Sorcha's old man stands around like a spare prick in a nunnery.

'This is the last of the Lytton Springs Zinfandel,' Sorcha's old dear goes. 'The man in Whelehans said he has no idea when or if they'll be getting more in.'

Sorcha's old man goes, 'The Taoiseach has made it clear, repeatedly, that it's going to take time for us to finally reap the rewards of this thing.'

Fionn goes, 'I see the *Times* has storted a regular *Can't Get X? Try Y!* column, offering people alternatives to foodstuffs they can't buy here any more.'

Sorcha goes, 'I know that you and I disagree on the merits of Irexit, Fionn, but the things that are missing from the supermorket shelves are all air-mile-intensive foods like goji berries and walnuts, which we should be phasing out of our diets if we want to achieve corbon neutrality.'

Her old man's like, 'Hashtag, Countdown to Zero.'

He really is a knob of the highest focking order.

I'm there, 'Can we stort? Because I'm a bit bored sitting here.' I grab a pen and the A4 notepad from the island. 'Alright, Brian, you first – what do you want from Santa? Here it comes!' and I close my eyes in mock fear. 'The avalanche!'

'A remote-control airplane,' Brian goes.

I open my eyes.

I'm there, 'A what?'

He's like, 'A remote-control airplane.'

I look at Sorcha and I'm there, 'This is the famous Mike's influence, is it?'

Sorcha's like, 'They were always airplane-mad, Ross.'

Which is horseshit. They used to watch YouTube videos of planes crashing and they'd focking cackle with laughter. That was back in the good old days.

I'm there, 'Fine, Santa will bring you a remote-control plane. What else, though?'

'Nothing else.'

'What about a robot dog?'

'I don't want a robot dog.'

'What about a drone? Yeah, no, instead of a remote-control plane, Santa will bring you a drone. Like the one that the Killiney and Dalkey Combined Residents Association flies over us twice a week to check on any unauthorized development happening in the area.'

'No,' he goes, looking at his granddad – the prick – for approval. 'I'd be happy with just one big present.'

I'm there, 'I'm putting you down for an airplane, a drone and a robot dog.'

Sorcha's like, 'Ross, he doesn't want those other things.'

I'm there, 'He's getting a drone and a robot dog – whether he likes it or not. Leo, what do you want?'

I shit you not, he goes, 'A chemistry set.'

I'm there, 'You're not getting a chemistry set. What kind of bullshit is this?'

'He wants a chemistry set,' Sorcha's old man goes. 'He's interested in science.'

I'm like, 'He is in his focking hoop interested in science. You've poisoned his brain.'

Fionn goes, 'I actually got a chemistry set when I was Leo's age.'

I'm there, 'My point exactly. I don't want him ending up like you, Fionn – and that's no offence to you.'

'I want a chemistry set,' Leo goes – and I swear to God, I think he's about to burst into tears.

I'm like, 'Fine, you can have your focking chemistry set, but you're getting a robot dog as well. And a drone. And loads of other shit. It's Christmas. Johnny, talk to me. What do you want from Santa?'

'A remote-control plane,' he goes.

I'm there, 'And?'

'And nothing,' Johnny goes. 'I'd be happy with that.'

I fock the pen across the kitchen in Sorcha's old man's direction. Sorcha goes, 'Ross!'

I'm there, 'One present each! What the fock, Sorcha?'

Sorcha's old man goes, 'I received one present every Christmas when I was their age.'

I'm there, 'He's ruined our kids, Sorcha. This used to be a mad night. There'd be focking killings. Who ported their hair to the side like that?'

Sorcha's old dear goes, 'I did – and I happen to think they look very smort.'

I'm there, 'They don't. They look like three focking knobs. They should have a blade one at the side and a quiff at the front like me. And, by the way, I do the mulled wine every year.'

'You don't live here any more,' Sorcha's old man makes sure to go. 'This is *our* home again.'

Sorcha goes, 'Can we all just calm down for one –?'

But before she can even finish her sentence, the kitchen door swings open and in walks her sister, holding the baby in her orms. This, like, silence descends on the room. She has that effect on people.

She goes, 'Are you making your Santa Lists, boys?'

Brian, Johnny and Leo just stare at her. I'd say Sorcha's old man has told them to be wary of her.

I'm just, like, staring at that tiny baby – can't help myself. The focking nose on him.

She goes, 'Hey, Ross!'

I'm like, 'Hey, em . . . Yeah, no, hi.'

She goes, 'God, I miss the days when your boys used to kill each other. When did they become such dry shites?'

Sorcha's old man is suddenly so tense, I can nearly hear his body creaking. The sister sits down in my old ormchair in the corner, opens her shirt, lops out her left lunchable and storts – I shit you not – breastfeeding Paavo in front of us. I'm just, like, staring at her, not for a potential glimpse of boobage, I should add. I'm just sitting there thinking, shit, is that my actual son?

'No, no, no,' her old man tries to go, 'you are *not* doing that here!'

The sister's like, 'What, feeding my child?'

He's there, 'There are children present!'

'So?' she goes. 'Sorcha, you fed Hillary in front of the boys, didn't you?'

Sorcha doesn't answer her. She's a feminist, but she's also a daddy's girl and she doesn't want to say anything to damage that.

'Ross,' the sister goes, 'you don't mind me feeding my baby in front of you, do you?'

Out of the corner of my eye, I can feel Sorcha's old dear staring hord at me.

'This is pure exhibitionism,' Sorcha's old man goes. 'Nothing more.'

Sorcha's there, 'Would you not be more comfortable doing that in your room – even though, as a feminist, I don't believe that breast-feeding a baby in public is anything to be *ashamed* of?'

The sister goes, 'Oh my God, Ross, what way are you staring at me?'

I'm there, 'Excuse me?'

I can feel my face burning.

She's like, 'Oh! My God! Ross, I'm your sister-in-law!'

I look down at my phone and I notice that I have a missed call from Honor. Shit, I think. It's a wonder I've never had a stroke.

I'm there, 'I just have to, em –' and I stand up and step out of the room.

Sorcha goes, 'You're not going, are you? We haven't done Hillary's list yet!'

I answer the phone.

I'm like, 'Honor, talk to me.'

She goes, 'Oh! My God!' and I'm listening carefully to figure out if she's drunk.

She goes, 'Oh! My! God!'

I'm there, 'Honor, what have you had?'

She's like, 'Sincerity just rang me! You talked to her mom!'

'I, er, did, yeah.'

'She's allowed to be friends with me again.'

'Yeah, no, that's good news, isn't it?'

She lets out this, like, piercing scream of excitement.

She goes, 'Oh my God! Oh my God! Oh! My God!' and then she just hangs up before she gets a chance to tell me that I'm the best father in the world.

★

Benny McCabe – aka 'Stacks of Money' – is working behind the bor of the Broken Orms in Finglas and he gives me a big hello when I step through the door.

He goes, 'How's Rosser?' with a big smile on his face, like he finds even the idea of someone like me ridiculous.

I'm there, 'Yeah, no, all is good in the hood, Benny.'

He's there, 'Call me Stacks, Rosser.'

I'm like, 'Okay, all is good in the hood . . . Stacks.'

He goes, 'Still looking for your boat, are you?'

Seriously, it's every focking time.

I'm there, 'Just because I wear sailing shoes, it doesn't mean that I have to sail a boat. It's, like, you wear Caterpillar boots, but you don't operate a focking, I don't know, JCB.'

He goes, 'I *can* operate a JCB – and I *have*,' and I realize that it was a bad analogy because, according to Ronan, Stacks has buried more bodies than Staffords.

Still, it's very hord to dislike him.

I'm there, 'Is he in?' meaning the man himself.

Yeah, no, he always comes here at six o'clock on a Friday.

'He's in the snug,' Stacks goes. 'He's learning to speak Rushidden, Rosser.'

I'm there, 'So I believe. Throw a pint of Heineken on for me, will you, Stacks?'

'It'll have to be Hanijan.'

'Sorry – yeah, no – force of habit.'

I push the door of the snug. Ronan is sitting there with his headphones on him. He's going, '*Nam nuzhno devyanosto . . . trillionov rubley . . . Nam nuzhno devyanosto . . . trillionov rubley . . .*'

He sees me standing there and he whips the things off his head.

I'm there, 'Sounds like you're really getting to grips with it.'

He goes, 'I'd wanton to be. Ine off to Moscow tomoddow – with Heddessy.'

I'm like, 'Moscow? The one in Russia?'

'The one in Rushidden, Rosser, yeah.'

'Why are you going there?'

'Thrust me, Rosser, you'd be bether off not knowing. What are you doing hee-or in addyhow?'

I grab a stool and I sit down next to him.

I'm there, 'I just wanted to hopefully clear the air between us.'

He goes, 'Are you throying to say soddy for your caddy-on at the house-warbon peerty?'

'Fine, yeah – I'm sorry, okay?'

'Apodogy accepted.'

Stacks of Money steps into the snug and puts my pint down in front of me. He goes, 'You alreet for anutter one, Ro?'

And Ronan goes, 'Ine moostard for the moment, Stacks,' and off the dude focks.

I'm there, 'Yeah, no, I'm sorry, Ro. For acting the dick. I was worried about you. I'm still worried about you.'

He goes, 'You caddent go slagging off Shadden's famidy, Rosser. You said thee were scummy fooken scumfooks.'

'Ro, when I was leaving the porty they were beating the shit out of the neighbours, who looked like good people – golf people. And you were right in the middle of it, getting stuck in.'

'It got ourra haddend. I'd be the foorst to admit it. But these are moy people now, Rosser.'

'And that's why I can't forgive myself, especially knowing what you gave up for me. I should have just gone to jail.'

'You woultn't hab lasted pissing toyum in jayult, Rosser. Ine tedding you that as a fact.'

'I might have surprised you.'

'You were shitting yisser paddants, Rosser. In addyhow, it's dudden now and I hab to joost gerron wirrit. Make the best of a bad situation.'

I'm there, 'Yeah, no, whatever.'

He knocks back a mouthful of whatever piss he's drinking, then he goes, 'So, er, how's Hodor?'

I'm there, 'Yeah, no, she's good, Dude.'

'Is she off the geergle?'

'Off the gorgle? Jesus, you make it sound like she has a drink problem.'

'A geerl of her age, thrinking spidits at eleben o'clock in the morden – that's a geerl with a thrink problem, Rosser.'

'Well, she's promised me it was just a phase she went through.'

'So why *was* she thrinking? Was it oaber a fedda?'

'No, it wasn't over a *fedda*. Look, this is strictly between us, Ro, and I'm only telling you because she's your sister. It was over a girl.'

'A geerl?'

'Yeah, no, she likes a girl. More than likes her, in fact.'

'So she's lesbiant?'

'Yeah, I mean, that's pretty much the definition, isn't it?'

'A lesbiant?'

'I know.'

'Not that there's athin wrong with that, Rosser.'

'Absolutely not.'

'There's nuttin wrong with it, in fact.'

'Nothing whatsoever. Nothing what-so-ever.'

'So who's the geerl?'

'I don't know did you ever meet Sincerity Matthews?'

'Siddenceditty?' he goes – definitely taken aback. 'I thought Hodor fooken hated her?'

I'm there, 'Love and hate are just two sides of the same board-room agenda.'

I don't even know what I mean by that. I just know that it sounds good.

That's when he goes, 'Hee-or, what are you doing for your beert-day, Rosser?'

I'm there, 'My birthday? I don't know. I haven't thought about it.'

'It's your bleaten fortieth. Hab to do something, Jaysus sakes.'

'I don't know, maybe I'll *have* a porty, then.'

He goes, 'What about habbon it hee-or?'

And I'm here, 'Here?' not wanting to come across as a snob.

Before I can say anything, he calls out for Stacks, who sticks his head in the snug again.

He goes, 'Is the funkshidden roowum free, Stacks – the steert of January?'

Stacks goes, 'What are you looken to hoyid?'

'Not looken to hoyid athin. It's Rosser's fortieth is cubbing up.'

Stacks turns to me then. He's like, 'So you're wanton it for yisser peerty?'

I'm there, 'No, no, definitely not.'

'Why?' he goes. 'Not good enough for you, is it not?'

I'm like, 'Yeah, no, it's not that.'

It is that.

Ro goes, 'Come on, Rosser! All yisser southside mates can hire a bleaten coach, like yous did when the rubby was at Croke Peerk!'

Stacks goes, 'Look at him, turdening he's nowuz up at it.'

I'm there, 'I'm not turning my nose up at anything,' and of course he shames me into saying yes then. 'Fine, I'll have it here.'

Ronan goes, 'I'll steert pladding it when Ine howum from Moscow, Ro.'

Stacks is there, 'When is it, Rosser?'

I'm like, 'It's the sixth of January.'

'It's a Muddenday,' Ronan goes. 'So we'll hab it on, what, the teddenth?'

Stacks is there, 'Gayum ball. It'll gib me a few weeks to get rid of the two bodies is in theer.'

I'm like, 'What the fock?'

The dude cracks his hole laughing, then he goes, 'The fooken bleaten face on him, Ro!'

'Smell that?' Roz goes. 'What do you think?'

I'm there, 'Is that not the same as the *last* one I smelled?'

Yeah, no, Sorcha used to pull that trick on me when she sensed that my enthusiasm for shopping was storting to flag and I was prepared to say just about anything to get the fock out of Brown Thomas.

Roz laughs. She goes, 'Ross, they're nothing like each other. That one's Mandarin and this one's Pomegranate Noir.'

Yeah, no, we're standing at the Jo Malone counter because she's buying a scented candle for the woman who waxes her eyebrows. Sometimes it feels like the Celtic Tiger never went away.

'So which do you prefer?' she goes.

I'm there, 'I think that one,' because it's a fifty-fifty shot.

'*That* one?' she goes. 'Because you said the other one a *minute* ago?'

Meaning it *was* a test. Seriously, do they teach them this shit in school?

'Okay,' I go, 'the other one, then.'

Roz laughs – which Sorcha *never* did, by the way.

She goes, 'Okay, I get the hint. We'll go and get a hot chocolate. I'll take the Pomegranate Noir one.'

The shop is absolutely rammers, what with it being the last late-night shopping Thursday before the big day. There's, like, Christmas music playing. 'Last Christmas' comes on.

'I love this song,' we both – at the exact same time – go.

Roz is like, 'Oh my God, no! It's my *actual* favourite!'

I'm there, 'Yeah, no, mine too. I love the video. George and Andrew in a chalet with a bit of a crew. I always thought the friends looked a bit racy. I don't know why, but I always think that all sorts went on once the cameras stopped rolling.'

Roz finds this hilarious.

She goes, 'Oh my God, don't ruin it for me!' and she slaps me – playfully, in fairness – with her glove. We both laugh and then we end up staring into each other's eyes and we're suddenly serious and I go, 'I love you,' and, for once in my life, I'm not saying it just to – whatever – get my hole off a girl.

She goes, 'I love you too,' and we both smile and we kiss and she tastes of coconut lip-balm and the turkey and brie toasties we had in Davy Byrne's. 'If someone had told me a year ago that I was going to be this happy, I never would have believed them.'

Then her eyes drift over to the Chorlotte Tilbury counter and she goes, 'Hey, Ross, look!'

Yeah, no, Sincerity is putting blusher on Honor's cheeks and Honor is just standing there, allowing it to happen.

'You look so pretty with colour in your face,' Sincerity is telling her.

And Honor is like, 'Do you think?'

'Oh my God,' Sincerity goes, rubbing it in. '*So*, so pretty.'

She adjusts the mirror on the counter so that Honor can see what she's talking about.

Honor's like, 'Oh my God, I *love* it!'

Roz goes, 'They're so good for each other.'

I'm there, 'Thanks again – for being so understanding about the whole Honor getting shit-faced thing.'

'Most young people experiment with alcohol,' she goes. 'And I don't think we could have stopped Sincerity from seeing Honor even if we'd wanted to. She absolutely loves her.'

'Loves her? Are you serious?'

'Is it not obvious?'

'I mean, I knew they were close.'

I notice that Sincerity has a bottle of perfume in her hand. She sprays some of it on her neck, then she invites Honor to smell it, and Honor doesn't need to be asked twice. She takes in a big, greedy lungful of it and her eyes nearly roll back into her head.

Then Sincerity sprays some on Honor's neck and leans in for a sniff. Honor laughs and pulls away – yeah, no, she's always been ticklish there – and the two of them collapse in hysterics.

I'm there, 'I think Honor loves Sincerity, too,' seeing as Roz was the one who brought up the subject.

She goes, 'We're talking about loving her in the way that you might love your sister, right?'

I'm there, 'Erika? Yeah, no, I suppose you *could* say that.'

'What I mean is, Honor is like the sister that Sincerity never had.'

Oh, fock, what have I just said?

I'm there, 'Yeah, no, that's what I meant as well. Sincerity is the sister that Honor never had. We're on the same page.'

I'm still staring at them. Sincerity has discovered that Honor has tickles and now she's *really* trying to sniff her neck and she has her orms pinned to her sides and Honor is trying to fight her off but at the same time she's, like, cracking her hole laughing.

Roz shakes her head and goes, 'Our daughters are as mad as each other. I'm going to go and pay for this candle.'

We're standing in the queue when she – totally out of the

blue – goes, 'Talking about that Wham! video has made me really excited about going skiing now.'

I'm there, 'When are you going skiing?' because it's the first I'm hearing about it.

She's like, 'Just after Christmas.'

'You never said.'

'I did. I told you we go to Gstaad for New Year's every year.'

'Who's we?'

'Me, Sincerity, Raymond –'

'Raymond?'

'– and obviously Gráinne.'

'And why wasn't I asked on this trip?'

'Because we booked it in, like, Morch, when you and I weren't even –'

'Apology not accepted.'

'I wasn't apologizing.'

'I just don't understand why you have to go with *him*.'

'Oh my God, you're jealous!'

'I'm not jealous.'

'Nothing's going to happen, Ross. His wife is going to be there.'

'I just find the whole thing a bit random, that's all.'

'What's random about it?'

'Just the way he's always, I don't know, hanging around. I don't trust him.'

'You don't trust *him* or you don't trust *me*?'

'I don't like it – that's all I'm saying.'

'What are you going to do – tell me that we can't take our daughter away skiing any more?'

'What if I said yes?'

She goes, 'Oh my God, you're just another misogynistic orsehole,' and this is, like, five minutes after telling me she never thought she'd be this happy again. 'I'm going to pay for this, then me and Sincerity are going home.'

I'm there, 'What about the hot chocolate? There was talk of hot chocolate.'

But she goes, 'I'm not in the mood for hot chocolate any more.'

★

Of course, the goys find the entire thing hilarious.

'What's this?' JP goes. 'The great Ross O'Carroll-Kelly is getting a taste of his own medicine and he doesn't like it one bit?'

I'm there, 'The dude is trying to break us up. He told me he was going to do it.'

Fionn – the focking relationship expert – goes, 'Can't you just tell her?'

I'm there, 'She won't believe me. She'll believe him. Every relationship she's had in the past ten years has ended because dudes *supposably* can't handle her still being mates with her ex. She told me that herself. I reckon he's pulled this stunt with every single goy she's ever been with.'

Christian goes, 'But his wife is going to be in Gstaad as well, right?'

I'm there, 'That's not the point. The dude is undermining me, using every dirty trick in the book. Just as an example? Do you remember that time, back in the day, when I was seeing those two birds from Cork – we're talking Vanessa and Anna?'

Christian laughs. He's there, 'You were definitely seeing Vanessa. Wasn't Anna going out with your twin brother?'

'Yeah, well, Raymond just so happens to work with Anna. And he arranged for us to bump into her, accidentally on purpose, in Kehoes one night. And Roz was like, "Why didn't you tell me you had a twin brother?"'

JP's like, 'Jamie!' suddenly remembering. 'Wasn't he deaf in one ear?'

I'm there, 'Yes, and he had a phobia about rubber, including condoms. That's not the point. The dude is using my past against me.'

Christian's there, 'I still say that if you trust *her*, then you've nothing to worry about,' and he's another one – divorced, bear in mind – who doesn't know what the fock he's talking about.

JP goes, 'Put your Santa hat on,' because – yeah, no – they're giving them out in The Bridge tonight as some kind of Hanijan promotion.

I throw it on – so as not to be a Johnny Buzzkill.

'By the way,' JP goes, 'is she still looking over?'

He's talking about Belle – as in, like, Delma's daughter – who showed up tonight with a couple of mates.

Christian's there, 'Yeah, she's still looking over.'

JP goes, 'What's she playing at? This isn't even her local?'

I'm there, 'Probably keeping an eye on you for her old dear – make sure you don't stray.'

Women. You couldn't be up early enough for them and I hope that doesn't come across as sexist.

I knock back a mouthful of Hanijan and then I notice Oisinn squeezing his way through the crowd towards us.

I'm like, 'O-zark! The Big O! *O de toilette!*'

He returns my high-five, but – yeah, no – there's no real *enthusiasm* in it?

Christian's there, 'How did it go?'

Oisinn's like, 'Not great, to be honest. He was no focking use at all.'

I'm there, 'What's this?'

'Me and Magnus went to see a solicitor about maybe going to court to get access to Paavo. The solicitor said we're going to have to go the DNA route.'

I'm there, 'Fock, Dude,' at the same time thinking, this is all getting uncomfortably close for me.

He goes, 'Have you seen her, Ross? With the baby, I mean?'

I'm there, 'I haven't laid eyes on the girl, Oisinn, and that's the honest truth.'

'Yes, you have,' Fionn goes. 'You saw her the night we wrote the children's Santa Lists.'

You can always trust Fionn to let you down.

I'm there, 'Yeah, no, I forgot about that. Hey, she storted breast-feeding the kid in front of us,' but nobody's in the mood to laugh along with me.

'Does he look like me?' Oisinn goes – sounding a little bit desperate. 'Or even Magnus?'

I'm there, 'I think he looks like both of you – as in, he has a mixture of *both* your genes?'

'Well, you know that's not actually possible?' Fionn goes – Mister Focking Facts and Figures. I'm trying to give the dude a bit of hope here while possibly taking the heat off myself.

Christian's there, 'Has she said who he is yet? As in, this other man who might be the father?'

Oisinn goes, 'Nothing. What about you, Ross?'

I'm like, 'Me?' a little bit too quickly. 'Why would you think I was the father?'

'I'm asking has she said anything to you,' he goes.

I'm like, 'Oh, er, nothing, no,' and then I quickly change the subject. 'I can't believe we're still drinking this piss, by the way. I wonder will we ever taste Heineken again?'

'I'll tell you something,' Christian goes, 'I don't believe for one minute that these shortages are temporary.'

JP's like, 'Me neither. Nothing is being imported and what we have is running out. I saw two men come to blows in Donnybrook Fair the other day – we're talking an actual fist fight – over the last tub of ricotta. There's huge tension out there. It's all going to kick off between now and Christmas. Mork my words, there's going to be riots.'

I look at Oisinn and he looks all, I don't know, lost and devastated. I decide that I have to get the fock out of there.

I'm there, 'Goys, I'm going to call it a night.'

They're like, 'What?' because I'm usually the *last* to leave?

I'm there, 'Yeah, no, it's the Roz going away skiing with *him* thing – it's ruining my buzz. I'll see you on Christmas Eve.'

As I step outside into the rain, my phone all of a sudden rings. It's Ronan, so I answer it.

I'm there, 'Ro!' at the top of my voice because I think I'm a bit jorred. 'How the hell are you? How was Moscow?'

'Keep yisser fooken voice dowun,' he goes. 'No one's apposed to know that we weddent.'

I'm like, 'Sorry, Dude.'

I can hear music in the background. Loud music. It's, like, 'Rhythm is a Dancer' and he's having to shout over it.

'Ine arthur habbon an idea,' he goes.

I'm there, 'Yeah?' my hand over my other ear to try to hear him better.

'This peerty Ine arranging for you. It's godda be faddency thress – noynties-themed, do you get me?'

I'm like, 'Was it "Rhythm is a Dancer" that put the idea in your head? Where are you, by the way? Because if you're in town, I'll come and meet you.'

But he goes, 'Er, no, you're alreet, Rosser. I've to go hee-or,' and he hangs up on me.

I'm just about to Uber when, all of a sudden, a voice behind me goes, 'Do you want a lift?'

It ends up being the famous Belle – all focking smiles, by the way.

I'm like, 'Er –' because I'm wondering why she's being suddenly *nice* to me?

She goes, 'It's okay, I haven't been drinking,' and not being able to come up with a reason to say no, I follow her back to her silver Hyundai Elantra, which is porked on Pembroke Place.

We hop in and a minute or two later we're driving up Anglesea Road.

'So what's going on with *him*?' she goes.

I'm there, 'As in?'

'My mom says things aren't going well. But she won't tell me the full story. She just keeps bursting into tears.'

'Hey, I'm as much in the dork as you are, Belle.'

She says nothing for a few minutes, then I go, 'Er, you know I'm living on Ailesbury Road?' because – yeah, no – she's missed the turn and suddenly we're passing Donnybrook Bus Depot.

She's like, 'I thought you might want to come back to mine for a nightcap.'

I'm there, 'Yeah, no, I like nightcaps,' but at the same time I'm thinking, er, what the fock is going *on* here?

She goes, 'I'm moving to London after Christmas. And I want to know that everything is okay between my mom and *him*.'

Yeah, no, her and Bingley didn't approve of their old dear getting hitched – especially to a man twenty-something years younger than her.

I'm there, 'Like I said, I know literally nothing.'

I look at her sideways as we're passing David Lloyd Riverview. I remember years ago asking her to give me Physics and Chemistry grinds when I went through a phase of liking girls who were cold and withholding and I thought she looked like a young Thora Birch, even though she doesn't any more.

She eventually pulls up outside a humungous gaff in Clonskeagh. It turns out she's renting the basement flat. As she's opening the door, she goes, 'Do you have condoms?' and it actually takes my breath away a little bit, the directness of it, the – big word alert – *presumptuousness* of it?

She hasn't even asked me if I *want* to have sex with her. I mean, obviously, I do – or I *would*, all things being equal – but I'm actually in a relationship now.

I'm there, 'I'm actually going out with –'

But then I think about Roz, heading off to Gstaad with her ex-focking-husband, and I think – in my drunken, horny state – that if I pre-cheat on her, then I won't feel half as bad if I find out that *she's* cheated on *me*?

It's the kind of thing that makes total sense after seven or eight pints of Hanijan.

'You're what?' she goes.

And I'm there, 'Nothing – forget I said anything.'

I follow her into the bedroom and she storts taking off her clothes.

I'm like, 'Correct me if I'm wrong, but you wouldn't be a regular in The Bridge, would you?' because I want to feel like I put a *bit* of effort in? 'Where do you tend to do your socializing normally?'

She rolls her eyes and goes, 'Ross, you don't have to chat me up. Just take your clothes off and get into the focking bed.'

So – yeah, no – I whip off the threads, remove my famous condom from my wallet – it's been there for donkey's years and I hope the rubber hasn't perished – and I slip between the sheets. It's freezing cold and we make an instant grab for each other for warmth.

We stort kissing. I've an instant boner on me and I can't help but smile.

She's like, 'What?'

I'm there, 'This is like getting off with a teacher.'

'I gave you one grind and you faked a migraine after fifteen minutes.'

'No, I meant that in a good way. I was thinking about Mrs Corish, who taught me Maths and Biz Org in third year. I didn't think you were into me, though. You always throw your eyes up to heaven when you see me coming.'

'Just stop focking talking, will you?'

So we stort going at each other in a serious way and the foreplay ends up being loud and sweary and grunty and jaw-clenchy.

I'm lying on the flat of my back and she's sitting on top of me, holding my wrists very tightly and pinning my orms to the mattress. At the same time, she's leaning forward so that her little jigglers are about three inches away from my mouth and I keep lifting my head to try to get my lips around them like it's Hallowe'en and I'm playing Snap Apple.

'Give me the condom,' she goes, so that's what I end *up* doing?

I'm there, 'Hopefully, it's still in date,' and she grabs a hold of Captain Winky and slips the old rain mac on him. Then she sort of, like, levers herself down onto me and we're suddenly off and running. She's, like, bouncing up and down on me like she's riding the waves on a jet-ski and I'm pulling my famous slow-motion-on-a-rollercoaster face.

I'm there going, 'That's it! That's it! Keep going, girl! That's it!' and she takes off my Santa hat – I totally forgot I was still wearing it – and stuffs it, bobble-first, into my mouth, presumably to shut me up.

I'm about ten seconds away from seriously, seriously disappointing her when she suddenly stops moving and withdraws the old – no other way of saying it – thrill drill from her.

I open my eyes and spit out the Santa hat. I'm like, 'What the fock?'

She goes, 'What's going on? Between my mom and *him*?'

I'm there, 'I honestly don't know. Please, you can't leave me with blue balls – not at Christmas.'

'Tell me and we can carry on.'

I'm there, 'This is blackmail,' because I'm lying there with a horn on me like the Wellington Monument.

She goes, 'Tell me.'

'Fine. He can't look at her. It's since she had her lips done. He thinks she's, like, destroyed her face.'

'That's not what he told her. He told her he didn't care what she looked like.'

'He lied. He can't have sex with her with the lights on. He has to do her from behind.'

'The bastard!' she goes, then she climbs off me.

I'm there, 'What about –?'

But she goes, 'Finish yourself off and then get the fock out.'

And I'm so thrown by all of this that it takes me a good seven or eight minutes to finally come.

'Sing "Adeste Fideles",' the old dear goes. 'I simply adore "Adeste Fideles".'

Seriously, she thinks Honor is here to sing Christmas carols for her and the other residents.

I'm like, 'Yeah, Mom, this is your granddaugh –'

But Honor suddenly bursts into song, there in the middle of the day room.

Adeste fideles, laeti triumphantes,
Venite, venite in Bethlehem,
Natum videte, Regem angelorum.

It was always my old man's favourite Christmas song and I get a sudden flashback to him, staggering around the house on Christmas Eve, half a bottle of Courvoisier inside him, dropping my Santa presents under the tree while singing it at the top of his voice, really hamming up the Latin, rolling every 'r'.

Venite adoremus,
Venite adoremus,
Venite adoremus,
Do-om-inum!

As a matter of fact, I think it was my old man who taught Honor the words – just like he taught Ronan and tried to teach me.

The old dear has her eyes closed and she's moving her head from side to side and I wonder if she's remembering him too.

Deum de Deo, lumen de lumine.
Gestant puellae viscera,
Deum verum, gentium non factum.

My eyes are all of a sudden drawn to – again – the TV on the wall, which always seems to be on mute. But I can't believe what I'm seeing on the screen.

I'm like, 'Jesus Christ, is that Glasthule?'

Yeah, no, a crowd of people have broken into Mitchell & Son Wine Merchants. And, judging by the admittedly shaky iPhone footage, they're kicking down the door of Cavistons as well.

I grab the TV remote and I turn up the volume.

Venite adoremus,
Venite adoremus,
Venite adoremus,
Do-om-inum!

The singing stops and I catch the end of the news report – Eileen Dunne says that the riot kicked off following rumours that a local wine merchants had managed to take delivery of a consignment of wines from France, rumours which proved unfounded.

I'm like, 'Jesus Christ.'

There's, like, silence in the day room. I'm not sure if half the people here even understand what's going on, but they too can sense that it's not good.

JP predicted this and he was right.

Dalisay steps into the day room and tells us that visiting time is over. I help the old dear out of her chair, then me and Honor walk her back to her room, each of us linking an orm.

She's there, 'I do love Christmas,' and then she goes, '*Laeti trium-phantes!*' except she sings it in a deep voice, really drawing out the 'r'.

I'm there, 'Do you know who you sounded like there? The old man.'

'What old man?'

'*My* old man – as in, *your* husband?'

'Conor? He died, Ross. You know, I don't think it's properly sunk in with you.'

We reach her room. Honor helps her take off her dressing-gown and the old dear must suddenly remember her because she goes, 'Thank you, Honor. You're such a sweet girl. You were a ghastly child, you know?'

Honor smiles. She knows she's telling the truth.

The old dear's like, 'Wasn't she awful, Ross?'

I'm there, 'A little bit – but I was always a fan.'

But – yeah, no – she really was awful, though.

The old dear picks up *Criminal Assets* and goes, 'Will you read to me, Ross?'

I'm there, 'Dalisay said visiting time is over.'

'It's absolutely filthy, you know? It's about a woman who redis-covers her lustful side after her husband is sent to prison. She's fantasizing about doing it with a woman she meets when she's walking her dog in Cabinteely Pork. Are you married, Honor?'

Honor's like, 'No, I'm not married, Fionnuala.'

I'm there, 'She's still at school.'

'She's what?' the old dear goes.

I'm like, 'She's still at school.'

She's there, 'Well, if you're still at school, you're far too young. Is there someone? A boy?'

I don't know where to look. It's, like, *awk! ward!*

'I don't like boys,' Honor goes – doesn't even bat an eyelid saying it. 'I like girls.'

I'm there, 'She likes *a* girl,' and I don't know what point I'm trying to make. 'So it's too soon to say if she's fully –'

'And have you told her?' the old dear goes.

Honor just, like, shakes her head.

The old dear smiles to herself. She goes, 'You know, I liked a girl once. Alison Prentice was her name. She was in my school. We used to play tennis together. I think I spent most of my teenage years fantasizing about her – like the woman in, what's that book called, Ross?'

I'm like, '*Criminal Assets.*'

'*Criminal Assets,*' the old dear goes.

Honor goes, 'So what happened, Fionnuala?'

'Oh, nothing at all,' the old dear goes. 'I never told her how I felt about her. I was too scared, you see. Scared she wouldn't feel the same way. Scared that she was interested in boys, like most of the other girls in school.'

'That's so sad, Fionnuala.'

'Well, years and years later – only two years ago, in fact – I bumped into her. She was having coffee in Powerscourt – with her wife.'

'What? She was gay all along?'

'Married to an American with a stud in her tongue. I thought to myself, I bet I know what that's for! "Oh," I said, "you're a lesbian now, are you?" And do you know what she told me? She said when we were in school, she had a huge crush on me.'

'Oh my God,' Honor goes, 'your life could have been – oh my God – totally different. You could have, like, ended up married to her.'

'Well, I'm glad I didn't,' the old dear goes, 'because she was an awful size and if there's one thing I can't abide it's people who let themselves go.'

I'm like, 'Yeah, great story, Mom.'

'But we could have had a lot of fun together,' she goes. 'Oh God, if you could have seen her, Honor, all sweaty in her little tennis whites.'

I'm there, 'Okay, we are definitely out of here.'

The old dear goes, 'Take my advice, Honor, if you like this girl, you should tell her.'

I bend down and I kiss the old dear on the cheek and I go, 'Merry Christmas.'

Honor does the same.

As we're leaving the ward, we can hear singing:

Venite adoremus,
Do-om-inum!

Honor goes, 'Do you think I should?'

I'm like, 'Should what, Honor?'

'Tell Sincerity,' she goes, 'that I like her.'

I'm there, 'Honor, you can't take advice from your grandmother. Her mind is gone. We don't even know if that story is true or if it's something that's in one of her books.'

Honor goes, 'Hmm.'

I'm like, 'What does that mean?'

But she's sort of, like, staring into space and I'm suddenly worried.

I'm there, 'Honor, I genuinely don't think it's a good idea.'

The old man is about to address the nation on TV following what Miriam Lord in the *Irish Times* is calling the Cab Sav Riots.

Helen sort of, like, chuckles to herself.

She goes, 'If I know Charlie, he'll appreciate that one.'

I'm there, 'Yeah, no, he rants and raves about Miriam, but he loves her one-liners. He must send her flowers ten or eleven times a year.'

Erika is just, like, glowering at us. We're obviously not allowed to talk about him in, like, a *fond* way?

I'm there, 'I must tell Honor that her granddad is about to be on TV,' and I whip out my phone – too lazy to stand up and shout up the stairs – to text her.

'Her grandfather who had a woman murdered,' Erika goes.

Helen's there, 'Not according to the report by independent crash investigators,' because even Simone's family have accepted that it was an accident now.

'So you're taking *his* side?' Erika goes.

And Helen's like, 'It's not about taking sides, Erika. If you don't want your father in your life any more, that's fine – but this fixation you have with him, it's not healthy for you.'

There's no reply from Honor. I'm about to stand up and call her when the old man's face suddenly fills the screen.

He's like, 'Good evening,' and there's no doubt he's had his wig plumped up for the occasion.

I'm there, 'He's had his wig plumped up for the occasion.'

Erika shushes me.

The old man goes, 'I want to speak to you tonight about the shocking events witnessed in the Dublin suburb of Glasthule yesterday – the so-called Cab Sav Riots!' and – yeah, no – you can see the corners of his mouth being tugged into a little smile.

He goes, 'Two years ago, Ireland voted by a narrow but decisive morgin to take back its independence and pursue its own destiny outside of the European Union! We knew that when we embarked on this bright, new future together that we would have to make sacrifices in the short term to gain benefits in the long term! That was made clear at the time! Divorce is difficult!'

Erika goes, 'Not for you, it's not.'

But Helen's like, 'Erika, just listen.'

He goes, 'Extricating oneself from a relationship, especially one that's as full of traps and snares as Ireland's relationship with our European neighbours, was never going to be easy! There was always going to be a period of adjustment and that is what we are seeing in the reported shortages of *some* food and drink products! I have stressed all along that this is a temporary state of affairs! As we speak, measures are being taken to rectify the situation, measures that will results in our supermorket shelves being full once again!'

I'm there, 'I wonder does that have anything to do with Ronan going to Russia?'

Erika's like, 'What? He went to Russia?'

'With Hennessy,' I go. 'Although no one's supposed to know.'

The old man's there, 'Unfortunately, this will not happen in time for Christmas, which means that many of us won't get to enjoy many of the special treats that we normally enjoy at this time of year! I want to let you know that I share your pain and your frustration! However, the scenes we witnessed on our television screens in both Cavistons and Mitchell & Son Wine Merchants yesterday are frankly unacceptable in a democratic country!'

'Focking democratic?' Erika goes – it's, like, a really sweary episode of *Gogglebox*. 'Focking spare me!'

He's there, 'Violence and destruction of property – in good areas – cannot be tolerated and it will not be tolerated! This act of wanton thuggery is aimed at loosening Ireland's resolve to go its own way – just like the orson attack that destroyed our national porliament!'

She goes, 'You focking did it! It was you!'

I'm there, 'Do you think he was behind the Glasthule attacks? Jesus, he's supposed to be mates with Peter Caviston.'

'I'm talking about the focking Dáil,' she goes.

The old man's like, 'As a democracy, we cannot allow dangerous extremists – be they Sea-mon Donne or the perpetrators behind yesterday's attacks – to knock our country from its current course!'

Erika jumps to her feet. She goes, 'He said her name! He said her focking name!'

The old man smiles into the camera and he's like, 'My wife, Fionnuala, and I would like to take this opportunity –'

I'm there, 'Wife? He hasn't seen her in months!'

'– to wish you and yours a Merry and a peaceful Christmas and a happy and prosperous New Year!'

Erika goes, 'That's it! That's the final focking –'

Helen's like, 'Erika, calm down.'

'Her poor parents watching that,' she goes. 'She was never found guilty in a court of law. Which means she's innocent.'

I'm there, 'Did he pronounce it right, Erika? I can never tell.'

She's like, 'Oh my God, that's it!' like something has suddenly dawned on her. 'I can't prove that Sea-mon was murdered. But I can prove that she didn't burn down the Dáil.'

I'm there, 'See-mon. See-mon. Am I saying it right?'

Helen goes, 'How are you going to do that, Erika?'

And Erika's like, 'By finding out who did.'

My phone all of a sudden beeps. It's, like, a text message from Honor telling me that she has zero focking interest in watching the old man on TV.

I excuse myself and I tip up the stairs. I knock twice on Honor's door and she goes, 'Fock off!' which is her way of saying, 'Come in!'

I push the door and I stick my head around it. She's lying on her bed with her hands behind her head, staring at the ceiling.

I'm there, 'What's wrong? You're not jorred, are you?'

She sits up and scowls at me.

She goes, 'How the fock could you ask me something like that?'

I'm thinking, oh, I don't know, might have something to do with the three or four times now that I've seen you absolutely wankered drunk.

I'm there, 'Sorry, Honor, that was uncalled for.'

That's when I realize that she's been crying.

I'm there, 'Jesus, Honor,' rushing over to her bed. I sit down on the side of the thing. 'What's wrong? Tell me.'

She goes, 'I wish I was dead. No, I wish I was never born.'

I'm like, 'Please don't say that. You being born was the best thing that ever happened to me,' and for once I don't even feel the need to add, 'Non-rugby-related'.

She goes, 'Why did you and *her* have to have children?'

And I'm there, 'Honor, being a father to you has been the greatest privilege of my life.'

Non-rugby-related. My point is that it doesn't require saying.

I'm like, 'Honor, why don't you tell me what happened?'

She looks at me with her big panda eyes.

'I took Fionnuala's advice,' she goes, 'and I told Sincerity how I felt about her.'

I'm like, 'Oh, Jesus, no – you don't want to take relationship advice from that mad old bint. Honor, what exactly did you say?'

'We were in the toilets,' she goes, 'in Dundrum Town Centre. We were in the same toilet cubicle. I was trying on a top because I was thinking of bringing it back to Massimo Dutti and she said that I had amazing boobs.'

I'm there, 'Oh, Jesus, I think I know where this is going.'

'And I tried to kiss her.'

'You made a lunge in other words.'

'She pushed me out of the way and she was like, "Oh my God! Oh my God! Oh my God!"'

'I can imagine.'

'She basically ran over me to get out of the cubicle and then –'

'What?'

'– I told her that I loved her.'

I'm there, 'And am I to take it that she didn't say it back to you?'

And she goes, 'No, she called me a focking weirdo and she said she never wanted to see me again.'

6.

All the Roads We Have to Walk are Winding

Roz says that was amazing and she's panting in my ear like she's just carried a suitcase up six flights of stairs.

I'm there, 'Yeah, no – no complaints from me either,' as we disentangle our limbs. 'I'm sorry again about, well, you know –'

She goes, 'About being jealous and possessive?' but she's smiling – seeing the funny side of it now.

I'm there, 'I don't usually *get* jealous?' snapping the old Santa sock off me and wrapping it in tissue. 'It's one of the things I love about myself.'

She goes, '*One* of the things?'

I'm like, 'You know what I mean.'

I get down off the bed and my knees nearly buckle. She really put me over the jumps tonight. It's like the day after Leg Day. I head for the bathroom and flush my muck down the jacks.

She goes, 'I probably shouldn't have sprung it on you like that. I thought I'd mentioned that we were going skiing.'

I'm there, 'You definitely didn't.'

She probably did. I'm not much of a listener.

'I hope you believe me now,' she goes, 'that you have absolutely nothing to worry about.'

I definitely don't feel as bad, having pre-cheated on her.

She goes, 'Raymond and I were always much better as friends.'

I'm there, 'Does *he* realize that?' as I slip between the sheets again.

'Yes, he realizes that. You know, he's a really nice guy, Ross. And you've got loads in common.'

'Do we?'

'Well, you played rugby and he played rugby.'

Don't be focking ridiculous, I'm nearly tempted to say – except it doesn't even deserve an acknowledgement.

I'm there, 'What else?'

She laughs – obviously can't think of anything.

She goes, 'He really likes you, Ross.'

I'm there, 'Does he now?'

'He was saying earlier how much he and Gráinne were looking forward to seeing you on Christmas Day. You are still coming to mine, aren't you?'

'Yeah, no, I'm having my dinner with my old dear out in Ongar and then I'll swing in to you around seven.'

'It was Raymond who persuaded me to be a bit more, you know, understanding about you being insecure.'

'Again, I'm not sure if I'd call it insecurity, Roz.'

'He said you're bound to have issues around trust – especially after the way Jamie treated you.'

I'm there, 'Who the fock is Jamie?' and I mean it.

She goes, 'Er, your *brother*?'

I honestly thought she was talking about Heaslip, who's never treated me with anything but respect, even taking me back into his boozer after the three or four times he's felt it necessary to ban me.

I'm there, 'My brother, yeah.'

'Jesus,' she goes, 'he really is dead to you, isn't he?'

'Sadly, yes.'

She's like, 'I hope you don't consider me forward in saying this,' and she storts playing with my hair.

I'm there, 'Go on, what?'

'Well, Raymond has done a lot of therapy.'

'Has he now?'

'He used to have issues around jealousy too.'

'Imagine that.'

'He was saying that jealous feelings are almost always rooted in some previous loss or trauma. He thinks it'd be a very healthy thing for you if you and your brother could put your differences behind you.'

The focking shit-stirring focker.

I'm there, 'No way.'

'I don't mean that you'd become bosom buddies or anything,' she goes, throwing back the sheets and getting out of the bed. 'But it might be good for you to meet him, just to say, you know, I'm sorry and let's move beyond this.'

She pulls on her G-er, then throws on her dressing-gown.

'Anyway,' she goes, 'I'm sorry for bringing it up again. I was going to grab a glass of wine. Do you want one?'

I'm there, 'Er, yeah, no, wine sounds great.'

'I was thinking we might wait an hour and then go again.'

Jesus, I think, what do you think I've got here, a focking telescope?

I'm there, 'We'll give it a crack.'

She steps out onto the landing, then a second later, she turns back.

'By the way,' she goes, 'what's going on with Sincerity and Honor?'

I'm thinking, oh, for fock's sake.

I'm there, 'In terms of?'

She goes, 'Honor was supposed to call in here last night. They were going to watch *Elf* together. It's Sincerity's favourite Christmas movie.'

'And, what, she didn't show up?'

'No, and when I asked her what time Honor was coming, she just changed the subject. I hope they haven't had a falling-out.'

'Who knows with girls of that age. I did warn you that it might not last.'

I'm sure Honor will be back to bullying her now that Sincerity knocked her back.

She goes, 'I hope they patch things up. They're so good together. I'll get the wine.'

She's been gone maybe thirty seconds when my phone all of a sudden rings. From the screen, I can see that it's Ronan, so I decide to answer.

I'm like, 'Ro, what's going on?'

He goes, 'Did you get me message, Rosser?'

'No, I didn't get any message.'

'I left you a bleaten voice message!'

He sounds upset about something.

200

I'm like, 'What's going on, Ro?'

He goes, 'Ine in a birra botter.'

'What kind of bother?'

'Ine arthur losing me wetton ring.'

'Your wedding ring? Where did you lose it?'

There's, like, silence on the other end of the line.

I'm there, 'Ro – *where* did you lose your wedding ring?'

'In Private Eyes,' he goes.

I'm like, 'On Dame Street? You mean the titty bor?'

'It's a gentlemen's club, Rosser.'

'If we're talking about the same spot, Ro, it's no gentlemen's club.'

Yeah, no, they were no strangers to my ugly mug in there back in the day.

I'm like, 'When were you there?'

'The utter night,' he goes.

'Is that where you were when you rang me? Rhythm is a focking Dancer?'

'I was out with Heddessy, cedebrating the thrip to Russia – it alt went to pladden, Rosser – and then we decided to hit a strip club.'

I actually laugh.

I'm there, 'So much for you making a go of it with Shadden.'

'I oately had the wooden dance,' Ronan goes, 'and I cadent eeben remember it, except that the boord's name was Zondra and she's woorking theer to put herself through coddidge.'

'Yeah, that's what they all say, Ro.'

'Will you go in and get it for me, Rosser?'

'Excuse me?'

'Me wetton ring. Zondra has it for me. It's joost Shadden keeps aston me why Ine not wearton it addy mower and Ine arthur tedding her I left it in the office. Go on, get it for me, Rosser.'

'Why me?'

'Because I'll be moordered if Shadden foyunts out. Ine only back in the big round bed –'

'I don't even want to think of you and your big round bed. Fine, I'll go and get it for you.'

I hang up on him and I throw on my threads just as Roz arrives back upstairs with two glasses of red.

She's like, 'Where are you going?'

I'm there, 'I have to head off. Something's come up.'

'Oh,' she goes, sounding disappointed. I honestly don't think I could persuade the big man to answer the bell again. 'Is it something to do with Sorcha?'

Yeah, now who's the possessive one?

I'm there, 'It's honestly nothing – a favour that I have to do for Ro. I'll text you tomorrow.'

Then off I go into the night.

It's a surprise to discover that the doormen haven't changed since I was a semi-regular back in the day.

'Russell!' one of them goes – he's from, like, Poland.

I'm there, 'Ross – near enough.'

He steps aside, no questions asked. Jesus, I was covering half their payroll when me and Sorcha were on a break around '08 or '09.

I make my way inside and I have a look around. A woman walks straight up to me and goes, 'You want to buy drink for me?' in a sort of, like, fake Bond girl accent.

I'm there, 'Yeah, no, I'm not here for a lap-dance.'

And then in a Liverpool accent, she goes, 'You pfookin taahm-wasteh!'

'I'm actually looking for someone. A girl called Zondra.'

'Mooch is it weerth to you?'

I whip out my phone.

I'm there, 'I've no actual cash on me. Can I tap?'

'What the pfook are you gonna tap iroff?' she goes. 'Me pfookin ahrse? That's Zondra theer, behand you.'

I turn around and – yeah, no – there's a skinny girl with hair like Rod Stewart, dancing on a table in a boob-tube with a length of tinsel for knickers.

I'll tell you one thing I already know for sure. Zondra is not in any college.

I'm there, 'Zondra?'

She smiles at me and goes, 'You want dance?' again with the put-on Russian accent, then she jumps down off the table, nearly turning her ankle in her clear-heeled platform sandals.

I'm there, 'Yeah, no, I'm not here for that.'

It turns out she's also from Liverpool and is just as quick to anger.

She goes, 'Stop wasting me pfookin taahm.'

I'm there, 'I'm Ronan's old man. He said you had his *wedding* ring?'

Her face lights up. He obviously made an impression on her.

'Arrr-eh!' she goes, 'Roh-nin! He's pfookin gorgeous.'

I'm there, 'Yeah, no, sorry if he was a bit, you know, handsy with you.'

'No, he were greash. He were a peerfict gent.'

'His wife wouldn't say that if she found out he was hanging around in a place like this. No offence. Do you have the ring?'

She bends down and unbuckles one of her sandals. Yeah, no, the ring is attached to the strap. She stands up to her full height and hands it to me.

I'm there, 'Why'd he take it off anyway?'

She goes, 'He were off his head drunk, like. He kept throwing it on the flaaaw.'

'On the –?'

'Flaaaw.'

'Oh, the floor.'

'I tuck 'im into one of the pravate booths – for a dance, like. All's he did was cry and tawk about how mooch he missed some Amedican geerl.'

'Avery?'

'Averdy, yeah – that were her name. Broken-arted, he was. I felt soddy for im.'

I'm like, 'Thanks, Zondra. Merry Christmas. And good luck with the exams, by the way.'

She goes, 'Whorr exams?'

Yeah, no, I'm never wrong.

★

It's, like, eleven o'clock on the day before Christmas Eve and me and Honor are in the cor on the way to Honalee to bring Brian, Johnny and Leo into town to soak up the Xmas atmos and spend whatever money they've managed to save during the course of the year.

Yeah, no, when they were born, I bought them money-boxes – sterling focking silver – in the shape of rugby balls and they put any money they happen to get into those, then we head for Grafton Street for a pre-Christmas splurge.

Honor is quiet. I know she's hurting.

I'm there, 'Any word from –?'

And she's like, 'I haven't texted her. What's Roz saying?'

'Just that – yeah, no – you were supposed to watch *Elf* with her in her gaff the other night and you were a no-show and that Sincerity –'

'What?'

'Well, she didn't want to talk about it.'

'That's what Roz said?'

I'm there, 'Honor –'

And she goes, 'Dad, I swear to God, if you're about to give me the plenty-more-fish-in-the-sea talk, then you can focking pull over now.'

I'm there, 'Fine – whatever.'

I blame the drink – either too much or the want of.

I'm there, 'So what's the plan? Are you going to go back to bullying her or what?'

She's absolutely – I *think* it's a word – *aghast* at that?

She's like, '*Excuse* me?'

I'm there, 'It's just that, you know, you victimized her for years and I just thought, well, now that she's ghosting you –'

'Is that what you honestly think of me?'

'Well, I just thought the easiest way of getting over her might be to go back to thinking she's a knob.'

'Dad, it's fine.'

'Is it?'

'I've moved on, okay?'

'Are you sure? I mean, that was very quick.'

'I fancy someone but she doesn't fancy me back. Boo-focking-hoo!'

'Good point. And we'll have a good day in town today, won't we?'

'As long as we can go for a drink. I am focking gasping.'

I look at her side profile.

I'm there, 'Please tell me you're shitting me.'

She goes, 'I'm shitting you! Just drive, will you?'

Twenty minutes later, we arrive at Honalee. The gaff has been decorated the way Sorcha's old pair always decorated it – we're talking tree in the window and blah, blah, blah.

Sorcha lets us in and goes, 'Hey, Honor! How are you? I've just made my famous mince pies if you want one!'

Honor's just like, 'I'm not hungry,' and she borges past her and up the stairs to see her brothers.

Sorcha goes, 'I'd love to know what I did to upset her.'

I'm there, 'She's a teenager, Sorcha. You know the score – you were one yourself.'

She sad-smiles me and goes, 'I just wish I was more present in her life. I literally don't know anything about my daughter any more.'

'What do you want to know?'

'Like, is there a boy on the scene?'

'Er, not at the moment, no.'

Sorcha laughs.

She's like, 'Oh my God, Ross, I know you don't want to hear it, but sooner or later there are going to be boys knocking on the door for Honor.'

I'm there, 'I'm not sure she'd have any interest,' because Sorcha genuinely hasn't a clue what's going on.

She goes, 'I'm sure every father thinks the exact same thing. You're still coming here on Christmas morning to see the children open their presents, aren't you?'

I'm there, 'Wouldn't miss it for the world.'

'Just to let you know, Mike is going to be here.'

'What, for Christmas dinner?'

'For the whole of Christmas. He's staying over Christmas Eve and –'

'You're obviously serious about each other.'

'We are, Ross. Very serious. He's great with the kids and Mom and Dad love him.'

'Sounds like he's ticking all the boxes.'

'Ross, don't be –'

'I'm sorry. I shouldn't have said that. It's just –'

'Strange.'

'Strange, yeah.'

'Anyway, Brian, Johnny and Leo are upstairs. They're really look-ing forward to going into town.'

I tip up the stairs to their room. When I get there, they're playing 'Ding Dong Merrily on High' for Honor – Johnny on the flute, Leo on the violin and Brian on the focking triangle.

I'm there, 'Ignore them, Honor. You don't want to encourage them.'

I walk across the room to the bookshelf where their money-boxes are.

I'm there, 'Right, let's see how much you've saved, will we?' and I pick up the first one. 'And bear in mind, I'll double what-ever's in –'

I give it a shake. And I'm in shock. Because it's literally empty.

I'm like, 'What the actual –?'

I put it down and I pick up the second one. Again, I give it a shake and – yeah, no – that one's empty too.

I'm there, 'What the fock is going on?'

I pick up the third one and it's, like, the same story. I turn around to the boys for, like, an explanation.

I'm there, 'A month ago, I picked up those money-boxes and they were, like, pretty much full.'

Brian looks at Leo, while Leo looks at Johnny, while Johnny looks at Brian, and nobody – not one of them – can look at me. They stort talking among themselves in German.

I'm like, 'No focking German, okay?'

Honor's there, 'Boys? Where has your money gone?'

Leo – his head down – finally goes, '*He* took it from us.'

I'm there, 'Who took it? Sorcha's old man?' because I'm looking for an excuse – any excuse – to deck him.

Brian's like, 'No, not Granddad Lalor!' like I'm a focking idiot or something. 'Morcus.'

Honor turns her head to look at me so fast that I'm surprised she doesn't break her neck.

She's like, 'Morcus?'

Johnny goes, 'Morcus and his friends. We have to pay them twenty euros each per week in tax.'

I'm there, 'Tax?' in the same contemptuous way my old man says the word. 'Focking *tax*?'

Honor goes, 'Where, boys?'

Brian's there, 'The library in Dalkey. Granddad Lalor brings us every week and they meet us there to collect it.'

'I'm going to kill him!' Honor goes, presumably meaning Morcus. 'I'm going to focking kill him!' and she makes a beeline for the door.

I'm there, 'Honor, come back,' and I chase after her.

She goes, 'I know where he lives, the little focker.'

I'm roaring after her, going, 'Don't do anything stupid – please!'

I catch up with her at the gate and she is seething. She's pretty much frothing at the mouth.

She goes, 'I'm going to rip his focking orms off! I'm going to tear off his focking testicles and I'm going to feed them to him!' and it doesn't take me long to realize that this little outburst isn't about Morcus bullying her brothers – well, it's not *just* about that?

I give her a hug and I'm like, 'Honor, it's okay! We'll sort the little focker out – him *and* his mates!'

She's, like, shaking in my orms and she could definitely – legally – kill someone right now.

'Focking, focking fock!' she goes, shrieking it out. 'Focking focker!'

I'm there, 'Honor, I've got you! I'm here! I've got you, okay?'

Suddenly, out of nowhere, she storts sobbing, going, 'I focked it up, Dad! I had her as a friend and I couldn't just be *happy* with that? I had to focking push it and now she doesn't want to know me! She thinks I'm a focking weirdo!'

I'm there, 'She's probably just in shock, Honor. It was a lunge, in fairness to it. She might come round.'

'I'm leaving school,' she goes. 'I can't face her in January.'

She's very dramatic.

I'm like, 'Seriously, Honor, I honestly think you two will look back on this one day and laugh about it.'

And I hate myself – *hate* myself – for lying to the girl.

There's, like, no food shortages here. I say it as well – to no one in particular.

I'm like, 'No food shortages here.'

Yeah, no, it's Christmas Eve and the old man is hosting a big bash in the Áras for his Cabinet and staff and there's a buffet laid out for a king.

And – yeah, no – he's up there talking about sacrifices.

He's going, 'The year of our Lord twenty hundred and nineteen will be remembered as a year in which we, the people of Ireland, agreed to forgo many of the little luxuries we enjoyed in life and offer it up in the national interest! We knew that extricating ourselves from our frankly abusive relationship with the European Uberstaat would not be without problems! We knew that they would make it difficult for us to go! And so they have! But I am confident that, by the end of 2020, Ireland will be basking in the sunlit uplands of its post-Irexit future!'

There's, like, a humungous cheer from the completely focking deluded in the room.

The old man continues droning on and I just zone out. I'm suddenly listening to Sorcha, who's standing by the buffet with Gordon Greenhalgh – yeah, no, the Minister for Housing – and she's going, 'Where did all this food come from?' and she doesn't mean it in a good way. 'I thought we couldn't *get* Camembert?'

Further up the table, I notice Kennet and Dordeen stuffing items from the table – turkey legs, a side of ham, a whole pudding – into a black refuse sack. When I catch his eye, Kennet goes, 'M . . . m . . . m . . . mire as weddle, Rosser. Shurden it's f . . . f . . . f . . . f . . . f . . . faree, idn't it? And you nebber know when you'll see a s . . . s . . . s . . . s . . . spread like this agedden.'

I never said a word about that family that wasn't one hundred per cent warranted.

I whip out my phone. I'd two or three missed calls earlier and I check my voicemail. It says I've no new messages but three *old* ones? The first one is from Sorcha's sister – she goes, 'This is your sister-in-law!' – and she says she can't believe that I called into the focking house yesterday and didn't ask to see my newborn baby son and that her solicitor wants me to get a DNA test. The second is from Ronan – last night – saying thanks for popping into the titty bor to get his wedding ring back. And the third one is from – yeah, no – Belle, saying that what happened between us the other night meant absolutely nothing and she can't believe I spunked all over her good silk pillow case.

And a Merry focking Christmas to you, I think.

I feel something – or someone – grab my leg then. I look down and it ends up being Mellicent, my little, I suppose you'd have to say, *sister*? I bend down to pick her up and, as I do, I hear a load of tiny voices going, 'Ross! Ross! Ross!' and suddenly they're all swarming around me – we're talking Hugo, we're talking Cassiopeia, we're talking Diana, we're talking Louisa May and we're talking Emily – all with their orms in the air. I just laugh.

I'm there, 'I can't pick you all up!' but I manage to scoop Hugo up into my other orm and the rest of them make do with grabbing hold of my legs.

Astrid, their German nanny, tips over to me.

She goes, 'Merry Christmas, Ross.'

I'm like, 'Yeah, no, Merry Christmas, Astrid.'

There's no attraction there – certainly not from *my* point of view?

She goes, 'All day they are excited you are coming. It's Ross, Ross, Ross, Ross, Ross, Ross.'

I'm like, 'That's a lovely boost for me to get.'

They're like superfans.

I'm there, 'How are they doing?'

She sort of, like, sad-smiles me.

'Oh, you know,' she goes, 'they miss your mother very much.'

I'm there, 'I can only imagine.'

'And also,' she goes, 'your father.'

I'm like, 'What do you mean by that?'

'Perhaps I should not have said.'

'Are you telling me that they never see him?'

'I don't wish to cause trouble. There are five nannies now and that is more than enough to manage.'

'But *he* never sticks his head around the door?'

'Sometimes he does.'

'How often are we talking in terms of?'

'Perhaps once a week.'

'Once a week?'

'But not every week.'

I'm just, like, staring at the dude, giving him serious daggers. He's still banging on, giving it, 'I want to leave you with the words of the late, great Winston Churchill, who said during Britain's own time of emergency: "Let the children have their night of fun and laughter! Let the gifts of Father Christmas delight their play! Let us grown-ups share to the full in their unstinted pleasures before we turn again to the stern task and the formidable years that lie before us, resolved that, by our sacrifice and daring, these same children shall not be robbed of their inheritance or denied their right to live in a free and decent world! And so, in God's mercy, a Happy Christmas to you all!"'

There's, like, a loud roar, followed by a round of applause and I notice that quite a few people are literally wiping away tears.

Let the children have their night of fun and laughter? The focking nerve of the man. I make my way towards him – slowly, because I've got two of his famous children in my orms and the other four are still clamped to my legs. I shove my way through the throng of people telling him that he's a great man altogether and I go, 'Let the gifts of Father Christmas delight their play? You've a focking neck on you like Ruby Walsh's undercrackers.'

He just goes, 'Merry Christmas, Kicker!'

I'm there, 'What are they getting for Christmas?'

'I beg your pordon?'

'*Your* children – what gifts from Father Christmas are going to delight *their* play?'

'Oh, there'll be, em, a trainset, I suspect,' and he's totally spoofing now, 'and a gun-and-holster or two!'

I'm there, 'You haven't a clue what Santa's bringing them, do you?'

'Well, Astrid and the others will look after all of that! Father Christmas and so forth!'

'You've no interest in them, do you?'

'That's rather horsh, Ross!'

'What are their names?'

'Well, they all have different names, don't they?'

'Yes, they do all have different names. What are they?'

He goes, 'Ross, I have far weightier matters on my mind –'

I'm there, 'Than the names of your children?' and then I look at each of them in turn, first the two that I'm holding in my orms. 'That's Mellicent and that's Hugo,' and then the two clinging to my right leg, 'Diana and Cassiopeia,' and my left leg, 'Emily and Louisa May.'

He doesn't even look ashamed of himself.

'Like I said,' he tries to go, 'far weightier matters on my mind! Affairs of state!'

I'm there, 'Why did you bring six children into the world if you had no interest in them?'

He's like, 'It was your mother's idea! I went along with it just to keep her happy!'

I can't believe what I'm actually hearing here.

I'm there, 'Dude, listen to yourself. They're *your* children and you don't even care about them.'

He's like, 'Of course I care about them! But I just think my time wouldn't be best spent hanging around the nursery playing nurse to them and singing "Rudolph the Red-nosed Reindeer" and whatever you're having yourself! I happen to think my time would be far more valuably spent ensuring that they grow up in a happy and prosperous Ireland, free from the enterprise-crushing strictures of Ursula von der Leyen and her great codocracy!'

'I'm sure they'll be very grateful.'

He decides that the conversation is over and he focks off then. No sooner has he gone than Hennessy decides to come and talk to me and it's not to wish me a Merry Christmas.

'I don't want you upsetting your old man,' he goes. 'He's got a lot on his mind.'

I'm there, 'But not the six children that he decided to bring into the world.'

Hennessy – I shit you not – goes, 'Well, you seem to get on very well with them.'

I'm there, 'Er, they're my sisters – and brother.'

'Well, why don't you take them?'

'Jesus Christ, they're not unwanted pets – they're children!'

He just shrugs like there's no real difference.

I'm there, 'Yeah, no, it's a wonder that Lauren turned out as well as she did.'

Actually, that's bullshit. Lauren is an absolute weapon and it's not difficult to see why.

I'm there, 'I believe you took my son to a focking lapdancing club.'

'As I remember it,' he goes, 'it was more a case of *him* taking *me*,' and then his expression suddenly changes. He looks over one of his shoulders and then the other. Then he goes, 'I hear the crash investigators turned up nothing.'

I'm there, 'Excuse me?'

'The crowd that was hired by the girl's family – to prove that we killed the girl to stop her testifying. Oh, I know all about it.'

'How?'

'Because it's my job to know. And now your sister is trying to prove that the girl had nothing to do with the fire.'

'The girl had a name. It was See-mon. Although I'm not sure if I'm pronouncing it right.'

Then he leans close to me – so close that Mellicent and Hugo end up turning away from his foul, cigor breath – and he goes, 'Tell her to stay out of it. You'd be doing her a favour,' and then *he* focks off, leaving his words hanging in the air like a threat.

I spot Ronan standing about twenty feet away and I manage to drag my legs over in his direction.

I'm like, 'Hey, Dude.'

And he goes, 'Howiya, Rosser? Ah, would you look at the size of them! Are yous looken forwurt to Saddenty cubbin?'

They've absolutely no idea what the fock he's talking about.

He bends down and picks up Cassiopeia.

I'm there, 'Be careful of her. She's a biter. Your wedding ring is in my pocket, by the way.'

He reaches into it with his free hand, pulls the thing out and manages to transfer it onto his finger.

He goes, 'You're a bleaten life-saber, Rosser.'

I'm there, 'I had a great chat with your mate – Zondra, was it?'

'I, er, don't remember mooch about the night.'

'Oh, don't worry, she remembered everything. She said you kept throwing your wedding ring away. She took it for safekeeping.'

'Feer fooks to her.'

'She said you also kept banging on about how you were still in love with some American girl called Avery.'

He just stares into space and blows out his cheeks. Suddenly, there's a scream. We both turn around. Kennet is holding a full lobster and he's chasing Dordeen with it.

She's going, 'Would you ebber fook off with that, Kennet!'

Ronan catches my eye and we both smile and it's the first time in a long time that I've felt we were on the same page.

Suddenly, out of the corner of his mouth, Ronan goes, 'The cunterdoddy's boddixed, Rosser.'

I'm there, 'Boddixed?'

He's like, 'Keep yisser voice dowun.'

So – yeah, no – I lower the old volume.

I'm there, 'People are saying that it's more serious than the old man is letting on.'

'I shouldn't be tedding you this, Rosser.'

'You might as *well* tell me? I probably won't understand it anyway.'

'The Gubderminth ren ourra muddy.'

'They what?'

'Thee ren ourra muddy.'

'No, it's not catching.'

'Thee.'

'They.'

'Ren.'

'Ran.'

'Ourra.'

'Out of.'

'Muddy.'

'Oh, muddy! Okay, I get you.'

'We caddent boddow muddy from addy wooden because we welched on isser debts.'

'Hang on – does this have anything to do with you and Hennessy going to Moscow?'

'We weddent to ast Vladimir Putin if he'd open up a credit loyun to the cunterdoddy.'

'Er, and *did* he?'

'He did, yeah.'

'Well, thank God for that.'

'Rosser, he ditn't do it as an act of chaddity.'

'Are you saying he wants something in return?'

'You bethor fooken belieb he wants something in retoorden.'

I'm like, 'Jesus Christ, what did you agree to, Ro?'

And he goes, 'You doatunt waddant to know, Rosser. You doatunt waddant to know.'

Christian says something is going on.

I'm there, 'What kind of something?'

'Something big,' he goes. 'Something very, very big.'

Yeah, no, we're in The Bridge and it's, like, Christmas Eve night.

He's like, 'I was in Malingrad yesterday and there were all these, I don't know, Russian naval dudes there.'

'And what were they doing?' Fionn goes.

Christian's there, 'Nothing. They were just having a look around. The question is why?'

No one seems to have any answers, so I get the round in. We're talking Hanijan for me, Fionn, Oisinn and JP and a Bally-go-on-go-on-go-on for Christian.

I'm like, 'Merry Christmas, goys.'

And they're all like, 'Merry Christmas,' except for Oisinn, who looks about as miserable as I've ever seen him look.

He goes, 'She wouldn't even let us see him,' because he's focking hammered.

I'm there, 'Who?'

I already know the full story – he's told us about seven times – but I'm trying to see if I can get a name out of him.

'Sorcha's sister,' he goes.

I'm like, 'Yeah, no, fair enough.'

Apparently, there was a scene outside Honalee this morning. Oisinn showed up with a present for Paavo. Sorcha's sister refused to open the door to him and her old man – the focking bell-end – threatened to call the Feds.

'Wouldn't even let me see him,' he goes. 'Focking Christmas and everything.'

JP's there, 'Dude, you just have to be patient. Go through the steps.'

Christian's like, 'What are the steps?'

'Oisinn's solicitor has been talking to Sorcha's sister's solicitor. He's given them a date for the DNA test.'

'And what about the other dude who's in the frame – the married man she was seeing?'

Oisinn's there, 'She's told him she wants him to take a test too. I think he's ghosting her.'

'What a prick,' Christian goes.

JP's like, 'She's talking about taking him to court, isn't she – to make him take the test?'

'Well, hopefully it won't come to that,' I go.

Oisinn's there, 'What does that mean?'

'I'm just saying, you know, hopefully you'll do the test and it'll prove straight away that you're the father – either you or Magnus.'

'Yeah, no, good point. She wouldn't let me see him, Ross. Focking Christmas.'

I'm there, 'I'd maybe make that one your last, Dude.'

And no sooner have I said that than Magnus arrives to bring him home.

We're all like, 'Merry Christmas, Magnus.'

And he's there, 'Merry Chrishmash, guysh. Oisinn, what the fock, man?'

'She said, "Talk to my solicitor!"' Oisinn goes.

Magnus is like, 'Who? Who shaid thish?'

Oisinn's there, 'Sorcha's sister.'

JP goes, 'He turned up at her house today.'

'I wanted to see my son!' Oisinn goes. 'It's focking Christmas!'

Yeah, no, the present is on the table in front of us. The wrapping paper is wet from all the spilled beer and it's storted to peel off. It looks like a Fisher-Price something-or-other.

Magnus goes, 'For fock shake, Oisinn, the sholishiter shaid not to contact her. We could loosh everything.'

'Wouldn't even let me see my own son,' Oisinn goes. 'Christmas focking Eve.'

Magnus apologizes to us, then he's like, 'Come on, Oisinn, letsh go home.'

And then off the two of them fock.

The subject turns to rugby then – or should I say *back* to rugby, because we never stray too far from it. I mention to the goys that I'm totally over the disappointment of the World Cup and I think four more years will make all the difference to this team in terms of six or seven goys coming into their prime and then a lot of young talent coming through.

I'm there, 'I'm making a prediction. Write it down. Because I certainly have – in block capitals in my Rugby Tactics Book. We won't be going out of the 2023 World Cup at the quarter-final stage. We're going to actually win it.'

No one says shit. They're not convinced.

'Speaking of rugby –' JP goes, then he looks at Fionn.

Fionn smiles. He's like, 'Ask him.'

I'm there, 'Ask me what?'

JP's like, 'We're re-entering the Leinster Schools Senior Cup – as in, like, Castlerock College.'

Yeah, no, they haven't competed in the thing since Tom McGahy – I won't speak ill of the dead – pulled the school out of it, claiming that rugby was fostering a culture of misogyny and bullying among the students, the focking prick with ears.

I'm there, 'Left it a bit late in the day, haven't you? Do you know how long it takes creatine to stort having an effect on performance?'

'It's not for 2020,' Fionn goes. 'It's for 2021. Which gives us a year to prepare for it. And that's what we wanted to ask you.'

I'm like, 'What?'

JP's there, 'Will you coach the team?'

They're obviously expecting me to say yes, judging from their reaction when I go, 'No – not a focking chance.'

JP's there, 'We'll pay you. I'm putting up the money to hire a world-class coach –'

I'm like, 'It's not about the money.'

'So why are you saying no?' Fionn goes.

I'm there, 'Because a co-education school has never won the Leinster Schools Senior Cup, Fionn.'

'We could be the first,' JP goes. 'Imagine it!'

I'm there, 'If you believe that, you're focking crazy.'

'Dude –'

'Forget it, goys. I don't want that on my CV. The answer is no.'

At some point just before midnight, Lauren – randomly – shows up.

'The fock is *she* doing here?' I go.

Christian's like, 'She's entitled to go for a drink, Ross.'

'Who's looking after the kids, though? And I'm only asking because I'm supposed to be godfather to your eldest.'

'Ross, for once in your life, try not to say something to piss her off.'

'She's hyper-focking-sensitive, Dude. Can't blame her, of course, having Hennessy as a father.'

She arrives over and it turns out that she's with someone – an absolute cracker, as it happens. Lauren introduces her as Sinead Roe, who lives three doors down from her. If I had to say – with a gun to my head – that she looked like anyone, it'd be Jodie Comer except with dorker hair and from – like Lauren said – Booterstown.

Slick Mick here manages to get all of the vital information out of her within, like, twenty seconds of the introduction. She went to Loreto Foxrock, she *was* married but she's now divorced, she has her own dentistry practice in Blackrock, specializing in non-surgical cosmetic treatments, and she does most of her socializing in Gleesons, although it's hard to get a night out when you have kids at home.

Lauren's there, 'Never stopped you, Ross, did it?'

I decide to just rise above it because me and Sinead are getting on like ketchup and mustard. But then I hear Lauren, out of the corner of her mouth, go, 'Don't believe anything he says – he's full of shit.'

And that's why I end up going, in a jokey way, 'Here, tell your old man to stop bringing my son to strip clubs, will you?'

Lauren loses it in a big-time way. She goes, 'What the fock does that mean?'

I'm there, 'They were in Private Eyes on Dame Street. I don't know if Hennessy had a dance, but I'd be shocked if he just sat there for the night with his orms crossed.'

She makes a grab for my throat and Christian ends up having to pull her away from me.

Then he goes, 'Ross, you should maybe –' and he nods in the direction of the door.

I'm there, '*I* should maybe? It's supposed to be *our* Christmas night out – as in just the goys? What the fuck is she even doing here?'

JP goes, 'Ross, I'm heading off anyway. Do you want to head back to mine for one last one?'

I'm there, 'Yeah, no, whatever.'

I wish Christian and Fionn a Merry Christmas and I tell Sinead that I hope to meet her again soon and then I give her a wink and go, '*Very* soon.'

Then me and JP head for his gaff – an aportment on the old Berkeley Court site.

We're walking along Shelbourne Road, past the Mercedes-Benz dealership, which is all lit up in Christmas lights, when JP turns around to me and goes, 'Ross, can I say something to you?'

I'm there, 'If this is about me coaching Castlerock College, you're wasting your focking breath, Dude. I have a reputation – well, I used to have one.'

He's like, 'No, it's not about rugby. It's about Delma.'

I'm there, 'Oh?'

He goes, 'I feel bad about telling you all that stuff – you know, about me not being able to look at her face when I'm having sex with her.'

I'm like, 'Dude, it went no further. I can one hundred per cent promise you that.'

'I've decided that I'm going to man up,' he goes, 'as a husband, I mean.'

I'm there, 'But you won't leave the light on when you're doing it, will you?'

'I'm just going to have to get over it. She's still the same person on the inside, right?'

'Absolutely.'

'I have to keep reminding myself how I felt about her before she let that butcher have a go at her face.'

'Do you remember when you were, like, fifteen or sixteen and she'd be having coffee with my old dear and I'd give you her cup out of the dishwasher so that you could lick the lipstick off it?'

'Well, I'm not talking about specifically that.'

'And the time she just left, but then she came back because she left her keys on the island, and she walked in to catch you sniffing her chair.'

'Again, I think I've nicer memories of her than that, Ross.'

We walk into the building and he says Merry Christmas to the concierge. He's in cracking form as he calls the lift. We step into it and he pushes the button for the penthouse floor.

I'm there, 'She won't mind me coming back for a drink, will she? We'll try not to wake her.'

JP goes, 'She'll probably still be up. Belle was calling in.'

Oh, fock.

I'm like, 'Belle?'

'Yeah,' JP goes, 'they were going to watch a Christmas movie – probably have a bottle of wine.'

We reach the penthouse floor and the doors open. We step out of the lift and walk down the hallway.

I'm there, 'If Belle's going to be there, I probably shouldn't go in.'

He goes, 'Why not?'

I'm like, 'I just don't think she's a fan of mine.'

But it's too late. JP puts his key cord in the door and opens it. I step into the aportment behind him.

'Delma?' he goes, walking into the living room and then the bedroom. 'Delma? Are you home?'

There doesn't seem to be any sign of her.

That's when I hear him go, 'What the fock? What the focking –?'

I follow him into the bedroom. He's actually in her walk-in wardrobe. I stick my head around the door and I straight away discover what he's so upset about. All of her clothes are gone – and so, it seems, is Delma.

JP's like, 'No! Please, no!' and he runs out of the wardrobe and out of the bedroom and out of the aportment.

I shout after him. I'm like, 'Where are you going?'

And he shouts back, 'I'm going to see is her cor downstairs. I might still have a chance to catch her.'

And that's when I notice the letter on the little table in the hallway. It's, like, a single sheet of paper, folded over, with 'JP' written on the outside.

I pick it up – I know I shouldn't – and I open it.

I give it the old left to right.

It's like, 'My dear JP. This is for the best. Ross told Belle everything – how you can't look at me when you make love to me any more. My heart is broken but it will heal in time. I'm moving to England with Belle. Please don't come after me. Love, Delma.'

I hear the lift doors open and JP goes, 'Her cor is gone! What the fock, Ross? What the fock is going on?'

I slip the letter into the inside pocket of my Henri Lloyd sailing jacket and I go, 'No idea, Dude. It's a definite mystery.'

When I arrive home, Erika and Helen are still up. They're, like, watching *It's a Wonderful Life* like they do *every* Christmas Eve?

Erika goes, 'How is everyone?'

I'm there, 'Yeah, no, a mixed bag actually.'

'What does that mean?'

'Oisinn turned up at Sorcha's, wanting to see the baby and the sister – actually, what's her name?'

'She wouldn't let him see him. He phoned me. He was hammered.'

'Yeah, no, he was hammered in The Bridge as well.'

'That focking bitch.'

Helen goes, 'Erika, come on, don't talk about people like that.'

She's there, 'I'm sorry, Mom, but that's what she is – to put Oisinn and Magnus through that. Although I did tell him at the time that they were mad having anything to do with her.'

Helen's there, 'Are you having Christmas dinner with us tomorrow, Ross?'

I'm like, 'Er, no, I'm having it with the old dear – in Ongar.'

She goes, 'That'll be lovely to spend the day with her.'

And I'm there, 'Yeah, no, it could be her –' and I suddenly stop because I can't bring myself to say the words 'last one'.

Erika goes, 'Do you want a drink?'

I'm there, 'What have you got?'

'I've just opened a bottle of Baileys,' Helen goes. 'It's on the island in the kitchen.'

Baileys. It *must* be focking Christmas.

I'm there, 'Yeah, no, I'll have a drop – just to be sociable. Where's Honor, by the way?'

'She's just gone to bed,' Helen goes.

Erika's there, 'She told me what happened with Sincerity.'

'Yeah, no, she made a move on her,' I go. 'And Sincerity wasn't into it.'

Helen's like, 'That's awful. She must be so embarrassed.'

I'm there, 'I think it was my old dear who put the idea in her head. I told her not to listen to her. I'm not being a dick here but even if Sincerity *was* into girls, I think she'd be way out of Honor's league.'

Erika's there, 'That's lovely, Ross.'

I'm like, 'Hey, I've never been afraid to call it,' then I tip out to the kitchen to grab myself a Baileys.

I see the bottle on the island. But when I pick it up, I discover – what the fock? – that it's *empty*? I'm thinking, did Helen not say that she'd just opened it?

And then the focking penny drops.

Up the focking stairs I go. I knock on the door, at the same time going, 'Honor? Honor?'

She goes, 'For fock's sake, come in, will you?'

She is *not* a good drunk.

Before I get to even open my mouth, she goes, 'Sincerity reposted a meme on Instagram saying that "Baby, It's Cold Outside" should be, like, banned?'

I'm suddenly thrown.

I'm like, 'Banned? I love that song.'

'It's supposedly problematic from, like, a consent point of view?'

'Tom Jones – with what's-her-name out of Catatonia?'

'Do you not get it, Dad? She having a focking dig at me!'

'Is she?'

'I tried to kiss her without asking for her permission.'

'Oh, we've to ask people for their permission before we throw the lips on them now, do we?'

'Yes, Dad, we do.'

'Honor, I honestly think you're reading too much into it.'

'Then why won't she return my text messages?'

'I don't know, Honor. I honestly don't know. How much have you had to drink?'

'I think I'm going to be sick.'

'If you necked that entire bottle of Baileys, then I'm not surprised.'

'It's, like, curdling in my stomach.'

All I can do is just sigh. What am I going to do with this girl.

I'm there, 'Honor, look –'

'You're going to ask me why I'm drinking, aren't you?'

'Well, yeah, I'm worried about you.'

'Alcohol stops me from feeling sad.'

'That's a hell of a lot to drink, though, Honor – albeit Baileys.'

'I only ever mean to drink a little bit – to make the sadness go away. But when I have one mouthful, I'm still sad, so I decide to have another, then another, then another, until I feel absolutely nothing at all.'

Jesus, I remember Christian explaining his alcoholism to me in exactly the same way.

I'm there, 'Honor –'

But she goes, 'I already know what you're going to say – that I can't keep getting drunk like this.'

'You definitely can't.'

'Then how do I stop myself from feeling sad all the time?'

'I don't know the answer to that question, Honor.'

She storts crying. I sit on the side of the bed and I hold her hand.

She goes, 'I don't want to be inside my head. I can't focking stand it.'

I'm there, 'Honor, can you make me a promise?'

'What?'

'When you feel sad like this, and you think that maybe a drink will take the edge off it, just ring me, okay?'

'How the fock will that help?'

'It's something I used to do for Christian. Just tell me that you feel like drinking. I won't try to persuade you *not* to drink – even though I can't believe I'm saying that to my fourteen-year-old daughter. But sometimes just explaining to someone the way you're feeling can really help.'

Jesus Christ, *I'm* crying my eyes out now.

She nods her head, at the same time wiping away her tears.

I'm like, 'Okay?'

And she's there, 'Okay.'

'I'll tell you what else I can do. I'm going to her dad's house tomorrow night for, like, Christmas drinks. Do you want me to put a word in for you with Sincerity? I don't mean tell her that you're a great catch and she must be mad knocking you back. I mean tell her that you're sorry – you maybe misread the signals.'

'She wasn't giving me any signals. Dad, please don't say anything to her.'

'Fine – yeah, no, I won't, then.'

We're both quiet for a little bit, then she goes, 'I don't like her dad.'

I laugh.

I'm there, 'Why don't you like him, Honor? And bear in mind, you're pushing an open door here.'

She goes, 'I just hate the way he's real touchy-feely around Roz. He's, like, her *ex*-husband – but he carries on as if there's still something between them.'

I'm there, 'I'm glad it's not just in my head.'

She goes, 'It's not, Dad,' and she hands me her phone.

On it, there's a photograph that Roz posted on Instagram two hours ago of the two of them kissing each other underneath the mistletoe – with their eyes closed, on the *literally* lips?

I feel my blood stort instantly boiling.

Honor goes, 'They look like an actual couple in that photograph. I don't know how you and Gráinne are so cool with it.'

I'm there, 'Yeah, no, I've had to stop myself from offloading once or twice. Are you going to be okay?'

She's like, 'I don't know.'

I'm there, 'Hey, why don't I grab my pillow and my duvet from my bed and I'll sleep down there on the floor like I used to when you had nightmares as a child.'

She goes, 'I'd like that.'

I'm there, 'Just don't focking puke on me, okay?'

She laughs and she's like, 'I can't promise that.'

I don't actually care. She can puke on me however much she likes.

'Dad?' she goes as I make a bed for myself next to hers.

I'm like, 'What is it, Honor?'

She goes, 'I feel like drinking.'

I'm there, 'Okay, maybe we'll stort it from tomorrow.'

I'm like, 'How's the head?'

This is as we're pulling into Honalee.

'My head is focking killing me,' Honor goes, 'and I feel sick.'

I'm there, 'Well, you drank a serious skinful in fairness to you.'

We get out of the cor and I grab the presents from the boot.

It's Sorcha's old man who answers the door. He's wearing a red Christmas jumper with *Sexy and I Snow It* on it and I somehow manage not to comment on it.

He's like, 'You were supposed to be here at nine.'

I'm there, 'So?'

And he goes, 'So you've missed the boys opening their presents,' and he sounds delighted with himself. 'Oh, well, there's always next year.'

Honor has no time for his shit this morning. It's probably The Fear. She literally shoves him aside and I follow her into the gaff and I'm like, 'Sexy and I Snow It? Yeah, you focking wish.'

The boys are in the living room with Sorcha and her old dear and they're all, like, gathered around the Christmas tree. The TV is on and it's, like, a carol service from St Paul's Cathedral. The floor is covered in torn wrapping paper and – yeah, no – like the dickhead said, everything has been already opened.

Sorcha goes, 'Merry Christmas, Ross!' and we do the whole air-kissing thing and then she turns to Honor and it's the same thing.

Honor goes, 'Merry Christmas – whatever!' and it's nice to see her making the effort. Sorcha's old dear says fock-all to either of us.

Brian, Johnny and Leo, I notice, are all wearing pilot caps, which are too big for their heads.

I'm there, 'Where did they get those?' because they definitely weren't on their Santa List.

'I got them for them,' I hear a voice go, then I turn around to see that the famous Mike has entered the room. He's in his pilot's outfit again – seriously, I don't think I've ever seen him in civvies.

He goes, 'Merry Christmas, Ross,' and – I swear to fock – I end up just staring at him with my mouth slung open like a bird waiting for a worm to be dropped in.

I'm like, 'Your voice is so –'

He's there, 'My voice? What about it?'

It's so focking weird because I feel it in my knees.

I'm there, 'Nothing,' quickly getting my act together. 'You're not flying off somewhere, are you? Seriously, I don't think I've ever seen you in civvies.'

Sorcha's old dear goes, 'He's just arrived back from Washington. He flew overnight.'

'And he still managed to get here in time to see the boys open their presents,' Sorcha's old man goes.

Mike smiles and goes, 'I really had to put my foot down when I was crossing Greenland!' and everyone laughs like this is somehow hilarious.

I'm there, 'Have you ever thought of being a DJ?'

He's like, 'A DJ?' like no one has ever said it to him before, which I refuse to believe.

I'm there, 'You could *be* one. If you wanted.'

He goes, 'Thank you, Ross. I must remember that.'

'Daddy, look what Santa brought me!' Leo goes and he shows me his – yeah, no – remote-controlled Boeing 747.

Brian and Johnny each have one in their little hands too.

I'm there, 'Yeah, no, you must have been a very good boy, in fairness to you. I've got one more present for each of you here. These are, like, Daddy presents,' and I hand them out.

They tear off the wrapping and they look at the things like they've no idea what the fock they are or – worse – what the fock they're even *for*?

Sorcha's old man goes, 'Are those baseball bats?'

And I'm there, 'I didn't think you knew anything about sport,' which is a real dig at him, because he *doesn't*? I remember once he was in my old man's corporate box for one of the autumn internationals – might have been South Africa – and he went, 'Are there any points awarded for kicking the ball *under* the bor?'

Ollie Campbell happened to be there as a guest of my old man and I could have cried for the dude.

'Baseball?' Sorcha goes. 'But they play hockey, Ross.'

They focking don't play hockey, I'm very tempted to go.

I'm there, 'Well, it's good for kids to try a lot of different sports.'

Which I don't believe, by the way – not for a focking second, whatever Josh van der Flier might think.

'Where did you get those?' Sorcha's old dear goes.

I'm there, 'Ronan's mate, Buckets of Blood, has a brother who's just opened a mortial orts shop on Capel Street.'

Sorcha's looking through the torn packaging. She goes, 'Ross, did you get them a ball?'

And I'm there, 'No, he doesn't sell the balls for some reason. There's no real call for them – that's according to him.'

'I know what these are intended for,' Sorcha's old man goes, 'and I'm confiscating them.'

He takes them and the boys raise no objection. Honor *does*, though?

She goes, 'They're for their own protection, you focking thundering focking prick.'

Yeah, no, the hangovers definitely don't suit her.

He's like, 'How *dare* you speak to me like that!'

But she's there, 'How dare *you* stand by and allow my brothers to be bullied!'

'Bullied?' Sorcha goes.

I'm there, 'Yeah, no, there's a kid called Morcus. Him and his mates have been extorting money from them – every time Sexy and I Snow It there takes them to the library in Dalkey.'

Sorcha looks at the boys and goes, 'Is this true?'

I'm there, 'It is true – their money-boxes were empty.'

The boys have their heads down. They're ashamed, and rightly focking so.

Sorcha's old man goes, 'Well, this is the first I'm hearing of it.'

And Honor's like, 'Yeah, that's the focking problem – you're not looking after them.'

Sorcha's sister all of a sudden steps into the room, going, 'What's all the shouting?'

She's carrying little Paavo in her orms.

Sorcha's old dear straight away loses it with her. She's like, 'Don't you *dare* stort feeding that child in here!'

The sister goes, 'Er, he's already *fed*? Although he can't keep his sticky little hands off my breasts. Like father, like son!'

I can feel my face getting hot.

I'm there, 'Right, let's go and fly these things, will we?' and I lead Brian, Johnny and Leo outside to the back gorden to try out their planes, with the rest of the crew following behind us.

I take one plane, Sorcha's old man takes one and Mike takes the third one. Out of the three of us, *he* manages to get his plane airborne first – he flies the Government jet for a living, so he'd *want* to be focking good at it? I take off second, and then Leo has to actually take the remote control from Sorcha's old man to get his in the air.

I think about cracking some joke about Sorcha's old man not being able to get it up, but then I decide, fock it, it's Christmas – maybe keep it festive.

Behind me, I hear Sorcha go, 'Can I have a little hold of him?' and I turn my head to see her taking the baby from the sister. 'Look at you! Aren't you beautiful! Fionn will be arriving with Hillary in a few minutes!'

Brian is going, 'Daddy, can I have a go?' and he's trying to take the remote control *from* me?

I'm there, 'Hang on, let me see can I get the hang of it first,' because my one is wobbling in the air like a miskicked conversion, while Mike is flying Leo's plane in perfect circles, round and round the house, making me look bad in the process.

Sorcha's sister sidles up to me and, out of the corner of her mouth, goes, 'When are you taking the test?'

I'm there, 'I was going to wait for Oisinn and Magnus to do theirs first. You've broken their horts, I want you to know. Oisinn was in The Bridge last night and the poor dude was in bits.'

'Ross, Paavo is your son. If I have to take you to court to get you to do the test, I'll focking do it.'

Brian goes, 'Daddy, I want to fly my plane!' because Leo and Johnny both have the controls in their hands at this stage and they're getting the definite gist of it.

I'm there, 'In a minute,' because I'm enjoying myself here. I've managed to get it high in the sky over the sea.

Over to my right, about twenty feet away, I can hear Sorcha's old pair deep in conversation.

He's going, 'Even if they are being bullied, violence is not the answer. Violence is never the answer.'

That's when Honor snatches the remote control out of my hand.

I'm there, 'What are you doing?'

She goes, 'I want to try something.'

Sorcha's old man is like, 'I've *seen* this Morcus fellow talking to the boys in the library. He seems like a very agreeable chap to me.'

Honor has got this look of, like, grim determination on her face as she brings the plane in from over the sea.

Sorcha's old man goes, 'Of course, if *he* had his way,' because he can't bring himself to say my name, 'they'd still be three little thugs with a notorious reputation.'

She storts to bring the plane down towards the house, except it's not *slowing* down? She's biting her bottom lip – concentrating hord, in fairness to her.

'I'm sure the entire thing is a misunderstanding,' Sorcha's old man keeps going. 'I'll talk to Morcus's father. He's an orchitect.'

The thing is coming down towards us at a shorp angle and suddenly we can all hear it, like a focking whip-crack, as it flashes past just above our heads.

Sorcha and her sister scream when they realize what's happening.

It's like, *'Aaaaaarrrrrrgggggghhhhhh!!!!!!!'*

And even Mike, who you'd imagine would have nerves of steel, goes, 'Watch out!' in his sexy voice.

'A bloody good orchitect as well,' Dick Brain goes. 'I think he may have had a hand in designing that wonderful new building on Sir John Rogerson's –'

The plane hits him just above the knees – he doesn't even see it coming – but the impact is so hord that it ends up literally flipping him over, so that he lands on his back with a sickening thud.

'Oops!' Honor goes – the old gorgle really brings out her nasty side.

And I'm there, 'Sexy and You Snow It? Focking decked and you snow it more like!'

As a gag, I'm not sure if it works for everyone – but, hey, it works for me.

Erika rings me and she's not a happy bunny rabbit.

She's there, 'Did you drink all of my mother's Baileys last night?'

I go, 'What kind of question is that to ask me?' because I'm playing for time here.

She's like, 'The bottle was nearly full, Ross. And this morning it's empty.'

I can't rat Honor out, so instead I go, 'Yeah, no, it's very easy to drink, in fairness to it.'

She's like, 'So what the fock did you do – neck the entire bottle?'

I'm there, 'Well, it's more like a dessert than a drink, isn't it?'

'You've got a focking problem,' she goes. 'You need, like, an intervention or something.'

I'm there, 'Erika, can we maybe talk about this later? We're just about to eat here,' because – yeah, no – it's three o'clock on Christmas Day and I'm in the nursing home in Ongar.

She hangs up on me and I tip back into the dining room, where thirty patients, along with their plus-ones, and about ten members of staff, are about to be served dinner.

'Have you been wanking?' the old dear shouts and – I swear to fock – the entire room looks up. 'I think he's been wanking!'

I'm like, 'No, I haven't been wanking,' and I can feel my face turn red. 'And can you maybe keep your voice –?'

She's there, 'He has a very high sex drive, you see,' again announcing this information to the entire room. 'He was forever going at himself.'

'Like Valerie Amburn-James,' some old dude at the end of our table goes, because – yeah, no – her book is obviously doing the rounds in here.

The old dear's like, 'Yes, just like Valerie! Sex on the brain!'

I'm there, 'If you must know,' although I'm looking at Dalisay for some reason, 'I was on the phone to my, technically, *sister*?'

'You don't have a sister,' the old dear goes. 'Conor and I just had you, Ross – and that was quite enough for me, thank you very much!'

She's sitting there in a cerise twinset and a paper crown with a slightly confused look on her face. I sit down next to her – and opposite Dalisay – and I try to change the subject.

I'm there, 'Dalisay, I'm guessing you don't have anything like this back home?'

But she goes, 'Yes, we celebrate Christmas. The Philippines is a Christian country, Ross – mostly Catholic.'

I'm like, 'That's one fact about the Philippines that I didn't know.'

Listen to Michael Palin here – I don't even know where the fock it is.

She goes, 'We have Christmas trees. We have Santa Claus. We have Simbang Gabi.'

I'm there, 'What's that – as in, specifically, like?'

'We prepare to celebrate the birth of Jesus by going to Mass every day for nine days.'

'*Nine* days?'

'Nine days.'

'I always forget that Jesus was actually *born* on Christmas Day. I mean, a lot of people believe that's how the whole thing got going, don't they? God, I'm storving, though. I could eat a former's orse through an electric fence.'

The old dear goes, 'What are we having for the dinner?'

'Presumably, it'll be turkey and ham – what with it being, you know –'

'What? What is it?'

'Er, *Christmas*?'

'Oh, good. I do love Christmas. And who are all these *other* people, Ross?' and this is at, like, the top of her voice.

I'm like, 'They're all you're, em, friends.'

'God, I don't think so! Look at the state of them! They're all . . . elderly people! This one here smells of –'

'Please don't say it.'

'Piss, Ross! He smells of piss!'

It's at that exact moment that the kitchen staff stort arriving with plates of food for us all. It smells – yeah, no – great and we all horse into it.

I'm there, 'And what do you tend to eat in the Philippines, Dalisay – on the big day, like?'

She goes, 'We have Christmas dinner on Noche Buena – the night of Christmas Eve. We have ham and roast pork with sweet liver and sometimes spaghetti noodles with a banana-ketchup sauce.'

'And does that ever seem random to you? Presumably not – if it's what you're used to, right?'

The old dear goes, 'What's Conor doing that's so important that he can't have Christmas dinner with his family?'

I'm there, 'He's working,' but then – for some reason – I just throw in, 'And so is Chorles – presumably.'

She's like, 'Who on Earth is Chorles?'

And then I stort, again, just randomly trying to remind her of – yeah, no – Christmases past, hoping that it'll somehow jog her memory.

I'm there, 'Do you not remember the Christmas morning when you were sick – in inverted commas – and you asked *him* to cook the turkey? And he forgot to take the little bag of giblets out of it and the whole thing ended up tasting of melted plastic?'

She just looks back at me blankly.

I'm like, 'And then there was the Stephen Zuzz Day when he was at the Leopardstown Races – again, drink was involved – and he leaned too far forward and fell over the edge of the stand. There wasn't a bother on him, Dalisay, even though he fell, I don't know, however many feet.'

Again, there's not even a flicker of memory from the old dear.

I go, 'And what about the year he took Honor to see the live animal crib outside the Mansion House and he dropped a half-smoked Montecristo into the hay and ended up nearly borbecuing a cow, three sheep and a focking donkey?'

I suddenly hear the scrape of chair legs off the floor. Dalisay is standing up and I notice that she's got, like, tears in her eyes.

'Excuse me,' she goes – then she sort of, like, rushes out of the room.

After a minute or two – I finish my roast potatoes because they're incredible – I get up to go and check on her. She's standing outside in the hallway with her face in her hands – yeah, no, *sobbing*?

I'm there, 'Dalisay, this isn't about the donkey, is it? Because all of the animals made it out alive.'

It turns out that it's not that at all.

She goes, 'Hearing you speak about your father, it makes me miss my father.'

I'm there, 'Is he –?' meaning dead.

'He is like Fionnuala,' she goes. 'He has dementia also,' and I feel suddenly shit that she's here – I'm *guessing*? – hundreds of miles from home, caring for my old dear in her old age while her old man is going through exactly the same shit.

I'm like, 'You should be with him – if there was any justice in the world.'

I don't even know what I'm saying.

She goes, 'My brothers and sisters are there. But sometimes I get sad that I will perhaps never see him again.'

I give her a hug and – yeah, no – it doesn't feel in any way inappropriate.

When she stops crying, I let go of her and I'm like, 'Do you want to ring home? On my mobile, I mean?'

She's there, 'No, it's okay.'

'It's not a big deal. My old man pays all my bills anyway.'

'No, it's very late at night in the Philippines. And I spoke to them this morning on FaceTime.'

FaceTime, of course – no one rings anyone any more.

She goes, 'You are very sweet,' and I notice that she's looking at me very, very intensely.

Suddenly, with no pre-warning, and certainly no consent check, the girl throws the lips on me. Hand on hort, I don't exactly push her away. I don't want to embarrass the girl and I think I mentioned that she looks like Angel Locsin.

We kiss for maybe thirty or forty seconds. Her mouth tastes of sausage-meat stuffing and her face has that Dettol smell that's common to nurses the world over.

Suddenly, from inside the dining room, I hear the old dear go, 'Where's Ross gone? And where's Dalisay?' and that's when Dalisay suddenly stops kissing me. She looks like, I don't know, a deer that's been stortled by the snap of a twig.

'If I know Ross,' the old dear goes – again, top of her voice, 'he'll be trying to have sex with her.'

Dalisay goes, 'I am sorry. I am so, so sorry,' and she turns and hurries away down the corridor.

Roz kisses me, then she says I smell of Dettol.

I'm like, 'Dettol? That's random.'

Seriously, it's uncanny. Sorcha always knew if I'd cheated on her in Copper Face Jacks. Even after a shower, the smell lingers on. This time, at least, I have an excuse.

I'm there, 'Yeah, no, I had my Christmas dinner in a *nursing* home, remember?'

She's like, 'Oh, God, I'm sorry, I didn't mean to sound –'

I'm there, 'Hey, it's cool. Merry Christmas!' and I kiss her back.

She goes, 'Everyone is here! My mom and dad are dying to meet you!'

I'm like, 'What? Your old pair are here?'

The only reason I sound worried is because I always seem to get off on the wrong foot with parents. I'll never forget the night that Sorcha brought her old pair into The Wicked Wolf to meet me for the first time and I was standing on the bor with my chinos around my knees while JP and Oisinn were trying to light a length of toilet paper that was sticking out of my orse. I don't think there was any coming back from what the goys still refer to as the Chariots of Fire Incident.

I'm there, 'I just wish you'd given me a bit of, I don't know, notice.'

She goes, 'Ross, I told you that my parents were coming for Christmas dinner.'

I'm there, 'I know, but I didn't think they'd still be here at, whatever, nine o'clock.'

She's like, 'Stop being weird – they're going to love you,' and she takes me by the hand and leads me down the hallway to the living room.

There's, like, a porty in full swing in there. Raymond – the focking prick – and Gráinne are there, then a load of neighbours and then four or five Mount Anville moms that I recognize from doing the school run.

'Most of you already know him,' she goes, as she pulls me to the centre of the room. 'But for those of you who don't, this is Ross, my' – and she looks at me as if she's seeking my permission – 'portner?'

I'm like, 'Yeah, no, portner works for me.'

Everyone laughs. I've no idea why.

'Ross,' she goes, 'this is my mom and dad,' and she leads me over to this woman and man, who look definitely younger than *my* old pair. 'Mom and Dad, this is Ross.'

I'm like, 'Hey, how the hell are you?' because I forget sometimes how much of a people person I am when I can be focking orsed.

'I'm Alan,' her old man goes, 'and this is Cherie.'

I'm like, 'Cherie – that's a gorgeous name,' and I'm off to a flyer.

I can feel Raymond just, like, staring at me.

'We met you, very briefly,' Cherie goes, 'at Strictly.'

She obviously means the Mount Anville father-and-daughter ballroom dancing competition, which me and Honor won.

'Well, I remember him playing rugby,' the dad – Alan – goes.

I'm there, 'Are you serious?' and I can't keep the smile off my face.

'Against Newbridge College,' he goes, 'in the final in 1999. You were out of this world. I remember saying at the time that this guy is going to play number ten for Ireland one day.'

Raymond – can't help himself – goes, 'But he didn't – did you, Ross?'

And Alan goes, 'Says the man who played rugby for Bective's – what was it? – third team?' and he says it without even looking at him.

And that's when I suddenly pick up on the fact that Roz's old pair have zero time for the dude.

Roz goes, 'Ross, there's Hanijans in the fridge if you want one,' so – yeah, no – I take my leave of them and tip down to the kitchen.

I walk in and Sincerity is in there, putting cocktail sausages wrapped in bacon and other porty nibbles on plates, presumably as soakage for the adults.

I'm there, 'Hey, Sincerity – how the hell are you?'

She's like, 'Hi, Mr O'Carroll-Kelly,' and – yeah, no – it's *awkward*?

I'm there, 'Come on, Sincerity, it's Ross, Rosser or The Rossmeister. I've told you that.'

I notice a pair of brand-new ski boots on the kitchen counter.

I'm there, 'Did you get those for Christmas?'

She goes, 'No, my mom bought them for my dad.'

'Look, Sincerity, I'm just going to come out and say it. Honor really misses you. She's sorry that she tried to, you know – blah, blah, blah. In her defence, she's been drinking so much lately, she doesn't know up from down.'

'The thing is, Ross, that I'm not actually gay?'

'Yeah, no, she copped that from your reaction.'

'Like, I don't even *care* that she's gay? I was just shocked when she tried to –'

'Let's not go into the ins and outs of it. You're the best friend she's ever had, Sincerity. You're the only friend she's ever had. She really misses you.'

'I miss her too. But it's just, well, she didn't ask for my consent.'

'Sincerity, a great man named Father Denis Fehily used to say this thing – to forgive someone is to set a prisoner free and discover that the prisoner was you.'

She thinks about that for a good ten seconds and I can tell she likes it. She's a great kid.

I'm there, 'I've loads of his quotes written into my Rugby Tactics Book. I read them every day.'

She goes, 'I better bring these into the room,' and off she goes.

As she walks out, Raymond walks in.

I pull open the fridge door and I whip out a bottle of what Jamie Heaslip has storted referring to as Chinaken. I'm always telling him that he should stort a podcast.

I close the fridge. Raymond is eating a cocktail sausage, trying to act shit cool, but he's obviously still smorting from the putdown he got a few minutes ago.

I'm there, 'He's sound, that Alan, isn't he? He's no fan of yours, or am I picking that up wrong?'

He goes, 'Well, he's certainly been taken in by you. Like father, like daughter.'

I knock back a mouthful of the stuff.

And that's when he goes, 'I know your secret.'

I'm like, 'What secret would that be?' thinking he's bluffing. 'The one about me not having a twin brother?'

'No,' he goes, a smile suddenly erupting across his face, 'the one about you being the father of your wife's sister's baby.'

I end up nearly dropping the bottle.

I'm like, 'Wh . . . wh . . . wh . . . what?'

He goes, 'So when are you taking this DNA test?'

I'm there, 'How do you know about –?'

He goes, 'I've been listening to your voicemail messages. You know, someone with as many dirty secrets as you have should really think about changing his pin from four zeroes.'

What the fock? I say it as well.

I'm like, 'What the fock?' and then I'm like, 'Shit, what other messages did you hear?' because I need to know everything he has on me.

'Is that not big enough?' he goes – information is power and he knows it. 'I take it you haven't told Roz that your sister-in-law has just had your baby?'

'Illegibly,' I go. 'As in, nothing's been proven yet. So what are you going to do? Tell her?'

He laughs and he's there, 'Don't need to – no, I'm going to sit back and enjoy watching all of your lies unravel.'

He goes to walk out of the kitchen, then he stops at the door and turns back.

'Oh,' he goes, 'a woman named Dalisay left you a message about an hour ago. She sounded Spanish.'

Oh, fock.

I'm there, 'She's from the Philippines.'

'Right,' he goes. 'Well, she said that what happened between you earlier can never happen again. She's supposed to be nursing your mother and it was highly unprofessional of her.'

And with that, he just focks off, delighted with himself.

I'm, like, staring at his brand-new ski boots and you can probably guess what pops into my head in that moment. I decide to take a shit in them.

I'm actually unbuttoning my chinos when I suddenly change my mind. Knowing my previous form with in-laws, I think, Alan and Cherie will probably walk in on me while I'm still in the process of crimping one off.

And that's when I spot a small box of thumb tacks on the kitchen counter. Roz has obviously used them to hang up the decorations.

I pick up the left ski boot and I peel back the insole. I take a thumb tack from the box, then I push it through the insole, halfway down the boot, with the point sticking up. Then I press the insole back down.

I decide to rejoin the porty and just, like, front it out, thinking that I've nothing to worry about yet, especially if Raymond is serious about saying nothing and watching me slowly blow myself up.

A few of them are playing some kind of board game in the living room.

Roz goes, 'General knowledge – Ross, you'll be good at this!' and I'm thinking how right Raymond is when he says that I have her totally fooled. 'You can be on our team!'

And that's when Raymond – totally out of nowhere – goes, 'Oh, by the way, Ross has a little secret, Roz! Are you going to tell us what it is, Ross?'

The focker is just, like, grinning at me – he has me by the balls and he knows it.

I'm there, 'I'd be interested in hearing what you have to say first.'

'Okay,' he goes, 'I'll say it. Ross was in a strip club last Friday night.'

Every single conversation in the room suddenly stops.

Roz is like, 'What?'

I'm there, 'It's bullshit, Roz. It never happened.'

But *he* goes, 'Really, Ross? Are you actually going to lie to her face like that?' and I watch him reach for his phone.

Yeah, no, I still haven't changed my pin and he could play

presumably Ronan's thank-you message on speaker right now if he wanted.

I'm there, 'Fine – yeah, no, I was in Private Eyes on Dame Street. And it's more of a lapdancing club than an actual strip club.'

I don't know why I think this detail makes the story sound better.

Roz goes, 'You were here with me on Friday night. You said you had to go because something came up.'

Her old pair are just, like, staring at me – *literally* open-mouthed?

As a matter of fact, pretty much everyone is looking at me in exactly the same way.

I'm there, 'I didn't go there to get a dance, Roz. My son lost his wedding ring in there and I popped in to get it back from a dancer slash prostitute named Zondra.'

'You *what*?' Alan goes.

I'm getting the feeling that he's no longer a fan.

I'm there, 'You know what? I might call it a night. I'm a bit wrecked.'

And, as I head for door, I can nearly *hear* the smile on Raymond's focking face.

7.

All My People Right Here, Right Now

'Can you get me, like, a Bacordi and Coke?' Honor goes. 'With or without the Coke – and can you make it, like, a double?'

She's a focking comedian, in fairness to her.

I'm there, 'Honor, I am not getting you a double Bacordi – end of story.'

She goes, 'You said that I should tell you when I felt the urge to drink.'

I'm like, 'Yeah, no, I meant that more in terms of me being, like, your sponsor – rather than in terms of you asking me to, like, order for you.'

She's there, 'I wouldn't have agreed to it if I'd known that was the deal.'

Yeah, no, this is us on, like, Stephen Zuzz Day in the old man's box at Leopardstown. We're, like, waiting for him and Ronan to arrive.

Honor goes, 'What about just a Bacordi then – as in, like, one shot?'

I'm there, 'Honor, I am not buying you drink. Not until you're sixteen.'

And that's when her *phone* all of a sudden rings? She looks at the screen and her face lights up like the Bellagio fountain.

'Oh! My God!' she goes. 'It's Sincerity!'

I'm there, 'Are you going to answer it?'

She's like, 'Did you say something to her?'

And I go, 'Yeah, no, I know I said I wouldn't say anything to her, but we just got talking and – Honor, answer it.'

She takes, like, a deep breath and then she does as I suggested.

She's like, 'Hello?' and she listens for a bit – which is new for her – and then she goes, 'Sincerity, will you hang on for, like, two seconds? I'm just going to take this outside.'

She puts the call on hold, then just throws her orms around me and whispers in my ear, 'Thank you, Dad. Thank you, thank you, thank you!'

Then she lets go of me and heads outside to talk.

'Do you not want that Bacordi?' I shout after her – it's, like, a test really. 'A double, wasn't it?' but she suddenly has zero interest in drink and all I can do is just smile to myself. It's, like, mission accomplished in terms of this particular parenting job.

I knock back a mouthful of Hanijan and I'm studying the names of the horses running in the next race when I suddenly hear a voice go, 'Rosser, you fooken bender!' and I turn around and there's Ronan in a coat identical to the one my old man wears to Leopardstown every year.

I'm like, 'Ro, how the hell are you?'

And he goes, 'Ine moostard, Rosser.'

'Did you have a nice Christmas?'

'Ah, it was gayum-ball. You know yisser self. Kennet and Dordeen invirrit us in next doh-er.'

'Sounds great.'

'Whorr about you? How was yisser Christmas?'

I'm there, 'Highs and lows, Dude. Speaking of which, I need you to talk to Roz and explain to her why I was in Private Eyes on Dame Street last week.'

He goes, 'What are you thalken about, Rosser?'

'Ro, don't act the focking innocent. Roz's husband knows that I swung in there last Friday night and he just so happened to mention it to Roz in front of her old pair and all of the neighbours and one or two Mount Anville moms last night.'

'And what are you wanton me to thoo?'

'I'm *wanton* you to text her – or preferably phone her – and tell her that the only reason I went in there was to get your wedding ring back.'

He goes, 'I caddent thoo that, Rosser. What if it gets back to Shadden?'

243

I'm there, 'Seriously, Ro, this is my focking relationship on the line here.'

He's like, 'Ine oatenly yanking yisser chayin, Rosser. I'll gib her a beddle – and I'll teddle her the scower.'

I'm there, 'Much appreciated. What the fock are you wearing, by the way?' because – like I said – he's like a Mini-Me version of my old man.

'What are you odden about?' he goes.

I'm like, 'Er, the *coat*?'

'It was a Christmas president,' he goes, 'from Cheerlie.'

I'm there, 'Is that his *actual* coat – as in, the one he wears to Leopardstown every year?'

He's like, 'Habn't a clue, Rosser,' and then he checks his pockets, then reaches inside and pulls out – yeah, no – a newspaper cutting, which turns out to be the racing form for Leopardstown a year ago. 'Moy fooken Jaysus – I think it might be, Rosser.'

I'm there, 'Where the fock is he?' because the first race is about to stort. 'I thought he was supposed to meet us here?'

He goes, 'He caddent make it this year. He towult me to teddle you he's soddy. He's a phowun conference with the madden heself.'

'Who's that?'

'Putin.'

'Oh, right. What's the story there, Ro?'

'What do you mee-un?'

'As in, what the fock happened in Moscow? As in, what was the agreement?'

'I caddent teddle you, Rosser. It's a State secret.'

'You can tell me – I'm your old man.'

'Seerdiously, Rosser – doatunt ast me. Wheer's Hodor, by the way? She texted me this morden. Said she was cubbin today.'

'Yeah, no, she's outside – on the phone to Sincerity.'

'What, they're back thalken?'

'Looks like it. I'd a word with Sincerity last night. One of Father Fehily's quotes seems to have done the definite trick.'

'Ah, Ine delirrit, so I am. Hee-or, Sincedity's not a lesbiant arthur awl, is she?'

'Fock, no – she made it very clear to me that she has zero interest in Honor unless it's as a friend.'

'And Hodor's happy with that, is she?'

'She must be. I offered to buy her a Bacordi as she was walking out the door and she didn't look over her shoulder.'

'Ah, moostard,' he goes. 'Fooken moostard. Hee-or, I meant to say, Stacks of Muddy is veddy excirrit about this fortieth peerty of yooers.'

I'm there, 'Dude, I was thinking, don't go to any trouble on my account. I can have it in The Bridge. As a matter of fact, Seán O'Brien and the rest of the goys will be devastated if they find out I'm having it somewhere else.'

'It's too late, Rosser. Ine arthur senton out all the invitashiddens and I've sebbenty RSVPs seddent back. Heer-or, now that I think abourrit, I'd one back from Roz this morden saying she couldn't make it.'

'Ro, you need to focking talk to her.'

'I'll rig her, Rosser – and I'll say you werdent in addy sthrip club.'

'No, I *was* there. I've already admitted that. But I was only in there to get your wedding ring back.'

'Leab it wit me. Hee-or, what are you going as, by the way?'

'What do you mean?'

'It's faddency thress – noynties-stoyle. I was thinking, we could go as the Gaddagher brutters.'

'That what?'

'The Gaddagher brutters.'

'Ronan, I have literally no idea what you're trying to say.'

'The Gaddagher brutters.'

'Don't keep saying the same thing. We'll be here until the final race.'

'The Gaddagher brutters – ourra Oasis.'

'Oh, the Gallagher brothers!'

'That's what ine arthur saying. I was thinking I could be Liam and you could be Noelt.'

'No, I want to be Liam. It's my porty, bear in mind.'

'Feer denuff.'

Suddenly, he goes, 'Hee-or, Heddessy geb me a tip for this next race. Thracer Foyer. He said to back him to widden.'

I'm like, 'Tracer Fire?' checking out the race cord. 'He's like twenty-to-one. Should we not back him each way?'

He's there, 'Rosser, this is Heddessy we're thalken about,' meaning that the race is almost certainly fixed.

I'm thinking, what a focking crook he's ended up working for.

But then I'm like, 'Yeah, no, stick a grand on for me, will you?' and I hand him a roll of fifties.

He focks off to put the money on and that's when I hear two beeps. It's, like, a text message for Ronan – yeah, no, he left his phone on the table. I shouldn't look at it. It's, like, a massive invasion of his privacy. But on the home screen, I notice, there's a text message and I can see that it's from Avery. So – fock it – I end up picking it up and just reading the thing.

And it's like, 'You need to get out of Ireland, Ronan. And I'm not just saying that because I want to be with you. I'm saying it because I love you and I don't want you to spend the rest of your life in prison.'

Honor asks me if I'm nervous.

Yeah, no, we're in the cor and I'm dropping her to Sincerity's gaff for, I don't know, the teenage equivalent of a playdate.

I'm like, 'Why would *I* be nervous?'

It's their first time seeing each other since Honor tried to throw the lips on her.

'Sincerity said you went to a strip club,' she goes. 'And her mom found out about it.'

Yeah, no, it'll be the first time I've seen Roz since Christmas night.

I'm there, 'It was actually a lapdancing club, Honor. There's a big difference.'

There's no difference.

I'm there, 'What about you? Any nerves?'

She's like, 'No, I talked to her that day in Leopardstown and then I talked to her for, like, two hours last night and then I talked to her again for, like, an hour this morning.'

I smile – just at how easily young people seem to get over shit. I wish it was like that for adults.

'Oh! My God!' she goes. '*Guess* who me and Sincerity are dressing up as for your porty!'

I'm there, 'I don't know – who?'

She goes, 'John Travolta and Uma Thurman – from, like, *Pulp Fiction?*'

I'm like, 'Hey, that's cool,' and then I ask what is almost certainly a stupid question. 'Which one of you is going to be John Travolta?'

She goes, 'I am.'

'Yeah, no, I thought as much.'

'And we're learning the dance.'

'What, from the actual movie?'

'Oh my God, we've watched it, like, a hundred times on YouTube.'

'That's, em, cool.'

I pull up outside the gaff.

I'm like, 'Okay, just give me a second here to think about my opening line – something preferably tactical.'

But Honor gets out of the cor and heads for the front door like me, back in the day, attacking the opposition twenty-two.

It's, like, Roz who answers her knock. I'm still walking up the path. She looks absolutely incredible, standing there in the light of the doorway, dressed all in black, her boppers looking like two ripe cantaloupes in her tight-fitting, cashmere sweater.

She smiles at Honor and steps aside to let her in.

I'm there, 'It's great how easily young people seem to get over shit, isn't it? I wish it was like that for adults.'

She goes, 'Is that some kind of dig at me?' and she folds her orms in, like, a definitely *defensive* gesture?

'It was just an observation. Did, em, Ronan ring you by any chance?'

'Yes, he did.'

'And did he explain that the only reason I was in that, again, lap-dancing club was to try to get his wedding ring back? A woman called Zondra had it.'

'He told me that.'

'It's such a random name, isn't it? Although I doubt if that's what's on her birth cert.'

There's not a flicker of reaction from her. She's not ready to forgive me yet.

I'm there, 'He was saying that you RSVP-ed no – as in, you're not coming to my porty? I don't know how you're going to break the news to Sincerity because Honor and her have been practising the dance from *Pulp Fiction*.'

She goes, 'It's not that you went to a strip club that upset me, Ross. It's that your first instinct – yet again – was to lie about it.'

'I was embarrassed.'

'*You* were embarrassed? Imagine how *I* felt! My parents were sitting there!'

'I don't see why Raymond had to bring it up in front of them – in front of everyone.'

'Mom was like, "If he could lie to you as easily as that, then what kind of a relationship is it?"'

'And what about your old man? What was his take?'

She laughs – but not in a good way – then shakes her head.

'Oh, he totally took your side,' she goes. 'Rugby boys always stick together.'

Yeah, no, if he's ever travelled to an away Six Nations match, he'll be no stranger to women called Zondra. I don't mention that, though.

I'm there, 'So he had a totally different view of the matter. That's interesting.'

She's like, 'But my mom is right, Ross. If you can lie like that, with so little effort, then I have to wonder, what else aren't you telling me?'

'There's nothing else.'

'You've no more secrets?'

'No, that's your lot.'

I realize that this puts me even more at Raymond's mercy, but I can't exactly tell her – yeah, no – I think I might have accidentally had a baby with my wife's sister, and I got off with my old dear's

Filipino nurse – oh, and I had sex with a woman named Belle, even though I finished *myself* off?

I'm there, 'You know everything now.'

I smile at her and she smiles and looks away and sort of, like, shakes her head, like she's storting to see the funny side of it.

She unfolds her orms and with a slight flick of her head gestures for me to come in.

I'm good at talking my way out of situations. Let's be honest, I've had plenty of focking practice.

I'm there, 'Are you all packed?' because – yeah, no – they're heading off first thing.

She goes, 'Yeah, it's much easier to pack for a skiing holiday. It's mostly just sweaters.'

I'm there, 'I was just admiring the one you have on you.'

I've got the total gift of the gab.

I'm like, 'It's cashmere, I'm presuming?'

She's there, 'Yeah, I've had it for years, but it's, like, so warm.'

'Yeah, no, it looks warm. I'd totally understand if your answer to this question is no –'

'Ross, our children are in the kitchen?'

'– but do you want me to pop in to feed your tarantula while you're away?'

She laughs. She really *gets* me – even though she hasn't a focking clue what I'm really like.

She goes, 'I've asked my dad to do it – no offence.'

I'm like, 'Yeah, none taken.'

She's there, 'By the way,' changing the subject, 'I never got to ask you, how's your mom? How did Christmas go?'

I'm like, 'Yeah, no, it was obviously different from previous –'

And that's when it happens. I hear my voice suddenly crack. I don't know where it comes from and I don't know why now, but I've got, like, tears rolling down my cheeks and I'm going, 'I don't want her to die, Roz. I don't want her to –'

She throws her orms around my shoulders and she's going, 'You poor thing, Ross. You poor, poor thing,' and I'm crying like a child and holding onto her for dear life, feeling the warmth of her hetta googies pressed against my chest.

After thirty seconds or so, I stop crying and I pull back and we look into each other's eyes. She's an incredible woman.

She goes, 'I know it's none of my business, Ross, but have you thought of having, like, a Living Funeral for her?'

I'm there, 'What's a Living Funeral? As in, what pacifically?'

'Well, there's a girl who used to be in my Rebound Exercise class and her father was, like, terminally ill. And she just thought, well, what's the point in all of us getting together and saying nice things about him after he's dead? Let's do it while he's still here.'

'So it's, like, a roast – except you're saying, like, *nice* shit about the person?'

'I suppose that's one way of looking at it.'

All of a sudden, we hear the sound of music coming from the kitchen. It's, like, the song from Pulp Fiction – "You Never Can Tell" by, I don't know, whoever.

'Come on,' Roz goes, taking me by the hand, 'let's go and watch.'

She pushes open the door of the kitchen and we slip in. Honor and Sincerity don't seem to even notice us standing there – they're, like, so lost in the moment.

They're standing opposite each other, their hips and elbows swinging to the rhythm of the music, and they've got it down – we're talking moves, we're talking timing, we're talking eye-contact, we're talking everything.

Roz links my orm and the two of us stand there watching them, grinning like idiots, until the song ends, then they turn and see us there.

Honor goes, 'Dad, where would I get a bootlace tie?'

And I'm there, 'We'll find you a bootlace tie.'

JP says he can't believe that Delma would just walk out like that – without an explanation, without even a *note*?

I'm there, 'But she did, Dude – a fact is a fact.'

I must remember to burn that focking note.

'It's just very unlike her,' he goes.

I'm there, 'Have you considered that maybe she –'

'What?'

'– picked up on the fact that you wouldn't look at her boat race when you were having sex?'

Yeah, no, it's, like, ten o'clock on New Year's Eve and we're standing on the balcony of his aportment in Ballsbridge, staring across at the Aviva Stadium. Yeah, no, he's invited a crowd around to watch the fireworks at midnight.

He goes, 'Do you think that's what happened?'

I'm there, 'She knew you were losing interest, Dude. You didn't turn up to her birthday dinner in The Ivy that day – you stayed in The Bridge, boozing with us.'

He just shakes his head and goes, 'I'm such a piece of shit.'

I'm there, 'Take my advice and move on, Dude. You can't keep holding on to the past,' and then I make a subtle attempt to change the subject. 'Lansdowne Road, huh? Where it all happened! Can you believe it's going to be, like, twenty-one years in Morch?'

He goes, 'Move on? She's my focking wife, Ross.'

'Well –'

'What do you mean by that?'

'I just mean that you weren't married for very long. I always thought the whole thing was a bit of nostalgia on your port for a woman – a much, *much* older woman – who you had a bit of a perverted fixation with as a teenager.'

'I'm going to find her.'

'Er, maybe she doesn't *want* to be found?'

'I'm entitled to know why she decided to end our marriage.'

I'm like, 'Just keep remembering what she did to her face. Would you want to open your eyes to that every morning for the rest of your life? Ask yourself that question before you go chorging over there.'

'Over where?' he goes.

Oh, shit, I've said too much.

I'm there, 'I don't know – over anywhere.'

He's like, 'Dude, do you know where she's gone?'

'Of course I don't. Er, how *would* I?'

'Over *there* – it sounded like you had, I don't know, somewhere specific in mind.'

'I just, I don't know, assumed she was in London with the famous Belle.'

He's there, 'She's in London!' like he hadn't thought of it before. 'Of course! Belle got that big job in HSBC!'

Jesus, I'm suddenly wondering did Raymond hear the voice message she left me about blowing my beans all over her silk pillow case. The answer is probably.

I'm like, 'London is a big place, though. Write her off, Dude. Keep remembering her face. She looked like something I'd draw with a focking pen in my mouth.'

He just nods – he's hopefully hearing me.

A second or two later, the patio door slides open and Oisinn and Magnus step out onto the balcony.

I'm like, 'Hey, goys – how was your Christmas?'

'Pretty shit,' Oisinn goes. 'Not surprisingly – given, well, you know.'

I flick my thumb in the direction of the stadium and I'm like, 'I was just saying to JP, twenty-one years, huh? In Morch.'

Magnus goes, 'Well, at leasht we'll know the truth very shoon.'

I'm like, 'In terms of?'

Oisinn's there, 'We're having our DNA tests done next week. We should know within a week to ten days of that whether one of us is the biological father.'

I'm like, 'It's not actually definitive, though, is it?'

'Ninety-nine-point-nine-nine per cent definitive,' Oisinn tries to go. 'And there's probably a few more nines on the end of that as well.'

I'm there, 'It's still not one hundred per cent, though. Bear that in mind.'

Magnus goes, 'JP, I was sho shorry to hear the newsh about Delma. Do you think there ish any hope for you guysh?'

JP's like, 'Ross thinks she might have gone to London with Belle. I was half thinking of going over to look for her.'

I'm there, 'Bad idea.'

But Oisinn goes, 'At the very least, she owes you an explanation, Dude. I mean, to leave like that – without even leaving a note.'

I can't listen to any more of this, so I slip back into the aportment. The porty is in – yeah, no – full swing. I spot Erika – didn't even know she was coming – deep in conversation with Christian and I tip over to them.

Erika is telling him that Amelie is growing up so fast and Christian says we should all get together soon with the kids and maybe do a walk up Killiney Hill.

I'm there, 'I'd be up for that – big time. Have you both RSVP-ed, by the way? For my fortieth?'

Christian goes, 'Yeah, I sent Ronan an e-mail.'

I'm there, 'And you know it's, like, 1990s-themed fancy dress?'

'Yes, Ross,' Erika goes, 'we read the invitation.'

I'm like, 'Dude, you'll probably come as someone from Stor Wors, will you? Jor Jor Binks or one of that crew?'

He's there, 'Maybe.'

I'm like, 'And if you're worried about it being in Finglas –'

'*I'm* not,' Erika goes. 'It's nice to do something outside your comfort zone, isn't it?'

'– there's going to be buses going from outside the Horse Show House – just in case you *are* worried – and then dropping people back there afterwards.'

I suddenly spot Fionn arriving – late, by the way. And he's with a girl who looks definitely familiar.

I'm like, 'Who's that bird with Fionn?'

'That's Sinead,' Christian goes. 'She's a friend of Lauren's.'

I'm there, 'Lives three doors down. I met her on Christmas Eve.'

Erika's like, 'Wasn't she in, like, Loreto Foxrock?'

I'm there, 'So when the fock did this happen? Was he with her that night in The Bridge?'

Christian goes, 'No, but they got on very well and I think they swapped numbers.'

I'm there, 'I didn't see *that* coming.'

He's like, 'I think they might have went on one or two dates over Christmas.'

'Well, this has pissed me off,' I go.

Erika's like, 'Why?'

I'm there, 'I don't know. Look at her and look at him.'

Fionn leads her over to us with a big smile on his face. I think I mentioned that she looks like Jodie Comer. He's punching and he knows it.

I'm there, 'I don't remember JP saying we could bring a plus-one,' which is petty of me, I realize. 'I'm only mentioning it because you're usually such a stickler for the rules.'

He goes, 'Sinead, this is my friend, Erika.'

Erika smiles and goes, 'You went to Loreto Foxrock, didn't you?' and it's hord to know whether she's saying it to be a bitch or not.

Sinead is like, 'I did, yeah,' not even attempting to deny it, taking it on the chin.

Fionn completes the introductions. He's there, 'Christian, you obviously know – and do you remember Ross?'

She's like, 'I do, yeah – hi, Ross.'

I'm there, 'How are things in the dentistry game?' just to remind Fionn that I put in a lot of vital spadework the night he met her.

She goes, 'Good – although the practice was closed all over Christmas.'

I'm there, 'And you're not in Gleesons tonight, no? And I only mention Gleesons because it's where you said you tend to do your socializing.'

She looks at me like I'm a genuine weirdo.

'Ross,' Erika goes, 'can I have a word with you about something?' and she sort of, like, indicates the kitchen with a nod.

I follow her in there.

I'm there, 'There's no focking justice in the world, is there? Although that was a nice dig you got in about Loreto Foxrock.'

She's like, 'What the fock are you on about?'

I'm there, 'That's not what you wanted to talk to me about, no?'

She just rolls her eyes – isn't even worthy of an answer.

'Mom ran into an old friend of hers in The Westbury over Christmas,' she goes. 'Liam Lysaght.'

I'm like, 'Don't know the dude. Has he any connection to rugby?'

'He's an Assistant Gorda Commissioner.'

'That'd be a no, then.'

'They went out together when they were younger. She actually went to his debs.'

'Tipperary, I'm guessing – or somewhere like that.'

'No, Ross, it was in Dublin.'

'I don't know why I presume all Gords are from the country. Prejudice, I suppose.'

'They went for a drink together.'

'I think I know where this is going.'

'And they ended up talking about Dad.'

'Okay, that wasn't the twist I was expecting.'

'He said a lot of senior Gords are convinced that Hennessy was behind the fire.'

'Was it just one drink they had or did they kick on from there?'

'Ross, he said that Hennessy is still a suspect. They're, like, dying to chorge him. But they need evidence.'

'I honestly hoped the punchline was going to be that Helen clicked.'

'Can you talk to Ronan?'

'About?'

'About getting something on Hennessy.'

I suddenly remember something. The text message from Stephen Zuzz Day.

Erika's like, 'What?'

I'm there, 'Yeah, no, Ronan's in some kind of trouble, Erika.'

'Trouble?'

'I was at the races with him in Leopardstown, as you know, and he left his phone – yeah, no – unattended while he went off to place a bet. Anyway, he got a text message. I shouldn't have read it, but I did – and here we are.'

'Who was it from?'

'It was from Avery.'

'Avery? Are you saying they're still in contact?'

'Yeah, no, they *must* be? And he's obviously told her shit. Because she told him that he needs to get out of Ireland or he could spend the rest of his life in prison.'

'Did you ask him about it?'

'No, because it was a private text. And he wouldn't tell me anyway. But I think it has something to do with Moscow.'

'Moscow?'

'Yeah, no, Hennessy brought Ronan over there. He had him learning Russian and all sorts.'

'Ring Avery.'

'Do you think?'

'Ross, your son needs your help.'

And that's when my phone all of a sudden rings. I check the screen and it turns out that it's Roz.

I'm there, 'It's my, em, girlfriend. Not trying to make you jealous. Probably ringing just to wish me a Happy New Year.'

Erika just shakes her head and then leaves me alone.

I answer the phone. I'm like, 'Hey, Babes – how's the skiing?'

'Ross,' she goes, sounding upset, 'there's been an accident.'

I'm there, 'An accident? Are you okay?'

'Those ski boots that I bought for Raymond,' she goes, 'there was a thumb tack in one of them.'

Shit, I forgot I did that.

I'm like, 'A thumb tack?' wondering is she *accusing* me here? 'How did that get in there?'

She's there, 'I've no idea. But Raymond was putting them on in the ski lodge, standing at the top of the stairs –'

I'm thinking, oh, my God – *please* let him have amnesia.

She goes, '– and he fell, Ross –'

I'm there, 'Put me out of my misery here – are we talking in terms of a head injury, or at least a very bad concussion?'

'No, he fell on Gráinne,' she goes, 'who just happened to be walking up the stairs at the time.'

I'm there, 'So, what, she broke his fall, did she?' and I'm thinking, fock her and her focking interference.

She's like, 'Well, yes, but she has a suspected broken ankle.'

I'm there, 'But *he's* okay – that's what you're saying, is it?'

She goes, 'Apart from a nasty cut on the sole of his foot that needed two stitches, he's fine.'

I'm like, 'Fock.'

She's there, 'What do you mean by that? You sound almost disappointed.'

I'm like, 'Sorry, I meant fock in relation to – yeah, no – Gráinne's news. What an absolute bummer that is for everyone involved. Er, Happy New *Year*, by the way?'

They're staying on. That's the latest from Gstaad. Gráinne's ankle is definitely broken but she doesn't want to ruin the holiday for everyone else, so she's staying in the lodge all day with her leg in one of those giant space boots while Roz, Raymond and Sincerity play happy families on the slopes.

I'm pissed off – not half as pissed off as Gráinne, I suspect – but pissed off all the same.

Honor goes, 'Oh my God, did you see the photographs of Sincerity's stepmom on crutches?'

I'm like, 'Yeah, no, with the big, comical boot – I was checking out her Instagram as well.'

She's there, 'I wish it had happened to Sincerity's dad instead.'

I actually laugh.

I'm there, 'You shouldn't wish horm on other people, Honor.'

'Why not?' she goes.

'I don't know – you always hear people say that.'

'You were thinking the exact same thing as me.'

'Yeah, no, I was hoping he'd have some sort of head injury and not be able to remember anything.'

'Why?'

'Doesn't matter. It's grown-up shit.'

I'm standing at the door of her bedroom. She's practising the *Pulp Fiction* dance again.

She's like, 'Dad, can you *not* do that?'

I'm there, 'What was I doing?'

She goes, 'You're sniffing the air to find out if I've been drinking.'

'I'm allowed to be worried about you, Honor.'

'Well, you don't *need* to be? I'm fine.'

'That's good to hear. Right, I've to make a phone call. What time is it in Boston, by the way?'

'I don't know. They're, like, five hours behind so it's, like, eleven o'clock in the morning.'

'It's so random, isn't it?'

'What is?'

'That it can be one time of day here and a totally different time of day in the States. Like, just think about it.'

'I'm stunned that I'm related to you. Can you please fock off now?'

I leave her to it. A second or two later, I hear the sound of 'You Never Can Tell'. I walk across the landing to my room and I dial Avery's number.

She answers on, like, the third ring and she must still have me in her contacts because she goes, 'Hey, Rosser!'

Yeah, no, that's what she calls me – she'd be used to hearing it from Ro.

I'm there, 'Avery, how the hell are you?'

She goes, 'I'm good.'

'And Horvord? How's all that going?'

'It's a lot more work than I expected it to be – but I'm really enjoying it.'

'Yeah, no, good to hear – very good to hear.'

'Was there, um, something you wanted to talk to me about? I've got a lecture in, like, fifteen minutes.'

Jesus, she actually *goes* to lectures. I'm guessing Horvord Law is a lot different from doing a SportsMan Dip. in UCD.

'Ronan,' I go.

She's like, 'Ronan? Er, what about him?'

'I know you've been in touch with him.'

'Look, I don't want to cause any trouble in his marriage. It was Ronan who contacted me.'

'I don't care about his marriage. I just want to know what's going on.'

'He was just, like, drunk-texting me over Christmas.'

'I read one of your texts back to him, Avery.'

She's, like, shocked by that. She obviously takes the whole privacy thing very seriously.

She goes, 'You know that's a serious violation of my –'

I'm there, 'He's in some kind of trouble, Avery. As his father, I'm entitled to know –'

'As his father, why don't you ask him?'

'Because he won't tell me. He keeps saying that I *doatunt waddant* to know.'

She goes quiet for a moment, then she's like, 'Rosser, I have this lecture –'

I'm there, 'You said he needed to get out of Ireland, Avery. What's he done? What went down in Moscow?'

'Rosser, I'm not sure this is something we should be talking about over the phone.'

'You said he could spend the rest of his life in prison.'

'Please, Rosser, he told me in confidence.'

'Avery, what has he done? What crime has he supposably committed?'

'Rosser, I have to go.'

I'm like, 'Just say it, Avery. Give it to me in one word.'

And that's when she says it.

She goes, 'Treason.'

Dalisay can't even look me in the eye. It might not be a quality I possess, but I definitely recognize embarrassment when I see it.

I'm there, 'Dalisay, you had a little nip – I wouldn't worry about it.'

'If they find out,' she goes, 'I will lose my job.'

'I'm hordly likely to complain, am I? I mean, I wasn't exactly shoving you off me.'

'I crossed a line –'

'I've crossed many lines. I've crossed many, many, many lines.'

'I don't know why I did it.'

'Look, don't be hord on yourself. A lot of girls get the urge to kiss me.'

'Do they?'

'A hell of a lot. Ask around. It's not a biggie.'

'So you will not report me?'

'Report you? Dalisay, I was, like, fully into it at the time.'

My phone beeps. It's, like, a text message from Roz, who got in from Gstaad in the early hours. She's like, 'Happy birthday, my love x.'

Dalisay goes, 'It won't happen again.'

And I'm there, 'Well, let's not go making rash promises. How's the old dear this morning?'

She's like, 'She is very tired today,' and I follow her – yeah, no – into her room.

She's asleep on the bed with – oh, for fock's sake – the top buttons of her dressing-gown opened to the point where I can see her left stonk sticking out of it.

I'm like, 'Jesus Christ, can you maybe –?'

Dalisay rushes over to her, going, 'Fionnuala, I am just going to button you up.'

That's when the old dear wakes up and she storts getting a bit – this is a definite Ronan word – but *obstreperous*?

She's like, 'Who the fock are you? Take your filthy hands off my jewellery!'

Dalisay goes, 'She is very confused when she wakes up. Sadly, it is all part of her dementia.'

But then I'm thinking, it might *not* be? She used to think all foreigners were trying to steal from her. I think she went through about three hundred cleaners during the course of my childhood. At one point she had, like, an airport body-scanner fitted at what she used to call the tradesman's entrance at the side of the house. Everyone who was born outside of the country or born working class had to pass through it as they were leaving the gaff.

I don't mention that, though, in case it sounds racist.

Dalisay goes, 'You are here, Fionnuala. You are safe. Your son has come to see you.'

She's like, 'Ross? Where are you?'

I'm there, 'Yeah, no, I'm *here*?' and I take a couple of steps forward.

She goes, 'Oh, good – because I know what day it is today. It's your birthday.'

It's, like, so random the things that she can and can't remember.

Dalisay goes, 'Do you want to sit up, Fionnuala?' and I help her winch the old dear up in the bed.

'It's his *fortieth* birthday!' the old dear goes. 'Isn't that right, Ross?'

I'm like, 'That's right – the big four-oh!'

Dalisay smiles at me across the bed and goes, 'Happy birthday, Ross!'

The old dear's like, 'Oh, don't encourage him, Dalisay. He'll be trying to get your knickers off like that ghastly man.'

I'm there, 'What ghastly man is this?'

'This awful, awful person,' the old dear goes, 'who Valerie Amburn-James has got herself mixed up with.'

I'm like, 'Oh, this is in your book.'

'It's not my book. It's this other Fionnuala person's. You know, I think she's sexually frustrated.'

'So you said.'

'Now, I'm sorry, Ross, but I have nothing for you because I've been so busy here that I haven't been able to get out to the shops.'

'I don't need a present.'

She goes, 'You know, Dalisay, I put on thirty-four pounds when I was pregnant with Ross.'

I'm like, 'Yeah, no, you don't have to tell the story of my birth again,' because it's had more airings that the nativity story at this point.

She's there, 'I had cravings, you see. Chocolate profiteroles. Sixty or seventy a day. By the third trimester, I was –'

I'm like, 'Ninety percent choux pastry,' because I'm hearing it for the thousandth time.

She goes, '– ninety per cent choux pastry. I was ten days overdue when he finally decided to make an appearance. And he chose to do it when I was in –'

I'm like, 'The National Gallery.'

'– the National Gallery,' she goes. 'With my friend, Angela. I was standing in front of Gabriël Metsu's *Woman Reading a Letter* when I felt this very, very intense urge to pee. But it turned out it wasn't an urge to pee.'

I'm there, 'Her waters had broken.'

'I literally flooded the floor,' she goes. 'Buckets and buckets of the stuff. Angela, my friend, said, "We'd better get you to Holles Street." And I said, "Oh no you focking won't! I'm going to Mount Cormel or I'm going nowhere!" But there wasn't time!'

I'm there, '*It was rush-hour*,' and I'm doing an impression of her now.

'It was rush-hour,' she goes. 'I remember gripping her hand in the back of the taxi – I might have even sunk my nails in – and I said, "Angela, in the name of all that is holy, do *not* bring me to focking Holles Street!" But by that stage, I think the head was already showing, so Holles Street it had to be. And it was even worse than I thought it'd be. Some of the things I witnessed in there, I'll never forget.'

Clearly, I think. Even dementia hasn't dislodged the details from her mind.

She goes, 'I saw babies coming out of the womb –'

I'm there, '*With tiny little cigarettes burning between their fingers.*'

She's like, '– with tiny little cigarettes burning between their fingers.'

Dalisay smiles. I think she gets a good kick out of our double-act.

'And it was straight into the delivery room,' the old dear goes, 'and my feet were put in the stirrups.'

I'm like, 'Okay, let's maybe leave the story there, will we? Did I tell you I'm having a porty on Saturday night? In Finglas, of all places. Yeah, no, Ronan's throwing it for me in the function room at the back of the Broken Orms.'

She goes, 'The second I storted pushing – oh Jesus, it storted coming out of every focking orifice. There was shit and piss and sick everywhere.'

I'm like, 'Mom, can you maybe *not*?'

She's there, 'I said to Conor –'

'You said to Chorles.'

'– that this would be my first and last pregnancy. If there was to be any more of that business between us, he would have to have a focking vasectomy.'

She stops talking, then a second or two later this confused look comes over her face and her eyes are suddenly all glassy.

She goes, 'Who's Ronan?'

I'm there, 'Ronan is my son.'

'No, Honor is your son – he's been here.'

'No, Honor is my daughter.'

'What, she's a girl?'

'Of course she's a girl. Ronan is my eldest son.'

'I don't think I've met him.'

'You've met him loads of times. He calls you Fidooda.'

'Why does he call me Fidooda?'

'Because he's from, like I said, Finglas.'

'You won't let him anywhere near my jewellery, will you, Ross?'

I laugh. I can't help it.

I'm like, 'No, Mom, I won't.'

I watch her close her eyes. She's worn out already. And I stort thinking about what Roz said about getting a crew together – we're talking family, we're talking friends, we're talking maybe even fans of her books – to let people say goodbye to her while she's still *kind* of here?

Dalisay goes, 'Now we must let her sleep.'

So me and Ronan are in the toilets of the Broken Orms in Finglas and – yeah, no – we're getting ready for the porty.

I'm like, 'What do you think?' checking out my humungous stick-on eyebrows in the mirror.

He goes, 'Throw on the hat theer.'

So – yeah, no – I throw on the bucket hat.

'Moy Jaysus,' he goes, 'you're the ibage of Liam Gaddagher, Rosser.'

I'm like, 'Right – and you're the image of Noel,' because it's actually uncanny.

I'm there, 'Where did you get all of this clobber anyway?'

'A cousint of Nudger's was the thrummer in No Way Sis,' he goes, adjusting his wig in the mirror. 'Thee were a thribute band from Deerndale back in the day.'

With the stick-on sideburns, he looks the definite port.

'I belieb you reng Avoddy,' he goes.

There's no point in me denying it. But I give it a shot anyway.

I'm there, 'Avery?' raising a giant caterpillar eyebrow. 'I honestly haven't spoken to that girl since –'

He goes, 'She toawult me she was thalken to you, Rosser – the utter day.'

I'm like, 'Fine – yeah, no, I rang her, but only because I was worried about you.'

'She said you were reading me bleaten text messages as weddle.'

'Correction – I read one text message. It popped up on your screen. She said you needed to get out of Ireland or you could spend the rest of your life in prison.'

'It's nutting to woody about, Rosser.'

'She mentioned treason.'

'Ah, she overreacted, Rosser.'

'You're not going to tell me what it's about, then?'

'It's gubbermint bidiness, Rosser. I caddent discuss it with you. Hee-or, what do you think?'

He puts on a pair of round glasses with, like, red lenses in them. He's an absolute ringer for Noel – or Noelt, as he calls him – just like I'm the spits of Liam.

I'm there, 'Yeah, no, you look the definite port. Dude, there's no point in telling me that it's nothing to worry about. I worry about you in the same way that you worry about Rihanna-Brogan.'

'Look, alls it is,' he goes, 'is a birrof a diplomathic thing to be woorked out. It'll be sorthed, Rosser – be moostard.'

I'm there, 'But you're back texting Avery again, huh?'

'That was a woodence-off.'

'Just like the strip club was a once-off, huh?'

'Rosser, please, just leab it for toneet, will you?'

And that's when I hear the bus pull up outside.

I'm there, 'That'll be everyone. It was picking them all up outside Madigan Square Gorden.'

He laughs and goes, 'Because God forbid thee should spend addy mower toyum on the northside than thee hab to!'

I laugh and I'm like, 'Amen to that, Dude.'

We head out into the function room. We're the only ones here. The DJ is playing 'Livin' La Vida Loca' by Ricky Mortin. A minute later, the doors open and in they all troop, all my crew, in fancy-dress. It takes me a good while to recognize some of them, although I spot the goys straight away, dressed up as the Spice Girls, we're talking Christian as Scary – although he hasn't blacked up – Fionn as Sporty, JP as Posh, Magnus as Baby and Oisinn – absolutely bet into a tiny Union Jack dress – as Ginger.

It's, like, high-fives and chest-bumps all round. Christian says that me and Ronan make a great Liam and Noel and I tell Oisinn that he's managed to cure me of my obsession with Geri Halliwell and that Magnus has managed to do something similar for my pigtails fetish, which he finds hilarious.

I'm looking around the room and it's great to see that everyone has made the effort. Chloe, Sophie, Amie with an ie – and then three random birds I don't recognize but have almost certainly had sex with – have come as the characters from *Friends*. Claire from Bray of all places and Garret – her complete and utter knob of a boyfriend – have dressed up as Buzz Lightyear and Woody from, like, *Toy Story*. One F has come as Austin Powers. Lauren and Ross Junior have come as Anakin Skywalker and Queen Amidala from *The Phantom Menace*. And Jamie Heaslip and Seán O'Brien – focking priceless! – have come as the two dudes out of *Wayne's World*, and Dave Kearney – it was good of him to come, given that I'm pretty sure I'm fighting with his brother at the moment – has turned up in a pair of MC Hammer trousers.

'Ah, here's the boys,' Ronan suddenly goes and I turn around to see his crew come through the double doors – we're talking Nudger, we're talking Gull, we're talking Buckets of Blood, dressed as characters from *Lock, Stock and Two Smoking Barrels*. Buckets is great as Vinny Jones – he even has two fake sawn-off shotguns, although, when I think about it, I realize that they're almost certainly real.

I turn around to the bor and I catch Benny 'Stacks of Money' McCabe's eye.

He goes, 'Where did you peerk the boat, Rosser?'

Seriously, it's getting really old at this stage.

I'm there, 'On the focking Tolka, Dude. Can we get some Hanijans out here?'

And that's when he says *the* most incredible thing.

He goes, 'No Hanijan toneet, Rosser. Heideken addy good to you?'

I look at the goys. JP's mouth is open, forming a perfect O, which makes him look even more like Victoria Beckham.

We're all like, 'Heineken? Where the fock did you get Heineken?'

Stacks goes, 'From that madden behoyunt you theer.'

I turn around and who's standing there only the old man and Hennessy, the old man dressed as Bravehort – with the blue-and-white face paint – and Hennessy just in his regular civvies.

I'm there, 'How did you get your hands on it?'

'Twelve fooken baddles of the stuff,' Stacks goes.

The old man's there, 'Well, what's the point in being the leader of a country,' and he says it in this terrible Scottish accent, 'if you cannae enjoy the occasional privilege, eh, Ross!'

I get this sudden flashback to the six weeks he spent on the stand at the Mahon Tribunal and how he used to get up at, like, five o'clock every morning to watch *Bravehort* to psych himself up for his evidence that day.

He goes, 'Happy fortieth birthday, Kicker!'

I'm like, 'Yeah, no, whatever.'

Hennessy says nothing. His eyes – along with everyone else's – are drawn to Erika, who's walking across the floor dressed up as Britney Spears in the sexy schoolgirl outfit.

'Focking hell,' I hear myself go. 'Jesus focking –' and I make a beeline for her.

The song playing is 'Ooh Aah . . . Just a Little Bit' by Gina G.

She goes, 'Happy birthday, Ross.'

I'm like, 'I've had this exact dream. You in this outfit. Loads of times, in fact.'

She gives me a peck on the cheek and a hug and goes, 'For one night of the year, Ross, can you *not* act like a weirdo?'

I'm there, 'Yeah, no, sorry.'

She goes, 'It's bad enough being in the same room as *him*,' meaning the old man, 'and Hennessy – and Sorcha,' and she looks around for her.

I'm there, 'She's not here yet. She's driving over – as is Roz, by the way, with Honor and Sincerity.'

Erika goes, 'Oh my God, look at Ro dressed as Noel Gallagher! Did you talk to him yet?'

I'm like, 'As in?'

'About what Avery meant – when she mentioned treason?'

'Yeah, no, he wouldn't tell me anything.'

The old man gives her a smile and a wave, but she looks away, while Hennessy looks her up and down, licking his lips and doing fock-knows-what to her in his mind.

She goes, 'Okay, I'm going to go and talk to Ronan myself,' and off she goes, leaving me with a boner on me like a focking Pringles can.

The cast of *Friends* arrive over to me while I'm throwing back my second pint of the night. Amie with an ie wishes me a happy birthday and then immediately takes it back by telling me that I'm losing my looks.

She goes, 'I always said, back in the day, when you were the goy every girl wanted to be with, that your looks would be gone by the time you hit forty.'

I'm about to tell her that she's no Jennifer Aniston and that wig is focking wasted on her when Chloe turns around and goes, 'Hey, Ross, did you hear I'm on the spectrum?' like it's something that I should be *congratulating* her about?

Sophie goes, 'Oh my God, I forgot to tell you, the girl who colours my hair got tested as well. I think it was, like, a birthday present from her husband. And she's on the spectrum too!'

'Oh! My God!' Chloe suddenly goes. 'Here's Sorcha with her new boyfriend! Could he *be* any hotter?'

Which, by the way, is the only reason I know that she's supposed to be Chandler. Otherwise, she's just a girl wearing a dude's clothes.

Sorcha comes over to us with the famous Mike and – yeah, no – surprise, sur-focking-prise, he's in his pilot's outfit yet again and she's just wearing a leather flight jacket over a white t-shirt with a frizzy blonde wig.

The song playing is 'All That She Wants' by Ace of Base.

'Oh! My God!' Chloe goes. 'Could you *be* any more Tom Cruise and Kelly McGillis?'

Sorcha gives me a big smile and a kiss on both cheeks, then a hug and goes, 'Happy fortieth, Ross! Oh my God, is that Heineken? Where did you get actual Heineken?' and the others are all staring at me to see what my reaction to Mike is going to be.

I'm there, 'Dude, I honestly have never seen you *not* dressed as a pilot.'

He goes, 'Happy birthday, Ross,' offering me his hand. I take it. 'This is some turnout.'

Again, I'm momentarily mesmerized by his voice. I just find it really, really soothing.

I snap out of it and I go, 'Wasn't *Top Gun* more of, like, an eighties thing?'

Chloe goes, 'Oh my God, Ross, could you *be* any more jealous?'

It's becoming *very* focking annoying.

I'm like, 'I'd hordly say that I'm –' and that's when Claire and Garret arrive over – Buzz and focking Woody – and Sorcha introduces them to Mike.

'Oh my God,' Claire goes, 'I have heard *so* much about you!'

Chloe, Sophie and Amie with an ie just stare at her. They hate her for refusing to stick to her own side of the Dorgle and who can blame them?

She's like, 'Sorcha, did you hear the news? Garret and I are setting up a coffee shop on the seafront in Bray and it's going to be run by sex offenders!'

At least that's what I *think* I hear?

I'm there, 'A coffee shop run by sex offenders?'

'By *ex*-offenders,' he goes. 'They're people who've been to prison – usually as a result of addiction or mental health issues – and we're giving them a second chance.'

I'm there, 'Because I was going to say, a coffee shop run by sex offenders would be a hord sell – even in Bray.'

'Oh! My God!' Chloe goes. 'Could you *be* any funnier?'

And that's when I decide to go back to the bor. As I move away, Sorcha tells me that she has something for me and that she's given it to Ronan.

I'm like, 'What is it in relation to, Sorcha?'

But she goes, 'It's a surprise,' and she gives me an incredible smile. 'I can't wait to see your reaction.'

I'm storting my third pint of Heineken – God, I've missed the stuff – when Lauren and Ross Junior sidle up to the bor beside me.

The song playing is 'We Like to Porty' by The Vengaboys.

Ross Junior goes, 'Roth, I'm drethed up ath Anakin Thkywalker and my mom ith drethed up ath Queen Amithala.'

I'm like, 'Yeah, no, I can see that, kid,' because Lauren is staring at me and she knows I think he's a focking weirdo, despite everything I tried to do for him as his godfather.

He goes, 'Doethn't she look really thexthy, Roth?'

I'm there, 'Er – yeah, no – I suppose she does look sexy,' because she hates it when I ignore him. She expects everyone to validate the kid. 'Very focking sexy.'

He goes, 'I thold her before we left the houth that I would marry her like Anakin Thywalker married Queen Amithala in *The Phantom Menath*.'

Jesus focking Christ, I think – although I suppose I'm one to talk, given my obsession with my half-sister, who I can't help but notice is chatting away to Buckets of Blood in the corner. She seems to be – what the fock? – flirting with the dude, laughing at his one-liners and letting him touch her without threatening to break his orm in three places. And you can see that *he* is loving the attention.

'Sorry we're late,' I hear a voice go.

I turn around and it ends up being Roz, dressed as Slash from Guns N' – yeah, no – Roses and Honor and Sincerity dressed up as the – like I said before – John Travolta and Uma Thurman characters from *Pulp Fiction*.

I'm like, 'You look amazing!' and that's directed at all three of them.

Roz goes, 'I'm so sorry we're late. Honor had a bit of a panic attack when we were driving over the Rosie Hackett Bridge.'

I'm like, 'Yeah, no, I usually take the M50 when we have to drive northside – that way, she has no idea when we've crossed the Liffey, aport from a – as she says herself – vague sense of *foreboding?*'

Roz wishes me a happy birthday, as does Honor and as does Sincerity, and it ends up being hugs and air-kisses all round.

Honor's like, 'Oh my God, Dad, you are *so* focking old!'

I laugh, and I can feel Sorcha and Chloe and Sophie and Amie with an ie – but mostly Sorcha – staring over, taking a massive interest in what's going on.

And, meanwhile, I'm doing the same to Erika, who's still chatting away to Buckets of Blood, laughing at his jokes, fluttering her eyelids at him, touching him on the orm to tell him to stop – oh my God! – being *so* funny.

The song is '2 Become 1' by the Spice Girls.

I'm thinking, she's not going to *be* with him, is she? Focking Buckets? A literally debt-collector whose business cord refers to him as The Attitude Adjuster. Even though – having said all that – I've a hell of a lot of time for the dude.

Roz suddenly goes, 'Oh my God, why are you staring at your sister like that?'

I'm there, 'Like what?'

Then I end up being rescued by – of all people – my old man. The music stops and the dude suddenly has the mic in his hand and he's going, 'Ladies and gentlemen – if I could just have your attention for a moment! As I said in the Convention Centre recently, when Deputy Varadkar asked me whether the Irish people might be offered a second referendum on EU membership, I will be brief!'

Everyone laughs. People like the dude – I've never *understood* why?

He goes, 'Forty years is, em, a relatively short period of time! And yet, in that time, Ross has achieved so much! Who will ever forget his try against St Mary's in the 1999 Leinster Schools Senior Cup? Or his penalty from fifty metres out against Gonzaga – same competition, same year? Or his drop goal against Newbridge College – also in the 1999 Leinster Schools Senior Cup?'

I'm like, 'Jesus Christ, is winning the 1999 Leinster Schools Senior Cup the only thing I've achieved in your eyes?'

Brian, Johnny and Leo wander over to me. I put my orms around them and pull them close to me. They're wearing Republic of Ireland soccer jerseys, which is obviously a reference to Italia '90, which I wasn't allowed to watch as a kid. Yeah, no, the old man was terrified that I'd find something I loved more than rugby, so he took the plug off the TV for the month.

He finishes up his speech, going, 'And I am desperately, desperately proud of him – as I am of all of my children!' and I notice Erika giving him a serious filthy from the other side of the room. 'Happy birthday, Kicker!'

And everyone laughs and goes, 'Happy birthday, Kicker!'

The dude hands the mic to Ronan, who then makes his own speech.

He goes, 'The foorst toyum I ebber met Rosser, he turdened up at the house in Figglas in he's sailing jacket and he's sailing shoes and I remember I says to me ma, "Who's this sham?" and she says, "This is your fadder, Ronan." And I says to her, "This bleaten flute? Moy fooken Jaysus – what were you thinking, Ma?"'

Everyone cracks their hole laughing, including Tina, by the way, who's come as Ali G, and Tom, her fireman boyfriend, who's come as Hulk Hogan.

Ro goes, 'Oaber the years – and meddy, meddy unsupervised access days, spent mostly in Dr Quirkey's Goodtoyum Empordium, me booting the fook out of the Coin Cascades to make the muddy fall – me and Rosser clicked. Mathor of fact, it's mower thrue to say, we bonded. And now I look back on the day he knocked on the doher as the most impowartant day of moy life.'

Fock, I'm already in tears here.

He goes, 'I've nebber calt him Da – it was altways Rosser, because to me he's altways been a mate, the best mate I ebber had. But I know that to him, I am, foorst and foremost, he's sudden. He nebber stops woodying about me, joost like he nebber stops woddying about Hodor, Brian, Johnny and Leo. You can say what you like abourrum – and quite a few wooben out theer have had loawuts to say –'

That gets a humungous laugh.

'– but he's the best fadder in the wurdled. And that's why I joost wanthed to take this opportudity to say, Thanks – and Happy Boortday . . . Da.'

There's, like, a huge roar followed by a round of applause. I wipe away tears and I go to grab the mic from him.

He goes, 'Hang on, Rosser – foorst, I've a little surproyuz for you. Wooden peerson who woulda luvven to be hee-or toneet but unfortunately caddent is your mutter, Fidooda. Which is why Sudeka throve out to Ongar this morden to record a little video wirrer.'

I look around for Sorcha and I catch her eye and smile at her. Then, suddenly, up on the TV screen on the wall pops the old dear's face.

She goes, 'Hello! What, do I just talk to this thing? Happy birthday to my beautiful, beautiful boy, Ross – my pride and joy for forty years!' and I am instantly in floods. 'I remember the day he was born. I was screaming, "Don't bring me to focking Holles Street!" Anyway, I hope you have a lovely day,' and she sort of, like, blows a kiss to the camera, then just before the recording is ended, she goes, 'Which one are you, then? Has he tried to have sex with you? He tries to have sex with everyone, you know?'

Everyone finds this absolutely hilarious, of course.

I grab the mic with just, like, tears streaming down my face and I go to say something, except no actual words come out of my mouth.

Ronan shouts, 'Quick! Purron 'Woddender Waddle'!' and then five seconds later – like he said – "Wonderwall" comes on and he throws his orm around my shoulder and the two of us stort belting out the words like Noel and Liam.

It ends up being quite possibly the best night of my life – and in Finglas! It's, like, who'd have predicted it?

Just before midnight, the old man tips over to me and tells me that he has to be off because he has a video conference with Vladimir Putin in the morning. Even with all the face paint on him, I can tell that he's rattled from seeing the old dear's face.

I'm there, 'I'm going to arrange a living funeral for her.'

He goes, 'What on Earth is a living funeral?'

I'm there, 'Er, it's *like* a funeral? Except all the mourners sit around and say nice things about the person while they're still here.'

I watch tears stort to form in his eyes, then they stort spilling down his cheeks, ruining his make-up.

He's like, 'I, em, have to –' and he turns to leave.

Ronan goes, 'Doatunt go addywheer yet, Cheerlie,' and – yeah, no – he has the mic in his hand again. 'Hodor and her friend Siddencedity hab a little surproyuz for us. Hit the music theer.'

Honor and Sincerity walk to the middle of the dancefloor to a humungous round of applause. Sincerity steps out of her shoes – just like Uma Thurman does in the actual movie. Then they stand opposite each other and the music comes on.

This, like, wave of excitement hits the function room. Everyone's like, 'Whoa!' because they have every single step absolutely perfect.

I notice Sorcha walking towards me, her face absolutely beaming with pride and seeming to say, 'Can you believe that's our daughter out there?'

She's just about to open her mouth when someone on the other side of me grabs my hand and – yeah, no – it ends up being Roz. She looks so excited.

She goes, 'That's our daughters out there!'

I'm like, 'Yeah, no, I know.'

She goes, 'I missed you, Ross.'

I'm there, 'I missed you too,' and I kiss her on the lips.

And, out of the corner of my eye – again, using the peripheral vision that so mesmerized Denis Hickie – I watch Sorcha pull a disappointed face, then turn and walk away.

Sorhca's sister rings me and she asks me – yeah, no, she actually *tells* me? – to meet her in Storbucks in Blackrock at eleven o'clock.

I'm like, 'What's the occasion?'

But she goes, 'Just focking be there,' because, like I said, it's not an invitation. 'I have some big news for you.'

I'm there, 'Big news? What kind of –?'

But she hangs up on me and I end up having to drive there in an absolute daze, my pulse racing, my hands literally trembling on the wheel, knowing in my hort of horts that Oisinn's and Magnus's

DNA results have come through and I'm about to find out if I'm the father of their baby.

I drive past Blackrock College and I don't even raise my middle finger – that's what a state I'm in. When I hit the next orange light, I don't fly through it like I *usually* would? I decide that I need to be forewarned, so I send Oisinn a text, going, 'Any news?'

There ends up being no reply from him. I throw the cor into a space on Idrone Terrace and I somehow manage to feed the coins into the meter with my trembling fingers.

A minute or so later, I walk through the door of Buckys and I spot her straight away. She's sitting at the back of the place with the famous baby in her orms.

She gives it to me straight away – we're talking both barrels.

She's like, 'So now it's confirmed – you're Paavo's father.'

I end up making this noise. It's not exactly a *scream*? It's, like, a painful yowl. I've only ever made it once before and that was the night Sorcha went to pull me off as a birthday treat but forgot that she'd been chopping chillies an hour earlier for her famous Otto-lenghi rendang beef.

It's like an animal's dying agonies.

She goes, 'Sit down – everyone is looking.'

Which is true. It's Blackrock, bear in mind.

I'm there, 'We don't know that it's me. I haven't taken a test.'

'Well,' she goes, 'Oisinn's test came back negative and Magnus's test came back negative. So that just leaves –'

She puts her finger to her lips and pulls a face like she's me trying to add three numbers.

I'm there, 'Not necessarily. You might have slept with someone else.'

She's like, 'Are you calling me a slut, Ross?'

'No, I'm not calling you a slut. I'm just saying that, you know, until I take the actual test myself, we'll never know for sure – so I'm just not going to take the test.'

'Do you want to hold him?'

'No, I don't want to hold him.'

'Ross, you're hyperventilating.'

'It's a shock, that's all.'

'Come on, Ross, you knew all along he was yours. Now we need to decide what we're going to do.'

'In terms of what?'

'Are we going to get married?'

'Married?'

'You have to marry me, Ross. You've ruined me.'

'But I'm still married to your sister.'

'But you're getting divorced, aren't you?'

'Yeah, but –'

'I can't wait to see the look on her face when I tell her that you're Paavo's father.'

'Jesus.'

'Are we going to buy a house?'

'A house? What, together?'

She goes, 'Er, I *hordly* think my parents are going to let me carry on living in Honalee when they find out that I got pregnant by Little Miss Perfect's husband.'

I'm there, 'Shit, I need to think about this.'

She's like, 'You've had plenty of time to think, Ross.'

And that's when I hear my phone ring in my pocket. I whip it out. Shit – it's, like, Oisinn.

I answer it, sounding – yeah, no – *cautious*?

I'm like, 'Yo, Big O, I was only texting to find out was there any news.'

He goes, 'Yeah, we got word from the clinic this morning,' and he sounds so low that I wonder will the dude ever know happiness again.

I'm there, 'Dude, I'm genuinely, *genuinely* sorry.'

But then – out of nowhere – he storts laughing and I can hear Magnus in the background laughing as well.

I'm like, 'Dude, what the fock?'

And he goes, 'I was yanking your chain, Ross! Paavo is our son! Well, technically, Magnus is the father, but you know what I mean!'

I'm there, 'Jesus! That's . . . that's . . .' and I'm looking across the table at Sorcha's sister, who's got a big grin on her face, '. . . focked up.'

I hear Magnus go, 'What doesh he mean by focked up?'

I'm like, 'Yeah, no, I meant that in a good way. I'm delighted for you, Dudes.'

Oisinn's there, 'We're on our way to Blackrock – to collect him from Sorcha's sister!'

I'm like, 'Yeah, no, I can't wait to meet him – properly, like.'

Oisinn hangs up on me.

I'm like, 'What the actual –?'

Sorcha's sister shrugs and goes, 'I was just focking with you. I wanted to see what your reaction would have been.'

'So he's *not* mine?'

'Well, if his DNA is a perfect match with Magnus's DNA, then he can't be, can he?'

'I don't know, I was wondering –?'

'What?'

'Well, the day I rode you, or the day we had sex down in Brittas, I was wondering could any of my DNA have somehow gotten into the baby's bloodstream?'

'Jesus, did they teach Biology in your school?'

'I've no idea. I was on the Senior Cup team.'

The story of my life.

I'm there, 'So what's happening – you're just going to hand him over to them?'

She goes, 'That was the deal.'

I'm like, 'In a Storbucks, though?'

She goes, 'Doesn't matter where we do it. It'll still break my hort.'

I know I shouldn't, but I suddenly feel sorry for her.

I'm there, 'You and him – I'm talking about Paavo – really bonded, didn't you?'

She goes, 'Of course we did. I'm his mother, Ross – whatever else I might be.'

I'm there, 'So what are you going to do?'

She's like, 'I got my passport renewed this morning,' and she takes the thing out of her jacket pocket and puts it down on the table. 'I'm going to go back to Australia.'

I'm like, 'Are you serious?'

'There's nothing here for me – not now.'

'What about Paavo? You've presumably got rights.'

'I'm sure Oisinn and Magnus wouldn't want me in his life. And I wouldn't blame them – after what I've put them through.'

'You've still got your family here.'

'Ross, I get a sexual thrill thinking about my sister walking in on me while I'm having sex with her husband. Does that sound like a normal family to you?'

'Who's to say what a normal family is? I mean, *I'd* be the last person.'

There's a real, I don't know, hopelessness about her and I feel like nearly giving her a hug.

She goes, 'I saw all the photographs from your fortieth.'

I'm there, 'Honor and Sincerity stole the show. Did you see the video?'

'On Sorcha's Insta,' she goes. 'Yeah, no, I did.'

Then, completely out of nowhere, she goes, 'So does my sister know that her daughter is a lesbian?'

I'm there, 'A lesbian?' pretending that I've no idea what she's even talking about. 'What makes you think –?'

She goes, 'Oh, please, Ross! I'm ninety per cent that way myself. I can see it even if my sister can't. There's nothing wrong with it, by the way.'

'I know there's nothing wrong with it.'

'Good for Honor. She'll have a much happier life having fock-all to do with men.'

'You're not going to tell Sorcha, are you?'

'Come on, Ross. I might be a bitch but I'm not a focking orsehole.'

'That's true – in fairness to you.'

'I can imagine her reaction, though. *I had, like, loads of gay friends in UCD.*'

I laugh. It's funny, in all fairness. Then I suddenly find myself staring down at her passport on the table and I end up having one of my famous brainwaves. Her name. It's right there underneath that green cover.

I reach for the thing, going, 'Oh, are these the new non-EU Irish passports? I haven't seen one yet!'

I flip it open and I see her picture and then my eyes look for her name. I see it there. It's –

And just as my eyes manage to focus on it, she whips the thing out of my hand.

She's like, 'You'd better go. Oisinn and Magnus will be here any minute.'

It's, like, a freezing cold morning on Killiney Hill. One of those ones where you can see your breath in front of your face and feel the crunch of frost under your Dubes.

We're the last to arrive and the entire crew is waiting in the cor pork for us – we're talking Christian with Ross Junior and Oliver, we're talking JP with Isa, we're talking Fionn with Hillary, we're talking Oisinn and Magnus with little Paavo and we're talking Erika with Amelie.

I pork the cor. Honor gets out of the front and Brian, Johnny and Leo get out of the back.

Johnny goes, '*Es ist eiskalt!*'

And I'm like, 'Speak English, guys. It's not fair on everyone else if the three of you are chatting away in your own secret language. And, remember, this isn't a focking nature trail. The idea is all of us getting together with our kids, so I don't want you banging on about acorns and whatever else.'

A year ago, they'd have told me to go and fock myself and probably flipped me off as well – you couldn't tell them anything – but now the three of them just nod, meek as lambs.

Everyone is making a fuss of Paavo. Erika is having a little hold and – yeah, no – JP is asking Oisinn and Magnus how the little lad is sleeping.

Oisinn goes, 'He's up all night, screaming the house down, but we honestly don't care. We're just happy to have him.'

I'm there, 'He's possibly pining for his mother,' and I know instantly that I've said the wrong thing.

Christian goes, 'What's the story with Sorcha's sister?'

And Magnus is like, 'She hash gone back to Aushtralia. And, by the way, Rosh, we told her that we were happy to forget the pasht and she should play a full and active part in hish life.'

Oisinn's there, 'We even told her that she could move back in with us.'

Yeah, no, that'd be just like them. You wouldn't find two more decent blokes.

'Shadly,' Magnus goes, 'she shaid no – she'd prefer to cut her tiesh altogether,' and then he catches Honor's eye and goes, 'Your dansh at the party was fantashtic. You and your friend shtole the show, yeah?'

Erika's like, 'Hear, hear!' and Honor smiles. She loves a compliment. The apple doesn't fall far from the tree.

We stort walking and – yeah, no – it's lovely to see all of our children mixing with each other. Oliver is chasing Amelie – he clearly has an eye for her – and Honor is holding Hillary by the hand. Leo points out a squirrel to Ross Junior and I end up having to go, 'What did I say about this not being a nature walk?'

He's like, 'Sorry, Daddy!' and that's, like, word for word.

Christian's there, 'The difference in those boys, Ross.'

I'm like, 'I know, right? Sorcha's old man has focking ruined them.'

'I don't know about that. They were an absolute nightmare before.'

'I actually preferred them when they were a nightmare. They're being bullied, Christian.'

'What?'

Yeah, no, I tell him about Morcus and his mates and the three empty savings boxes. And, in fairness to him, he goes, 'Fock!'

I'm there, 'A year ago, they'd have torn this dude's orms out of his focking sockets. Now, the three of them just stand there and let him do whatever he wants to them.'

I look over my shoulder and Fionn is walking just behind us.

I'm there, 'What's the story with you and that dentist one?' just making conversation. 'It's really pissed me off, by the way.'

He's like, 'Why has it pissed you off?'

'Because I saw her first.'

'How old are you? Six?'

'I not only saw her, I laid the groundwork for you.'

'By asking her where she did her socializing?'

'That and other questions. What's her name again?'

'Her name is Sinead.'

'And does she ever mention me? As in, would I have had a shot if I hadn't left with JP that night?'

'Ross, you're going out with someone.'

'I'd still love to know.'

'Believe it or not, it hasn't come up, Ross.'

'Hell hath no fury – blah, blah, blah.'

Hillary says he's tired and I bend down and pick him up and tell him we'll be stopping for hot chocolate soon.

JP is up ahead, walking with Isa. I catch up with him.

I'm like, 'What's the story, Dude? No word from hopefully Delma, no?'

He's there, 'Nothing. I'm still thinking of going to London – to look for her.'

'Take the hint, Dude. She's not coming back to you.'

'I need to hear it from *her*, Ross. I can't move on until I do.'

A few minutes later, we stop at the little coffee shop halfway up the hill. I get the round in – we're talking hot chocolate for the kids and coffee for the grown-ups.

I end up talking to Erika.

I'm there, 'You were getting on very well with Buckets of Blood at the porty, by the way. I was nearly getting jealous.'

She looks at me like I should be in psychiatric care – which I probably should.

She goes, 'I was trying to get information out of him.'

I'm there, 'You were borking up the wrong tree, then. Ronan told me once that Buckets has spent more than a thousand hours being questioned by the Gords in the course of his life and he's never said a single word to them.'

'Well, they clearly don't have what I have.'

'Yeah, no, I saw him checking out your yams. And your legs. Hang on, are you saying he told you something? Fock, was it about Ronan? Does he know what went down in Moscow?'

'No – but he knows who burned down the Dáil.'

'What?'

'He knows who Hennessy hired to do the actual job.'

'Did he give you a name?'

'Not yet. But he will.'

'What does that mean?'

She goes, 'He's asked me out. I'm going for a drink with him on Friday night.'

I'm there, 'Oh my God, you're going to make him fall in love with you!'

Suddenly, I hear this commotion coming from about fifty feet away. All the kids are shouting over at us in these, like, panicky voices.

I hear Honor go, 'Dad! Quick! It's Leo!' and my first thought is that they've run into Morcus and his mates and they've done something to him.

But it ends up not being that at all. As I make my way over to them, the crowd ports to reveal Leo standing there with his tongue – quite literally – stuck to a lamp-post.

I'm like, 'What the fock?'

Ross Junior goes, 'Oliver thold him to lick the lamp-potht,' ratting his little brother out.

I look at Leo – disgusted with him.

'He told you to lick the lamp-post and you just did it?' I go. 'What kind of a focking idiot are you?'

He goes, 'Thime thothy, Thad,' because the thing is really frozen to it.

Brian's there, 'Dad, what are we going to do?'

And I'm like, 'We're going to leave him here,' because I'm bloody furious.

Johnny goes, 'We can't leave him here!' and he storts – I am *so* focking embarrassed – *crying*?

I'm there, 'It's natural selection, Johnny. It separates the weak from the strong.'

But then one or two of the other kids – mainly Ross Junior – stort crying as well and I go, 'Honor, lace over to the shop there and ask them for a cup of boiling water.'

Honor's like, 'Dad, you can't pour boiling water on his tongue.'

Fionn suddenly steps forward. The brains of the operation.

He goes, 'Here, my coffee is cool. This should do the trick.'

'We're not allowed to drink coffee,' Johnny goes.

I'm like, 'He's having a focking coffee and that's that.'

Fionn storts pouring the stuff onto Leo's tongue.

Brian, who's a little focking worrier, goes, 'We have to be home by twelve o'clock because Granddad Lalor has to give us our medication.'

It actually goes straight over my head at first. I'm still too angry with Leo for it to sink in. It's Honor who ends up pulling him up on it.

She's like, 'What medication, Brian?'

He instantly clams up.

I'm there, 'Yeah, no, what medication – good point.'

Honor goes, 'Daddy won't get angry.'

I'm like, 'Whether I do or not is, I don't know, irregordless. Brian, I want to know right now. What medication is Granddad Lalor giving you?'

And Brian goes, 'He's giving us Somnabien – for our ADHD.'

8.

How Many Special People Change?

So this is it. Today is going to be the day when the decking finally happens – me being the decker and Sorcha's old man being the deckee.

He can't say he hasn't had it coming to him.

Honor goes, 'When you say you're going to deck him –?' and I honestly haven't known her to be this excited by someone else's misfortune since her mother got staphylococcal scalded skin syndrome during a skin peel the day before she was supposed to lead the Rosary at the Mount Anville Past Pupils Networking Union's inaugural Bottomless Brunch morning in The Dean Hotel.

I'm there, 'When I say I'm going to deck him, I mean he's going to be decked. He's going to be the subject of a decking and it'll be the decking of a lifetime.'

She goes, 'Oh my God, are you going to hit him?' and she's really, really up for it.

I'm there, 'He has my kids on drugs, Honor. For no reason at all.'

'Well, for Attention Deficit and Hyperactivity Disorder.'

'Whose side are you on, Honor?'

'I'm on your side – especially if you're going to hit him.'

'Focking Somnabien. It's no wonder they've turned into three dry shites.'

I look in the rear-view mirror and – yeah, no – the three of them are sitting in the back with their heads down, not a focking peep out of them.

Honor goes, 'Oh my God, do you know what would be *so* funny? If you were to, like, hit him so hord that he ended up with, like, a brain injury and that stupid bitch he's married to –'

I'm there, 'Legs like the Bride's Glen viaduct. I'm on the record as saying it.'

'– had to push him around in a wheelchair for the rest of his life.'

Yeah, no, she hates them even more than I do?

Five minutes later, I pork the cor in the driveway and get out. I absolutely hammer on the front door. Twenty seconds later, Sorcha answers it.

She goes, 'You're late, Ross. You were supposed to have the boys back an hour ago.'

I'm there, 'I would have done except Leo got his tongue stuck to a focking lamp-post.'

She's like, 'How did that happen?'

I'm there, 'Yeah, like you don't know. Is your old man home?'

'Ross,' she goes. 'I don't need any disruption in my life today. Your dad has called an emergency Cabinet meeting for this afternoon –'

I'm there, 'In the kitchen, is he?' and I borge past her into the house.

He *is* in the kitchen – eating boiled eggs with soldiers while reading the *Irish Times*.

When he hears me step into the room, he obviously thinks it's Sorcha because he goes, 'If the rumours you've heard about a deal with Russia are true, you really need to stort publicly distancing yourself from An Taoiseach, Dorling.'

I'm there, 'I'm not your focking dorling.'

He looks up in fright, but then he sort of, like, resets his features and goes, 'What time do you call this? You're an hour late – and I shall be deducting it from your access time next weekend.'

I'm there, 'Dude, I think it's only fair to warn you that you're about to be decked.'

He must see the anger in my face because he jumps to his feet and he scurries around to the opposite side of the island.

He goes, 'What is the meaning of this?'

By now, Sorcha has taken the boys out of the back of the cor and arrived down to the kitchen to find out what all the shouting is about.

I'm there, 'You put my kids on drugs.'

He actually laughs. He's either very, very brave or very, very foolish.

He goes, 'Are you talking about their medication?'

I'm there, 'Whatever it is that's turned them into weedy little victims with zero craic out of them and zero interest in rugby.'

I look over my shoulder and notice they're standing behind Sorcha in the doorway of the kitchen. I should feel bad for them, but I don't. They *need* to hear this?

'Ross,' Sorcha goes, 'it's only Somnabien.'

I'm like, 'So you did know about this?'

She's there, 'The boys have Attention Deficit and Hyperact –'

I'm like, 'Says who?'

He goes, 'Says the specialist who diagnosed them.'

I'm like, 'And why wasn't I told about this?' and I walk around the other side of the island to try to get within punching distance of her old man, but he moves too, staying well out of range.

Sorcha's there, 'Because you were in total denial about their behaviour.'

'I wasn't in denial,' I go. 'They were three focking brats, that's all.'

Sorcha's like, 'That's not all. They were out of control, Ross. Mom and Dad couldn't bring them anywhere. They were banned from every pork and play centre on this side of the city. They were banned from the Disney Store, from Tayto Pork, from the zoo.'

I'm like, 'They were dicks – I'm not denying that,' and I change direction and try to go around the other side of the island, like Jamison Gibson-Pork sneaking around the blind-side of a scrum. He sees the move – even though he couldn't tell Jamison Gibson-Pork from the Herbert focking Pork – and he sort of scuttles a few feet to his left.

'Look at them now,' he tries to go, because that polished morble countertop is the only thing standing between him and a dislocated jaw and he knows it. 'They're absolutely thriving!'

I'm like, 'They're focking boring,' and I've got my fist cocked and ready to fire.

Sorcha goes, 'We didn't bring children into the world so that they could amuse you, Ross.'

I'm there, 'Well, they don't – not any more.'

That's when Leo, then Johnny, then Brian, all burst into

tears – presumably at the thought of what I'm going to do to their beloved grandfather.

I'm like, 'Listen to that! Three focking wusses.'

He's there, 'They're doing wonderfully well in school,' and he's only digging a bigger hole for himself now.

I'm like, 'They can't even get on the focking hockey team.'

He goes, 'They're polite and mannerly.'

I'm there, 'They're licking focking lamp-posts and being focking bullied.'

'If you're referring to the business of their money-boxes,' he has the actual balls to go, 'I spoke to that boy's mother and she explained that the entire thing was a misunderstanding.'

Sorcha goes, 'Ross, you need to leave now.'

I'm there, 'Just let me hit him once.' And then I look at him and go, 'Just let me get one punch in on you and we'll leave it at that. One punch and we're quits.'

He goes, 'Sorcha, call the Gords,' because he knows if I hit him, there's a chance he wouldn't wake up this side of the summer.

I suddenly make a grab for him across the island and I manage to get a good fistful of his Pringle focking cordigan, then I pull him across the countertop towards me.

Sorcha screams and the three boys stort crying even louder.

The dude's little feet are off the ground and I suddenly don't know my own strength. I drag him across the island with one hand and I'm ready to unload the other one on him when someone suddenly grabs me by the wrist.

I turn around and it ends up being – yeah, no – Mike.

I almost don't recognize him because he's wearing a dressing-gown rather than his work clothes.

I'm there, 'Dude, let go of my hand – the focker has had it coming for a long, long time.'

But Mike just goes, 'Ross, do you really want your children to see you do this?' and – honest to fock – his voice instantly calms me down. 'Look, what's going on between you two is really none of my business. You're upset, Ross, but if you hit him, bear in mind, there's a chance you'll never see your kids again.'

It's like focking catnip. I let go of Sorcha's old man and I uncock my fist.

Mike's like, 'Whatever is wrong, Ross, you can sort it out without resorting to, you know –'

I'm there, 'Decking people.'

'Well, yes.'

'Your voice –'

'My voice?'

I'm there, 'I don't know, it's like a superpower. And that's not a gay thing,' and then I look at Sorcha and I go, 'I like this dude,' and I actually mean it. 'He's a keeper.'

I walk past the boys, who've stopped crying now, then up the hall-way and outside to the cor. Honor is sitting in the front passenger seat.

She goes, 'Did you deck him?'

I'm there, 'Yeah, no, I didn't in the end,' and as I put my hands on the steering wheel, I notice that they're shaking – yeah, no – violently. 'Where were you, by the way? I needed you in there. You could have chased the focker around the other side of the island for me.'

'Well, while you were in the kitchen, shouting your mouth off and then *not* decking him, I went upstairs.'

'Upstairs? Why?'

'I went into his bedroom to get this.'

She opens her hand to reveal – yeah, no – a small white tablet.

I'm there, 'What, you only stole one of them?'

She goes, 'Stealing them wasn't the plan. You're going to switch them – for a placebo.'

I'm like, 'Whoa . . . right . . . very good . . . very, very good.'

She's there, 'You don't know what a placebo is, do you?'

I'm like, 'Not a clue, Honor, no.'

She goes, 'Well, in this case, it's a tablet that looks like the real thing, but it's actually *fake*? I was thinking, these kind of look a bit like Tic Tacs, don't they?'

And I'm there, 'Oh my God, Honor, you are a focking genius.'

So – yeah, no – it's, like, Saturday morning and I'm out for a run with Roz – we're talking from Dún Laoghaire Pier down to the

Joyce Tower, around it and back again. I honestly haven't run since I was coaching the Ireland women's team and it definitely shows, although Roz is being very decent about it, even pretending to have a stitch so it doesn't look like I'm slowing her up.

We're actually taking the steep road to the tower, with the Forty Foot just up ahead of us, when Roz – and this is, like, totally out of the blue – goes, 'I think Sincerity might be a lesbian.'

Oh, fock.

I'm there, 'Er, why do you *think* that – as a matter of interest, like?'

'Oh, she just started asking me all these questions last night about why some girls are into boys but other girls are into girls. And then she asked me how would someone know if they *were* a lesbian.'

'I thought she was going out with what's-his-name – the Protestant?'

'I think she may have cooled on him.'

'That's a pity. I liked him. Like I said, I like all Protestants.'

'Ross, can I tell you something – in confidence, like?'

'Yeah, no, big time.'

'I'm wondering does she like Honor.'

'Er, as in, like, *like* like her?'

'I was looking at the two of them at your fortieth, doing their dance. They just seemed –'

'Seemed what?'

'Well, more than just friends. There was just something about the way that they were looking at each other. What would *your* reaction be, Ross?'

'In terms of?'

'If Honor came to you and told you that she was, like, you know, gay?'

'Honestly, Roz, if Honor told me she'd fallen in love with the fridge, I wouldn't give a monkey's. All I care about is that she's happy.'

'You're an amazing father – you do know that, don't you?'

'Yeah, no, I've always said it's one of the few things that I'm genuinely, genuinely good at.'

'What's that rattling sound, by the way?'

'Rattling sound? Oh, yeah, no, I've got Tic Tacs in my pocket.'

'It sounds like a lot of Tic Tacs.'

'I bought them this morning and meant to throw them in the old glove box.'

'Do you want to stop for a breather?'

'If that's cool with you.'

We've gone right the way around the tower and we stop at the low wall overlooking the tiny beach. There's, like, forty or fifty people in the water, even though it's the middle of January and absolutely freezing. Of course, sea-swimming is suddenly all the rage. Or – as it used to be called – swimming.

Roz puts her foot up on the wall to stretch out her right calf. I stort thinking about those long legs of hers wrapped around the back of my neck and I'm thinking of asking if we could go back to hers for a bit of horizontal refreshment.

'How's your mum?' she goes.

I'm there, 'Yeah, no, I saw her on Friday, although it wasn't a great day for her. She was mostly sleeping and she's got these, like, bed sores on her legs, which are weeping,' and I realize that I've talked myself out of wanting sex.

She goes, 'Is it all arranged – the living funeral, I mean?'

I'm there, 'Yeah, no, I sent out the invites. It's the second Sunday in February.'

She goes, 'I was telling Raymond all about it – I hope you don't mind.'

I'm there, 'Er, no. Er, whatever –' because I've suddenly spotted a familiar face – in fact, *four* familiar faces? – on the other side of the beach. It's, like, Christian and he's sitting on a bench on the concrete platform – and with him are Lauren, Ross Junior and Oliver. Which shouldn't strike me as weird. He's with his kids and – yeah, no – their mother. But there's something about them, all dressed in identical Dryrobes, that has me wondering are Christian and Lauren back together again.

You focking mug, I think to myself.

'Raymond thought it was a beautiful way to honour your mother,' Roz goes – she's been talking the entire time. 'He said he wishes he'd thought of doing something similar for his own mother.'

All of a sudden, her *phone* storts ringing? She has it in one of those, like, ormband phone-holders.

She whips it out and goes, 'Oh! My God! Speak of the devil!' and then she answers it and goes, 'Your ears must have been burning!'

Why can't the focker just leave us to enjoy our day in peace?

She's like, 'Where are you? Oh my God, no way!' and then she looks at me and goes, 'Raymond, Gráinne and Sincerity are having brunch in Fallon & Byrne in the People's Pork!'

If I didn't know better, I'd say he has some kind of GPS tracker hidden somewhere in her cor.

'Yeah, we'll pop in,' she goes – without even asking *me*, by the way? 'We won't stay long, though – it's *your* day with Sincerity.'

She hangs up.

I'm there, 'That's a coincidence, isn't it? Of all the places they could have gone this morning –'

And she's like, 'Oh my God, right?' and she doesn't even pick up on the fact that I'm being a dick about it.

So back down to the People's Pork we tip – we actually run there.

I'm already in a fouler, so much so that I've totally forgotten about my best friend throwing his focking life away by getting back together with his ex-wife.

Raymond stands up with a big grin on his boat when we walk through the door. Gráinne is sitting there with her big space boot propped up on the seat beside her. Sincerity is eating pancakes.

She goes, 'Hi, Ross!' because she's a great kid.

He's like, 'Oh my God, can we get this man a chair? Ross, you look like you're about to have a hort attack!'

What a focking wanker.

I'm there, 'No, I'm fine. I don't need to sit down.'

Roz goes, 'Maybe you should sit down, Ross. You're very red in the face.'

I'm like, 'No, no, you take that chair there. I'm going to go and grab us some menus.'

Raymond goes, 'I'll go with him. Roz, what are you doing to the poor man?' and I hear the legs of his chair scrape off the floor.

I'm standing at the counter and I'm trying to catch the barista's eye when Raymond sidles up beside me.

He goes, 'A thumb tack in my ski boot. That was a bit nasty, Ross, wasn't it?'

I'm there, 'I don't know what you're banging on about.'

'Oh, well, it was poor Gráinne who got the worst of it – as you can see. Any word on your wife's sister's baby? Are congratulations in order?'

I actually laugh.

I'm there, 'It's not mine. Magnus is the father – as in, one of the *sperm* donors?'

This seems to come as a genuine disappointment to him.

I'm like, 'So you can't hold that one over me.'

He's there, 'Oh, there are plenty of other things, Ross. I am going to have so much fun making your life as difficult as I can before you finally take the hint and fock off out of Roz's life.'

The barista raises his eyebrows to me.

I'm there, 'Can I get two menus, please?'

He hands them to me and I head back to the table, where Gráinne is telling Roz that her ankle is healing a lot more slowly than the consultant thought it would and the physio said she's going to have to wear the boot for another four weeks.

I'm there, 'Bummer,' and I suppose I *should* feel bad, but I don't.

Raymond does a bit of a theatrical throat clearance then, like he's got some big announcement to make, which it turns out he *does*?

He goes, 'I have a bit of a surprise for you, Ross. Although I'm a bit worried telling you now, given how much strain you've already put on your hort this morning. I'm afraid you might keel over.'

Roz is there, 'What's the surprise, Raymond?'

And that's when he says it.

He goes, 'I met your brother.'

Roz is like, 'Oh my God! You met Jamie?'

'I met Jamie,' he goes. 'And he is the spitting image of you.'

Roz is like, 'Well, he would be. They're identical twins. How did you meet him?'

'Well,' he goes, really warming up now, 'as you know, I work with Anna, who used to go out with him when Ross here went out with her friend. Vanessa, wasn't it, Ross?'

I'm like, 'Keep going.'

'Well, we were in The Ivy last week – we delayed our Christmas porty until January because we had one or two people out on maternity leave – and who should walk up to our table only –'

'Jamie!' Roz goes – then she looks at me, her mouth slung open like she's singing hosannas.

He's there, 'What a brilliant goy. He's just like you, Ross. Straightforward. There's no sides to him. What you see is what you get.'

Roz goes, 'Was he with Harissa?'

He's like, 'Harissa?'

'Harissa,' she goes. 'As in, his *wife*?'

He's there, 'Oh, Harissa! Yes! And she's absolutely gorgeous – I can see why you two fell out over her, Ross. Anyway, I hope you don't mind, but I mentioned to him that your mother was ill. I kind of put my foot in it. He hadn't heard, Ross. He was in shock.'

Roz goes, 'Oh my God, he doesn't even know his mom has dementia?'

I'm there, 'It's not *my* job to tell him.'

Raymond goes, 'I also mentioned – I'm sorry, I've got such a big mouth – that you were having this living funeral thing for her. And he said – and again, I don't want to interfere – that he would love to go.'

Roz turns to me and she's like, 'Ross, this is it! This is your chance to finally put it behind you!'

I'm there, 'I honestly never want to see the dude again.'

But Roz looks at me like she's disappointed with me.

'Ross,' she goes, 'your brother is reaching out to you. Jesus, you can't deny him the chance to see his mother before she, well –'

I'm there, 'I don't even have his number.'

Raymond grins at me across the table.

He's there, 'Don't worry, I got it! I'll text it to you here.'

Roz goes, 'Ross, please promise me you'll ring him.'

I'm like, 'Yeah, no, fine – I'll try.'

My phone beeps.

Raymond goes, 'He said you can ring him any time, day or night.'

I look at my phone. On the screen is a text message from Raymond. It's, like, three laughing emojis and then it's like: 'How are you going to get out of this one, Houdini?'

I'm looking at the Tic Tac in one hand and the boys' ADHD medication in the other and I honestly can't tell the difference between them.

Honor's like, 'See?'

Yeah, no, we're sitting at a red light on Johnstown Road and I'm just, like, staring at them, thinking there's no way Sorcha's old man will be able to tell, unless he sniffs one, of course.

I'm there, 'They're a bit minty, aren't they?'

'You're forgetting,' Honor goes, 'that he has no sense of smell.'

Of course, he had, like, nasal polyps – which sound focking revolting, by the way – two or three years ago. He can't taste anything either. I've had his wife's cooking and, believe me, that's a focking blessing.

I'm like, 'It sounds like you've thought of everything, Honor.'

The cor behind me gives me a long, impatient beep. Yeah, no, the light has turned green.

Honor goes, 'Do you want me to get that?'

I'm there, 'Yeah, please do,' and she opens her window and sticks an upturned finger out of it, while I lean on the accelerator.

She's in cracking form this afternoon and I'm wondering is it just because we're about to switch the meds that are making her brothers dopey for breath mints.

I'm there, 'You're in cracking form today, Honor.'

And she's like, 'Am I?'

'I hope you don't mind me remorking on it.'

'I don't mind at all. By the way, Sincerity broke it off with Johnny Prendergast.'

'Poor Johnny. Any idea why?'

'She just said she didn't fancy him any more.'

Out of the corner of my eye, I can see a little smile playing on her lips. That'll be the hope.

We eventually arrive at Honalee and I swing the cor into the driveway.

'No one here,' I go.

And Honor's like, 'Er, I *told* you that? I texted Leo. *She's* at work and her focking dickhead parents have taken Brian, Johnny and Leo to the Royal Irish Academy of Music.'

'What a focking waste of time.'

I pull up in front of the gaff.

I'm there, 'This is, em, definitely a good idea, isn't it, Honor?'

She goes, 'Er, *yeah*?'

'I'm sorry, Honor – I don't know why I doubt myself sometimes.'

'They're walking around like focking zombies.'

'Zombies with zero interest in rugby.'

'And they're being bullied.'

'What kind of a father would I be if I just stood back and allowed that to happen? Come on, Honor, let's do this thing.'

We get out of the cor. I take out my front door key and I let us into the gaff. Up the stairs we go, the two of us laughing our heads off – that's how good we feel about the plan.

We go into *his* bedroom and then into the en suite.

I'm there, 'Where are they?'

She goes, 'They were in here.'

She opens the medicine cabinet and pulls out a lorge tub. Honor gives it a shake.

She's there, 'Okay, we have to make sure that we put the exact same number of Tic Tacs in here as there are tablets. Because I wouldn't be surprised if he, like, counts them every night.'

'He's such a dick,' I go.

She takes the tub into the bedroom and tips the pills out onto the bed, then she storts counting them. While she's doing that, I notice his slippers – ugly, brown tortan things – on the floor next to the bed.

I'm there, 'The old me would have probably taken a shit in one of his slippers. Actually, will I take a shit in one of his slippers?'

Honor goes, 'Dad, focus, will you?' because she's an absolute pro at this kind of thing. 'If he finds out that someone has shat in his slipper, the first person he's going to think of is you. And then he'll stort asking why you were in his bedroom and what else you did while you were here.'

I'm like, 'See, I always get carried away. That's why you're the brains of the outfit, Honor.'

'Okay,' she goes, 'count out one hundred and eight Tic Tacs, will you?'

I'm there, 'Would *you* mind doing it?' pulling the boxes out of my pocket and handing them to her. 'Like I said, you're the brains.'

So she counts out – exactly like she said – one hundred and eight Tic Tacs and puts them into the tub.

I'm there, 'What are we going to do with the actual tablets? Will I flush them down the jacks.'

She goes, 'No, don't chance it. We'll take them with us and flush them down the toilet when we get home.'

So I stort shoving handfuls of the things into the pocket of my sailing jacket and that's when I discover that there's a piece of paper in there. I pull it out. Shit, it's the goodbye note that Delma left for JP.

Honor goes, 'What's that, Dad?'

And I'm there, 'You don't want to know, Honor. Something I meant to throw out except I forgot all about it.'

She puts the tablet box back in the medicine cabinet and we head off, although I take one last look at his slippers. It's a missed opportunity – like having to take the three points when you knew there were seven right there – but the priority has to be the welfare of my children.

There'll be other chances to shit in his slippers.

We hop into the cor and I stort the engine. And that's when my *phone* all of a sudden rings?

I answer it and it ends up being Erika.

She's like, 'Where are you?'

I'm there, 'I was collecting Honor from school – and we had a short detour to make on the way home.'

Honor laughs. I can be very funny.

Erika goes, 'Are you listening to the news?'

I'm there, 'Erika, you do know you've phoned Ross, don't you?'

She's like, 'Switch it on, Ross.'

So I switch it on and I flick through the pre-sets until I hear my old man's voice and – yeah, no – I just presume that this is what she's banging on about.

The old man is going, 'The Deputy is talking out of his rear end – as he has been since the very first day he walked into this chamber!' and you can hear all this angry shouting and roaring in the background. 'Let me repeat, for those of you who are hord of hearing, there *is* no deal with Russia! There has *been* no deal with Russia! And there will *be* no deal with Russia!'

I'm there, 'Erika, I've no idea what I'm supposably listening to here.'

She goes, 'The CIA have said they've noticed unusual things happening off the north-western coast of Ireland.'

I'm like, 'In terms of what, Erika?'

'A build-up of ships,' she goes. 'Russian ships.'

I'm there, 'That's, em, interesting,' because I remember Christian said there were a bunch of Russian Navy heads hanging around Malingrad before Christmas. 'Is this the CIA in, like, the States that we're talking about?'

She goes, 'Ross, this has something to do with Ronan going to Moscow with Hennessy. You need to get him to talk to you.'

I'm there, 'I tried. He wouldn't tell me anything.'

And she goes, 'Well, you need to try focking horder.'

'What are we doing hee-or?' Ronan goes.

He can't believe I dragged him out of work to go to an amusement orcade – even this one.

I'm there, 'I thought it'd be nice for old times' sake. You mentioned it in your speech at my fortieth and I just thought – yeah, no – we haven't been to Quirkey's in, like, years.'

And to think I watched him grow from a child to a teenager to a man in this place. The bells, the chink of coins, the flashing lights – they're bringing back a lot of memories.

He goes, 'Hee-or, what's going on between Edika and Buckets of Blood?'

I'm there, 'In terms of?'

'She's arthur going out on tree dates wirrum. He took her out the utter night for didder. Thee weddent to Dim Sum and Den Some in Artane.'

'Sounds like a classy joint.'

'It's a fruddent for muddy-launthering. What's her gayum, Rosser?'

'In terms of?'

'A geerl like Edika would have no bleaten inthordest in the likes of Buckets. She's obviously using him for sometin.'

'Maybe she has a debt she wants recovered and she hasn't heard yet that the buckets of blood spilled are usually his.'

'He's an auld softy, Rosser – whatebber she's at, joost ted her not to break he's bleaten heert.'

Ronan is nervous – keeps looking over his shoulder, like he's nine years old again and he's expecting to see László, the bouncer who focked him out of here so many times that they actually became friends. I think Ronan might have even arranged a marriage for him when his work permit ran out.

He's obviously waiting for me to say something.

He goes, 'Rosser, *you* ast *me* to go for luddench. You said it was an emeergedency.'

I'm there, 'I wanted to bring you somewhere noisy – so there's no chance of anyone listening in.'

He just stares at me. He's got, like, tears in his eyes. He's ready to offload.

I'm like, 'Ro, that thing on the news about Russian ships off the coast of Donegal. Does that have anything to do with you?'

He looks around. He's trying to find a corner where the music is louder. He spots Dance Dance Revolution. If you totted up all the hours we spent on that thing, it'd be weeks out of our lives.

He goes, 'Mon, let's daddence.'

We make our way over it to it, passing – speak of the devil – László on the way.

He goes, 'Hello, Ronan. Hello, Rosser.'

And Ro's like, 'Howiya, László? How's Jacintha?'

Jacinta. That was it. I think they've actually got kids now.

I put the money in the slot and he chooses 'Pocketful of

Sunshine' by Natasha Bedingfield. We both step up onto the boards as the music comes on. We stort dancing – and Ronan storts talking.

He goes, 'The cunterdoddy was broke, Rosser. And when I say broke, I mee-un *broke*. No one would leddend us addy muddy arthur Cheerlie welched odden all eer debts. So he did a deal with the Rushiddens.'

I'm there, 'What kind of a deal are we talking in terms of?'

'A hunthrit biddion up fruddent –'

'A hundred billion what?'

'US doddars, Rosser. Then a hundred biddion for each of the next fowur yee-ors.'

'In return for?'

'The Rushiddens are wanton to serrup a nabal base in westorden Eurdope.'

'I'm presuming we're talking about Malingrad?'

'Madingrad was apposed to be biddilt for gas and oyult explordation. But Cheerlie knew Putin wanthed if for mower than that. And he knew if the cunterdoddy ebber ren ourra muddy, he had that to offert him.'

I have to say, I love Natasha Bedingfield.

I'm there, 'So is that why you and Hennessy went to Moscow?'

He goes, 'To fidalize the dea-ul, yeah.'

'And it's definitely a bad thing, this, is it?'

'For Putin to hab a nabal base in Westorden Europe? Wirrin sthriking distance of Amedica? Rosser, when this gets out, it's godda be anutter Cuban bleaten Missile Crisis.'

I'm like, 'Fock!' even though I've no idea what that even means. 'Hang on, did my old man not deny all of this? I heard him with my own ears.'

'He loyut to the Doddle, Rosser.'

'He what?'

'He loyut to the Doddle.'

'Ro, all I can hear coming out of your mouth is noise.'

'He loyut –'

'Oh, he *lied*.'

'– to the Doddle.'

'Lied to the Dáil – got it. And I'm presuming that's, like, a no-no, is it?'

'He's boddixed, Rosser. It'll all cub out. It's altready cubbing out. The ships are theer. And submardines – wit nuclear capabidity.'

The song ends. I don't know about Ronan, but I'm absolutely focked from dancing.

I'm like, 'Ro, Avery's right. You need to be ready to run when this thing breaks.'

He goes, 'I caddent, Rosser. Ine up to me boddicks in it. And Heddessy says if he goes dowun for threason, I'll be going dowun wirrum.'

Sorcha rings and she sounds in a bit of a state.

She goes, 'Ross, where are you?'

And I'm there, 'I'm just about to meet the goys in The Bridge,' because – yeah, no – it's Sixmas Eve and they'll all be dying to hear whether I think Ireland can bounce back against Scotland tomorrow after the disappointment of the World Cup.

She goes, 'Oh, right – look, it doesn't matter.'

I'm there, 'What's up, Sorcha? Is this about the Russia thing?' because it's still all over the news.

She's like, 'I can't talk about that, Ross. It's, like, Cabinet confidentiality.'

I go, 'So, em –' meaning, why the fock are you ringing me, then, and I'm only saying that because it's lashing rain.

She's like, 'I don't even know why I'm ringing you. It's just, well, a combination of things.'

'As in?'

'Leo got suspended from school today. For calling his German teacher a prick with ears and a thundering fockpig.'

I laugh. I know I *shouldn't*? But here we are.

She goes, 'It's not funny, Ross.'

I'm there, 'I'm sorry.'

I'm not sorry.

She's like, 'I don't know what's going on with the three of them this week but their behaviour is as bad as it was a year ago.'

I'm there, 'Oh?'

She goes, 'Brian tore up all of the daffodils in the gorden yesterday and Johnny told my mom that she had legs like the Bride's Glen viaduct.'

Kids are like sponges, aren't they?

I'm there, 'Jesus. And what's *he* saying? As in your old man?'

'He can't get his head around it?'

'So he doesn't know as much about raising boys as he *thought* he did?'

'He just doesn't understand why their meds don't seem to be working any more.'

'Serves him focking right. Anyway, I'd better –'

She goes, 'It's over between me and Mike,' and she just, like, blurts it out like that. 'I was the one who ended it.'

I'm there, 'Oh, em, I'm sorry to hear that. I'll miss his voice. I hope that doesn't sound weird. Do you mind me asking what happened?'

She goes, 'I found out that he flew the Government jet to Amsterdam to collect the Heineken for your fortieth birthday porty – using his diplomatic badge to avoid the usual customs checks.'

I'm just like, 'Fock,' because I'm getting lashed on here.

She's there, 'Then he told me he's been flying all over Europe to collect cheese and wine and cigors and God knows what else for the Áras. It turns out that An Taoiseach has been eating and drinking and smoking as normal while the rest of the country has been making sacrifices for Irexit.'

I'm like, 'Sorcha, I told you not to trust my old man. He's been different ever since he put that wig on his head.'

She's there, 'Sorry, Ross, I have to go. It sounds like one of the boys has just smashed a window.'

She hangs up and I head inside – my focking jacket saturated by the way. There's a definite buzz when I walk through the door. The goys are all delighted to see me and even Dave Kearney looks up from the pint he's pulling and goes, 'No Tactics Book with you tonight, Ross, no?'

No, I think, but it'll be on my focking lap in the Aviva tomorrow like it *always* is?

Christian, Fionn, Oisinn and JP are standing around in a huddle. Oisinn is talking about changing nappies like he invented fatherhood and I just think, fock it, he deserves this.

I'm there, 'How's the little goy doing?'

He's like, 'He's doing great, Ross,' and I've honestly never seen him happier.

I take off my jacket and hang it on the back of the chair to dry. Then I turn around to Christian and I'm like, 'You're a focking dork horse, by the way, aren't you?'

He's there, 'What do you mean?' like he doesn't know.

'I saw you in Sandycove – near the Forty Foot. Playing happy families with Lauren and the kids.'

'I went sea-swimming with my kids and their mother.'

'Don't give me that. I know what I saw. The four of you in matching Dryrobes.'

He shrugs like there's no point in lying any more.

'Fine,' he goes. 'Lauren and I have decided to get back together.'

JP's like, 'That's great news.'

Oisinn's there, 'The kids must be delighted.'

Fionn's like, 'I'm very happy – for all of you.'

But I go, 'You're a focking mug. And I'm saying that as both your best mate and someone who's not afraid to call it – unlike these three.'

Christian goes, 'Ross and Oliver are happy. I'm happy. Lauren is happy.'

I'm there, 'Lauren is never happy. Her old man is Hennessy Coghlan-O'Hara.'

He's like, 'Yeah, thank you for your concern, Ross.'

I go, 'It'd be like this dude,' and I flick my head in JP's direction, 'getting back together with Delma.'

'That will never focking happen,' JP goes – and there's a real hordness in his voice, which makes it sound like he's finally accepted that she's gone. 'To just walk away like that and leave me in this, like, purgatory, she must have really focking hated me.'

Okay, time to change the subject, I think.

'You're probably wondering about my fifteen to face Scotland?' I go.

'Front row – Healy, Herring and Furlong. Second row – Henderson and Ryan. Then Stander, obviously, on one wing and van der Flier on the other. Doris at eight. Then Murray, Sexton, Stockdale, Aki –'

I notice Fionn pull a face.

I'm there, 'What – are you thinking Aki at thirteen?'

He goes, 'No, I'm thinking why do you spend so much time pretending to be a rugby coach when you could *actually* be one?'

This is him trying to persuade me to coach Castlerock again.

I'm there, 'Forget it, Dude. A co-ed school has never won the Leinster Schools Senior Cup.'

He's like, 'You could make rugby history. Our first thirty bursary students storted this week.'

'You mean non-fee-paying? Hang on, it's January.'

JP goes, 'Well, most of them have been expelled from other schools. One or two have just got out of Oberstown.'

I laugh – I *actually* laugh? – and I go, 'You two seem determined to drag that once-proud school into the gutter. Well, I'm not going to help you. You're on your own.'

JP goes, 'Ross, I've to head off early tonight. Have you got my ticket for tomorrow?'

I'm there, 'Before we come to that, I've something to tell you all. Jamie's back.'

Oisinn goes, 'Jamie?'

'My twin brother,' I go. 'I'm bringing him out of retirement.'

They all laugh, in fairness to them, even though they've no idea where this conversation is going.

I'm there, 'I told you that Roz heard that I had a twin brother. Well, she wants to meet him.'

Christian just shakes his head in wonder, obviously thinking, is the Rossmeister General *ever* going to change? Hopefully not.

JP goes, 'Why does she want to meet him?'

I'm there, 'So you know I'm arranging this living funeral for my old dear next week? Roz said she couldn't believe I'd even think of having it without telling Jamie and she sort of, like, guilted me into ringing him, even though we've been estranged for years.'

They're all just looking at me with their mouths open.

Christian goes, 'Ross, why don't you just tell her the truth – that you made him up?'

I'm there, 'Because I'm too far down the road, Dude. I've fully committed to the lie.'

Oisinn's like, 'So what are you going to do?'

I'm there, 'I'm going to arrange to meet her before the thing kicks off and I'm going to pretend to – yeah, no – *be* him?'

JP laughs – he can't help himself.

He goes, 'You're going to pretend to your girlfriend that you're your twin brother?'

I'm there, 'That's the plan.'

He goes, 'You'll never pull it off.'

I'm there, 'I seem to remember you saying something very similar when I attended the Loreto Foxrock and Loreto on the Green debses on the same night.'

Christian smiles at the memory. He goes, 'In fairness, it had never been done before.'

I'm there, 'I'd one in the Berkeley Court and one in Jurys. And they never knew about each other – until a week later, of course, when the story was all over town.'

I really *was* a legend when you think about it.

Fionn goes, 'Hi, Erika,' because – yeah, no – Erika has turned up.

She's like, 'Yeah, hi, boys,' except she's all business. 'Ross, can I have a word with you?'

She leads me over to the other side of the pub, then she goes, 'Did you talk to Ronan?'

I'm like, 'Yeah, no, I took him to Dr Quirkey's at lunchtime. I was feeling a bit – I think it's a word – *nostalgish?*'

'For fock's sake, Ross – what did he say?'

'I didn't understand a lot of it. But basically the old man sent Hennessy and Ronan to Russia looking for money – in return for which the old man agreed to let them keep their ships and possibly nuclear submarines in Donegal.'

That rocks her back on her kitten heels.

She goes, 'Oh my God, this could be another Cuban Missile Crisis.'

I'm there, 'That got mentioned. What actually *was* that? Was it, like, a major thing?'

She doesn't bother her hole even answering me.

I'm like, 'So what about you? Have you got anything out of Buckets of Blood yet?'

She's there, 'Not yet.'

'How many dates have you gone on with him? Three, according to Ronan. Hopefully, you haven't had sex with him. You haven't had sex with him, have you?'

'I've been playing the long game. I've been lavishing him with attention.'

'Lucky him.'

'And now I'm about to turn the tap off.'

But before I can say, 'The poor focker,' I hear JP shout at me across the bor.

He's like, 'Ross, where's my ticket for tomorrow?'

And, without thinking, I go, 'In my jacket pocket.'

It's only as he's reaching for it that I suddenly remember the letter from Delma and my life suddenly flashes before my eyes.

I'm there, 'Dude, wait!'

Except he's already reached into my jacket and pulled out the piece of paper, at the same time sending ADHD tablets flying everywhere.

I watch him as he reads his name on the outside, then he opens it up and gives it the old left to right with a look of, like, shock on his face.

And I catch Dave Kearney's eye and I go, 'Dude, is that side door open?'

Honor asks me if I'm going to take that call – yeah, no, this is while I'm dropping her to school – and I tell her that it's only JP and I'll catch up with him later.

She goes, 'That's, like, the third time he's phoned since we left the house. And wasn't he trying to get you yesterday as well – and on Saturday?'

I'm like, 'What are you, monitoring my phone now?'

'You've obviously done something to piss him off.'

'Can we *change* the subject? What about Brian, Johnny and Leo on Saturday, huh?'

Yeah, no, we were asked to leave Burger King because Brian smashed Leo in the face with a wet mop and Johnny tipped a bucket of sudsy water over his head.

Honor goes, 'Oh my God, it was *so* funny. Did you hear me tell that security gord to keep his focking nose out of other people's business?'

I'm there, 'I did, Honor – and you showed unbelievable restraint in the circumstances. It's great to have everything back to normal again, isn't it?'

And that's when she says it – totally out of left field.

She goes, 'So I got off with Sincerity on Saturday night.'

I'm like, 'What?' and I end up nearly wrapping the A10 around a lamp-post on Deepork Road.

She's there, 'Well, *she* kissed *me*. Oh my God, I don't know where it came from. And then – yeah, no – I kissed her back.'

I'm like, 'Jesus!'

'What?'

'I don't know.'

'Why did you say, "Jesus!"'

'I don't know. It's just big news.'

'Whatever.'

'And was it, I don't know, any *good*?'

'Oh my God, she's an amazing kisser. Dad, can you maybe drive in a straight line?'

'I'm sorry. So, like, how did it happen?'

'I don't know. We were watching a movie –'

'Which movie was it?'

'What does that matter? It was, like, *Fast & Furious: Hobbs & Shaw*.'

'Okay – continue.'

'And she kissed me.'

I'm there, 'I can't believe you waited until we were at the school gates before you dropped this bombshell.'

She goes, 'It's not a major deal, Dad,' but she can't wipe the smile off her face.

I'm like, 'I wondered why you were in cracking form. Well, you're certainly less of a bitch than you are most mornings.'

She's there, 'Thanks, Dad.'

I'm like, 'I notice these things.'

I pull into the cor pork.

I'm there, 'So, what, is Sincerity gay all of a sudden?'

And she goes, 'Oh my God, you are *so* obsessed with labels!'

She throws open the door.

I'm there, 'I'll see you later so,' and she gets out and she slams the door after her.

I'm back on the Stillorgan dualler when I stick on the radio and – yeah, no – there's a thing on the news about the old man.

Some dude says that he's fighting for his political future this morning after satellite images released by the CIA appeared to contradict his claims that there were no Russian warships off the coast of Donegal.

Holy focking shit, I think – even I know that this is major.

The dude goes, 'It's all rather reminiscent of 2010, when – if you remember – Fianna Fáil ministers Dermot Ahern and Noel Dempsey denied that Ireland was in negotiations for a bailout when, in fact, the IMF were already here. Fianna Fáil leader Micheál Mortin has said that Ireland's sovereignty has been compromised and that the Taoiseach has broken international law, while Fine Gael leader Leo Varadkar has called for an immediate General Election.'

I just think, fock, and I point the cor in the direction of the Áras.

There's, like, hundreds of protesters outside the gates, holding placords saying shit like, 'You Lied to Us!' and 'We Want Our Star Back!' and 'Where Has All the Brie Gone?' and they're shouting, 'CO'CK OUT! CO'CK OUT! CO'CK OUT!'

I manage to get through the crowd and through the gates.

When I walk into the gaff, all hell is literally breaking loose. From the hallway, I can hear the sound of, like, six or seven voices shouting, not to mention babies crying – and, above it all, my old man roaring the same words he roared when the Criminal Assets Bureau kicked down the door of his office back in the day, the same words that inspired the name of the document disposal business that he set up, years after he got out of the slammer.

He's going, 'Shred . . . focking . . . EVERYTHING!'

I tip up the stairs. The entire team of nannies are on the landing with my – yeah, no – brother and sisters in their orms and the kids are, like, bawling their eyes out.

Astrid goes, 'Ross, what is all this shouting?'

I'm there, 'Leave it to me, Astrid.'

I stand at the door of the old man's office and I just, like, observe the chaos. There's, like, twenty or thirty people in there, running backwards and forwards, shouting at each other while Hennessy – standing in the middle of this madness – borks out news updates from his phone.

He goes, 'The Minister for Housing, Gordon Greenhalgh, has said he would welcome further clarification from the Taoiseach on the matter!'

'The bastard!' the old man goes – he's sitting behind his desk, red in the face, a Cohiba the size of a giraffe turd burning between his fingers. 'You warned me against appointing him to the Cabinet –'

Hennessy's like, 'He's a snake!'

'– and you were absolutely right!'

There's, like, three giant shredding machines on a desk next to the far wall and I notice Ronan feeding fistfuls of documents into them.

He goes, 'What about these, Heddessy?'

And Hennessy's like, 'You heard the man! Everything! Shred everything!'

The old man goes, 'Can you get one minister – just one! – to say *something* in support of me?'

Hennessy's there, 'They're deserting the ship like rats, Taoiseach.'

The old man's like, 'What about Sorcha?'

'She's not answering her phone, Taoiseach.'

'A fine way to repay the faith I placed in her!'

That's when I decide to step into the office. Ronan is the first one to see me. He's like, 'Rosser!' and he gives me a look as if to say that the old man has lost his shit.

Then Hennessy cops me. He's there, 'What the hell do you want?'

The old man goes, 'Kicker, I'm rather busy, I'm afraid! Events, dear boy!'

I'm there, 'So it's all gone to shit, huh? Why don't you just give it up, Dude?'

'Give it up? Ross, there are people out there who are counting on me to steer the ship through this patch of political turbulence!'

'Dude, look out the window. People hate you. You've focked up the country. The supermorket shelves are empty and there's Russians in Donegal.'

The old man looks around me at Hennessy and goes, 'Let's release a statement saying that whatever bureaucratic blockages that existed with regord to food imports have been cleared and the shelves will fully stocked within a matter of weeks! Hurrah!'

I'm there, 'Dude, you're toast.'

Hennessy goes, 'Don't listen to him, Taoiseach.'

I'm there, 'The country can't wait to see the back of you. But you've got six children outside on the landing and a wife with senile dementia who all need you.'

Hennessy goes, 'What if we put out a statement saying that the CIA photos are fake – an attempt to discredit you? We buy ourselves a few weeks, stop the Cabinet defections, maybe announce a reshuffle, the money from Putin comes through –'

'And suddenly no one gives a bloody fig about Russian warships in Donegal!' the old man goes. 'I like the way you're thinking, Hennessy!'

And that's when I see it – the opportunity to do something that I've wanted to do for, like, years.

He's looking at Ronan now and he's going, 'The Parthians have been slaughtered, the Briton conquered – play on, Romans!' and I take advantage of this lapse in concentration to make a grab for his wig.

I take a firm grip of it between my fingers and – knowing that he uses some pretty strong adhesive to glue it to his head – I yank it hord. There's, like, a horrible ripping sound and he screams as the thing comes loose in my hand.

He goes, 'What in the name of Hades are you doing?' as he gets to his feet and storts coming around the desk towards me.

I turn around and I make a run for it.

He goes, 'Hennessy! Stop him!' but as the dude comes towards me, I feint one way, then go the other, totally wrong-footing him with a nice swivel of my hips.

Someone else – some office functionary – makes a grab for the thing then, but I put my hand in his face and push him off, then I basically knock over some much smaller dude who tries to stand in my way. And then suddenly it's only Ronan standing between me and the shredders.

Our eyes meet.

The old man goes, 'Ronan! In the name of humanity! All of my power comes from that wig! I'm nothing without it!'

Ronan carries on staring at me for a second or two, then he goes, 'Soddy, Cheerlie – it's for the best,' and he steps aside.

The old man goes, 'NOOOOOOOOO!!!!!!!!!' and he launches himself at me – we're talking about a full-on rugby tackle here. He hits me hord around the waist – a referee could have no issue with it if this were a match situation – and he knocks me to the ground.

But not before I manage to twist my body, Matrix-style, in mid-air and deposit the wig into the shredder, like the great Drico himself grounding the ball against Australia at the Rugby World Cup in 2003.

The machine storts coughing and spluttering, basically choking on the thing, before it storts spitting out chunks of that autumn ochre hair that I grew to hate so much.

I'm lying on the ground with the old man on top of me. Ronan and Hennessy are just, like, staring at him with shock on their faces. The old man storts patting his perfectly smooth, perfectly bald head.

He goes, 'What have you done, Ross? What in the name of Hades have you done?'

★

CAUTION

TURBO-SHRED

The timing is absolutely vital here. As with, I don't know, a single loop switch, everything has to happen at exactly the right moment to pull it off.

I ring Roz at, like, eleven o'clock in the morning from an old Pay As You Go phone that once belonged to Honor. Not recognizing the number, she answers with a dubious, 'Hello?'

I'm there, 'Howiya,' because I definitely mentioned to her that the dude spoke with a skanger accent. 'This is Jamie O'Carroll-Kelly. Ine Ross's brutter. So I am.'

She's quiet for a good five seconds and I can hear her gobbling for air. Then she goes, 'J . . . J . . . J . . . Jamie? Oh, em, how did you get this number?'

Fock, I didn't fully think this through. I consider hanging up, but then I go, 'Ross geb it to me. He said you toawult him to rig me – to tell me about me ma being in a bad way – and I wanthed to thank you peersonolly.'

I'm wondering am I over-egging the accent?

She goes, 'Where are you?'

I'm there, 'I'm in Ongar . . . Ine in Ongar.'

She's like, 'Oh my God! You're coming to the living funeral!'

I'm there, 'No, Ine not. Look, I doatunt wanth to create a bad atmosphere.'

'I'm sure you wouldn't. This could be an opportunity for you and Ross to put the past behind you.'

'No, I doatunt deseerve his forgibness. Especially arthur what I did.'

'I'm sure if you came to the nursing home –'

'Ine at the noorsing howum now.'

'Oh my God, I'm literally five minutes away from you! I'm on – let me check the satnav here – the Ongar *Distributor* Road?'

'Ine just arthur seeing me ma. The whole thing was veddy emotional.'

'Please don't move, Jamie. Stay where you are.'

'Right.'

'Ross is on his way as well.'

'He wouldn't wanth to see me, Roz.'

'I'm just going to ring him. Where *exactly* are you?'

'Roz, no. He did enough by tedding me that me ma was sick. You caddent ted him.'

'But Ross and I don't have *any* secrets from each other.'

Jesus, I think, you don't know the focking half of it.

I'm there, 'I'd luvven to meet *you* but.'

She goes, 'Okay – where?'

'There's a Patty Power – a bukies – in Ongar. And opposite that, there's a pork bench – I mean a peerk beddench. I'll you see theer in a few midutes.'

I'm already *sitting* on the bench, of course? I'm wearing – I shit you not – an old blue-and-yellow Pringle sweater that Sorcha bought me once when we talked to the priest about renewing our vows and a nerdy-looking pakamac that I stole from someone in a hostel while we were doing the Camino.

Oh – and I'm wearing a pair of wrecked Nikes that I've had for years instead of my trademork Dubes and I've combed down my famous quiff to give myself a bit of a fringe.

I hope it's enough.

I watch Roz pork outside the bookies and then get out of her cor. She sees me sitting there and she gives me a smile and a little wave as she walks towards me.

'Oh my God,' she goes, 'you are *so* alike.'

I stand up and I'm there, 'Yeah, I doatunt know if he said it to you but we're identhical twiddens.'

We exchange a hug and she goes, 'Oh my God, you hug like him as well! Is Harissa with you?'

I'm there, 'She's, er, not with me, no – so she's not.'

She goes, 'Will we –?' and she indicates the bench with a nod of her head.

We move towards it and she goes to sit down.

I'm like, 'Can I sit the utter side of you, Roz? It's just Ine deaf in this ear.'

Being a good liar is as much about having a head for details as it is about having no conscience whatsoever.

We end up sitting there for, like, ten minutes, most of which she spends trying to persuade me to go to the living funeral.

She goes, 'It needn't be awkward. It could be the opportunity that you and Ross need to reset your relationship and rebuild it again.'

She's such a good person. I wish I was a good person.

I'm there, 'Look, me and Ross are two veddy, veddy diffordent people. He's honest and he's loyal,' because I can't resist the temptation to give myself a little pat on the back, 'whereas Ine not. He has a rugby brain, whereas I doatunt. He's able to handle rubber, whereas Ine totally allergic to it, including condoms.'

She screws up her face. Yeah, no, it's definitely a random thing to say. But then she suddenly remembers the time.

She goes, 'Oh my God, I'm going to be late!' and she jumps up from the bench. 'Jamie, it was lovely to have met you!' and we share one final hug – a longer one this time – before Roz walks back to her cor.

The second she's out of sight, I peg it in the other direction. This is where the Nikes come into their own. I race along the road until I come to a wall that's maybe, like, seven feet high? I jump, grab onto the top and pull myself up *onto* it? Then I drop down onto the other side – into the grounds of the actual nursing home.

I push my way through all these, like, bushes, then I race across the grass to the cor pork, where Honor is waiting with my clothes.

She goes, 'Please don't tell me she fell for it.'

I'm there, 'I was very convincing, Honor. You should have heard me.'

She turns her back on me while I change into my usual chinos, Dubes and light blue Ralph – no sailing jacket, though, because I left it in The Bridge the night JP found the letter in my pocket and he's hanging onto it, according to Christian, until I grow a pair of balls and face him like a man – and those were his *exact* words?

Honor just shakes her head and goes, 'Oh my God, she's perfect for you, Dad.'

I've just finished getting dressed when I see Roz pulling into the cor pork.

Honor's like, 'Hair!' and I suddenly remember to stand my quiff back up.

I watch Roz get out of her cor for the second time this morning.

I'm like, 'Hey, Roz,' and I realize that I'm still trying to catch my breath.

She goes, 'Hi, Ross! Hi, Honor!' and she gives us both a hug.

She doesn't say a word about meeting my brother. I'm thinking, no secrets, huh?

Into the nursing home we go. The room is absolutely rammers. I spot Sorcha and Ronan and so many faces from the past – we're talking Angela and Dermot from the campaign to move Funderland to the northside. We're talking Ida and Clem from the campaign to stop the Luas from coming to Foxrock. We're talking Lucy and Aednat from the campaign to stop poor people being allowed into the National Gallery.

Sorcha catches my eye and smiles at me and then she looks down and notices that Roz is holding my hand and her expression changes and she looks away. We plonk ourselves down next to Ro.

I turn to him and I go, 'No sign of the old man, no?'

He's there, 'Said he couldn't face it, Rosser.'

'The coward.'

'He said he's consitherdin he's political future this morden.'

'The selfish fock.'

Dalisay is standing in the doorway. She goes, 'Ross, are you ready?'

I stand up and I'm there, 'Yeah, no, all set,' and I follow her outside.

The old dear is standing in the corridor with two other nurses. When she sees me, she goes, 'Oh, hello, Ross. What's going on? Why won't they let me sleep?'

I'm there, 'There's a few old friends in this room who want to tell you how much you've meant to them over the years.'

'Why?'

'Because, I don't know, they love you.'

'Is Conor here?'

'Er, no, he couldn't make it. Shall we –'

And – yeah, no – we sort of, like, guide her into the room.

Everyone claps when they see her. It's all a bit weird, especially when the old dear goes, 'I don't know any of these people.'

I'm there, 'You do. You know Honor over there, look. And do you remember Sorcha?'

'No, I don't remember anyone of that name. Are you trying to have sex with her? Is he trying to have sex with you, Sorcha?'

'I was married to her for, I don't know, a lot of years. And you remember Ida and Clem, don't you? You all went on hunger strike together until they agreed to reroute the Luas through Leopardstown Valley – although I did catch you once or twice eating on the sly.'

Everyone laughs and it breaks the definite ice.

I look around the room and I go, 'Okay, the reason we're here today is – well, it was actually *Roz's* idea?'

I smile at her and I notice Sorcha have a sly look for her reaction while pretending to pick a piece of lint off the shoulder of her jacket.

I'm there, 'The idea is that you all get to say what it is about my old dear that you love, or what it was about her that inspired you. Or she may have done something to piss you off. Now is the chance to get it off your chest.'

Everyone cracks up laughing. I know how to work a crowd. I'm just going to come out and say it – it's a focking disgrace that Leo Cullen has never picked up the phone to me.

I sit back down and Ida – out of Clem and Ida – is the first to get up to speak.

She goes, 'Fionnuala, I know you probably have no idea who I am, but we were dear, dear friends once. And I remember when we were fighting this Luas nonsense, I was storting to lose all hope. I'd been refusing food for about six days and I'd just fainted through hunger and dehydration. But you had this incredible strength – which makes complete sense now if what Ross just told us is true. But I remember you sort of slapped my face and I came around and you said, "We are fighting for the future of Foxrock, Ida – weakness is an indulgence that we can ill-afford." And many times since then, Fionnuala, I've stood at the top of Leopardstown Road and I've watched the Luas come around the corner from the direction of Sandyford – isn't that right, Clem? – and it *looks* like it's heading for Torquay Road, but then

318

it suddenly banks to the right and disappears off to, well, God *knows* where. And I always remember those words of yours.'

That gets a round of applause from everyone, except obviously the old dear, who has no idea who Ida is or why she's saying this shit.

The woman sits down and her orse has barely touched the chair before Sorcha is on her feet.

'Sorcha Lalor,' she goes – like anyone here doesn't *know* who she is? 'Member of Seanad Éireann and, well, still Minister for Climate Action. I'm also – again, still – Fionnuala's daughter-in-law. I just want to say that I always thought she was the most amazing, amazing person. She gave me – oh my God – *so* much advice over the years, especially when I was dating her son.'

Roz is holding my hand and I notice that her grip becomes suddenly tighter.

Sorcha's there, 'I'm guessing you don't remember this, Fionnuala, but I used to ring – oh my God, I'm so embarrassed about this – and I'd say, "Why is he such a Chandler!" because he had *such* commitment issues.'

Roz turns to me and goes, 'I don't think you have commitment issues.'

And I'm there, 'Yeah, no, I don't know where this is coming from.'

Sorcha goes, 'Anyway, what I wanted to say to you, Fionnuala, is thank you, thank you, thank you – for being not just a mother-in-law but a mentor and a definite friend.'

The old dear just stares at her – hasn't a clue who she even is.

Angela from the Funderland group stands up then and that's when Roz turns to me again and she goes, 'I met Jamie.'

I'm there, 'You're joking.'

She's like, 'Well, you gave him my number, didn't you?'

I'm there, 'Yeah, no, I did. But – yeah, no – you met him?'

'I did.'

'And how was it?'

'He saw your mom this morning. I tried to persuade him to stick around for this but he thought it might have been difficult.'

It would have been more than difficult.

She goes, 'You were right, though – about him being a sleaze.'

I'm there, 'Oh?'

She's like, 'He was trying to look down my top the entire time I was talking to him –'

Yeah, no, I'm a terrible man.

She goes, '– and then, when he was hugging me goodbye, I'm nearly sure he had an erection.'

Angela sits down. I didn't hear a word of what she said except the last line: 'You have inspired future generations to continue the battle to take Funderland out of Dublin 4.'

That gets a big round of applause.

The old dear goes, 'Ross, who *are* all these awful, awful people?'

And then – holy shit – Honor gets to her feet.

She goes, 'My earliest memory of Fionnuala is her telling me not to call her grandma. She said it made her feel, like, *old*? Then she showed me how to mix a Bloody Mary for her – just like she showed my dad when he was a child too. Over the years, I learned – oh my God – *so* much from her. It was from being around Fionnuala that I realized the importance of always, always being yourself, even if that means being a total bitch and maybe a few people get hurt along the way. The most recent lesson she taught me was that there's absolutely nothing wrong . . . with being gay.'

And then – I swear to fock – she just sits down again. It's a definite mic drop moment. I'm looking around me at a roomful of people with their mouths wide open like sex dolls.

Roz goes, 'Oh my God!'

And Sorcha's there, 'Gay? Oh my God, *are* you gay?' and it's clearly come as a major shock to her. 'Even though there's obviously nothing wrong with it. I had, like, loads of gay friends in UCD.'

The old dear goes, 'Ross, can you bring me back to my room, please?'

But we're all still digesting Honor's news when all of a sudden I hear a voice go, 'Hello, Dorling.'

I turn around and it ends up being like a movie moment.

Yeah, no, the old man is standing in the doorway, except he's the old man as I *used* to know him? As in, there's no wig. He's bald again and he's wearing – not a suit with his usual red tie – but the yellow trousers and the pink Lacoste polo shirt that used to draw shouts of 'Wanker!' even in Portmornock.

And he looks, I don't know, somehow *smaller*?

The old dear stares at him and I watch her glassy eyes slowly focus on him and become – yeah, no – suddenly aware.

And she goes, 'Oh look, Ross – it's Chorles!'

What's Erika doing here? That's what *I'm* wondering – except she actually laughs in my face when I ask her the question.

She's there, 'Are you *actually* serious?'

Yeah, no, we're sitting in the public gallery in the Convention Centre, where the old man is about to make a personal statement.

I'm like, 'Sorry, I forgot – you've been waiting for this day for a long time.'

She goes, 'Well, I can't deny that it's giving me a thrill to see him finally toppled. But this won't be over until I clear Sea-mon's name.'

I notice Sorcha looking up at us. She smiles at me, but it's Erika's eye that she's *trying* to catch? Except Erika is refusing point-blank to even look at her.

A hush suddenly descends over the Convention Centre as the old man stands up to speak. You can see people looking at him and nearly hear them saying to each other, 'There's something different about him! What's different about him?'

He goes, '*Leas-Cathaoirleach*, fellow Deputies and Senators. It has been the greatest privilege of my life these past few years to serve as the Taoiseach of this great country of ours. And it still *is* a great country, despite the many challenges that beset us at this time.

'To the more than one million people who voted for New Republic in the last General Election, I want to say thank you for the incredible mandate you gave us to do the work that was necessary to – quote-unquote – Make Ireland Great Again. I wish to stress, too, that the job is far from complete. However, after today it will continue under new stewardship.

'I have, this very morning, tendered my resignation as Taoiseach to the chairman of the porty and thus I must leave the office of

Taoiseach, which has been my job, my duty and my obligation, as well as a signal honour.

'I am stepping away from the role for personal reasons. As you know, my beautiful wife, Fionnuala, has been ill for some time now and I wish to dedicate to her the care that she so richly deserves. Unfortunately, the demands of looking after a wife with advanced dementia is not commensurate with the task of running a country embarking on an exciting new future, having shaken off the shackles of the failed European project. And, in this, I must concede defeat.

'At this moment in time, it is clear to me that Ireland requires someone with fresh ideas to take it forward. In looking back at my life – and not just my political life – the words of Polybius, the wonderful Greek historian of the middle Hellenistic period, come to mind. He said, "I produced offspring. I sought to equal the deeds of my father. I won the praise of my ancestors so that they are glad I was born to them. My career has ennobled the family line." Thank you all – and goodbye.'

There's, like, a spontaneous round of applause, in fairness, but I think it's the line about ennobling the family line that pushes Erika over the edge.

She stands up and roars, 'You focking murderer! You burned down the Dáil and you murdered Sea-mon to stop her testifying against you!'

And you can see all the other, I don't know, TDs and whatever else, looking up at the public gallery. It's a hell of a line to just throw out there, in fairness to it.

'Murderer!' Erika goes – again, at the top of her voice. 'Murderer!'

Suddenly, the door of the public gallery is thrown open and two sort of, like, bouncer dudes walk in, pick Erika up like she's a sack of mail and carry her outside.

I probably should maybe orgue with them, but it all happens so quickly, and anyway Erika is hysterical. So I give it five minutes before I leave the public gallery. Kennet is waiting outside the door for me.

He goes, 'Are you r . . . r . . . r . . . r . . . r . . . r . . . reet, Rosser?'

I'm there, 'What do you mean, am I *reet*?'

'Cheerlie waddants you in the keer wirrum – when he th . . . th . . . th . . . th . . . th . . . th . . . th . . . th . . . th . . . th . . . thrives ourra the place.'

I'm there, 'Whatever,' and I follow him down a corridor, through a door, then down three flights of stairs to the cor pork.

He goes, 'Did you hear about the utter f . . . f . . . f . . . f . . . f . . . fedda?'

I'm like, 'Which utter f . . . f . . . f . . . f . . . f . . . fedda?' really ripping the piss out of him.

He goes, 'Yisser sudden.'

I'm there, 'Ronan? What about him?'

'Shadden's thrun him out. She was looking through he's text messages – as you do – and she f . . . f . . . f . . . f . . . fowunt out he was texting that b . . . b . . . b . . . b . . . b . . . b . . . b . . . b . . .'

'Yeah, I know who you mean, Kennet.'

'. . . b . . . b . . . b . . . b . . . b . . . b . . .'

'Kennet, there's no need to say it.'

'. . . b . . . b . . . b . . . black boord.'

'So he's out of the house?'

'Back in he's ma's in F . . . F . . . F . . . Figlas is the stordee Ine arthur hearton. But d . . . d . . . d . . . d . . . doatunt be woodying yisser self abourr it, Rosser.'

'I'm not the slightest bit worried. I'm focking delighted.'

'Ine godda hab a woord with Shadden – ast her to take him back.'

'Yeah, you're only worried about losing your house in the K Club.'

'Coultn't be foorder from me th . . . th . . . th . . . thoughts. Shadden just needs to wontherstand that boys will be b . . . b . . . b . . . b . . . b . . . b . . .'

'Oh, for fock's sake.'

'. . . b . . . b . . . b . . . b . . . b . . . b . . .'

'The words is boys, Kennet! The word is focking boys!'

'. . . b . . . b . . . b . . . b . . . b . . . b . . . boys.'

By the time he's finished his sentence we're in the cor pork underneath the Convention Centre. I see the limo porked up and there's, like, three or four dudes in suits with radio mics standing around it.

The old man is in the back. He seems, I don't know, more relieved than sad.

I hop into the back seat and I go, 'Good speech.'

He's like, 'Thank you, Ross. I put the Polybius quote in for you because I know you're a fan.'

I've no idea who the fock he's talking about.

Up the ramp we drive and that's when I first hear the crowd. The electronic barrier lifts and we drive out onto the road. There's a crowd of honestly thousands outside and – yeah, no – they seem genuinely, genuinely angry. There's, like, a line of Gordaí trying to hold them back, but they don't manage it for long.

The line breaks and thirty or forty of them come streaming forward, their fingers pointing. Suddenly, there's, like, angry faces staring into the cor, shouting, 'You lied! You lied! You lied!' and 'You destroyed the country and now you're just walking away?'

They stort kicking the cor and gobbing on the windows and the hilarious thing is that my old man seems totally oblivious to it all. He's got a little smile playing on his lips as an egg explodes off the window right next to him.

'At least I'll get to enjoy the Six Nations now,' he goes. 'England up next, Ross, isn't it?'

9.

You're Half the World Away

I tell Sorcha that she doesn't *have* to do this, but she says – yeah, no – she *wants* to do it?

This is us in my old pair's gaff in Foxrock. The old man is taking the old dear out of the nursing home in Ongar next week and we're getting the place ready. Well, what we're actually doing is trying to fix the damage that Shadden did when she was living here.

'Oh my God,' Sorcha goes, pointing to three or four semi-circular-shaped dents in the good maple-wood floor, 'are those, like, hoof morks?'

I'm there, 'Yeah, no, they had the horse in the house.'

She goes, 'You don't mean Rihanna-Brogan's horse?'

She's lived a sheltered life.

I'm there, 'Yes, I mean Rihanna-Brogan's horse. Kennet storted building a stable for the thing in the gorden – without planning permission, of course. One or two of the neighbours complained, so they storted bringing it inside at night.'

She goes, 'That would certainly explain why I keep finding bits of straw everywhere.'

She's wearing yellow Marigolds and she's trying to scrub an especially stubborn stain off one of the kitchen counters.

I'm like, 'You know there's Flash Wipes in that cupboard over there?'

But she goes, 'Vinegar and hot water is just as effective as bleach, Ross.'

I'm there, 'But then the place ends up smelling like a chip shop.'

She's like, 'These are the sacrifices we have to make if we want to live in a zero-corbon world,' and then, after a few seconds of silence, she goes, 'I've decided to resign, by the way.'

I'm there, 'What?'

'As the Minister for Climate Action.'

'But you loved that job.'

'I know I did. I *still* do? But, well, it looks like Gordon Greenhalgh is going to be the new Taoiseach. And I'm not sure how he'd feel about having his predecessor's daughter-in-law looking at him across the Cabinet table – especially because I'm not even a TD.'

'He'd be mad to get rid of you after everything you've done for the country.'

'Well, I just hope he doesn't reverse any of my policy initiatives. The ban on sheep- and cow-breeding. The restrictions on air- and road-miles. I'd like to have a legacy. I'm giving up my seat in the Seanad as well.'

'Fock.'

'That's what my dad said when I told him. We had an – oh my God – major row. He wanted me to stand in the by-election for Chorles' seat and then challenge for the porty leadership in three or four years. He got *so* angry with me, Ross. He said I was a self-saboteur – that every time I find happiness, I do something to destroy it.'

'What a dickhead.'

'I was like, "Be honest, Dad, you want me to have a political career because it makes *you* happy, not me!" I've never spoken to him like that before.'

'Well, he's had it coming.'

'Then my mom got in on the act. She was like, "Is this about your daughter being a –" and she couldn't even bring herself to say the word.'

'There's nothing wrong with being a lesbian, Sorcha.'

'Er, if anyone knows that, Ross, it's *me*? I had, like, *loads* of gay friends in UCD.'

'Yeah, you mentioned.'

'*So* many gay friends.'

'I remember them.'

'But my mom is right in a way. No disrespect to you, Ross, but it should have been me that Honor told first. And not just because

I had loads of gay friends in UCD, but because those are, like, the precious mother-daughter moments. And I missed out on it because I was trying to make the planet safe for our children and our children's children.'

'I wouldn't beat yourself up over it. I didn't see it either. It was actually Erika who copped it.'

'Erika? You're saying *she* knew before *I* knew?'

'Yeah, no, she just saw the way Honor was around Sincerity.'

'Of course, she would – she was with Meredith McTominay on the Sixth Year skiing holiday to Klosters.'

I'm there, 'I can't believe you never told me that, by the way.'

And then she stops scrubbing and goes, 'I'm sorry, but who stubs out a cigarette on a polished quartz worktop?'

I'm like, 'Scumbags, Sorcha – that's who. Anyway, hopefully, with Ronan thrown out of the house again, and you no longer having Kennet as your driver, we'll be seeing little or nothing of the Tuites in the future. Good riddance to bad rubbish – literally, in the case of this thing.'

I pick up the bamboo tiki bor – the last of Shadden's shit – and I carry it out to the front gorden. Brian, Johnny and Leo are in the skip, absolutely killing each other. Leo cracks Johnny across the back of the head with a piece of MDF that was once port of a wardrobe and I laugh because (a) it's great to have them back to normal again, and (b) I've always been a sucker for slapstick comedy.

I tip back inside.

Sorcha goes, 'Are the boys behaving themselves out there?'

And I'm there, 'No, they're behaving the way boys are *supposed* to behave?'

'I really don't know what to do about them. They're actually worse now than they were *before* they went on their medication.'

'I'm still waiting for an apology from your old man.'

At that exact moment, the boys come tearing through the house and into the kitchen, Leo first, then Brian and Johnny chorging after him. Brian makes a dive at Leo and brings him down with what I would have to describe as a textbook ankle-tap.

Sorcha goes, 'Boys, stop it! Stop! Stop! Stop!' and I can hear from her voice that she's at the end of her rope.

She has to live with them, I suppose.

I go, 'Come on, Sorcha, let's leave them to it. We'll go and bring the old dear's shit down.'

So we tip upstairs, then we climb the ladder up to the attic, where all the old dear's bits and pieces were stored while Shadden was living here.

I'm there, 'Any word from your sister?'

She goes, 'Just what I've seen on Instagram. She's back in Sydney. She got Paavo's name tattooed on the inside of her orm.'

'That's, em, heavy.'

'I don't like tattoos, as you know, but it's actually nice.'

'What's her, em, Instagram handle? I wouldn't mind checking that out.'

'It's just her full name and then 1984 – the year she was born.'

'Do you know what? It doesn't matter.'

'Oh my God!' she suddenly goes – yeah, no, she's opened a cordboard box and pulled out – yeah, no – a white dress. 'Is this –?'

I'm there, 'Her wedding dress.'

She goes, 'This is the one she was always talking about! Wasn't it modelled on Princess Anne's dress when she married, like, Mork Phillips?'

I'm there, 'Apparently, I used to get her to put it on her when I was a little boy and I'd pretend that I was marrying her and –' and then I hear my voice suddenly crack.

Sorcha smiles at me and squeezes my hand.

I'm there, 'I'm sorry. It's just, you know –'

She nods like she understands, then she goes, 'It's an amazing thing what your dad is doing – giving up everything to mind his sick wife and their children.'

I'm there, 'He's not going to be doing the actual minding.'

Which is true. He's poached Dalisay from the nursing home and Astrid and three other childminders from the Áras to do the actual grunt work.

She goes, 'You know what I mean, though.'

I'm there, 'Oh, wow,' because I've opened another box and found my old dear's Christmas wreath. 'This has been in the family for, I don't know, generations. She got it from *her* old dear, who got it from *her* old dear – who got it from, I suppose, *her* old dear?'

'It's beautiful,' Sorcha goes. 'Oh my God, do you know what you should do? You should hang it on the door for when she comes home.'

'It's February, Sorcha.'

'Some people have wreaths on their doors all year round.'

'Ronan's in-laws have a Christmas tree up all year round. They can never be orsed taking it down after Christmas, then it gets to Morch or April and they decide, sure fock it, another few months and it'll be just around the corner.'

'You really don't like the Tuites, do you?'

'I hate them. Hey, did you hear about Christian and Lauren?'

'About them getting back together? It's amazing news, isn't it?'

'No, it's a focking shitshow. He's a mug and I told him so. Are you going to his fortieth?'

'I am – on my lonesome.'

'Er – yeah, no – I'm sorry about you and Mike. I liked him. Well, I liked his voice. I don't know why, I just found it very soothing.'

'He flew all the way to Paris, Ross – to buy chorcuterie for your dad.'

'Is that a reason to end it with him, though?'

'That's exactly what my mom said. She said, "You and your principles, Sorcha. You're going to end up alone." But – oh my God – he knew how I felt about people taking unnecessary flights, Ross.'

I feel like nearly reminding her that she once flew to London to buy a pair of limited edition Loubs from the flagship store and then flew back to London a week later because they weren't the right shade of baby pink. But I wouldn't be thanked for mentioning it, so I say nothing.

She goes, 'It all seems to be going well between you and Roz. You've done well.'

I'm like, 'Yeah, no, thanks.'

'I know a girl who did jury duty with her in 2007 – it was, like, a personal injuries case. Ask her does she remember Réaltín Clarke.'

'I'll make sure to do that.'

'And then I know another girl whose sister runs a bake sale every year for different charities and she said Roz – oh my God – always, always bakes something.'

'I'll mention that one as well.'

Then she looks away – suddenly all coy – and goes, 'Can I confess something to you, Ross?'

I'm like, 'Yeah, no, shoot.'

'When I saw you two together at your mom's living funeral, I was jealous.'

'Genuinely?'

'It's only natural, I suppose. We were together for a long, long time. And seeing you upset and then seeing someone else comforting you, it made me feel, well, like that should be me there.'

I'm looking at her face. I used to think she looked like Jennie Gorth back in the day and I suddenly feel more attracted to her than I did even then. I reach out my hand and I touch her face. She leans into it and I rub her cheek with my thumb and suddenly I have a boner on me that could jemmy open a strongroom door.

She goes, 'I'll never *not* care about you, Ross.'

And I'm there, 'And I'll never *not* care about you.'

I lean in close to her and I press my lips against hers, then after a second or two she responds, kissing me back, the way we used to kiss when we were, like, seventeen, and I was too cool to admit that I was in love with her.

Then suddenly she pulls away and she goes, 'Ross, I think I'd better go – before we do something we *both* regret?'

So I'm sitting in the slow procession of 4 x 4, all-terrain vehicles that we, on the southside of the city, call the school run when Ronan all of a sudden rings.

He's like, 'Alreet, Rosser?'

I'm there, 'Hey, Ro – I'm on the way to collect Honor from school. I believe Shadden's focked you out again.'

He's like, 'Who toawult you?'

330

And I go, 'Your f . . . f . . . f . . . f . . . fadder-in-law. He said she went through your texts and found out you were messaging Avery.'

'Good newuz thrabbles fast.'

'Was it filthy stuff you were texting her?'

'Soddy?'

'Like a picture of your dick. I'm just trying to find out if there's any chance of you and Shadden getting back together?'

'I doatunt think she'll be gibbon me anutter chaddence, Rosser.'

'Well, if Kennet has anything to do with it, you'll have your feet back under the table within a week or two. So just be strong, okay? Where are you?'

'Ine in woork. There's moorder going on, but. Gordon Greenhalgh is arthur taking oaber as caretaker Taoiseach and he's arthur sacking Heddessy as the Atoordoddy Generdoddle.'

'So, what, are you out of a job as well as homeless?'

'Heddessy toawult me this morden that I'll altways hab a job wirrum – no mathor what happidens. Hee-or, what's Edika playing at?'

'In terms of?'

'She's arthur going on fowur dates with Buckets – and now she's bleaten ghosting him. Woatunt retoorden he's calls or athin.'

'He's not the first dude she's done that to and I dare say he won't be the last.'

'The poo-er fedda is going off he's head, Rosser. I think he's arthur fawding in lub wirrer.'

'I've been there. I've been that soldier.'

'You what?'

'Dude, he didn't really think he had a chance with her, did he?'

'So why'd she lead him odden, Rosser?'

'Look, he has something that she wants.'

'And what's that?'

'I can't tell you, Ro. Anyway, Dude, here come Honor and Sincerity. I'll give you a ring later.'

'You teddle Edika that she has a lot to addenser foe-er. Buckets is like a brutter to me, Rosser.'

I hang up just as Honor and Sincerity get into the back of the cor.

I'm there, 'Hey, girls, how was school?'

Sincerity's like, 'Hi, Ross!' but there's no hello and no great-to-see-you-Dad out of Honor. She's glued to something on her phone, which turns out to be a Taylor Swift video, because she suddenly syncs it with the Bluetooth in the cor and now I'm having to listen to it blaring out over the speakers, with the two of them singing along.

Except I honestly don't care because I've never seen Honor this happy – or happy at all – unless you count laughing at someone else's misfortune or something really sad on the news.

I'm actually smiling to myself as I pull up at a red light on Foster Avenue. And that's when a cor all of a sudden pulls in front of me diagonally, blocking me off. The driver's door is thrown open and out gets – oh, fock! – JP.

He storts walking towards the cor and I centrally lock all the doors.

He grabs the handle on my side and he goes, 'Ross, open this door.'

I'm there, 'Dude, we're in a bit of a hurry. We're going to Eddie Rockets.'

'Oh my God!' Honor goes – and she's laughing. 'He seems really angry!'

I'm there, 'JP, you're scaring the girls. Can I maybe ring you later?'

'Dude,' he goes, 'if you don't open this door, I'm going to put my elbow through the glass.'

The lights have turned green and the thirty or forty SUV drivers behind us stort leaning on their horns. I'm going nowhere. He has me trapped here.

So I go, 'Not the face, okay? And not in front of the girls.'

I stick on the hazards and I open the door.

He's like, 'I want a word with you.'

I get out of the cor and I'm like, 'Just not within earshot of these two, okay?'

So we walk a few feet away – to the other side of *his* cor. I consider making a run for it, but I know deep down that the game is up.

He goes, 'Why did you do it?'

I'm there, 'Do what, Dude?' because I've learned from experience to ask for the chorges to be spelled out to you just in case you confess to something that they don't even know about yet.

He goes, 'Why did you tell Belle that I couldn't look at her old dear's face when I was having sex with her?'

I'm there, 'Dude, she sort of, like, wheedled the information out of me.'

'What do mean by wheedled?'

'Yeah, no, she sort of took advantage of me one night when I'd a few Hanijans on me.'

It's funny that I still have the ability to leave him open-mouthed in shock, after all these years and after all I've done.

He goes, 'You had sex? With Belle?'

I'm there, 'For a little bit. Until she got what she wanted out of me. Then I ended up having to finish *myself* off?'

All the drivers who are having to go around us are leaning on their horns and shouting out of their windows at us.

JP just shakes his head and then – weirdly? – I notice a smile suddenly form on his face, which then becomes a laugh.

He goes, 'I can't believe you had sex with Belle.'

I'm there, 'Do you not remember the time I went through a thing of liking girls who were cold and withholding?'

'She's technically my stepdaughter, you know?'

'Well, if you see her, tell her I'll pay to have her pillowcase dry-cleaned.'

Another cor beeps as it rounds us, then another, then another.

JP goes, 'In a way, I should be thanking you.'

I'm there, 'Thanking me. I actually *like* the sound of this?'

'Delma leaving me was all port of His plan.'

'Dude, you never would have got used to looking at that face. It was focking hideous. Hang on – all port of whose plan?'

'God's plan.'

'God's plan? What are you banging on about?'

'I've decided to go back to Maynooth to complete my studies and become a priest.'

Now it's *my* turn to stand there in open-mouthed shock?

I'm there, 'Are you yanking my cord, Dude?'

He's like, 'I've been thinking about it for a while – on and off, really, ever since my old man died, but especially since the Camino last summer.'

'Dude,' I go, 'I'm delighted for you,' and I genuinely, *genuinely* am?

He's there, 'Thanks, Ross.'

'You know what this means, of course? Means you have to forgive me for spilling the beans to Belle and then hiding that letter. I mean, what kind of a priest are you going to make if you can't let shit go?'

He laughs. He loves me like a brother – always has.

'Come here,' he goes, then he grabs me close to him in a bear-hug.

Fock knows what Honor and Sincerity are making of this.

Another SUV drives around us and gives us yet another angry blast of the horn.

'Fock you!' I shout – we're still having a moment here – and I give the driver the finger. 'Shit – can I still swear in front of you if you're going to be a priest again?'

And he goes, 'Seriously, Ross – how the fock are we still friends?'

'I see Gordon Greenhalgh is already talking about the need to mend bridges with our – quote-unquote – estranged former friends abroad,' the old man goes. 'You mork my words, Ross, if he becomes the new Taoiseach, we'll be a vassal state within the European Union once again inside twelve months.'

We're sitting in the back of his State cor – or what *used* to be his State cor? – on the M50 and we're on our way to Foxrock. The old dear is just, like, staring out the window, saying nothing until she eventually goes, 'Where on Earth are we?'

The old man's like, 'Kennet, what is that place over there – you see it, to the left?'

'That's T . . . T . . . T . . . T . . . T . . . Taddagh,' Kennet goes, although we're nearly at the ramp for Sandyford by the time he gets the word out.

'Taddagh,' the old man goes. 'I think he's trying to say Tallaght, Dorling.'

And the old dear's like, 'Tallaght?' like she's never heard of it before, like the three years she spent campaigning to stop the linking of the Luas red and green lines never even happened. 'And are there people living in all of those houses?'

'Kennet,' the old man goes, 'are there people living in all of those houses?'

Kennet's like, 'Indeeden there are, T . . . T . . . T . . . T . . . Teashocked,' because he's a focking crawler. 'Hee-or, Rosser, you might w . . . w . . . w . . . w . . . w . . . w . . . w . . . waddant to listen to th . . . th . . . this.'

He turns up the volume on the radio and – yeah, no – the sound of Sorcha's voice fills the cor.

The old man goes, 'She's resigning this morning, isn't she? Personally, I think she's mad. I agree with her father. She should bide her time, run for my seat and wait until Gordon makes a bloody well bags of everything – which he will.'

I'm there, 'Will you shut the fock up? I'm trying to listen.'

So – yeah, no – Sorcha is going, 'Leading a political life is an all-consuming business, one that leaves little or no time for anything else, including family and friends. One of my proudest achievements is being a mother to five children and it's to them that I now intend to dedicate all my time.

'I have – oh my God – *so* loved my time in Seanad Éireann with a seat at the Cabinet table. I feel deeply, deeply privileged to have served in Government and I am proud of my achievements as Ireland's first ever Minister for Climate Action. I hope the new Minister – whoever that will be – will continue the work I've storted in culling the national herd and restricting people's movements via airplane and private cor. I hope that the new Taoiseach remains as committed as the previous incumbent to hashtag Countdown to Zero, so that one day, Ireland can stand up and proudly say – along with Suriname and Bhutan – that we've done our bit and now, Russia, India, China, the United States, it's up to you to follow our lead.'

The old man laughs.

He's like, 'Not a bloody chance of that. Gordon's going to tear it all down. He'll put Michael D. back in the Áras – and the Áras back on the northside. You watch.'

Sorcha goes, '*Go raibh míle, míle, míle maith agaibh,*' and it's followed by – yeah, no – a round of applause.

I whip out my phone and I send her a text message. It's like, 'I thought you did great,' and I add an 'x', but then I change my mind and I take it out.

The old dear's there, 'Where on Earth are we?'

'We're about to turn onto the Leopardstown Road,' the old man goes, meaning we're less than five minutes from home.

Kennet decides that it's time to make his pitch. He goes, 'D . . . D . . . D . . . D . . . Do you know what the stordee is w . . . w . . . w . . . w . . . wit me, Teashocked?'

The old man's like, 'You?' and he's obviously getting ready to cut the dude loose.

He goes, 'W . . . w . . . w . . . w . . . will I be kept odden – by the new madden? *Or wooban?*'

'It's entirely out of my hands, Kennet. I'm no longer the Taoiseach.'

'So it's the eddend of the r . . . r . . . r . . . r . . . roawut, is it?'

'No, it's just here on the left, Kennet, thank you.'

He pulls into the driveway. I get out of the cor and so does the old man and we help the old dear out.

She goes, 'Where on Earth are we?'

The old man's like, 'We're home, Dorling!'

Kennet stays in his seat, then he whistles at me and goes, 'Rosser – c'mee-or.'

I walk over to the window.

He's there, 'Will you hab a w . . . w . . . w . . . w . . . w . . . w . . . woord with Heddessy – ast him to take me odden as he's th . . . th . . . th . . . thriver.'

I'm like, 'And why would I do that?'

'Because,' he goes, 'Ine woodied Ine godda get the b . . . b . . . b . . . buddet.

I'm there, 'Why don't you ask him yourself? I thought you two were tight.'

'He woatunt retoorden me c . . . c . . . c . . . c . . . cawdles.'

'That's not my problem.'

'If you hab a woord wirrum – even ast Cheerlie there to hab a woord – I'll teddle Shadden not to take Ronan back under addy c . . . c . . . c . . . c . . . c . . . circuddemstaddences. He'll be f . . . f . . . f . . . f . . . f . . . free of us – forebber, Rosser.'

I'm there, 'Like you said, Kennet, it's the end of the r . . . r . . . r . . . r . . . r . . . r . . . rowaut.'

He goes, 'You're oatenty a bleaten b . . . b . . . b . . . b . . . b . . . boddicks.'

But, by that stage, I'm already linking the old dear's orm and escorting her to the house.

The front door is open and Dalisay is waiting there with a big smile on her face.

She goes, 'Hello, Fionnuala!'

And behind her is Astrid along with the other nannies and the children in their orms or at their feet.

As the old dear steps into the house, she happens to look to her left and she sees the wreath that I hung on the front door. She stops and she stares at it. She doesn't say anything, but I can tell that it stirs something in her.

The old man goes, 'Come on, Fionnuala – let's get inside, shall we?'

We lead the old dear down to the kitchen, which was always her favourite room in the house. Everyone piles into the room and it's filled with the sound of children talking gibberish.

She's like, 'Why does it smell like a chip shop in here?'

'When have you ever been in a chip shop?' the old man goes. 'I think we'll have some tea, will we?' and he looks around him, obviously wondering who's going to make it. No one offers. He's going to have to get used to people not dancing to his tune. He fills the kettle from the tap and – with some difficulty – switches it on and then I catch him staring at the maple-wood floor.

'Good Lord!' he goes. 'Did someone bring a horse into this house?'

My phone beeps. It's, like, a text message from Sorcha, saying, 'Thanks x.'

And that's when – totally out of nowhere – the old dear goes, 'I want to speak to Ross. Can you all leave, please?'

Everyone is just, like, staring at each other, wondering what to do.

Louder this time, she goes, 'Can you leave the room? I wish to speak to my son alone! Out – all of you! You included, Chorles!'

So – yeah, no – they all shuffle out into the hallway.

The old man goes, 'Who in the name of Hades brings a bloody well horse into a house?' and then it's suddenly just me and the old dear in the kitchen.

'Don't leave me on my own,' she goes.

I'm there, 'You're not *on* your own. You've got a house full of people here.'

She goes, 'I mean when I die, Ross. The night before the funeral. Stay with me, won't you?'

I'm there, 'You're not going to die,' even though I know it's not true. 'You've got, like, years ahead of you.'

'Just promise me,' she goes.

And I'm like, 'Yeah, no, fine – I promise.'

I didn't see it coming. I don't think *any* of us did? Except Fionn, of course, who thinks he knows everything.

'There were one or two moments when we were on the Camino,' he goes, 'when I noticed him –'

I'm like, 'What, praying? And you never told the rest of us? We could have had an intervention or something.'

'Not praying,' he goes, 'but just, I don't know, deep in reflection.'

The famous Sinead is standing beside him, hanging on his every word. There's still no acknowledgement from him that he only got lucky that night because I left The Bridge early.

'As well as that,' Fionn goes, pushing his stupid glasses up on his nose, 'I think being back at Castlerock has had a profound effect on him. Look, I don't believe in ghosts or any of that stuff, but there are times – honestly? – when you'd swear you can hear Father Fehily's big voice echoing along the corridors.'

This is us at Christian's fortieth birthday porty, by the way, in the Royal St George Yacht Club of all places. Not that Christian knows anything about sailing. He's seen about as much of the sea as my Dubes. But – yeah, no – Oisinn is a member and he got the room for him and for that he's getting a fair focks from me.

Sinead asks Fionn if he wants a drink and he says no, then she says she'll be back in a minute and she kisses him, even though she's only going as far as the bor.

I'm there, 'That all seems to be going well. Which is a little bit annoying. You only ended up with her because I left the pub early on Christmas Eve – trying to be a mate to JP.'

He goes, 'Oh, was that the night you stole the Dear John letter that his wife left for him?'

I say nothing because it's an – what's the word? – *oratorical* question? As in, he already *knows* the answer?

I'm staring across the floor at Christian and Lauren. She's giving out yords to him about something or other. Didn't take those two long to rediscover why they got divorced in the first place. Still, I've said my piece.

I'm there, 'So did you find a coach yet?'

Fionn goes, 'I've offered it to Gorvan Deery.'

'Gorvan Deery? You've *got* to be shitting me. I tackled him once when he played for Mary's and he ended up with a dislocated hip. And I got off with his girlfriend – now wife, by the way – when she was on a Jier in Ocean City and he, like a fool, was in Huntington Beach.'

'Weird, he never mentioned any of this at the interview.'

'The point I'm making is that he's coached everyone – we're talking Terenure, we're talking Gonzaga, we're talking Newbridge – and he's never made it beyond a quarter-final.'

'Well, as you know, Ross, my first choice for the job isn't interested.'

'Dude, we're not having this conversation again.'

I look around the room, which is packed, by the way, and I spot

Sorcha chatting to Roz – well, boring the ear off her. If I know her like I think I do, she'll be absolutely killed with guilt over kissing me and she'll have gone into verbal diarrhoea mode, telling her that her friend's cousin's next-door neighbour knows a girl that Roz used to do, I don't know, qigong with in Kilmacud.

I'm about to tip over there to rescue Roz when all of a sudden I spot Christian's old dear standing on her Tobler up at the bor.

It's been a while.

I tip over to her and I go, 'Hey, how the hell are you?'

And she's like, 'Oh – hello,' and she's being definitely *standoffish* with me?

I rode the woman on the toilet floor at Christian's sister Iseult's twenty-first birthday porty back in the day and it's been a bit awkward between us ever since.

Again, that's just background.

I'm there, 'What are you drinking?'

She's like, 'I *have* a drink,' and I notice the Vodka Mortini on the bor in front of her.

There's a real Stiffler's Mom vibe about her and it's not an act.

I'm there, 'So where do you tend to do your socializing these days?' because I'm like one of those T-Rex's in Jurassic Pork, testing the fence for signs of weakness.

She goes, 'Socializing? That's a joke.'

I'm there, 'Why do you say that? You're still a very attractive woman.'

She's like, 'You heard he's going to be a father again, did you?'

I'm there, 'You're shitting me! Christian?'

'No,' she goes, 'that focker over there!' and I follow her line of vision across the room to Christian's old man, who's standing there with a very much younger and – yeah, no – very much pregnant blonde.

I'm like, 'Shit.'

She goes, 'Can you believe he brought her here in *that* focking state? And this is how Christian's boys find out they're going to have an uncle or aunt who's, what, more than ten years younger than them?'

I remember hearing that she's become a big-time sauce junkie since the divorce. She knocks back her entire drink in one – you can see where Christian got it from – and she's like, 'Do you want to go somewhere?'

I'm there, 'Er, in terms of?'

'I'm talking about you and me,' she goes. 'Do you want to get out of here?' and I've suddenly got a horn on me that could beat sense into the entire cast of *The Only Way is Essex*.

The old me would have definitely said yes. But, instead, I'm like, 'Er, the thing is, I'm actually *here* with someone?'

She goes, 'If I remember correctly, you were at Iseult's twenty-first with someone too.'

Which is a valid point.

I'm there, 'Yeah, no, but I've hopefully matured since then.'

She's like, 'You weren't that good anyway,' and then she storts looking around the room. 'So who is she?'

'Hey, Ross,' a voice behind me goes. It ends up being Roz and – yeah, no – she's staring at Christian's old dear like we're at Electric Picnic and the woman is trying to edge in front of her in the queue for a chemical toilet. 'Is everything okay here?'

Christian's old dear looks her up and down and goes, 'Euuugh!' and then focks off.

Roz is like, 'What was all that about?'

I'm there, 'Ah, that's just Christian's old dear. She's gee-eyed.'

She goes, 'I was just talking to Sorcha. It turns out we both know Jeanetta Davy – she was the one who brought SoulCycle to Ballinteer.'

I'm like, 'Yeah, no, small world – hate to have to Hoover it.'

Then Roz's face all of a sudden lights up.

She goes, 'Oh my God, here comes Raymond!'

I'm like, 'Excuse me?' and I spin around and – yeah, no – there he is, making his way towards us, with the famous Gráinne following about ten feet behind him, still in her space boot.

Roz is like, 'What are you doing here?' and, to be honest, I was about to ask the exact same question.

Raymond's there, 'Gráinne and I were just having a drink in the bor.'

I'm like, 'Of all the bors in all the world –'

He goes, 'I used to play squash with the Commodore's brother.'

I'm there, 'Again, small world. Tiny, in fact. How's the ankle, Gráinne?'

'Not good,' she goes. 'The bone wasn't healing properly so they think they're going to have to rebreak it.'

I'm like, 'Jesus!' because I do feel a *little* bit bad about what happened to her?

I'm there, 'So, Raymond, do you want me to have a word with Christian – see if he's cool with you crashing his porty?'

He's like, 'Hey, there's no need for you to feel threatened by my being here, Ross. I won't be staying long – just wanted to stick my head around the door to offer Roz my condolences.'

I'm there, 'Condolences?'

Roz goes, 'Yeah, Tobey died today.'

I'm like, 'Oh, shit – oh no, that's a blow,' and I genuinely have no idea who Tobey even is. 'Do we know had he been sick for long?'

'Tobey was her tarantula,' Raymond goes. 'You remember the one you were supposed to look after – except Roz ended up with a plague of locusts in the kitchen? Look at his face there! I'm only winding you up, Ross!'

I'm there, 'I'm going to, em, see can I find Oisinn and Magnus,' because if I have to spend a second longer in the dude's company, I *will* end up decking him.

I go for a wander and – yeah, no – I end up running into Erika, who's standing on the edge of a group that includes Chloe, Sophie and Amie with an ie, except she's not talking to them – or even *listening* to them? Instead, she's sipping a glass of prosecco and staring across the room at Hennessy.

'Look at him,' she goes – she's giving him absolute daggers, as only Erika can. 'He thinks he's gotten away with it.'

I'm like, 'Maybe leave it, Erika – I'm not sure that tonight is the night for this.'

The dude looks over then and catches her eye, with a big, shit-eating grin on his face.

Erika mouths the words, 'I'll get you.'

Hennessy just gives her one of his sleazy winks and pops an unlit Cohiba between his lips.

There's, like, hush then, because Lauren is about to make a speech. She thanks everyone for coming and she talks about how forty is an important milestone birthday even though fifty seems to be the big one for a lot of people these days and then she storts banging on about what an amazing father and husband and friend Christian has been over the years.

Then suddenly, out of nowhere, she goes, 'What the fock is *your* problem?'

And I discover, to my absolute horror, that she's looking straight at *me*?

I'm there, 'Excuse me?' because this is in front of, like, two hundred people.

She goes, 'You pulled a face – when I said that Christian was my soulmate.'

I'm there, 'I don't think I did, Lauren.'

'You pulled a focking face. And Christian told me, by the way, what you said to him when you found out we were getting back together.'

He's a focking shocker for that kind of thing. Rule number – pretty much – one of the Bro Code is that when you get back together with an ex and she goes, 'What do your friends think? You can tell me – I won't be angry,' you don't say shit.

But Christian has always, always, always spilled the beans.

I'm there, 'I'm just wondering is it happening a bit *too* fast? I mean, the matching Dryrobes!'

And she goes, 'Why don't you stay the fock out of it, Ross? You're not exactly an expert on marriage, are you?'

Then she says a few more words and she hands the mic over to the man of the moment.

Christian storts off by thanking everyone for coming, and, as he's doing that, Sorcha suddenly sidles over to me.

She goes, 'Are you okay?' and she sort of, like, whispers it to me out of the corner of her mouth.

I'm there, 'Yeah, no, I'm not scared of Lauren.'

I am scared of Lauren. I'm focking terrified of her.

She goes, 'You did pull a face, Ross.'

I'm like, 'Matching focking Dryrobes, Sorcha – will you give me a focking break!'

'But I still thought she was out of order calling you out like that in front of everyone.'

'She's always been jealous of my relationship with Christian. She knows fock-all about rugby but she understands there's a special bond between backs and she realizes she can't compete with that.'

'I was talking to Roz earlier.'

'So I saw.'

'She said that she met your twin brother, Jamie.'

'Did she?'

'You kept *him* a secret from me, Ross, didn't you?'

'You didn't tell her the truth, did you?'

'No, I covered for you. I said it was terrible how you've been estranged for years. I can't believe you're already lying to her, though.'

'I was boxed into a corner. I had no other option. The good news is that that's the end of the lies now.'

'Well, like I said, I didn't let you down.'

Christian's speech ends and we all give him a roar. I try to stort a chorus of 'Castlerock Über Alles' but there's no takers.

I suppose the Royal St George isn't the place for that kind of thing.

Sorcha goes, 'I'm going to go and talk to Erika.'

I'm like, 'Are you sure that's wise?'

'Ross, we were best, best friends. I'm going to ask her if we can just, like, put the past behind us.'

I watch her tip over to her. After one or two, what look like, tense exchanges, Erika smiles and – yeah, no – they end up just hugging it out.

It actually puts me in cracking form. I've even got a smile on my face as I tip back over to Roz and the other two. I notice that Raymond and Gráinne both have drinks now – red wine for him and white wine for her.

I'm there, 'So you're staying after all, Raymond, are you?'

And the dude goes, 'I was just talking to Christian's mother at the bar,' and this is in front of Roz, bear in mind. 'She was very, very drunk. So drunk, in fact, that she told me – a total stranger – that you had sex with her on the bathroom floor at her daughter's twenty-first birthday.'

Roz looks at me with her eyes and mouth wide open – an expression I'm becoming more and more familiar with – waiting for an explanation.

And, despite what I told Sorcha earlier, I hear myself go, 'It's lies, Roz – all lies. Like he said, the woman is absolutely hammered.'

So I'm lying on my bed, with one hand down the front of my Cantos – the baggy ones with the focked elastic – and my other hand texting Roz to ask her what she's wearing, except she's not biting tonight, and I'm wondering does it have something to do with what Raymond told her about me riding Christian's old dear.

And that's when I hear the doorbell. From her bedroom, Erika goes, 'Ross, answer that, will you?'

I'm there, 'Er, can you not get it? I'm in the middle of something.'

She's like, 'Yeah, you're playing with yourself, Ross,' which is presumably a lucky guess. 'Just focking do it, will you?'

So – yeah, no – I've no choice but to get up off the bed, then tip downstairs to answer the door. When I do, I end up getting a bit of a shock. Because standing there, clutching a bunch of petrol-station flowers and smelling of *Joop!* and desperation, is Buckets of Blood.

I'm like, 'Oh, Buckets, no!' because I feel genuinely sorry for the dude.

He goes, 'Is Edika howum? I know she is because that's her SUV peerked out on the roawut.'

I'm there, 'She's really done a number on you, huh?'

He's like, 'I caddent eat. I caddent sleep. I habn't collected a bleaten peddy in three weeks, Rosser.'

I'm there, 'This is what she does to people, Buckets. She leads

345

you on, makes you fall in love slash lust with her, then she walks away. She's done it to better men than you, Dude – she did it to me.'

He looks at me very strangely and goes, '*You* were in lub wirrer?'

I'm like, 'I was big time in love with her – although I was only with her the once.'

'But she's your sister, Rosser,' he goes.

Me and Buckets of Blood come from two totally different worlds. He'll never understand mine and I – thank fock – will never understand his.

I'm there, 'My point is, Buckets, whatever you *thought* she felt for you, it was just bullshit. She led you on.'

'You doatunt wonderstand,' he tries to go. 'We connected, Rosser.'

'That's what she makes you think. Oh, she's very good – I'll give her that. She uses everything in her orsenal. Her eyes. Her smile. She's very good at wearing tops that show off her whammers. And her legs are probably her best feature. I often think about –'

Behind me, I hear Erika go, 'Thanks, Ross, I'll take it from here,' and I'm suddenly thinking, shit, I wonder how much of that she actually heard?

'Edika,' Buckets goes when he sees her. 'Ine going ourra me bleaten head, so I am.'

She smiles at him – did I mention her smile among her qualities? – and she goes, 'Buckets, you'd better come in,' and she opens the door wider for him.

It's while he's stepping past me into the hall that my *phone* all of a sudden rings? And – yeah, no – I can see from the screen that it's Ronan and I instantly know that it's somehow connected to Buckets being here.

I answer it.

Ronan goes, 'Is he they-or?'

I'm like, 'Who?'

'Buckets, Rosser. He said he was going to see Edika to ted her that he lubs her.'

'Yeah, no, he's here, Dude. Where are you?'

'Ine in a keer with Nudger and Gull. We're about five midutes away. Rosser, doatunt leab the two of them on their owen togetter.'

'Why not? He's not dangerous, is he?'

'Buckets was oatenly ebber a danger to heeself. Ine joost skeered of what he might say to her. I'll see you in five midutes.'

'I'll leave the door open for you.'

I hang up and I tip down to the living room. I listen at the door and I can hear Buckets declaring his undying love to Erika.

He's like, 'I've nebber feddelt like this befower – not even about the mutters of me childorden.'

It'd break your focking hort.

Erika goes, 'Ross, stop listening at the focking door and just come in, will you?'

So – yeah, no – I do.

Erika's like, 'Buckets, I'm sorry I led you on,' and I'm thinking she's letting him down way more gently than she did a lot of other dudes, me included. 'I was looking for information from you. What do you know about the fire that destroyed the Dáil?'

He's there, 'For Jaysus sakes – not this agedden?'

She goes, 'Yes, this again. Who did Hennessy get to do the job?'

'I caddent teddle you, Edika. Ine not a rat.'

'Was it you?'

'You've no idea what it mee-uns in my wurdled to be a tout.'

She's like, 'An innocent woman went to her grave being blamed for a crime she didn't commit.'

He goes, 'Ine not saying addything. Edika, you've no idea what Heddessy's like. The madden has no fooken conscience whatso-ebber. He'd cut your bleaten troat and say you did it shaving.'

I'm there, 'What if Erika let you get off with her for a little bit? Would you spill the beans then?'

Erika goes, 'Stay the fock out of this, Ross, will you?'

I'm there, 'I'll turn my back and I won't look.'

Erika's like, 'Shut the fock up.'

There's, like, a break in the conversation then. Buckets asks her if she likes the tulips he brought her and she says that petrol-station flowers give her rhinitis. Hell hath no fury – blah, blah, blah.

347

Erika tries to come in from a different angle then.

She goes, 'You love Ronan, Buckets, don't you?'

Buckets is like, 'Course I lub him. He's like a seventh bleaten sudden to me.'

He's got six sons? He's worse than me.

She goes, 'If you know what Hennessy's like, you'll know why me and Ross are so desperate to get Ronan away from him.'

This seems to work on Buckets better than, say, a flash of knocker, or – just throwing it out there – a glimpse at her purple, lacy thong over the waistband of her skinny jeans.

He sighs, then he goes, 'He should nebber hab come back from Amedica.'

Erika's like, 'But he did. And now the only way to get him away from Hennessy is to get Hennessy sent to prison. And he deserves to be in prison, Buckets. You know that, don't you?'

Buckets just nods.

I'm there, 'Dude, Erika is talking sense. You'd be saving Ronan from a life of literally evil.'

And that's when Ronan rushes into the room, followed by Nudger and Gull.

'Buckets, say nutten!' Ronan goes. 'You doatunt waddant to be known all oaber towun as a fooken rat!'

He looks at Ro.

Erika's there, 'If you love Ronan, Buckets, you'll tell us what you know. It's the only way to break Hennessy's hold over him.'

Ronan's like, 'Buckets, joost remembor your brutter getting teered and fettored arthur ratting out Coke Eyes Delahunt and Larry the Lifer?'

I'm there, 'He got what?'

'Teered and fettored,' Nudger goes.

I've no idea what he's saying and I decide to just leave it.

Erika's like, 'Buckets, it's as simple as this. If you don't tell the truth about what happened, Ronan is going to spend the rest of his days doing Hennessy's dirty work. That's if he doesn't go to prison for treason.'

Buckets looks at Ronan and he's got, like, real love in his eyes.

'Buckets,' Ronan goes, 'you doatunt hab to do this for me.'

But Buckets has made up his mind what he's going to do.

'Heddessy ast me to burden down Leddenstor House,' he goes.

I'm like, 'Whoa! That's massive!' because I presume that's enough to get Hennessy put away for a ten-stretch.

Erika's there, 'And did you – burn it down?'

'No,' he goes, 'I turdened dowun the job. So he ast two feddas from Coolock to do it. Maguire and Patterson, thee call them.'

I'm there, 'I'm presuming those are nicknames?'

'Of cowurse they're fooken nicknayums!' Nudger goes.

Buckets is there, 'If you waddant sometin to go on foyer addy-wheer on the Nort Soyud of the City, they're the main medden to ast.'

Erika's like, 'My mom is friends with an Assistant Commissioner. If I bring you to see him, will you make a statement?'

Ronan goes, 'Buckets, hab a think about what this'll mee-un. Doatunt do it for moy sake.'

Buckets is there, 'The fooken bastoord has you thrapped hee-or, Ro. I hab to get you out. Ine godda make a statementh.'

And I'm like, 'Surely, Erika, that deserves a kiss.'

So I'm in town and I'm buying a few bits and pieces for Ronan. I'm actually putting together a Go Bag for him in case he has to leave the country in a hurry. I'm guessing he doesn't still have the one I gave him the night before his wedding.

I'm downstairs in Dunnes Stores in the Stephen's Green Shopping Centre and I'm throwing a can of shaving foam into the basket when my *phone* all of a sudden rings?

It's a number I don't recognize, so I let it ring out, but then it rings again and I decide to – yeah, no – answer the thing.

'Hello?' a woman's voice goes. 'Is that Ross?'

I'm there, 'Er, what's this in connection with?'

'Ross,' she goes, 'it's Gráinne.'

I'm there, 'Gráinne? Er, I'm just in –'

She's like, 'Yeah, I know where you are. Can you pop into the restaurant?'

'Er, when?'

'This morning. Before you leave town. There's no one else here. I need to talk to you about something.'

She hangs up, leaving me – honestly? – mystified. I pay for what's in my basket and I'm thinking, why the fock does she want to see me? And how does she know where I even am?

I'm wondering is it some kind of trap, but then I'm also intrigued, so I tip up to Comté on Camden Street, swinging my little bag of toiletries by my side.

The place is closed – yeah, no, they don't *do* lunch? – but I can see Gráinne through the glass, limping around the restaurant floor in her space boot, setting the tables for tonight.

I tap on the door and she hobbles over and opens it.

I'm there, 'I was just grabbing a few bits and pieces for my son – he might have to go away.'

She goes, 'Don't look so worried, Ross, it's not a trap.'

She invites me in.

I'm there, 'When did you say they were operating on the ankle again?'

But she doesn't answer. She knows I'm just babbling because I don't know why I'm even here.

She's there, 'Doesn't it drive you mad, Ross?'

I'm like, 'Doesn't what drive me mad?'

'You know what I'm talking about,' she goes. 'Those two,' and it's obvious that she's referring to Raymond and Roz. '*We might be divorced but we're still best, best friends.*'

I'm there, 'Yeah, no, I'm on the record as saying that men and women *can't* be friends?'

She goes, 'It takes fourteen days for a locust egg to hatch.'

I'm there, 'Er, okay,' suddenly thrown by this conversational – I want to say – *pivot*?

'The adult female buries her eggs in soil or sand,' she goes. 'They don't hatch on tiled floors or kitchen countertops.'

I'm there, 'I'm storting to wonder where this is going, Gráinne.'

'It takes months, and the right conditions, for a plague of locusts to develop,' she goes. 'What happened in Roz's kitchen wasn't your fault. Someone put those locusts there.'

'Are you saying it was Raymond?'

'I checked his credit card statement. There was a €470 charge on it from an online petfood supply company. I rang them. Do you know how many locusts you can get for €470, Ross?'

'I'm guessing it's a lot.'

'A whole plague's worth. I know what he's been doing to you.'

'Do you?'

'I know he's been listening to your voicemail messages.'

'How does he always know where we are? The time we were at the Forty Foot. The night of Christian's fortieth.'

'He has some kind of GPS device hidden in Roz's cor.'

'You're shitting me.'

'I'm not shitting you.'

'Wait a second, how did you know I was in Dunnes Stores in the Stephen's Green Shopping Centre?'

'He hid one in the lining of that jacket you were wearing the night that you and Roz had dinner here.'

'Shit – there's a hole in my inside pocket. He must have slipped it in through that.'

'I was watching your movements on his laptop in the office.'

I can't believe what I'm actually hearing here.

She goes, 'He's obsessed with her.'

I'm there, 'He pretty much told me that himself.'

'He doesn't want her,' she goes, 'but he doesn't want anyone *else* to have her?'

I'm there, 'Random,' pretending it's a concept that's totally alien to me. 'So, so random.'

She goes, 'You know, Roz isn't exactly innocent in all of this.'

I'm like, 'What do you mean?'

'She's not a fool, Ross. She's flattered by his attention. And she likes that it makes whoever she happens to be seeing jealous. I've seen Raymond drive away six or seven boyfriends and Roz just pretends it was their possessiveness that was the issue.'

'Does it not drive *you* mad?'

'Of course it does. You know, when I broke my ankle, they didn't miss as much as a minute of skiing time. They just carried on as if I wasn't there. Raymond, Roz and Sincerity, a happy little threesome, while I was stuck in the chalet all day with my leg in this focking boot.'

'Why do you put up with it?'

'I don't know. Sometimes, I think – I don't know – maybe I should have an affair. Just to make myself feel better.'

I'm there, 'I'm a big believer in a thing called pre-cheating. I actually invented it.'

She goes, 'What is it?'

'Well, you basically cheat on someone, just to put something in the profit column, so that if you find out that they've cheated on you, there's no actual loss. Does that make sense?'

Suddenly – out of absolutely nowhere – she grabs my head in her two hands and she storts kissing me on the mouth.

I'm like, 'What the fo –' because I honestly didn't see it coming, although after ten seconds or so, I join in because it'd be rude otherwise and I'm nothing if not a gentleman.

She's not an unattractive woman, although kissing her is like eating a protein ball – the first time you feel her tongue in your mouth, you're thinking, oh, this is really nice, then ten seconds later you're wondering, what the fock am I eating here?

She pulls back and she looks into my face – for what, I have absolutely no idea – then she goes, 'Pre-cheating, huh?'

She grabs my hand and she leads me through the restaurant towards the kitchen, her limping in the big boot and me using the sleeve of my jacket to wipe her spit off my chin, cheeks and – disgustingly – neck.

In the kitchen, we kiss some more, then she peels off my jacket and unbuttons my shirt, and I suddenly remember that I went at myself this morning and I'm worried that I might be wankrupt.

But, no, she tears open my chinos, then she storts pulling my plonker with both hands, like a magician pulling a string of handkerchiefs from a box, while I unbutton her crisp white shirt and have a good old feel of her doo-dahs through her lacy bra, and I'm suddenly standing to attention like someone's struck up the opening notes of 'Ireland's Call'.

She goes, 'I want you inside me – right now,' and I am only too happy to oblige.

I open her trousers and I yank them down, along with her knickers, as far as her knees, then I go, 'How do I take the boot off?'

But she's like, 'You can't. I have to leave it on.'

She sits up on one of the counters – probably not the most hygienic thing that's ever happened in this kitchen – then rolls onto her back with her two legs pointing in the air, then I move the big number eight, as I sometimes call him, into position.

And it's there that I'm going to fade the scene to black, out of respect for a woman who's still married, bear in mind, however unhappily.

All I will say is that the entire exchange lasts – without exaggeration – fifteen to twenty minutes and ends with her shouting, 'You're doing it to me! You're doing it to me! You're doing it to me!' while pressing her fingers into the sides of my head like it's a stress ball, and me with her two legs slung over my left shoulder, banging my back out while staring at my reflection in a silver saucepan hanging from the pot rack above our heads, my face looking ugly and twisted like a pissed Lord Voldemort.

'That was fantastic,' I go when it's all over. 'Full credit to you.'

But she doesn't comment either way. She just goes, 'There's Flash Wipes in the second drawer there,' as she sort of, like, slides her orse off the counter, then wobbles a bit on the dismount, her hips and knees absolutely focked from the workout.

I grab the packet and I throw it to her. Sorcha wouldn't approve. But, like I said, it's a food preparation area and there'll be no Michelin Stor if they find out that this is the kind of shit that goes on in the same spot where the coriander gets chopped.

I get dressed, then I bend down to pick up my sailing jacket – and that's when something suddenly dawns on me.

I'm there, 'Hang on, if there's a GPS device in my sailing jacket, won't Raymond know that I'm here with you?'

And she goes, 'Oh, good point,' and I can tell that it's not the first

time this has occurred to her. 'You better get going, Ross. He's probably already on his way.'

'Okay,' I go – at the same time demonstrating what I'm talking
about, 'hold the ball in your two hands like this.'

I can't believe how much Brian, Johnny and Leo have forgotten
about rugby. I'm having to teach them the basics all over again. Sorcha's old man did a real number on them.

'I've never been a big believer in passing the ball just for the sake
of passing it,' I go. 'Before you release the ball, try to get at least one
defender to commit – in other words, tackle you. That way you take
him out of the game altogether. Brian, are you listening to me?'

The dude is in his own little world. He's there, 'Stupid focking
bitch.'

I turn around to Honor, who's sitting on a bench just behind me,
her nose stuck in her phone.

I'm like, 'Er, who's he talking about?'

Honor goes, 'I presume he means that woman who complained
about him.'

Yeah, no, there was an incident earlier on in McDonald's in
Stillorgan. Brian fished the slice of gherkin out of his Big Mac and
he just, like, focked it over his shoulder, which I thought was hilarious, except it hit this woman in the face, stuck to her glasses, in fact,
and she went straight to the manager.

The boys were already on a final warning from an incident involving Leo the previous week and Zhang – who presides over the entire
operation – told me that he had no option but to ban us from
coming in.

'Your children,' he went – because he was very polite about the
whole thing, 'out of control!'

I'm like, 'Brian, forget her, okay? Or, better still, learn how to use
that anger by channelling it. Now, when you're passing the ball – I
can't believe I'm having to go back to day one with you, but that's
cool – always turn side-on to the defence so that you're facing the
supporting receiver.'

I still can't believe that Fionn is thinking in terms of Gorvan

Deery. I've actually forgotten more about rugby than Gorvan Deery will ever learn.

I'm there, 'Before you release the ball, identify the torget area – we're talking chest-high, in front of the receiver.'

Honor's phone rings and she answers it. A second or two later, she goes, 'Dad, it's Ronan.'

I'm there, 'Ronan? Why doesn't he ring me on *my* phone?'

'He said he tried but there's no answer.'

Yeah, no, I switched it to silent. I'm working here.

I take the phone from Honor. I'm like, 'Ro, how the hell are you?'

He goes, 'Where are you, Rosser?'

'I'm in Cabinteely Pork, trying to teach my children the rugby fundamentals all over again. Still, there's something to be said for working with a blank canvas.'

'What Ine aston is, is there addy wooden listening in?'

'No, there's not – chat away, Dude.'

'He's godden, Rosser.'

'Gone? Who's gone?'

'Heddessy. He's arthur doing a rudder.'

'You're shitting me.'

'Buckets made a statement to the Geerds saying Heddessy ast him to burden Doddle Airdint. Then thee addested Maguire and Patterson, who sang like a couple of canardies. When thee weddent to pick up Heddessy, his place had been cleart out.'

'So has he, like, left the country?'

'I habn't a clue. I weddent into woork yesterday and the office was all closed up. Then I ren into Buckets and he toawult me the stordee.'

'Ro, you've got to get out of here.'

'I'd nuttin got to do with burdening Doddle Airdint.'

'But he had you doing all sorts of other dodgy shit. Look, I bought you a few bits and pieces in town yesterday and I've made you a Go Bag – for when the time comes.'

Ronan exhales loudly. This is heavy shit.

He goes, 'Thanks, Rosser. And turden your bleaten phowun odden, will you? Case I need you in a huddy.'

357

I'm there, 'In a hoodie?'

'In a huddy!'

'Oh, in a hurry – right.'

I hand Honor back her phone, then I whip out mine and take it out of silent mode. I notice that I've got a missed call from Sorcha from twenty minutes ago. I listen to her voice message, just in case it's about Hennessy.

She's like, 'Ross, hey, it's me. I went to visit your gorgeous, gorgeous mom this morning. She'd no idea who I was, but it was still lovely to see her. Em, while I was there, your dad said that the Gords think Hennessy may have had something to do with the burning of Leinster House. Which means that Erika was right about Sea-mon being possibly innocent – which is, like, Oh! My God! Hennessy's gone missing and the Gords even searched your dad's house for him. Your poor dad is in shock, Ross.'

Jesus, she loves a long voice message, does Sorcha.

She's like, 'Anyway, I'll talk to you about it when you drop the boys back. I hope they're not being too bold. I was thinking this morning that we haven't had a proper talk yet about Honor being, you know, *gay*? Not that there's anything wrong with it. By the way, are Honor and Sincerity, like, girlfriend-girlfriend? I was looking at her Instagram last night and it's *just* pictures of *them* together. Okay, I'm babbling now. I know you always laugh at me and my long voice messages. I'll see you later on.'

It's as I'm hanging up that I hear Honor suddenly go, 'Oh my God, Dad! Look!'

At first, I think she's talking about possibly Johnny finally throwing a decent pass to one of his brothers, but when I turn around to look, I see the famous Morcus and his two mates making their way across the pork towards the boys.

'Where the fock have you three been?' Morcus goes.

Johnny's there, 'We don't go to the library any more.'

Morcus is like, 'Why not?'

'Because libraries are shit,' Leo goes.

What actually happened was that Sorcha's old man was told to stop bringing them after Brian set off the fire alorm by cracking the emergency glass with Johnny's head.

Morcus stops walking. He's there, 'Are you getting smort with me? You owe me four weeks – plus interest. That's eighty euros each.'

I know this is slightly off the point, but that's actually quite reasonable as these things go. To put it in context, I was getting more than that from the five or six First Years that I used to bully in Castlerock and that was, like, twenty-something years ago. He clearly doesn't have a business head on his shoulders.

Neither Brian, nor Johnny, nor Leo makes a move to give him what he's looking for, so Morcus goes, 'Search their pockets,' and one of the dudes takes a step forward and reaches for Leo's trouser pocket.

And that's when all hell breaks loose.

People often talk about the punch that Sébastien Chabal threw at Morc Giraud. As a matter of fact, I watched it with the boys on YouTube hundreds of times when they were younger. And Leo obviously has some, I don't know, muscle memory of it because it's the exact same punch he throws at this dude – a sledgehammer right hook to the side of the jaw that puts the kid on the deck.

'Oh, that's lights out!' I laugh – and it is, because the poor dude doesn't even stir.

Morcus stares at Leo in shock. He can't believe what he's just seen. But it's nothing compared to what comes next. Brian, Johnny and Leo stort walking towards Morcus and his mate, then they set about them like Cork women going at a buffet breakfast table.

I'm just watching, totally mesmerized, while Honor offers them advice from the bench, shouting, 'Kick him in the focking balls, Johnny!' and similar encouragements.

There's, like, punching and kicking and headbutting and biting. And, at the end of it, Morcus scrambles to his feet and tries to make a run for it, leaving his two mates behind like a proper coward.

That's when I notice that Leo is holding the ball over his head like he's about to take a lineout throw and I know straight away what he's about to do.

I'm there, 'Keep your legs flexible, Leo,' because I played hooker for Seapoint, bear in mind. 'Your power comes from your core – and remember to finish with your hands high.'

But he doesn't *need* to be told? He lets go of the ball and I watch it fly through the air in what I would describe as a textbook orc, before coming down and cracking Morcus on the back of the head and sending him to the floor.

It's the proudest I've been of any of my children since the Castle Pork Dalkey Open Sports Day when Honor spear-tackled a girl who tried to cheat her out of first place in the sack race.

And I'm just like, 'Goys – it's great to have you back.'

So it's, like, six o'clock on Saturday evening and I'm in Morton's in Ranelagh with Roz, picking up something for our dinner tonight and our brunch tomorrow morning.

Yeah, no, we're living the southside dream.

As we pass through the refrigerated-foods section, Roz doubles back, then her face breaks into a smile.

'Ross,' she goes, 'look! Porma ham! Kalamata olives! Gorgonzola!'

And – yeah, no – she's right. The fridges are full of Spanish meats and French cheeses and Italian whatever-else and Roz doesn't know whether she can trust her eyes.

She goes, 'Does this mean –'

I look around and I notice that all of the other shoppers have full baskets and huge smiles on their faces.

She's like, '– that the nightmare has ended?'

But she jinxes it by saying that because it's at that exact moment that I notice Raymond coming steaming down the aisle towards us, his face an angry shade of red.

He goes, 'Roz, I need to talk to you – alone!'

Roz is like, 'Raymond? Oh my God, what's wrong?'

I'm there, 'Whatever he's about to say to you, Roz, it already sounds like bullshit.'

He goes, 'Roz, certain things have been going on – and they've been going on right under your nose.'

I'm like, 'See what I mean? It's his word against mine,' because

I still think this is about me and Gráinne rattling the crockery the other morning.

But he totally ends up blindsiding me when he goes, '*His* daughter – is a lesbian!'

All activity in Morton's seems to come to a sudden halt at that point.

'I know that,' Roz – in fairness to her – goes. 'So what?'

He's like, 'So you don't mind? You don't mind that she's corrupting our daughter?'

'Corrupting her?'

'She was perfectly happy with that boy – the Protestant boy – until *his* daughter got inside her head.'

'What are you talking about?'

'Even *his* wife thinks there's something going on between them. Take a look at the girl's Instagram – it's *just* pictures of *them* together.'

This conversation is storting to feel weirdly familiar.

I'm there, 'How do you know what Sorcha thinks?' and then I suddenly cop it.

Her voicemail message. I never did change my PIN from zero, zero, zero, zero.

Roz goes, 'Raymond, I can't believe you're being so uncool about this.'

He's like, 'So you're saying something *is* going on?'

'I have no idea,' she goes, 'and it's none of my business. Raymond, I never thought you were homophobic.'

He's there, 'I'm not homophobic. I just don't want someone catching our daughter at a vulnerable moment and persuading her to do something that she later regrets.'

I should deck him – Morton's or not – except the dude is doing a good enough job of blowing *himself* up? So I keep my mouth shut.

Roz goes, 'Maybe Sincerity *is* gay. Or maybe it's just a phase. I went through something similar when I was in first year in college.'

I know that this is neither the time nor the place but I would definitely like to hear more about that.

'Wait a minute,' she suddenly goes, 'how did you know we were here?'

He doesn't even get a chance to answer because another voice goes, 'He has a GPS device hidden in your cor,' and I turn around to see Gráinne hobbling down the aisle towards us in her famous space boot. 'He also hid one in the lining of Ross's jacket there.'

Fock, I forgot to take that out as well.

Roz's jaw is basically on the floor at this stage and she's not alone. Pretty much the whole of Morton's is listening with their mouths slung open. Raymond ends up turning on *me* then?

He's like, 'You see what you've done?' and he pretty much spits the words out. 'We were all happy until you came along!'

Roz goes, 'Raymond, is this true? Were you tracking our movements?'

Like a fool, he says yes. I'd have denied it and then gone on denying it, even in the face of – I think it's a word – *irreputable* evidence. That's why I'm a player and he's not.

He goes, 'He's not good enough for you, Roz. Look at him with his sailing shoes and his little quiff and that horrible, leering smile on his face.'

He's not the first person to comment on the smile.

Roz goes, '*I'll* decide who's good enough for me, Raymond – not you.'

'What I mean is, Roz, he's not worthy of you. He's a rugby . . . person. There's stories about him all over town. He's a liar and a cheat.'

People say it's expensive to shop in Morton's but the customers are certainly getting value for their money today.

I can't resist going, 'You wouldn't want to listen to rumours, Raymond.'

He goes, 'There's that focking smile again. Ask him, Roz, what he was doing in the restaurant on Thursday morning.'

I'm in the process of trying to come up with something when Gráinne suddenly goes, 'I asked him to come and see me. Because I found out you spent €470 on locusts.'

Roz goes, 'Locusts?'

'They didn't breed in your kitchen after Ross knocked the box over,' Gráinne goes. 'Raymond put them there. He's been conducting a campaign against Ross.'

'Only because I know what he is,' Raymond goes. 'You know he doesn't even *have* a twin brother?'

Roz goes, 'What are you talking about? I met him.'

He's like, 'No, you met Ross pretending to be him.'

'Seriously, Raymond, I can't believe that you would go to these lengths to try to stop me from being happy.'

'Roz, you have to believe me – there *is* no Jamie.'

'But you said you met him yourself – in The Ivy, wasn't it?'

'I just made that up.'

'You're storting to sound unhinged.'

He goes, 'Something else happened – between him and his mother's nurse.'

I'm there, 'It's desperation stakes now.'

Roz just fixes him with a look and she's like, 'Raymond, I understand that you're always going to be in Sincerity's life – but you and I will never, ever be friends again.'

Then she bursts into tears and runs out of the shop, leaving her basket of goodies behind.

I look at Gráinne and I go, 'Thanks,' and then I give Raymond one of my famous wink-and-smile combinations, then I go outside to check on Roz, although not before hearing *him* go, 'I know that something happened between you two – and you did it just to punish me.'

Roz is sitting in her cor on Dunville Avenue, her face in her hands, crying her eyes out. I get into the passenger seat beside her and she throws her orms around my shoulders and storts *really* sobbing.

She's there, 'Oh, Ross, I'm so sorry. I had no idea he was doing that to you.'

I'm like, 'Hey, it was very much a case of give a dog a bad name.'

'Why didn't you say something?'

'I don't know. I just thought, fine, let him do his worst, then I'll come back stronger and prove my class in the second half. Do you remember the 2011 Heineken Cup final, by any chance?'

'No,' she goes, dabbing at her eyes with a tissue. 'What happened in it?'

I'm just grateful that Johnny Sexton isn't in the cor to hear her say those words.

I'm there, 'I'll put it on for you sometime. I have the DVD.'

She goes, 'Your brother said you were an amazing person.'

That was nice of me.

I'm there, 'Did he?'

'He said that people look at you and they automatically think rugby,' she goes, 'but that you have loads of other amazing, amazing qualities. Ross, I love you.'

I'm there, 'Yeah, no, I love you too.'

'As in, I really, *really* love you.'

'Hey, it's *all* good. What are we going to do about –?'

'Honor and Sincerity?'

'I was actually going to say the shopping. We left a basket full of groceries in the middle of the aisle.'

'I don't think I could go back, Ross. I'd be too embarrassed.'

'I'll go.'

'Are you sure?'

'I've *no* embarrassment. Our family just doesn't possess the gene. I'll be back in five.'

So I tip back into the shop and I retrieve the basket. Raymond and Gráinne have gone, although there's still quite a few people in there who witnessed the drama earlier and they're all shocked to see me picking up meats and cheeses as if nothing happened.

I carry the basket to the checkout and the girl storts putting my shit through. And that's when my phone rings. I can see from the screen that it's Sorcha so I decide to answer.

I'm there, 'If you're ringing about Morcus – and you've had a call from his old dear – all I'll say is that the little focker got what was coming to him.'

She's like, 'Okay, I don't even want to *know* what that's about? Ross, I've been trying to pluck up the courage to say something to you – trying to come up with different ways to bring it up as a subject? – but I'm just going to come out and say it. Is that okay?'

I'm there, 'Er, yeah, no, fine – make it quick, though, because this gorgeous-looking girl is nearly finished putting my groceries through.'

And she goes, 'I want you back, Ross. I want us to get back together.'

10.

We're All of Us Stars, We're Fading Away

I ask Sorcha what's changed and it's a genuine question. She didn't want anything to do with me four months ago – she was threatening to deny me access to my own children – and now she's all over me like a millennial on free wi-fi.

'So it's a no?' she goes.

This is us in the kitchen in Honalee, by the way.

I'm there, 'I'm not saying it's a no. I'm just saying, well, I'm confused, that's all. You threw me out, Sorcha.'

She goes, 'Because you cheated on me with Honor's teacher from the Gaeltacht.'

I'm like, 'So what's changed?'

She's there, 'I don't know,' and she looks away, then shrugs. 'I think at the living funeral for your mom, then also at Christian's birthday porty, I realized that – yeah, no – I still had *feelings* for you?'

'Right.'

'What does that mean?'

'Well, was it just because I was there with Roz?'

'Yeah, you're one to talk about jealousy, Ross. You were – oh my God – delighted when I ended it with Mike.'

'No, I wasn't. I actually liked the dude. I'm just wondering why the sudden change of hort? I mean, is it because –'

'What?'

'– because you've suddenly got no career, no boyfriend –'

'Oh, thanks very much, Ross.'

'I'm entitled to ask. In case you haven't noticed, Sorcha, I'm actually *with* someone at the moment?'

'Is that why you kissed me in your mom's attic?'

'Er, *you* kissed *me* in my mom's attic?'

366

'We kissed each other, Ross. Which goes to prove my central point.'

'What central point?'

'Ross, I really like Roz. A girl who I was in UCD with – and who I reconnected with recently on LinkedIn – runs an animal shelter just outside Enniskerry and Roz has a direct debit with her for twenty euros per month. Although she technically shouldn't have told me that because of GDPR rules –'

'Where's this going, Sorcha?'

'I'm saying Roz is a gorgeous person – but you're not serious about her.'

'I'm one hundred per cent serious about her. There's talk of us going to Portugal together for the Easter holidays – provided it doesn't clash with a Leinster home match.'

'You may have storted out serious about her, Ross, but now she's just another one of your girls.'

'That's horsh.'

'You told her you had a twin brother.'

'I told one or two lies to get myself out of a sticky situation caused by her ex, Raymond. But that's hopefully the end of it now that he's off the scene.'

'Ross, I know from the way you kissed me that you still love me.'

I do still love her. I can't lie – well, not about that. But I also have feelings for Roz. In a perfect world, I'd be with both of them – then, for one mad minute I actually think, what if I finished it with Roz but then Jamie re-entered the picture and told her that he had feelings for her? But then I realize it's crazy talk. I'd never pull it off – well, I probably would pull it off, but I don't need any more complications in my life.

I'm there, 'Can you give me some time, Sorcha – to think about it?'

She goes, 'Yes, but I'm not going to wait around until you've finished having your fun with Roz.'

And that's when I hear a loud bang coming from upstairs. It sounds like someone has kicked open a locked door. My money would be on Johnny. Sorcha doesn't even react. That's how bad their behaviour has become these days.

She goes, 'Dad wants to send them to this boarding school in Meath.'

I'm like, 'My children are not going to boarding school, Sorcha,' and I mean every word of it.

She goes, 'Mom and Dad play backgammon with a couple whose two grandsons had behavioural problems. They went there and they've literally *thrived*?'

I'm there, 'I repeat – my children are *not* going to boarding school.'

She goes, 'They're out of control, Ross.'

I'm there, 'I'm going to pop upstairs and see if they're ready,' because – yeah, no – we're supposed to be heading for Herbert Pork to throw the ball around.

I think it's best to stay away from Killiney slash Dalkey in case Morcus's old dear is on the warpath.

I'm walking past Sorcha's old man's study when I suddenly hear him call out, 'Ross?' which is weird because he never uses my name, preferring to call me 'you' or 'you, there' or 'you, boy'.

I push the door and – yeah, no – I step into the room. I look around at all the empty shelves and I have a little smile to myself remembering me and Honor burning all of his books in a skip that time.

He goes, 'So you've spoken to Sorcha, then?'

I'm there, 'Er, yeah, I have.'

He's like, 'And she's told you what she wants?'

I'm there, 'Yeah, no, she wants me back. The girl is clearly gagging for me,' because I can't help myself – he brings out the definite worst in me.

He smiles at me and goes, 'I held a gun to your forehead in this room – do you remember that?'

I'm like, 'It's not the kind of father-in-law moment you forget in a hurry.'

I shat my chinos.

He goes, 'I often think about how all of our lives might have turned out if I'd pulled the trigger that day.'

I'm there, 'You'd have gone to jail.'

He goes, 'I'd be out by now. And Sorcha would have, no doubt, gone on to conquer the bloody world.'

'She was working in a clothes shop in the Powerscourt Town-house Centre. Would you wind your focking neck in?'

'We're not happy about this – Sorcha's mother and I. But we accepted a long time ago that you have some kind of hold over her, impossible as it is for us to fathom.'

'Dude, I haven't said yes to her.'

'And we also know from experience that what Sorcha wants, well, she generally gets. So I'm asking you, what would it take for you to move back in here?'

'Dude, are you deaf? I'm actually *with* someone at the moment? She's an absolute cracker as well – probably the best I've ever been with if we're basing it on pure looks.'

He goes, 'Sorcha's mother and I would move out – if that's what it took.'

I'm like, 'What?'

'We'd rent a little aportment somewhere – and we'd stay out of things. You could go back to raising the boys. They wouldn't have to go to boarding school.'

Suddenly, we hear the sound of something – or, more likely, someone – come tumbling down the stairs. My money would be on Leo.

And that's when something suddenly occurs to me.

I'm there, 'You're using the threat of boarding school to get me to move back in?'

He's like, 'I did everything I could for those boys.'

That's the point at which I *should* mention switching their ADHD medication for Tic Tacs – except when have I ever done what I *should* do?

I'm there, 'And, what, now you want to wash your hands of them?'

He goes, 'They're *your* children, not mine. So either you move back in here and act like a proper husband and father – or it's Naomh Aodhán's in Ballivor for them.'

Ballivor. He should be ashamed of himself. I turn around and I head for the door.

I'm there, 'Like I said to Sorcha, I'll think about it. Right now, we're going to the pork – to play a bit of rugby.'

He doesn't like hearing that. Hates the game.

As I step out of the room – yeah, no, it's Leo in a heap at the foot of the stairs – I hear the dude go, 'I really should have killed you all those years ago.'

'What's wrong?' Roz goes.

And this is while we're having sex at eleven o'clock on a weekday morning. Her Reformer Pilates class got cancelled. I'm lying on the flat of my back and she's sitting – again, that word – *astride* me, moving her hips like she can hear a Shakira song that the rest of us are deaf to.

She's like, 'Something's wrong,' because her two venti lattes are bouncing up and down six inches from my face and there might as well be hurling on the television for all the interest I'm showing in them. 'Are you thinking about your mom?'

I'm there, 'What the fock kind of question is that?'

She goes, 'No, I didn't mean it in *that* way. You said she was more confused than usual the last time you saw her – I was wondering were you worried about her?'

I'm thinking – yeah, no – maybe *stop* grinding on me while we're talking about my old dear?

I tap out – two little slaps on her flanks with both hands – and she dismounts.

She's like, 'So it's me, then. Look, I'm sorry again about Raymond. I admit it, Ross, I was too flattered by his attention to realize what a psychopath –'

I'm there, 'It's not Raymond, Roz.'

She searches my face and she quickly finds her answer.

She goes, 'It's Sorcha – she wants you back, doesn't she?'

I'm there, 'Yeah, no, she does.'

'I knew it from the way she was looking at you at the living funeral for your mom and then at Christian's fortieth. You know she only wants you because she has nothing else in her life.'

Oh, the claws are coming out now.

I'm there, 'I realize that.'

'I mean, she helped completely fock up the country,' she goes, 'and now she wants to go back to her old life as if nothing happened.'

'I know.'

'And you're, what, actually considering it?'

She sounds angry. I'm stiff as a board, by the way – still.

I'm there, 'They're threatening to send Brian, Johnny and Leo to boarding school unless I move back in.'

She goes, 'So you're just going to give in to them? And throw away what we have? We were talking about going to Portugal for the Easter holidays.'

I'm there, 'I just –'

She's like, 'You need time to think – fine,' and she bends down and storts picking my clothes up off the floor, then throwing them at me. 'You know, if you're not sure whether you want to be with me any more, then you shouldn't be here having sex with me. I want you to go.'

I go, 'Roz, don't be like –'

But she's like, 'Ross, get out! Now!'

So I throw my clothes on – ever the gentleman – bending my boner into my chinos before hitting the road.

I get into my cor and I check my phone. I've a missed call from Erika from, like, five minutes ago. I ring her back.

I'm like, 'Hey, Babes – what's the story?'

I must stop calling her that.

She's there, 'Where are you?'

I'm like, 'I've just left Roz's gaff.'

'Stay there. I'm coming to collect you.'

'Collect me? As in?'

'I've found Hennessy, Ross.'

I'm like, 'Where?' but she's already hung up on me.

Fifteen minutes later, I'm getting into her cor, going, 'I thought you said he'd probably fled the country.'

She's like, 'He mustn't have had time to get out.'

'So where is he? You smell gorgeous, by the way.'

'That orsehole who you call a father –'

'He's your old man as well.'

'– owns a little mews house in Quinn's Lane, just off Pembroke Street. He offered it to me years ago. It was just after I found out –'

'– that he was your old man.'

'I walked past there last night. There's someone in there.'

'He might have rented it out.'

'There was a window open. I could smell cigor smoke.'

My hort storts to suddenly quicken.

I'm there, 'So what are we doing? Why don't we just call the Feds?'

She's like, 'I'm *going* to call the Feds. I just want to look into his eyes as I'm doing it.'

'And why do you need me there, can I just ask?'

'You're going to stop him getting away.'

I thought that might be the case alright.

She throws the cor in Fitzwilliam Square and we tip around to – like she said – Quinn's Lane. It's a quiet morning and there's, like, very few people about.

We stop outside the house and – yeah, no – I get the smell of cigor smoke straight away.

I'm there, 'What'll I do – knock?'

'Knock?' Erika goes. 'Yeah, that's a great idea, Ross! Or why don't we just shout through the letterbox that we're outside and could he give himself up, please?'

I'm like, 'What, then?'

And she goes, 'Kick the focking door down.'

So that's what I do – or what I *try* to do? I show the sole of my right Dube to the thing three times in quick succession. I hear the splitting of wood, but then Erika loses patience with me, pushes me out of the way and finishes the job I storted with a mule-like kick from her knee-high Stuart Weitzman's.

The door gives way.

And, standing there in the hallway, with a look of total shock on his face, is the man himself. He puts his head down and makes a run at me, driving his shoulder into my solar plexus, but I've played against bigger men that Hennessy and I wrap my orms around him,

372

absorb the contact – it's textbook defending – and stort driving him backwards into the living room.

Erika closes the front door behind us.

I keep pushing the dude backwards – all within the rules – and I can feel the resistance suddenly go out of him. I shove him into an ormchair in the corner and he has the look of a beaten man, resigned to his fate.

Erika goes, 'You're going to spend what remains of your sorry life in prison.'

Unless he went to school with the judge, of course.

Hennessy's like, 'We'll see about that,' because this is Ireland and he knows it.

Erika whips out her phone and dials a number.

Hennessy goes, 'She was a fucking headbanger,' meaning presumably Simone. 'She belonged in a psychiatric institution.'

Erika – with the phone to her ear – goes, 'You thought your life was worth more than hers – and you were wrong. Hello, could I speak to Liam Lysaght?'

Hennessy turns his eyes to me.

'Liam Lysaght?' he goes, his voice dripping with contempt. 'The Assistant Commissioner? I knew him in UCD. He stood against me for the auditorship of the L&H and beat me by one vote!'

It's typical Hennessy – he holds onto shit like Kim Cattrall.

Erika goes, 'Yes, I can tell you what it's in connection with. I've found Hennessy Coghlan-O'Hara. He's in Quinn's Lane . . . Quinn's Lane . . . Hello? . . . The focking signal in here.'

She steps outside to try to get coverage. Over her shoulder, she goes, 'Ross, don't let him move from that ormchair.'

No sooner has she left the room than Hennessy goes, 'So you're going to send me to jail – your own godfather?'

I'm there, 'Don't you dare try to play the godfather cord with me!' and I actually *shout* it at him? 'You never took that seriously. You brought a prostitute to my christening as your plus-one.'

'I didn't know she was a prostitute –'

'She's down on my birth cert as my godmother!'

'– until her pimp showed up at the church and strong-armed me for money.'

'We've never had a relationship and you know it.'

'Never had a relationship? I've spent half my life cleaning up your fucking messes! Who fought your corner when you threw eggs at that girl from Sion Hill who was allergic to alpha-livetin and her head blew up like a fucking basketball? Who put his reputation on the line when you were arrested for exposing yourself in a pub in Ocean City? Who went to the High Court to get an injunction stopping you from being stripped of your Leinster Schools Senior Cup medal?'

'You didn't do any of that for me! You did it for my old man! Because he was worried about it affecting my hopefully rugby career!'

He goes, 'Your fucking rugby career!' and he laughs like the whole thing was never more than a joke. 'What's going to happen to the people you love if I go to jail? Did you ask your sister that or were you still too busy drooling over her?'

I'm like, '*Half*-sister?'

'Listen to me, you sick fuck. I go to jail – everyone goes to jail.'

'Everyone?'

'You think Charlie didn't know about the plot to burn the Dáil? It was his idea!'

'Have you got proof of that?'

'I'm Hennessy Coghlan-O'Hara! I've got proof of everything! You want him to spend the rest of his years in prison? Who'd look after your mother then? And those little kiddies? You?'

'Dude –'

'And then there's Ronan.'

'Ro had fock-all to do with the fire.'

'Hey, if I'm going to prison, I'm taking everyone down with me. He had nothing to do with the fire but he was up to his neck in all sorts. Tapping the phones of TDs. Reading their e-mails. Searching through their bins. And then there's what happened in Moscow.'

'Which was?'

'We sold Ireland's sovereignty for a few hundred billion dollars. That's treason, Ross. And Ronan did all the talking. He was the only one of us who spoke Russian.'

'You'd actually do that? You'd send my son and my old man to prison – out of pure spite?'

'But I don't have to, Ross. If I disappear, it all disappears. Ronan can go back to America. Back to Harvard. Back to the black girl.'

'I'm pretty sure that's racist.'

'All you have to do is let me use the bathroom. I'll do the rest.'

I'm, like, staring at the door, wondering what to do. I can hear Erika outside talking to presumably the Feds, going, 'He's here now. Send a cor.'

Hennessy goes, 'Fine, send us all to prison, then.'

I'm there, 'Just let me think, will you?'

He's like, 'The clock is ticking. You hear it? Tick fucking tock.'

'Okay,' I hear myself suddenly go, 'you can use the jacks.'

He stands up and goes, 'I'm pretty sure I'm entitled to under the rules of the Geneva Convention,' and he gives me a solid shoulder nudge as he passes me and heads for the old Josh Ritter.

Literally sixty seconds later, Erika steps back into the room, going, 'There's a cor on the way,' and then she cops the empty orm-chair and she's like, 'What the fock, Ross?'

I'm there, 'He needed the jacks. The something Convention got mentioned.'

She runs over to the jacks and throws open the door. The window is open and there's no sign of Hennessy.

'You focking idiot,' she goes, then she runs – in high-heeled boots, bear in mind – out of the mews and up Quinn's Lane with me following closely behind.

'There he is!' Erika goes and – yeah, no – I can see Hennessy up ahead, running towards Fitzwilliam Square, where – like I said – we're *also* porked?

He throws open the door of a silver Nissan Almera and jumps in, while me and Erika run for her cor. He pulls out of his space and Erika tears after him as he swings right onto Fitzwilliam Street, then left onto Leeson Street and over Leeson Street Bridge.

'You focking idiot!' Erika is roaring at me as she drives straight through a red light in pursuit of him.

I'm there, 'He said he needed a slash.'

She goes, 'Bull! Shit! He got into your head. Jesus, I was out of the room for one minute.'

'He didn't get into my head.'

'Probably told you that Ronan would end up going to prison, did he?'

'It got mentioned, yeah.'

Hennessy tears through Donnybrook, breaking every red light along the way, and we do likewise.

Erika's like, 'Where the fock is he going?' as he suddenly – without even indicating – swings the wheel right, crosses two lanes of oncoming traffic – seven or eight cors end up having to slam on their brakes – then flies up Belmont Avenue.

Erika does the exact same thing and we carry on after him as he turns left onto Sandford Road, then right onto Milltown Road.

I'm there, 'He must be heading for the golf course.'

She's like, 'Why would he be heading for the golf course?'

'He's a member. I don't know – maybe he wants to play it one last time before he gets sent down.'

'Seriously, Ross, what goes on in your focking – hold on, where's the Russian Embassy?'

'You're asking the wrong man, Erika.'

She goes, 'Focking Google it.'

Which is what I do.

I'm there, 'It's on Orwell Road.'

She goes, 'That's where he's heading. We can't let him get there.'

She puts her foot down – we're talking pedal to the metal – until we're right on his rear bumper, then she shunts him.

I'm like, 'Jesus, Erika, you're going to kill us!'

She's going, 'You're not getting away with it. You are not getting away with it!'

And then she swings the wheel right to try to overtake him, except *he* puts his foot down then, so suddenly we're haring up Milltown Road in the wrong lane, and now there's a number 44 bus flying towards us, with its horn blaring, and Erika pulls us back into the lane a split-second before we end up being creamed by the thing.

Hennessy turns left at the Dropping Well onto Churchtown

Road Lower, then a minute or so later he pulls hord on the wheel – again, across oncoming traffic – to take the right onto Orwell actual Road.

Erika considers going too but the close shave with the bus means she hesitates and we have to wait for seven or eight cors to pass, by which time Hennessy has managed to put a lot of distance between us.

'Foooooooooock!' Erika screams, thumping the steering wheel. 'Fooooooooock! Fooooooooock! Fooooooooock!'

But then a second later we hear a loud bang up ahead and Erika's face suddenly lights up.

We round the bend and I'm the one who ends up copping it first – a silver Nissan Almera wrapped around a lamp-post.

I'm like, 'Holy fock!' and it's weird because – despite everything – I don't want the dude to die.

Erika pulls in. We throw open our doors, get out and run to the front of the cor – only to find it empty.

I'm there, 'Shit! Where the fock is he?'

The airbags didn't deploy – they must have been switched off – and there's a ginormous hole in the windscreen through which Hennessy was obviously thrown on impact, because Erika goes, 'There he is!' and we see him maybe twenty or thirty metres ahead of us, moving fast but limping, leaving a slug trail of blood in his wake.

We're running after him, although I'm trying *not* to catch him, remember? Erika switches on what Ryle Nugent used to call the afterburners and storts closing the distance between her and him.

Hennessy turns into a gaff and we can see him maybe ten metres away pressing the intercom button on the wall outside. A second later, a gate pops open – just as Erika gets there – and Hennessy slips through it and slams it closed in her face.

She's, like, furious with herself.

She goes, 'Foooooooooock! Foooooooooooooooooock!'

I reach there a few seconds – on purpose, though – too late.

Hennessy stands on the other side of the black railings of the embassy, cuts all over his face and hands, pieces of shattered glass sporkling like diamonds in his hair and his moustache. From his

inside pocket, he takes out a cigor the size of Eben Etzebeth's fore-orm, then, as cool as you like, sticks it between his teeth and lights it.

He takes a long blast off the thing, then blows smoke through the railings into our two faces. Then he smiles at us, turns and heads for the open door of the embassy building. A flash of memory comes back to me, a piece of advice he gave me on my tenth birthday: 'Always walk like you're carrying a gun, kid, even if you're not.'

He stops at the door, looks back at us and – randomly – salutes us goodbye. And in my hort of horts I know that it's the last time I'll ever see Hennessy Coghlan-O'Hara.

Ronan goes, 'Probiss me, Rosser.'

And I'm there, 'Promise you what?'

'You know what Ine thalken about. Probiss me there's not godda be a big crowd at the depeerture gate to see me off. I doatunt waddant a big scene, do you get me?'

I'm there, 'Dude, I haven't said anything to anyone, okay?'

He lifts his hold-all – yes, his check-in bag is a hold-all – onto the scales and the machine spits out his luggage tag, which he attaches to the handle of the thing.

'So is Avery meeting you at the airport?' I go.

He's like, 'She is, yeah.'

'What city is Horvard in again?'

'It's in Bostodden, Rosser.'

'Yeah, no, I knew that.'

I didn't know that.

I'm there, 'And what's the story with the job? Did you ring Hazel?'

I'm talking about Hazel Rochford, his boss in Shlomo, Bitton and Black – Civil Rights Attorneys, who offered him the apprenticeship.

'I was thalken to her last night,' he goes. 'She said she'd luvven to teddle me the offer was stiddle on the table, but she'd hab to check it out wirrer colleagues foorst.'

I'm there, 'That's fair enough, I suppose,' because he did dick her around.

He goes, 'Eeben if she says no, I doatunt care, as log as Ine wit Avoddy.'

He puts his – again – hold-all on the conveyor belt and we watch it disappear, then we take the two escalators up to Deportures.

'So what's the stordee wit you?' he goes. 'Hab you decided yet – is it godda be Roz or Sudeka?'

I'm there, 'I've decided about thirty times. Then an hour later, I've changed my mind again. I'm not exaggerating, Ro, it might end up coming down to a coin toss.'

He goes, 'You doorty-looken doort-board, Rosser,' because – yeah, no – we've reached the top of the second escalator and he's spotted the crowd that's waiting to see him off.

There's Erika and Honor and Rihanna-Brogan. There's Tina and Anto and Tina's old pair. There's Nudger and Gull. There's Buckets of Blood and Benny 'Stacks of Money' McCabe.

He goes, 'You fooken boddicks, Rosser,' but he means it in a good way because he's half laughing and half crying.

Nudger goes, 'You ditn't think we were godda let you sneak ourra the cunterdoddy wirrout saying goodbye, did you?' and he walks up to Ronan and throws his orms around him – as do the *other* three amigos?

'Buckets,' Ronan goes, 'I caddent belieb what you're arthur gibbon up for me,' because – yeah, no – the story that Erika told me was that Maguire and Patterson have put a hit out on him and he's basically on the run.

So it's nice of him to show his face, in fairness to him.

Next, it's his old dear, his Uncle Anto and his Granny and Grandda Masterson. They're telling him how proud they are of him and how they'll visit him in the summer.

I catch Buckets staring longingly at Erika across the, I want to say, *concourse*?

I'm there, 'I know how you feel, Dude. She's like a drug.'

He doesn't know *how* to respond to that? I'm basically telling him that I want to have sex with my own sister – but then he doesn't know the context.

I'm there, 'Erika said you're going on the run.'

'Ine on the rudden now,' he goes. 'I've me boarden pass in me sky rocket, Rosser.'

'Where are you headed?'

'Well, obviously, I caddent teddle you that. I'll go away for a few years. Hopefully, the boys will forgib me when I doatunt show up to testify – and let me come back a year or two arthur.'

'Dude, I just want to say thank you. You put your life on the line – literally – for Ronan.'

'And for *her*,' he goes – staring at Erika, who just so happens to catch his eye and gives him a humungous smile that you know will keep him going for however long he'll be on the run.

Honor, I notice, is in bits. When she hugs Ronan, it's like she's planning to never let go.

'You keep on being yisser self,' he tells her. 'And take no shit from addbody, do you hear me? I fooken lub you, Hodor.'

And she goes, 'I focking love you, Ronan.'

Then it's Erika's turn.

She goes, 'Please don't take this the wrong way, Ro, but I've never been so happy to say goodbye to someone.'

He laughs – even though he's got tears spilling down his face.

He goes, 'You said you'd get me out, Edika – and you did.'

She's like, 'I'll be over at Easter to see you,' and she kisses him on the cheek.

He's there, 'I'd luvven that.'

Rihanna-Brogan is sobbing her hort out. He takes her by the hand and goes, 'Mon up to the gate wit me, Ri.'

As they're walking past me, Ronan throws his free orm around my waist and hugs me.

'This is what I ditn't waddant,' he goes into my shoulder, 'you fooken boddicks. Croying me eyes out hee-or – making an expedition of meself.'

I laugh.

I'm there, 'You're very welcome, Ro. I'll probably head over with Erika at Easter.'

He goes, 'You woatunt be allowut into the States, Rosser. You've a conviction for indecent exposhodder.'

I just laugh. That better not be focking true.

The last thing he says in my ear is, 'You were mower of a best mate to me, Rosser, than you ebber were a peerdent.'

It's all that any South Dublin dad – or mom – wants to hear.

But then he adds, 'I doatunt waddant to woody you, Rosser, but there's a teddible smeddle of thrink off Hodor's brett.'

Oh, fock, I think.

He walks up to the gate, still holding Rihanna-Brogan's hand, then he gets down on his hunkers and storts – I don't know – dispensing a few last words of wisdom to her.

There's a TV overhead and for some reason my eyes are drawn to it. Eileen Dunne is reading the news. She says that Gordon Greenhalgh has been elected Taoiseach by the Dáil. She also mentions that all Russian ships have left Irish waters and that Gordaí have storted a manhunt for the former Attorney General, Hennessy Coghlan-O'Hara, whom they wish to question in relation to a number of alleged offences.

Ronan points at me and then Erika and I hear him go, 'Whateber happidens, that madden theer, and that wooban theer, will always be theer for you.'

Then he storts walking through the maze of security barriers with retractable belts and Rihanna-Brogan totally loses her shit.

She's like, 'I doatunt wadden you to go, Daddy! I doatunt waddant you to go!'

It's Honor who goes to comfort her – and she does look a bit unsteady on her feet alright.

I suddenly feel someone's hand in mine. I turn to my right and it ends up being Tina. She goes, 'The best thing that ebber happened to that fedda, Rosser, was the day he's daddy knocked on my doh-er.'

I give her a kiss on the cheek. And now it's *my* turn to cry? The tears come in pretty much rivers as we all stand there – me and Tina holding hands, Ronan's grandparents holding hands, Honor and Rihanna-Brogan holding hands, and – yes, it'd put a smile on your face just to see it – Erika and Buckets of Blood holding hands, while Anto, Nudger, Gull, Buckets and Stacks cry openly, as we wave and wave at Ro until, finally, he's gone.

So it's, like, Wednesday night and we're all in The Bridge and I'm filling in the goys on everything that's happened over the last few days. We're talking Hennessy winning the race to the Russian Embassy. We're talking Ronan heading back to the States. We're talking – yeah, no – Sorcha wanting me back.

'But, Dude,' Oisinn goes, 'aren't you and Roz all loved up these days?'

I'm there, 'Yeah, no, we are.'

'So there's no decision to make, right?'

'Except Sorcha's old man is threatening to send Brian, Johnny and Leo to boarding school unless I move back in. They're back to being a focking nightmare again.'

'Sorcha mentioned that,' Fionn goes. 'It's weird – they were doing so well.'

I'm there, 'It's a genuine mystery alright.'

Christian goes, 'There is something to be said for, you know, putting the family back together again,' because that's exactly what *he's* done, 'even if you're not *in* love with Sorcha.'

I'm like, 'The thing is, I do *love* her? And I always will. But I also love Roz. So it's a mess. There's even a little bit of me that almost feels like –'

'Don't even think about it,' JP goes.

I'm there, 'You don't even know what I was going to say.'

He's like, 'You're thinking of bringing Jamie back.'

'Would it be the worst thing in the world? We'd all be getting what we wanted out of it. I could be with the two women I love. Sorcha could have her husband back. And Roz could be with someone who looks very, very like me – albeit a skangery version.'

He goes, 'Ross, you've got to stop making things difficult for yourself – you're forty now.'

I'm like, 'True that! Speaking of which . . .' and I raise my glass to him, '. . . happy birthday, Dude.'

Him and Fionn exchange a look of, I don't know, something. I cop it straight away.

I'm there, 'What the fock is going on?'

JP goes, 'It's, em, not really my fortieth today, Ross. It's actually not until April.'

I'm like, 'So what am I doing in a pub drinking on a Wednesday night?'

Yeah, like I had to be dragged here, kicking and screaming.

Christian goes, 'Ross, this is a kind of intervention.'

I'm there, 'Oh, just because you're a sauce junkie, you want to spoil the fun for the rest of us.'

He's like, 'It has nothing to do with your drinking, Ross.'

I look at the four of them and I suddenly notice the air of – I want to say – *conspiracy* between them?

I'm there, 'So what is it about?'

Fionn goes, 'Ross, we think you should take the job.'

I'm like, 'Coaching Castlerock? What happened to Gorvan Deery?'

'He quit,' Fionn goes. 'After one day.'

I'm like, 'Because?'

JP's there, 'Because the job was too big for him.'

I go, 'Bullshit – it was because he saw the material that he had to work with and he knew he couldn't turn them into a winning side.'

'No, he couldn't,' Fionn goes. 'But you could.'

I'm like, 'I've zero interest in Gorvan Deery's sloppy seconds.'

'Only one non-fee-paying school has ever won the Leinster Schools Senior Cup,' Fionn goes. 'That was Pres Bray. And I was privileged to be in the dressing-room when their coach delivered his big speech before they played Blackrock College in the final.'

I'm there, 'Dude, stop,' because I can already feel myself getting emotional.

He goes, 'I recorded it, Ross, on my phone. And I've listened to it so many times over the years – just as an example of how one man can motivate a group of young people to do anything – that I nearly know it off by hort. *"They don't even hate us. We're not even worthy of their contempt. Focking Blackrock College. Well, we're not here to watch them win. We're here to ruin their focking day."* Those kids would have walked into machine-gun fire for you, Ross.'

I'm there, 'Fionn, stop it, please,' because the tears are genuinely storting to flow now.

Oisinn gets in on the act then. He's like, 'Ross, the five of us have been friends since we were, like, thirteen years old. And you're the glue that's held us together that entire time. You've never given up on any of us – even in the worst of times. But do you know what makes me sad, Dude? You've given up on yourself.'

He's obviously been told to handle the tough love end of things.

He goes, 'We go to the RDS or the Aviva Stadium with you and you sit there with your Rugby Tactics Book on your lap. And you're making calls minutes before they occur to anyone else in the stadium – including, by the way, the actual coaches. And every year, you talk about the big breakthrough for you being just around the corner. But you've stopped believing it. Because, as Father Fehily used to say, "One of these days is none of these days." You can diss Gorvan Deery for being a mercenary, Ross, but at least he's doing something with his talent.'

I'm there, 'You can't use Father Fehily's words against me – that's out of order.'

'You led Pres Bray to the Leinster Schools Senior Cup,' JP goes. 'You led the Ireland women's team to the Grand Slam.'

'I had to resign one match early,' I remind them, 'because I took my orse out in a pub in Cork back in the days when that was considered hilarious.'

He goes, 'You're the most arrogant bastard any of us has ever met. And yet, one, two, three, four of us believe in you more than you believe in yourself.'

I'm like, 'Goys, you're working me over here. This is unfair.'

Christian's there, 'I remember when you helped Seapoint escape relegation to Division 2C of the All Ireland League. I was going to tell the coach that you had concussion and then you made a little speech, which I'll never forget. You said you'd realized lately that you'd been walking around for years feeling like you'd a hole in your chest. And the shape of that hole was –'

'Rugby,' I go.

'– the shape of that hole was rugby. You told me you'd no exams and no qualifications. You were a shit husband and a shit son. The only thing you were ever good at was rugby. *"This is my last shot. The dream kick and the jackpot focking question all rolled into one."* Do you remember that?'

I'm there, 'Of course I remember it,' and I'm in floods.

He goes, 'Well, it's that time again, Ross.'

Fionn's like, 'I'm offering you a thirteen-month contract – up to St Patrick's Day of next year.'

I'm there, 'Thirteen months? Shove it up your focking hole.'

'I'm only offering you thirteen months,' he goes, 'because I don't expect you to be around after that. You'll lead Castlerock College to victory – I know that as sure as I know my own name – then it'll be the Irish schools, the Irish Under-20s, Leinster, then Ireland.'

It's un-focking-believable. JP is right. These four dudes believe in the Rossmeister General even more than *I* believe in him?

Fionn goes, 'What do you say, Ross?'

I'm just looking at the four of them – yeah, no, we've had our differences in the past – but I realize that I love them and will until the day I die.

I'm like, 'Fine, I'll do it. I'll want focking expenses, though.'

JP catches Jamie Heaslip's eye as the dude is rolling a barrel across the floor of the pub towards us. He goes, 'Jamie, can we get another round of Hanijans – and a Diet Coke for Christian?'

But Jamie goes, 'If you wait five minutes, you can have Heineken.'

We're all like, 'What?'

And he goes, 'It's back. And we've the new Taoiseach to thank for it apparently.'

The old dear is stretched out on her favourite chaise.

'Whose children are these?' she goes, looking completely and utterly bewildered, like me when I've accidentally pressed the Irish language option on an ATM but decided to push ahead with the transaction anyway.

I'm like, 'They're *your* children.'

She's there, 'My children? I *have* no children, Ross – other than you.'

The drawing-room floor is like a bucket of worms – or a box of locusts. There's kids crawling and toddling everywhere. I'm holding little Hugo and he's trying to fight his way out of my orms. He's turning into a little bruiser, in fairness to him. He'll definitely play front row.

The old man steps into the drawing room with a copy of the *Irish Times* under his orm. He goes, 'I see An Taoiseach – inverted commas – has indicated his desire for a second referendum on our EU membership.'

I'm like, 'Dude, you destroyed the country – can you not leave him alone while he fixes the damage you did?'

The old man chuckles to himself and goes, 'I know what you're doing, Kicker. Subjecting your old dad to your famous devil's advocate act to try to persuade him to come out of the political wilderness. Well, it won't work, Ross. This is where I'm meant to be.'

'Chorles,' the old dear goes, 'whose children are these?'

The old man's like, 'They're our children, Dorling,' and then he looks around the room, pointing to each of them in turn, going, 'Cassiopeia . . . Mellicent . . . Deirdree . . . Louisa May . . . Emily . . . and Hugo!' and he's got a big, shit-eating smile on his face, like remembering the names of your own children is something that's worthy of a parade.

I'm there, 'There's no Deirdree.'

'Are you absolutely sure?' he goes.

'Yes, I'm absolutely sure.'

'Why did I think there was a Deirdree?'

I don't think he'd like the answer to that question.

I'm there, 'Her name is Diana. Dude, I offered to write the names down for you.'

He goes, 'Diana. That's it. Although we'll probably just change it to Deirdree – if I can't remember it. Simpler all round really.'

I'm like, 'I'm going to write the names down for you.'

There's a knock on the door and in walks Astrid with the other nannies – none of them great to look at.

She's like, 'Now it is bath time for the small ones.'

The old man goes, 'How many times do I have to tell you, Astrid, that you don't need to knock before you enter a room? This is your home as much as it is ours.'

I watch this look of horror cross the old dear's face and I smile because there are still times when the old Fionnuala O'Carroll-Kelly reveals herself.

I'm there, 'He doesn't mean it literally, Mom.'

And the old man goes, 'Oh, God, not literally – of course not.'

Astrid and the other nannies stort gathering up the kids and the old dear goes, 'Yes, take them away. I really can't abide children.'

They take off and then it's just me and the old pair in the room. The old man sits down in his ormchair and opens up his newspaper. A second or two later, he looks at me over the top of it and goes, 'Have you heard from young Ronan?'

I'm there, 'Yeah, no, I was talking to him last night. Him and Avery have a gaff in Boston. He's storting in Horvard in September.'

He goes, 'Pity it didn't work out with Hennessy,' and the level of denial is off the focking scale.

I'm like, 'What do you mean, it didn't work out with him?'

'What with, you know, Hennessy's legal troubles and so forth. You know they're saying that he paid a couple of chaps to burn down Leinster House.'

He's going to actually deny knowing anything about it. But for some reason, I decide to let it go.

He goes, 'Dear, oh, dear. You think you know someone, eh? He's, em, holed up in the Russian Embassy, I believe.'

I'm trying to figure out if *he* knows that *I* know?

'Claiming political asylum,' he goes, 'quote-unquote. Oh, well. I shall miss him at Cheltenham this year. What was it he used to call it?'

I'm there, 'Glastonbury for wankers. Sorry, no, that was me.'

'The Irish professional classes at prayer. That was it. Oh, he had a way with words, did Hennessy.'

'Bit of a sad end for him all the same – living out the rest of his days in an embassy on apparently Orwell Road.'

He smiles to himself, then goes, 'Oh, he'll get out of the country, Ross. This time next year he'll be on a bloody well beach somewhere. This is Hennessy Coghlan-O'Hara we're talking about.'

I think, fock it, I'm actually going to call him out here.

So I'm there, 'You're saying you knew literally nothing about Hennessy burning down the Dáil?'

'Left me completely in the dork,' he tries to go. 'I expect the chap knew what I would have said. I'd have told him, "We're democrats, old scout – we don't do that type of thing."'

I'm like, 'That's funny because he told me the opposite – he said you knew all about it.'

He suddenly looks like he's seen a ghost. His jowls stort wobbling like he's got a hot sprout in his mouth.

He's there, 'Wh . . . wh . . . wh . . . where did you see him?'

I'm like, 'Where? In that little mews house you own in Quinn's Lane. It was Erika who figured out where he was hiding. She was the one who phoned the Feds. But I let him go – to stop you and Ronan from going to prison.'

He doesn't know what to say.

'I, em, need the bathroom,' he goes, getting to his feet. 'Thanks for popping in to see your mother, Kicker.'

Off he focks.

'Where on Earth is Dalisay?' the old dear goes.

I'm there, 'She popped down to the village to get your meds, remember?'

She's like, 'Oh, yes. You're not going to try to have sex with her, are you, Ross?'

I'm there, 'I wasn't planning on it, no.'

'Because you try to have sex with everyone, don't you?'

'Not everyone – but I take your point.'

'I like her, Ross. I don't want you to frighten her off.'

Then – out of literally nowhere – she goes, 'Shall we go to The Gables?'

I actually laugh.

I'm like, 'What?'

'Let's go to The Gables,' she goes. 'For coffee. Like in the olden days. Do you remember?'

I get this sudden flashback to when I was, like, six or seven years old and she'd keep me off school so that we could have lunch together. She'd send me back and forth to the bor for Gin Mortinis – she'd even give me a little sip when the borman wasn't looking – and then I'd hold the wheel steady for her while she drove home, half shit-faced, to Glenageary slash Sallynoggin.

I'm there, 'We can't go to The Gables.'

She's like, 'Why not?'

And I honestly don't *know* why not?

So I go, 'Er, okay – I'll go and grab your coat.'

I tip out to the hallway just as Dalisay is walking through the front door.

I'm there, 'Hey, Dalisay.'

She smiles at me and goes, 'Hello, Ross.'

I wouldn't be a major fan of the phrase *She has a serious wide-on for me*, but she's definitely keen on me – that much is obvious.

I'm like, 'Would you have any objection if I took my old dear out for a cup of coffee?'

She goes, 'Of course not.'

'Yeah, no, we thought we'd maybe hit The Gables – for old time's sake. She used to bring me there when I was a little kid and I'd drive her home if she had one or two cocktails too many. Well, she'd work the pedals and I'd steer and tell her when she'd driven through a red light or hit a cyclist.'

Her mouth falls open. It must still be a big culture shock being so far from home. Again, I'm just presuming that the Philippines *is* far away?

'Actually,' I hear myself go, 'do you fancy coming with us?'

She's like, 'For coffee?' and her face is suddenly lit up like Pride Month.

'Yeah,' I go, 'come with us. You might get to meet one or two of her old mates. They're horrific people.'

She's there, 'That would be very nice, Ross.'

I'm like, 'I'll just throw her coat on her,' and I lift it off the hook on the wall.

I tip back into the drawing room and I'm there, 'Dalisay is going to come with us, Mom? Is that cool?'

But she doesn't say anything. She's lying back on – yeah, no – her favourite chaise with her eyes closed and the tiniest smile on her face.

And straight away I know in that moment that my old dear is dead.

Sorcha says she'll make the sandwiches and I tell her – yeah, no – thanks.

'No, I can do better than sandwiches,' she goes. 'This is for your mom – your gorgeous, gorgeous mom. I could do smoked salmon blinis. And grilled aubergine stacks. And serrano, pear and goat's cheese skewers.'

She's writing all of this into her phone.

I'm there, 'Yeah, no, whatever, Sorcha,' because my head is focking spinning.

It's been like this since about six o'clock last night, when the news got out – family, friends, neighbours, even fans of the old dear's books, calling to the house to offer their condolences.

Honor is lying on the old dear's chaise, holding one of her – genuine seal fur – stoles to her face. Probably because it smells of her *Chanel No. 5*. Or – Jesus Christ – maybe because it smells of gin.

'It seems it was a hort attack,' the old man is telling Zara Mitten, who picketed Thomas's with the old dear when the shop storted selling National Lottery scratch cords. 'I thought we'd have more time together, but it's probably kinder on everyone that it was quick.'

I feel like nearly saying, no, it focking wasn't – I'd have been happy if she'd lived for years, even with her mind the way it was.

I'm there, 'I still haven't cried.'

Sorcha goes, 'I'd imagine you're still in shock. What about falafel dippers – for the vegans?'

I'm like, 'Sorcha, I honestly don't give a fock about falafel dippers.'

She's there, 'Ross, *I'm* only doing this so that you and your dad can focus on celebrating Fionnuala's life with the people who loved her. What about butternut squash and spinach rotolos? Again, I'm thinking about the vegans.'

I'm there, 'Excuse me a minute, Sorcha,' because – yeah, no – Delma has just walked into the house.

She's straight over to me, going, 'I'm so sorry for your loss.'

I'm like, 'Yeah, no, thanks for coming.'

Poor Zara Mitten obviously hasn't heard the news about Delma's face and when she see her she shouts, 'Jesus focking Christ!'

Delma ignores her. I'd imagine she's used to it at this stage.

She goes, 'I tried to get a flight home last night, as soon as I heard, but I was too late.'

I'm like, 'You're here now, Delma, that's all that matters.'

'Poor Fionnuala,' she goes. 'Your mother was a one-off.'

'Yeah, no, she was definitely that.'

'A true original. With a poet's soul.'

Steady on, I think.

She goes, 'How are you bearing up?'

I'm like, 'Surprisingly well. I still haven't cried.'

'I expect you're still in shock,' she goes. 'Chorles said it was you who found her.'

I'm there, 'Yeah, no, we were about to go to The Gables.'

She's like, 'Sad that she didn't get to see the place one last time.'

I'm there, 'You heard about JP going back to study for the priesthood?'

She goes, 'I spoke to him on the phone about having our marriage annulled. I said I wouldn't stand in his way. When is the –?'

I'm like, 'She's coming here tomorrow. The removal is in Foxrock church at six and the funeral is the following morning.'

I manage to catch Honor's eye.

'You okay?' I mouth.

She nods, even though I know she's not. It'll take her a long time to get over this.

Delma goes, 'I'm so sorry for your loss, Ross,' and then she goes over to offer my old man her condolences, leaving a trail of shocked exclamations – 'What the fock has she done to her face?' – in her wake.

393

I spot Dalisay, hanging around in the doorway, looking nervous. I grab her hand and pull her into the room.

'I am so sorry,' she goes. 'I don't want to –'

I'm there, 'Dalisay, don't be ridiculous. You only knew her for a short time but you were a massive port of her life.'

'How are you feeling?'

'I still haven't cried.'

'There will be lots of time for crying, Ross.'

'I feel bad for you, by the way. I mean, you quit your job to look after the woman and she didn't even last a month. I hope my old man is going to look after you in terms of bunce.'

'Bunce?'

'Means money.'

'He gave me two years' wages, Ross.'

Two years? What a focking mug, I nearly feel like saying, except it's Dalisay and she earned every focking cent of it.

'What about beetroot and rye tartines?' Sorcha goes – she's really wearing me out at this stage. 'I did them when my gran died and everybody commented on them. Hello, I'm Sorcha – Fionnuala's daughter-in-law.'

Dalisay goes, 'Yes, we have met before.'

Sorcha's like, 'Oh my God, Dalisay! I'm so sorry! I've got my catering head on!'

Behind me, I hear the old man telling four or five of the, I don't know, *mourners* that Hennessy phoned him last night.

'Typical of the chap,' he goes. 'There he is, stuck in the Russian Embassy – accused of all sorts of crimes, of which he is innocent, I'm one hundred per cent sure – and his first thought is for someone else. They broke the mould when they made that man.'

Everyone seems to agree that that's the case.

He goes, 'He was telling me about this *thing* in China – Covid-19, I think he said it was called – that they're saying *could* become a pandemic. I said, "Good Lord, old scout, it's not coming here, is it?" And all I could do was imagine Fionnuala's likely reaction to such a question: "To Foxrock? I seriously doubt it, Dorling!"'

Everyone laughs. It's a good line, in fairness to it.

Sorcha is telling Dalisay that she went to an amazing Filipino restaurant in London once and she – oh my God! – loved their sharing plates, although it might have *actually* been Filipino Fusion, even though she can't remember what kind of cuisine it was fused with. She says she's going to Google it.

I'm there, 'I'm just going to, em –' because I need to get out of here to just think.

I step out of the room, then out of the house. It's been raining all morning, coming down in literally sheets. I'm standing out in it, letting myself get absolutely soaked, breathing in and out, trying to calm my – I want to say – *mind*?

I hear yet another cor pull up on the road outside. A second or two later, I see Roz and Sincerity walking up the driveway with an umbrella.

'Ross, I'm so, so sorry,' Roz goes.

I'm there, 'Yeah, no, thanks for your text last night. Sincerity, do you want to go inside? Honor's in the drawing room.'

She goes, 'I'm sorry too, Ross.'

She's a brilliant kid.

I'm like, 'Thanks, Sincerity,' and then into the gaff she goes.

Roz covers us both with the umbrella.

I'm there, 'I haven't even –'

She puts her free orm around me and pulls me close to her. She doesn't say shit about grilled aubergine stacks or falafel dippers or butternut squash or spinach rotolos. She just holds me. I can feel her wet hair against my cheek and our breathing syncs and suddenly I'm sobbing like I'm never going to stop.

Fionn looks at me with just, like, *shock* on his face?

He goes, 'Ross, what are you doing here?'

JP's the same. He's there, 'I was going to take training this morning.'

Yeah, no, he's standing outside the staffroom in a pair of shorts that make me think of Father Fehily.

I'm there, 'Why would *you* take training? *I'm* the coach of this team, aren't I?'

The two of them just look at each other like they're wondering how easy it is to section someone.

Fionn's there, 'Ross, your mother has just died. The funeral –'

'The funeral is tomorrow,' I go. 'Today, I need to coach.'

They care about me – and I love that – but I am one hundred per cent serious here.

JP goes, 'Ross, I just think you should give yourself a few days,' because he lost his old man, bear in mind – he knows the terrain.

I look him in the eye, then I look Fionn in the eye, and I go, 'Rugby,' and nothing needs to be said after that.

Nothing ever does.

I take the bag of balls out of his hand, throw it over my shoulder and head for the brand-new, freshly laid rugby pitch, which Tom McGahy – in an act of sacrilege – turned into a morket gorden after banning the sport from the school.

There's, like, thirty or forty kids waiting for me – all Fourth and Fifth years – standing around in five or six little huddles. I can already see the cliques that I'm going to make it my business to break up.

I stand and watch them for about thirty seconds, remembering when I was standing where they're standing and Father Fehily was where I'm standing now.

One by one, they stort to notice me and a sort of, like, hush descends on the group, a lot of them no doubt thinking, holy fock – are we being coached by *the* Ross O'Carroll-Kelly?

'Who the fook is the fedda?' some dude goes.

He's definitely not paying fees.

I clear my throat and I go, 'For those of you *not* from a rugby background, my name is Ross O'Carroll-Kelly.'

The dude says something under his breath – which I *don't* hear? – but ten or fifteen members of the group crack their holes laughing.

I know I have a job on my hands getting their attention here, so I kick off with a quote from my famous Rugby Tactics Book.

I'm there, 'The shortest word for me is I, the sweetest word for me is love – but the only word for me is rugby.'

It doesn't go down as well as I expected.

'The oatenly woord for you is wanker,' the same dude goes.

He's tall – we're talking six foot – with a blade-one all over.

Every single one of them laughs – even the ones who, presumably, *know* who I am and what I've achieved in the game?

I fix the dude with a look and I'm like, 'What's *your* name?'

He goes, 'Gunther.'

Again, this is *supposably* hilarious.

I'm there, 'That's not your name. What's your actual name?'

The dude goes, 'My name is Gareth. Gareth Hunt.'

I'm there, 'You're a bit full of yourself, Gareth Hunt, aren't you?'

He's like, 'Yeah – so fooken what?'

'No, I'm saying it's good,' I go. 'Because you're going to be my captain.'

Oh, that knocks the wind right out of his sails.

He's there, 'Soddy?'

You can tell that he's just a mixed-up kid from the wrong side of the tracks and it's the first time in his Godforsaken life that anyone has ever believed in him – or maybe I over-binged on *Dangerous Minds* when I went through a period of fancying Michelle Pfeiffer to a degree that wasn't healthy for my marriage or my eyesight and I'm – what's the word? – *projecting* here?

I'm there, 'I'm saying that you're going to lead us into the Leinster Schools Senior Cup next year – unless it's too big for you, of course?'

He fixes me with a look. He knows what I'm doing here. What he doesn't know is that it's the exact same thing that Father Fehily did to me.

He goes, 'It's not too big for me.'

I'm there, 'Are you sure? You might be just a talker – and a funny-man. Maybe I'll pick someone else.'

He's like, 'I fooken want it,' and I can tell that he means it.

I'm there, 'That's good news. Because there will be times when it feels like a burden and I want to know that you're strong enough to carry it. Now, let's train.'

And just like that, I know what I'm going to do. There's nothing like throwing a rugby ball around in the fresh air for clearing the old head. I'm in the cor and I text Roz to ask if she's home. It turns out that she *is* home?

Fifteen minutes later, I'm standing on her front step and she's opening the door to me. She looks incredible. She's wearing a black cashmere sweater that really shows off her milk monsters.

She smiles at me and there's genuine love in it. She's one of the best people I've ever known. An angel. I'm convinced of it.

She goes, 'How are you doing?'

And I'm there, 'I'm, em, doing okay.'

She reads something from my hesitation – or maybe it's from my face.

'You're breaking up with me?' she goes.

And I just nod.

Her eyes go sort of vacant and she shakes her head. She wasn't expecting this.

'So, what,' she goes, 'you're going back to Sorcha?'

I'm there, 'It has nothing to do with Sorcha. I just had a rare moment of – I want to say – *clarity* while I was training the Castlerock College Senior Cup team this afternoon and I decided that it was time to do the right thing for once in my life – for every-one's sake, including my children.'

She nods like she understands, even though she probably *doesn't*?

She's there, 'Was it the business with Raymond?'

And I go, 'Raymond was right about me, Roz. Yes, he's a dick, and obviously a stalker, but he was bang on when he said that I was pretending to be someone else.'

She's like, 'You weren't pretending to be someone else, Ross.'

I was *literally* pretending to be someone else. I end up nearly telling her about Jamie – there on the doorstep.

I'm there, 'I enjoyed every minute we spent together. I enjoyed the dinners and the laughs and the sex that took ages. And I enjoyed being the person I was when I was with you. But it wasn't me, Roz. Father Fehily, my former schools coach –'

She smiles to herself.

She goes, 'I know who Father Fehily is, Ross. There's barely an hour goes by when you don't mention him.'

I'm there, 'Well, one of my favourite of his sayings was, "No matter where you go, there you are." I think what it means is that you can change your environment, but you can't really change who you are. Or you can change it for a little bit, but sooner or later – yeah, no – we all go back to being ourselves. I loved who I was whenever I was with you, Roz, but it wasn't me. And I wasn't going to be able to keep up the act forever.'

I can see little pools of tears forming in the corners of her eyes.

She goes, 'You won't be happy with Sorcha. It won't be long before you're back cheating on her.'

I'm there, 'Like I said, all we can be is who we are – I'm sorry if that sounds deep.'

She smiles and dabs at her eyes with the tips of her fingers.

I'm there, 'I just hope that us breaking up doesn't affect Honor and Sincerity's relationship.'

'Honor and Sincerity don't have a relationship,' she goes.

'Excuse me?'

'They kissed – that was all. And it was just the once. Sincerity was curious. She doesn't think she's gay after all.'

'And, what, she's springing this on Honor the week her grandmother died? Yeah, great timing, Sincerity.'

'She told Honor last week.'

Okay, that would explain why she was gee-eyed at the airport.

'She's back with Johnny Prendergast,' she goes.

I'm there, 'The Protestant?' and I don't know but I'm weirdly pleased for him.

Again, it's just Protestants. I couldn't wish enough good things for them.

'So this is it,' she goes and her eyes fill up again.

I'm there, 'I'm sorry, Roz,' and I go to give her a hug, except she folds her orms and turns away from me.

She's like, 'No – just go, Ross.'

So I turn to leave. There's something about seeing women crying that I can't handle – especially when *I'm* the one who *caused* it? I've always preferred to leave them hating me rather than wanting me.

So I put a bit of distance between us – as a matter of fact, I slip out through the gate and I make sure to close it behind me – before I tell her what I should have told her a long time ago.

I go, 'Roz?'

And she looks at me with tears streaming down her cheeks.

I'm there, 'I don't have a twin brother named Jamie. That was me that day, trying to see down your shirt.'

Her mouth falls open. It's a hell of an exit line, in fairness to it. Then I get into my cor and I drive away.

Fifteen minutes later, I'm on the Stillorgan dualler and I decide to check in on Honor. She answers on the third ring.

She's like, 'Where are you?' and I'm trying to figure out from her voice whether she's been drinking or not.

I'm there, 'I was at rugby training. I don't know if I mentioned it, but I'm back at Castlerock College coaching – back to where it all storted.'

'What time . . . is the chhh . . . the chhhurch?'

Yeah, no, she's focking jorred alright.

I'm there, 'Six o'clock, Honor. I just have to go and see your old dear first.'

She goes, 'You're not getting back together with the fffocking bi –'

I'm there, 'Honor, I thought we had an agreement that you'd tell me if you felt the urge to drink.'

'I just felt . . . sssad, is all . . . I wish Fffionnuala was . . . ssstill here.'

'I do too, Honor. Look, just promise me you won't have any more before the removal, will you?'

I can hear her putting the top back on a bottle of something.

I'm like, 'There's a good girl. Maybe try and get your head down for a few hours – oh, and drink loads of water – just so you don't have a head on you later on.'

Fifteen or twenty minutes later, I pull into Honalee.

Sorcha opens the door and smiles at me. I smile back at her.

Somewhere inside the house, I can hear Brian, Johnny and Leo tearing the place asunder. I hear a loud bang and then the sound of breaking glass and then Sorcha's old man shouting, 'The sooner you three thugs are out of this house, the better!'

I'm there, 'It sounds like your old man is really at the end of his tether.'

She goes, 'They're storting boarding school next week. He says he hopes that it'll straighten them out.'

I feel terrible – like I should *say* something?

I'm there, 'Anyway, I just wanted to –'

She goes, 'Ross, I already know,' and she's beaming from ear to ear.

I'm there, 'Do you?'

'I got a text message from Roz,' she goes. 'She told me *Well done!* and she said I was focking welcome to you.'

'That was, em, nice of her.'

'I told her that she didn't have to be such a bitch about it and she said that she can't believe that I let her think you had a twin brother named Jamie.'

'Yeah, no, I decided to, er, come clean about that one.'

She takes a step forward and – without saying a word – presses her lips against mine and suddenly we're kissing each other with, like, proper passion. She's running her hands through my hair and I'm squeezing her orse cheeks like I'm testing avocados for ripeness.

Her old man suddenly appears at the front door, going, 'Sorcha, the little shits have broken the skylight in the –' and then he obviously sees us wearing the face off each other – as we used to call it back in the day – and he goes, 'Jesus Christ!' and he scuttles back to the kitchen.

Sorcha storts laughing mid-snog because – yeah, no – it *is* funny.

'So how are we going to tell people?' she goes. 'I was thinking maybe we'd have a big porty and announce it at that. I was also thinking we might go to Rome this summer to renew our vows.'

I'm there, 'Sorcha, you've got the wrong end of the stick. I'm not coming back to you.'

Her jaw hits the floor. It's not what she was expecting to hear – especially because I've still got my two orms around her waist.

She suddenly shoves me in the chest.

I'm like, 'Jesus Christ, Sorcha.'

She goes, 'What the fock are you doing getting off with me, then?'

I'm like, 'Er, you threw the lips on me, Sorcha, and it was kind of nice and I didn't want to be rude.'

'Oh my God,' she goes, 'you're finishing it with me and you have a focking erection.'

That wouldn't be a first for me.

I'm there, 'I didn't say I wasn't attracted to you, Sorcha. I just said I can't go back to you, that's all.'

She's like, 'Why not?'

And I go, 'Because you deserve better. Because you've always deserved better. I could come back here and tell you that things were going to be different from now on and within a week or two, I'd be back cheating on you. You know it and I know it. The thing is, Sorcha, I know who I am now. I'm a wanker – a *rugby* wanker, in fairness to me. And, despite your best efforts – and even Roz's best efforts – I can't *be* anyone else?'

She sort of, like, huffs, then shakes her head. She knows I'm talking sense.

Sorcha's old man has obviously told Sorcha's old dear that the two of us are bet into each other in the front gorden because she's suddenly in the hallway going, 'For God's sake, Sorcha, bring him in! Does he need a hand with his bags?'

But Sorcha – over her shoulder – goes, 'It's fine – he's not staying, Mom.'

And there's just, like, silence from her then.

Sorcha goes, 'I can't believe that I'm, like, forty-one years old and I've ended up back where I storted – living in this house on my own with my mom and dad.'

Jesus, I end up nearly feeling sorry for her, especially when the *tears* stort to flow?

She goes, 'Oh my God, when Roz finds out she's going to be so focking smug.'

I'm there, 'Sorcha, I have to go. The removal's at six. I'll see you at the church.'

I head back to the cor and I look at her as I'm opening the door. She's really bawling now – the kind of sobbing you do as a kid when you can't even catch your breath. And in that moment, I know I have to do for Sorcha what I did for Roz and give her a reason to be happy to see the back of me once and for all.

'Sorcha,' I go, 'the reason the boys have turned into little pricks again is because I switched their ADHD medication for Tic Tacs.'

Then I get into the cor, stort her up and drive out of Honalee without even looking in my rear-view mirror.

Epilogue

Honor tells me that Sorcha is pissed off with me. I tell her – yeah, no – I definitely picked up on that myself.

She goes, 'Oh my God, Roz is pissed off with you as well. Er, she didn't even come to the *church*? Is it because you finished it with her?'

I'm there, 'In a roundabout way, yeah.'

This is us sitting in Foxrock church – Our Lady of Perpetual Sexual Frustration, as we used to call it. It's, like, eight o'clock at night. The two or three hundred people who came to the removal to pay their respects have gone, but I'm keeping my promise to my old dear not to leave her alone in the church.

The old man is just leaving.

He's like, 'I'm going to head back to the house, Kicker. See the children before Astrid puts them down for the night. You staying, are you?'

I'm there, 'I told her I would.'

He looks so ordinary without the wig – and ten years older than he did before.

'Okay,' he goes, 'well, I'll see you both in the morning. I don't know how I'm going to get through the day, never mind the days and weeks and – who knows? – maybe even years ahead. Anyway, night, Ross. Night, Honor.'

Honor goes, 'Night, Granddad,' and I listen to the sound of his John Lobbs retreating to the back of the church.

Then the noise stops and I turn around and he's standing at the door, looking back up the aisle at me. I'd never say it to him, but it's great to have him back.

He goes, 'She really loved you, Ross. I know she wasn't always good at showing it, but you were her *raison d'être*, if you'll pordon the French. And, well, mine too.'

He smiles at me, but there's real sadness in it. I smile back at him. Under my breath, I go, 'Yeah, whatever – Dick Features,' just for old times' sake. And then he's gone.

Honor goes, 'I feel like drinking.'

I'm there, 'See? All you have to do is tell me. And then I can at least try to talk you out of –'

She takes a shoulder of voddy out of her jacket pocket, unscrews the lid and knocks back a mouthful.

I'm like, 'Jesus, Honor.'

And she goes, 'I'm going to stop. I'm just going through some shit.'

'You're fourteen years old, Honor.'

'Er, I'm *fifteen* now?'

'You're fifteen, then.'

'I think I might be an alcoholic.'

'Well, that's another thing you have in common with your grandmother. You're a chip off the old sot.'

We both crack up laughing. It's amazing that I still *can* laugh?

'That joke just came to me there and then,' I go. 'And it worked, didn't it?'

She's like, 'It was very funny – although that could be the drink talking.'

'Jesus, Honor – seriously, though, you don't want to turn out like my old dear.'

But of course she *totally* does?

She goes, 'I love the way she was a total bitch to everyone.'

I'm like, 'Being a total bitch to everyone is fine. It's the idea of you drinking that I wouldn't be one hundred per cent –'

She knocks back another mouthful right in front of me.

I'm there, 'Okay, Honor, let that be your hopefully last. They do say alcoholism is genetic, of course. Funny that it's never affected me. Must skip a generation.'

She wipes her mouth with the back of her hand and laughs.

'You *are* focking joking,' she goes, 'right?'

I actually *wasn't?*

'A chip off the old sot,' I go. 'She'd have appreciated that one.'

Honor goes, 'She totally would have. Hey, Dad, I didn't lick it up off the ground – but I would if it was more than forty per cent proof.'

I'm there, 'I'm laughing because it's a funny one-liner, Honor, not because I approve.'

I look at the Christmas wreath that's beside the coffin. I've decided that I'm going to have it cremated with her tomorrow.

I'm there, 'I'm sorry about you and Sincerity – you know, that it didn't work out.'

She goes, 'She says she doesn't think she's gay after all.'

'I heard she got back with Johnny Protestant – I mean, Prendergast.'

'I think it was, like, pressure from her dad. He's a total homo-phobe.'

'And a dick.'

'She wants us to still be *friends*, though?'

'And how do you feel about that? Can you handle it?'

'I don't know. One minute I'm cool with it, then the next minute I think I might just go back to bullying her.'

'Well, take your time to decide, Honor. She owes you that space.'

I'm looking at the framed photograph of me and the old dear that's standing on top of the coffin. It was taken outside our first gaff in what I like to call Glenageary Although Let's Be Honest Sallynoggin. I can't be more than, I don't know, six months old – although you couldn't miss me with the humungous nose and the low-slung ears. And the old dear has this nervous expression on her face as if someone outside a shop had asked her to mind their dog and she was storting to wonder whether they were coming back.

The world is going to be a lot less colourful without her – that's for sure.

All of a sudden, I hear snoring. Yeah, no, Honor has fallen asleep sitting bolt upright in the pew. She still hasn't developed a tolerance for the spirits. I take off my sailing jacket and I put it around her shoulders to stop her from getting cold, then she snuggles in close to me, resting her little drunken head on my shoulder.

My phone beeps. It's, like, a text message from Ronan.

It's like, 'How'd the removal go?'

I text him straight back.

I'm there, 'Church was packed. Didn't realize she had so many fans?'

He goes, 'How are u bearing up?'

I'm there, 'I've no idea. Ok at the moment.'

He goes, 'I'm getting up 5 tomoro to watch it.'

Yeah, no, it's being broadcast live on the church website.

I'm like, 'Thanks Ro.'

He goes, 'Avery says hello btw.'

I'm there, 'Hello to Avery. I miss you, Ro. I love you.'

He's like, 'That's bent,' and I laugh out loud because that was his, like, catchphrase when he was a kid. Everything was bent. Rugby was bent. Grafton Street was bent. Wearing a scorf was bent. Sushi was bent. I'm still laughing when he sends another text, going, 'I love you too, Rosser. Hope you get thru tomorrow ok.'

I downloaded Tinder earlier on and I stort flicking through the rogues' gallery of single women out there who are looking for Mr Right – or at least Mr Right You'll Focking Do.

I spend, like, two hours flicking through them and I can't help but think that Raymond did me a massive solid in reminding me who I actually am. I'm not a domesticated animal – and there are rich pickings out there to be had.

I recognize quite a few girls on there from back in the day. A few of them had the pleasure of my company. I spot Freya, who worked in her old man's veterinary practice in Wicklow Town. I stole a sleeping seal from her, covered it in oil and pretended to Sorcha that I'd saved its life. I spot Oreanna, whose cat I accidentally ran over and then threw into the boot of my cor without telling her, in case it cast a shadow over our romantic evening – but then she found it the next morning. I killed her dog as well – another accident. And, it's only fair to mention, her cousin's snake. I spot Melanie, who was absolutely mad about me until I fished a humungous turd out of her toilet bowl that simply refused to flush away and I focked it out the window, only for it to land on the roof of her conservatory with the room full of guests.

All of these women and more are out there and – whatever twists and turns their lives have taken in the meantime – they're free and single and looking for love.

Jesus Christ, Claire – as in, like, Claire from Bray of all places is on there – and I'm wondering is it all over between her and Garret or are they doing the whole polygamy thing, which I heard that Garret was big into. I'll just say Greystones and leave it at that.

I swipe left.

Fock, even Christian's old dear is on there. For one mad moment I consider it – I genuinely do – but then I decide no, I'm going to keep things simple, for now anyway.

I'm scrolling and scrolling and scrolling while Honor is snoring away on my shoulder, sleeping off the booze. And that's when I see her beautiful face. I actually scroll past it at first, but then I remember that I know her and I go back.

It's Dalisay. It's a fantastic photograph of her as well. Angel Locsin. I said it from day one. I swipe right. I think, fock it, if nothing happens, I can always pass it off as a joke.

I sit there in the church, staring at the box that contains my old dear, dressed in her favourite outfit – a blush pink, Dior shift dress, which just so happens to perfectly match the silk lining of her coffin, hair done by Dylan Bradshaw – her 'soulmate' – which was another of her final requests. I'm thinking to myself whatever differences we had, I still loved the woman, and it feels like a big, empty space has opened up in my life.

And that's when my phone pings, and I automatically smile, because it's a message to say that I have a match.

Acknowledgements

After writing the Ross O'Carroll-Kelly series for twenty-four years, offering thanks to all of those who helped me along the way would take up a book of similar size to the one in your hands. But I can't say goodbye without acknowledging some very important people.

Rachel Pierce has edited all twenty-four novels in the series, as well as the three spin-off books. I've always considered her more than an editor and more like a producer – my own George Martin. The longevity of the series owes so much to her endless well of enthusiasm, the ideas she brings to every book and her determination that every instalment in the series should be better than the one that came before.

Faith O'Grady has been my agent for almost twenty years, and it wouldn't be overstating the case to say that she changed my life. Without her, I would never have become a full-time author and I want to thank her from the bottom of my heart.

I owe an enormous debt of gratitude to Alan Clarke, whose artwork helped to transform the series by bringing the characters to life and who made each book in the series a collector's item.

When you write books for Sandycove (formerly Penguin Ireland), you get to work with the very best people in the business. I want to say a massive thank you to Michael McLoughlin and Patricia Deevy for the vision and ambition that made the series such a commercial success. They really care about their authors and I have loved working with them. Over the years, I've spent hundreds of hours in the company of Penguin staff, past and present, who have made my job so easy as to call it fun. I especially want to thank Cliona Lewis, Patricia McVeigh, Brian Walker, Carrie Anderson, Aimée Johnston, David Devaney, Louise Farrell, Sorcha Judge, Joyce Dignam, Keith Taylor, Tom Weldon and Joanna Prior. And also Emma Brown, Ellie Smith, Annie Underwood, Richard Bravery, Chris Bentham, Josie Staveley Taylor, Alisha Kruse, Meredith Benson and Lottie Chesterman. I've loved working with you.

It has been a real pleasure also to work with the amazing Donna Poppy, who has been proofreading the Ross books for years. Her eagle eyes have saved me from professional embarrassment hundreds of times, and her feedback on the text has always been kind and encouraging.

Thank you to Rory Nolan, one of the great Irish actors of his generation, who brought Ross to life on stage and voices the audiobooks. And thank you to Paul Fegan of bitsixteen, sound engineer par excellence, who produces the audio versions of the books.

Thank you to my former *Sunday Tribune* colleague Ger Siggins, a mentor for over thirty years, who edited the first two self-published Ross books back in 2000 and 2001 and who stood with me on Baggotrath Lane when a delivery truck pulled up and we discovered what 5,000 books looks like. Also, I am greatly indebted to the late Michael O'Brien and all of the staff of The O'Brien Press, past and present, especially Ivan O'Brien, Emma Byrne and Kunak McGann.

Three real-life people made cameo appearances in this book. I want to say a huge thanks to the real Benny McCabe for your generosity towards the Cork Simon Ball and to Sinead Roe and Gareth 'Gunther' Hunt for your kindness towards the equally worthy GOAL Global.

This book is dedicated to Humphrey, a basset hound who, for thirteen and a half years, shared a workspace with me, not to mention the two-hour daily commute to and from the office. I'm sorry that I wasn't always attentive to your needs, Humps, but, whenever I took a break from work and saw the collection of toys you'd brought to try to entice me away from the computer, I always remembered the lesson you were forever trying to teach me – that life is supposed to be fun.

Huge thanks to my family and most of all my wonderful wife, Mary McCarthy, whose love means more to me than anything else.

People may not appreciate this, but when you write a book in Ireland, you end up on first-name terms with dozens of wonderful booksellers. I can't thank you all by name here but I really appreciate everything you did for me.

Lastly, I want to thank you, the readers, for following Ross O'Carroll-Kelly's story through two and a half decades of books. All good things come to an end. I suspect that I will miss it more than I realize right now. None of it would have happened without readers – without you.

Thanks. You total ledge-bags.